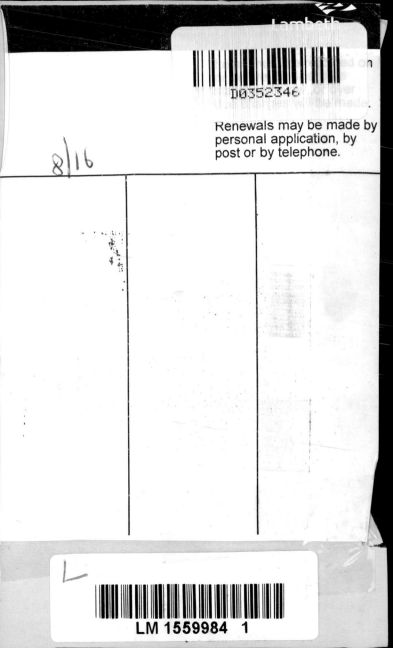

STEPPING INTO THE PRINCE'S WORLD

BY

MARION LENNOX

MILLS & BOON

First Published in Great Britain 2016
By Mills & Boon, an imprint of HarperCollins*Publishers*
1 London Bridge Street, London, SE1 9GF

ISBN: 978-0-263-92015-4

23-0916

Our policy is to use papers that are natural, renewable and recyclable products and made from wood grown in sustainable forests. The logging and manufacturing processes conform to the legal environmental regulations of the country of origin.

Printed and bound in Spain
by CPI, Barcelona

Marion Lennox has written more than one hundred romances and is published in over a hundred countries and thirty languages. Her multiple awards include the prestigious US RITA® (twice), and the *RT Book Reviews* Career Achievement Award for 'a body of work which makes us laugh and teaches us about love'. Marion adores her family, her kayak, her dog and lying on the beach with a book someone else has written. Heaven!

For Doug and Natalia.
Wishing you a fabulous wedding and
an amazing, fulfilling Happy-Ever-After.
Welcome home.

With grateful thanks to Jennifer Kloester,
who certainly knows where and how to kick.

If Our Jen met a prince on a dark night
she'd know what to do. :-)

CHAPTER ONE

You're to take your place as heir to the throne and find yourself a bride.

If Crown Prince Raoul Marcus Louis Ferdinand could cut that last order from his grandmother's letter he would, but he needed to show his commanding officer the letter in its entirety.

He laid the impressive parchment of his grandmother's letter before his commanding officer. Franz noted the grim lines on Raoul's face, picked up the letter and read.

Then he nodded. 'You have no choice,' he told him.

'I don't.' Raoul turned and stared out of the window at the massive mountain overshadowing Tasmania's capital. It was a mere shadow of the mountains of Marétal's alpine region.

He needed to be home.

'I've known my grandfather's health is failing,' he told his commanding officer. 'But I've always thought of the Queen as invincible. This letter might sound commanding, but it's a plea for help.'

'It is.' Franz glanced at the letter again. It was headed by the royal crest of Marétal and it wasn't a letter to be ignored. A royal summons… 'But at least it's timely,' he told Raoul.

Marétal's army had been engaged as part of an international exercise in Tasmania's wilderness for the last couple of months. Raoul's battalion had performed brilliantly, but operations were winding down.

'We can manage without you,' he told him. He hesitated. 'Raoul, you do know…?'

'That it's time I left the army.' Raoul sighed. 'I do know it. But my grandmother effectively runs the kingdom.'

'The Queen's seventy-six.'

'Tell *her* that.' He shook his head at the thought of his

indomitable grandmother. His grandfather, King Marcus, even though officially ruler, hardly emerged from his library. Queen Alicia had more or less run the country since the day she'd married, and she suffered no interference. But she was asking for help now.

'Of course you're right,' he continued. 'My grandparents' chief aide, Henri, has written privately that he's worried about the decisions my grandmother's taking. Or not taking. Our health and legal systems need dragging into this century. More immediately, national security seems to be an issue. Henri tells me of threats which she refuses to take seriously. He suggests increasing the security service, making it a force to be reckoned with, but the Queen sees no need.'

'You're just the man to do it.'

'I've never been permitted to change anything,' Raoul said flatly. 'And now…' He turned back to Franz's desk and stared morosely at the letter. '*This*. She wants me home for the ball to celebrate her fifty years on the throne.'

'It'll be a splendid occasion,' Franz told him. He, too, glanced back at the letter—particularly at the last paragraph—and try as he might he couldn't suppress a grin.

'You think it's *funny*?' Commanding officer or not, Franz copped a glare from Raoul. 'That the Queen decrees I bring a suitable partner or she'll provide me with one herself?'

'She wants to see you married, with an heir to the throne. She fears for you and the monarchy otherwise.'

'She wants me under her thumb, with a nice aristocratic bride to match.'

'You've never been under her thumb before.'

Franz had known Prince Raoul ever since he'd joined the army. Raoul presented to the world as the perfect Prince, the perfect grandson, but Franz knew that underneath his mild exterior Raoul did exactly what he wanted. If the Queen had known half of what her grandson had been doing in the army she'd have called him home long since.

But therein lay the success of their relationship. To his

grandmother, Raoul was a young man who smiled sweetly and seemed to agree with whatever she decreed. *'Yes, Grandmama, I'm sure you're right.'* Raoul never made promises he couldn't keep, but he certainly knew the way to get what he wanted.

'Our people will approve of me in military uniform,' he'd told the Queen when he'd announced his decision to join the army. 'It's a good look, Grandmama—the Crown Prince working for the country rather than playing a purely ceremonial role. With your approval I'll join the Special Forces. Have you seen their berets? It can do the royal image nothing but good.'

His grandmother had had to agree that his military uniform suited him. So had the country's media. At thirty five, with his height, his jet-black hair, his tanned skin and the hooded grey eyes that seemed almost hawk-like, the added 'toughness' of his uniform made the tabloids go wild every time they had the opportunity to photograph him.

'His uniform makes him look larger,' the Queen had told a journalist when Raoul had completed his first overseas posting.

Franz had read the article and thought of the years of gruelling physical training turning Raoul into a honed Special Forces soldier. His admiration for his royal charge had increased with every year he knew him.

Now he came round and gripped his shoulder. Franz had been Raoul's first commanding officer when he'd joined the army fifteen years ago. As Raoul had risen up the ranks so had Franz, and over the years they'd become friends.

'If you were a normal officer you'd be taking my place when I retire next year,' Franz told him. 'The army wouldn't give you a choice and that'd mean desk work. You know you hate desk work. There's so much more you can do working as heir to the throne—and you'll wear a much prettier uniform.'

Raoul told him where he could put his uniform and the older man chuckled.

'Yes, but you'll be wearing tassels, lad, and maybe even a sabre. There's a lot to be said for tassels and sabres. When do you need to leave?'

'The ball's in a month.'

'But you need to leave before that.' Franz glanced at the letter and his lips twitched again. 'According to this you have a spot of courting to do before you get there. First find your bride…'

Raoul rolled his eyes.

'I may have to go home,' he said carefully. 'I may even have to take up the duties of Crown Prince. But there's no way my grandmother can make me marry.'

'Well,' Franz said, and grinned again, 'I know Her Majesty. Good luck.'

Raoul said nothing. Some comments weren't worth wasting breath on.

Franz saw it and moved on to practicalities. 'Let's consider you on leave from now,' he told him. 'We'll work out discharge plans later. You can fly out tonight if you want.'

'I don't want to fly out tonight.'

'What *do* you want?'

'Space,' Raoul told him. 'Space to get my head around what I'm facing. But you're right. I need to go home. My grandparents are failing. I know my country needs me. I *will* go home—but not to find a bride.'

If she edged any closer to the end of the world she might fall off.

Claire Tremaine sat on the very highest cliff on the highest headland of Orcas Island and thumbed her nose in the direction of Sydney. It was Monday morning. In the high-rise offices of Craybourne, Ledger and Smythe, scores of dark-suited legal eagles would be poring over dull documents, checking the ASIC indexes, discussing the Dow Jones, making themselves their fifth or sixth coffee of the morning.

She was so much better off here.

Or not.

She sort of...*missed* it.

Okay, not most of it—but, oh, she missed the coffee.

And she was just ever so frightened of storms. And just a bit isolated.

Would there be a storm? The forecast was saying a weather front was moving well east of Tasmania. There was no mention of it turning towards Orcas Island, but Claire had been on the island for four months now, and was starting to recognise the wisps of cloud formation low on the horizon that spelled trouble.

A storm back in Sydney had meant an umbrella and delays on the way home to her bedsit. A storm on Orcas Island could mean she was shut in the house for days. There was a reason the owners of this island abandoned it for six months of the year. This was a barren, rocky outcrop, halfway between Victoria and Tasmania, and the sea here was the wildest in the world. In the worst of the storms Claire couldn't even stand up in the wind.

'But that's what we put our names down for,' she told Rocky, the stubby little fox terrier she'd picked up on impulse from the animal shelter the day she'd left to come here. 'Six months of isolation to get to know each other and to forget about the rest of the world.'

But the rest of the world had decent coffee.

The supply boat wasn't due for another week, and even then on its last visit they'd substituted her desired brand with a no-name caterers' blend.

Sigh.

'Two more months to go,' she told Rocky, and rose and stared out at the gathering clouds.

To come here had been a spur-of-the-moment decision, and she'd had plenty of time to regret it. She was looking at the rolling clouds and regretting it now.

'I'm sure the weather forecast's wrong,' she told her dog. 'But let's go batten down the hatches, just in case.'

* * *

He should tell someone where he was going.

If he did his bodyguards would join him. That was the deal. When he was working within his army unit his bodyguards backed off. As soon as he wasn't surrounded by soldiers, his competent security section took over.

Only they didn't treat him as a colleague. They treated him as a royal prince who needed to be protected—not only from outside harm but from doing anything that might in any way jeopardise the heir to the throne of Marétal.

Like going sailing on his own.

But he hadn't let them know he was on leave yet. As far as they were concerned he was still on military exercises, so for now he was free of their watch. He'd walked straight from Franz's office down to the docks. He was still wearing his military uniform. In a city full of army personnel, based here for multinational exercises, his uniform gave him some degree of anonymity. That anonymity wouldn't last, he knew. As soon as he shed his uniform, as soon as he went home, he'd be Crown Prince forever.

But *not* married to a woman of his grandmother's choosing, he thought grimly. He knew the women she thought suitable and he shuddered.

And then he reached *Rosebud*, the neat little yacht he'd been heading for, and forgot about choosing a bride.

This was Tom Radley's yacht. Tom was a local army officer and Raoul had met him on the first part of their combined international operation. They'd shared an excellent army exercise, abseiling across 'enemy territory' in some of Tasmania's wildest country. Friendships were forged during such ordeals, and the men had clicked.

'Come sailing with me when we're back in Hobart,' Tom had said, and they'd spent a great afternoon on the water.

But Tom had been due to take leave before the exercises had ended, and a mountain in Nepal had beckoned. Before he'd gone he'd tossed the keys of the yacht to Raoul.

'Use her, if you like, while you're still in Tasmania,' he'd said diffidently. 'I've seen your skill and I know you well enough now to trust you. I also know how surrounded you are. Just slip away and have a sail whenever you can.'

The little yacht wasn't state-of-the-art. She was a solid tub of a wooden yacht, built maybe forty years ago, sensible and sturdy. Three weeks ago he and Tom had put up a bit too much sail for the brisk conditions, and they'd had fun trying to keep her under control.

And now… Conditions on the harbour were bright, with enough sun to warm the early spring air and a breeze springing up from the south. Clouds were scudding on the horizon. It was excellent sailing weather.

He didn't want to go back to base yet. He didn't want to change out of his uniform, pack his kit and head for home.

He should tell someone where he was going.

'It's only an afternoon's sail,' he said out loud. 'And after today I'll have a lifetime of telling people where I'm going.'

He should still tell someone. Common sense dictated it.

But he didn't want his bodyguards.

'I'll tell them tomorrow,' he said. 'For today I owe no duty to the army. I owe no duty to my country. For today I'm on my own.'

Prince Raoul's movements were supposed to be tracked every step of his life. But it drove Raoul nuts.

Even his afternoon's sail with Tom had been tracked. Because he'd been off duty that weekend, his bodyguards had moved into surveillance mode. He and Tom had had a great time, but even Tom had been unsettled by the motorboat cruising casually within helping distance.

'I couldn't bear it,' Tom had said frankly, and Raoul had said nothing because it was just the way things were.

But this afternoon was different. No one knew he was on leave. No one knew he was looking at Tom's boat and thinking, *Duty starts tomorrow.*

No one saw him slip the moorings and sail quietly out of the harbour.

And no one was yet predicting the gathering storm.

'I'm sure it's a storm,' she told Rocky. 'I don't care what the weather men are saying. I trust my nose.'

Clare was working methodically around the outside of the house, closing the great wooden shutters that protected every window. This house was a mansion—a fantastical whim built by a Melbourne-based billionaire financier who'd fancied his own island with its own helicopter pad so he could fly in whenever he wished.

He'd never wish to be here now, Claire thought as she battened down the house. In the worst of the Bass Strait storms, stones that almost qualified as rocks were hurled against the house.

In the early days, Mrs Billionaire had planted a rose garden to the north of the house. It had looked stunning for half of one summer, but then a storm had hit and her rose bushes had last been seen flying towards the Antarctic. It had then been decided that an Italian marble terrace would look just as good, although even that was now pitted from flying debris.

'I hope I'm imagining things,' she told Rocky. Rocky was sniffing for lizards under the carefully arranged rock formations that during summer visits formed a beautiful 'natural' waterfall. 'The forecast's still for calm.'

But then she looked again at those clouds. She'd been caught before.

'If we lose sun for a couple of days we might even lose power. I might do some cooking in case,' she told Rocky.

Rocky looked up at her and his whole body gave a wriggle of delight. He hadn't been with her for two weeks before he'd realised the significance of the word 'cooking'.

She grinned and picked him up. 'Yes, we will,' she told him. 'Rocky, I'm very glad I have you.'

He was all she had.

She'd been totally isolated when she'd left Sydney. There'd been people in the firm she'd thought were her friends, but she'd been contacted by no one. The whispers had been vicious, and who wanted to be stained by association?

Enough.

She closed her eyes and hugged her little dog. 'Choc chip cookies for me and doggy treats for you,' she told him. 'Friends stick together, and that's you and me. That's what this six months is all about. Learning that we need nobody else.'

The wind swept in from the south—a wind so fierce that it took the meteorologists by surprise. It took Tasmania's fishing fleet by surprise, and it stretched the emergency services to the limit. To say it took Raoul's unprepared little yacht by surprise was an understatement.

Raoul was an excellent yachtsman. What his skills needed, though, was a thoroughly seaworthy boat to match them.

He didn't have one.

For a while he used the storm jib, trying to use the wind to keep some semblance of control. Then a massive wave crested and broke right over him, rolling the boat as if it was tumbleweed. The little boat self-righted. Raoul had clipped on lifelines. He was safe—for now—but the sail was shredded.

And that was the end of his illusion of control.

He was tossed wherever the wind and the sea dictated. All he could do was hold on and wait for the weather to abate. And hope it did so before *Rosebud* disintegrated and left him to the mercy of the sea.

CHAPTER TWO

TWO DAYS INTO the worst storm to have hit the island since the start of her stay Claire was going stir-crazy. She hadn't been able to step outside once. The wind was so strong that a couple of times she'd seriously worried that the whole house might be picked up.

'You and me, Rocky,' she'd told him, when he'd whimpered at the sound of the wind roaring across the island. 'Like Dorothy and Toto. When we fly, we'll fly together.'

Thankfully they hadn't flown, and finally the wind was starting to settle. The sun was starting to peep through the clouds and she thought she might just venture out and see the damage.

She quite liked a good storm—as long as it didn't threaten to carry her into the Antarctic.

So she rugged up, and made Rocky wear the dinky little dog coat that he hated but she thought looked cute, and they headed out together.

As soon as she opened the door she thought about retreating, but Rocky was tearing out into the wind, joyful at being allowed outside, heading for his favourite place in the world. The beach.

The sea would look fantastic. She just had to get close enough to the beach to see it. The sea mist was so heavy she could scarcely see through it—or was it foam blasted up by the wind? She could scarcely push against it.

But she was outside. The wind wasn't so strong that it was hurling stones. She could put her head down and fight it.

Below the house was a tiny cove—a swimming beach in decent weather. She headed there now, expecting to see massive damage, expecting to see…

A boat?

Or part of a boat.

She stopped, so appalled she almost forgot to breathe. A boat was smashed and part submerged on the rocks just past the headland.

The boat wasn't big. A weekend sailor? It must have been trying to reach the relative safety of the beach, manoeuvring into the narrow channel of deep water, but the seas would have been overwhelming, driving it onto the rocks.

Dear God, was there anyone…?

And almost as soon as she thought it she saw a flash of yellow in the water, far out, between the rocks and the beach. A figure was struggling through the waves breaking around the rocks.

Whoa.

Claire knew these waters, even thoughtshe'd never swum here. She'd skimmed stones and watched the tide in calm weather. She knew there was a rip, starting from the beach and swinging outward.

The swimmer was headed straight into it. If he was to have any chance he had to swim sideways, towards the edge of the cove, then turn and swim beside the rip rather than in it.

But he was too far away to hear if she yelled. The wind was still howling across the clifftops, drowning any hope of her being heard.

Was she a heroine?

'I'm not,' she said out loud. But some things weren't negotiable. She couldn't watch him drown—not when she knew the water. And she was a decent swimmer.

'You know where the dog food is, and the back door's open,' she told Rocky as she hauled off her coat and kicked off her boots. 'If I disappear just chew a hole in the sack. Tell 'em I died trying.'

But she had no intention of dying. She'd stick within

reach of the rocks, where the current was weakest. She was not a heroine.

Her jeans hit the clothes pile, and then her windcheater. *Okay, then—ready, set, go.*

He was making no headway. The current was hauling him out faster than he could swim.

Raoul had been born tough and trained tougher. He hadn't reached where he was in the army without survival skills being piled on to survival skills. He couldn't outswim the current, so he knew he had to let it carry him out until it weakened—and then he had to figure out a way back in again.

The problem was, he was past exhaustion.

By the time he'd reached this island the yacht had been little more than a floating tub. The torn sails were useless. He'd used the motor to try and find some place to land, but the motor hadn't had the strength to fight the surf. Then a wave, bigger than the rest, had hit him broadside.

The boat had landed upside down on the rocks. He'd hit his head. It had taken him too long to get free of the wreck and now the water was freezing.

If he let the current carry him out, would he have the strength to get back in again?

He had no choice. He forced his body to relax and felt the rip take him. For the first time he stopped trying to swim. He raised his head, looking hopelessly towards the shore. He was being carried out again.

There was someone on the beach.

Someone who could help?

Or not.

The figure was slight—a boy? No, it was a woman, her shoulder-length curls flying out around her shoulders in the wind. She had a dog and she was yelling. She was gesticulating to the east of the cove.

She was ripping off her windcheater and running down to the surf. Heading to the far left of the beach.

If this was a local she'd know the water. She was heading to the left and waving at him.

Maybe that was where the rip cut out.

She was running into the water. She shouldn't risk herself.

He tried to yell but he was past it. He was pretty much past anything.

The woman was running through the shallows and then diving into the first wave that was over chest high. Of all the stupid… Of all the brave…

Okay, if she was headed into peril on his behalf the least he could do was help.

He fought for one last burst of energy. He put his head down and tried to swim.

Uh-oh.

There'd been a swimming pool in the basement of the offices of Craybourne, Ledger and Smythe. Some lawyers swam every lunchtime.

Claire had mostly shopped. Or eaten lunch in the park. Or done nothing at all, which had sometimes seemed a pretty good option.

It didn't seem a good option now. She should have used that time to improve her swimming. She needed to be super-fit or more. There was no rip where she was swimming, but the downside of keeping close to the rocks at the side of the cove was the rocks themselves. They were sharp, and the waves weren't regular. A couple picked her up and hurled her sideways.

She was having trouble fighting her way out. She was also bone-chillingly cold. The iciness of Bass Strait in early spring was almost enough to give her a heart attack.

And she couldn't see whoever it was she was trying to rescue.

He must be here somewhere, she thought. She just had to fight her way out behind the surf so she could see.

Which meant diving through more waves. Which meant avoiding more rocks. Which meant…

Crashing.

Something hit him—hard.

He'd already hit his head on the rocks. The world was feeling a bit off-balance anyway. The new crack on his head made him reel. He reached out instinctively to grab whatever it was that had hit him—and it was soft and yielding. A woman. Somehow he tugged her to face him. Her chestnut curls were tangled, her green eyes were blurred with water, and she looked almost as dazed as he was.

He'd thumped his head and so had she. She stared at him, and then she fought to speak.

'You'd think…' She was struggling for breath as waves surged around them but she managed to gasp the words. 'You'd think a guy with the whole of Bass Strait to swim in could avoid my head.'

He had hold of her shoulders—not clutching, just linking himself with her so the wash of the waves couldn't push them apart. They were both in deadly peril, and weirdly his first urge was to laugh. She'd reached him and she was *joking*?

Um… Get safe first. Laugh second.

'Revenir à la plage. Je suivrai,' he gasped, and then realised he'd spoken in French, Marétal's official language. Which would be no use at all in Tasmania's icy waters. *Get back to the beach. I'll follow,* he'd wanted to say, and he tried to force his thick tongue to make the words. But it seemed she'd already understood.

'How can you follow? You're drowning.' She'd replied in French, with only a slight haltingness to show French wasn't her first language.

'I'm not.' He had his English together now. And his tongue almost working.

'There's blood on your head,' she managed.

'I'm okay. You've shown me the way. Put your head down and swim. I'm following.'

'Is there anyone…?' The indignation and her attempt at humour had gone from her voice and fear had replaced it. She was gasping between waves. 'Is there anyone else in the boat?'

Anyone else to save? She'd dived into the water to save him and was now proposing to head out further and save others?

This was pure grit. His army instructors would be proud of her.

She didn't have a lifejacket on and he did.

'No one,' he growled. 'Get back to the beach.'

'You're sure?'

'I'm sure. Go.' He should make *her* wear the life jacket, but the effort of taking the thing off was beyond him.

'Don't you dare drown. I've taken too much trouble.'

'I won't drown,' he managed, and then a wave caught her and flung her sideways.

She hit the closest rock and disappeared. He tried to grab her but she was under water—gone.

Hell...

He dived, adrenalin surging, giving him energy when he'd thought he had none. And then he grabbed and caught something…

A wisp of lace. He tugged and she was free of the rocks, back in his arms, dazed into limpness.

He fought back from the rocks and tried to steady while she fought to recover.

'W…wow,' she gasped at last. 'Sorry. I…you can let go now.'

'I'm not letting go.' But he shifted his grip. He'd realised what he'd been holding were her knickers. He now had hold of her by her bra!

'We surf in together,' he gasped. 'I have a lifejacket. I'm not letting go.'

'You…can't…'

He heard pain in her voice.

'You're hurt.'

'There's no way I can put a sticking plaster on out here,' she gasped. 'Go.'

'We go together.'

'You'll stretch my bra,' she gasped, and once again he was caught by the sheer guts of the woman. She was hurt, she was in deadly peril, and she was trying to make him smile.

'Yeah,' he told her. 'And if it stretches too far I'll get an eyeful—but not until we're safe on the beach. Just turn and kick.'

'I'll try,' she managed, and then there was no room for more words. There was only room to try and live.

She couldn't actually swim.

There was something wrong with her arm. Or her shoulder? Or her chest? She wasn't sure where the pain was radiating from, but it was surely radiating. It was the arm furthest from him—if he'd been holding her bra on that side she might have screamed. If she *could* scream without swallowing a bucket of seawater. Unlikely, she thought, and then wondered if she was making sense. She decided she wasn't but she didn't care.

She had to kick. There was no way she'd go under. She'd risked her life to save this guy and now it seemed he didn't need saving. Her drowning would be a complete waste.

Some people would be pleased.

And there was a thought to make her put her head down, hold her injured arm to her side as much as she could and try to kick her way through the surf.

She had help. The guy still had his hand through her bra, holding fast. His kick was more powerful than hers could ever be. But he still didn't know this beach.

'Keep close to the rocks,' she gasped during a break in the waves. 'If you don't stay close you'll be caught in the rip.'

'Got it,' he told her. 'Now, shut up and kick.'

And then another wave caught them and she had the sense to put her head down and kick, even if the pain in her shoulder was pretty close to knocking her out. And he kicked too, and they surged in, and suddenly she was on sand. The wave was ripping back out again but the guy was on his feet, tugging her up through the shallows.

'We're here,' he gasped. 'Come on, lady, six feet to go. You can do it.'

And she'd done it. Rocky was tearing down the beach to meet them, barking hysterically at the stranger.

Enough. She subsided onto the sand, grabbed Rocky with her good arm, held him tight and burst into tears.

For a good while neither of them moved.

She lay on the wet sand and hugged her dog and thought vaguely that she had to make an effort. She had to get into dry clothes. She was freezing. And shouldn't she try to see if something was wrong with the guy beside her? He'd slumped down on the sand, too. She could see his chest rise and fall. He was alive, but his eyes were closed. The weak sunshine was on his unshaven face and he seemed to be drinking it up.

Who was he?

He was wearing army issue camouflage gear. It was the standard work wear of a soldier, though maybe slightly different from the Australian uniform.

He was missing his boots.

Why notice that?

She was noticing his face, too. Well, why not? Even the pain in her shoulder didn't stop her noticing his face.

There was a trickle of blood mixing with the seawater dripping from his head.

He was beautiful.

It was the strongest face she'd ever seen. His features

were lean, aquiline…aristocratic? He had dark hair—deep black. It was cropped into an army cut, but no style apart from a complete shave could disguise its tendency to curl. His grey eyes were deep-set and shadowed and he was wearing a couple of days' stubble. He looked beyond exhausted.

She guessed he was in his mid-thirties, and she thought he looked mean.

Mean?

Mean in the trained sense, she corrected herself. Mean as in a lean, mean fighting machine.

She thought, weirdly, of a kid she'd gone to school with. Andy had been a friend with the same ambitions she'd had: to get away from Kunamungle and *be* someone.

'I'll join the army and be a lean, mean fighting machine,' he'd told her.

Last she'd heard, Andy was married with three kids, running the stock and station agents in Kunamungle. He was yet another kid who'd tried to leave his roots and failed.

Her thoughts were drifting in a weird kind of consciousness that was somehow about blocking pain. Something had happened to her arm. Something bad. She didn't want to look. She just wanted to stay still for a moment longer and hold Rocky and think about anything other than what would happen when she had to move.

'Tell me what's wrong?'

He'd stirred. He was pushing himself up, looking down at her in concern.

'H…hi,' she managed, and his eyes narrowed.

Um…where was her bra? It was down around her waist, that was where it was, but she didn't seem to have the energy to do anything about it. She hugged Rocky a bit closer, thinking he'd do as camouflage. If he didn't, she didn't have the strength to care.

'Your arm,' he said carefully, as if he didn't want to scare her.

She thought about that for a bit. Her arm…

'There…there does seem to be a problem. I hit the rocks. I guess I don't make the grade as a lifesaver, huh?'

'If you hadn't come out I'd be dead,' he told her. 'I couldn't fight the rip and I didn't know where it ended.'

'I was trying to signal but I didn't know if you'd seen me.' She was still having trouble getting her voice to work but it seemed he was, too. His lilting accent—French?—was husky, and she could hear exhaustion behind it. He had been in peril, she thought. Maybe she *had* saved him. It was small consolation for the way her arm felt, but at least it was something.

'Where can I go to get help?' he asked, cautious now, as if he wasn't sure he wanted to know the answer.

'Help?'

'The charts say this island is uninhabited.'

'It's not,' she told him.

'No?'

'There's Rocky and me, and now there's you.'

'Rocky?'

'I'm holding him.'

Silence. Although it wasn't exactly silence. The waves were pounding the sand and the wind was whistling around the cliffs. A stray piece of seaweed whipped past her face like a physical slap.

What was wrong with her arm? She tried a tentative wiggle and decided she wouldn't do *that* again in a hurry.

'Do you live here?'

'I caretake,' she said, enunciating every syllable with care because it seemed important.

'You caretake the island?'

'The house.'

'There's a house?'

'A big house.'

'Excellent,' he told her.

He rose and stared round the beach, then left her with

Rocky. Two minutes later he was back, holding her pile of discarded clothes.

'Let's get you warm. You need to put these on.'

'You're wet, too' she told him.

'Yeah, but I don't have a set of dry clothes on the beach. Let's cope with one lot of hypothermia instead of two. Tug your knickers off and I'll help you on with your jeans and windcheater.

'I'm not taking my knickers off!'

'They're soaked and you're freezing.'

'I have my dignity.'

'And I'm not putting up with misplaced modesty on my watch.' He was holding up her windcheater. 'Over your head with this. Don't try and put your arm in it.'

He slid the windcheater over her head. It was long enough to give her a semblance of respectability as she kicked off her soggy knickers—but not much. She should be wearing wisps of sexy silk, she thought, but she was on an island in winter for six months with no expected company. Her knickers were good solid knickers, bought for warmth, with just a touch of lace.

'My granny once told me to always wear good knickers in case I'm hit by a bus,' she managed. Her teeth were chattering. She had her good arm on his shoulder while he was holding her jeans for her to step into.

'Sensible Granny.'

'I think she meant G-strings with French lace,' she told him. 'Granny had visions of me marrying a doctor. Or similar.'

'Still sensible Granny.' He was hauling her jeans up as if this was something he did every day of the week. Which he surely didn't. He was definitely wearing army issue camouflage. It was soaking. One sleeve was ripped but it still looked serviceable.

He looked capable. Capable of hauling her jeans up and not looking?

Don't go there.

'Why…? Why sensible?' she managed.

'Because we could use a doctor right now,' he told her. 'Your arm…'

'My arm will be fine. I must have wrenched it.' She stared down. He was holding her boots. He must have unlaced them. She'd hauled them off and run.

She took the greatest care to put her feet into them, one after the other, and then tried not to be self-conscious as he tied the laces for her.

She was an awesome lifesaver, she thought ruefully. *Not.*

'Now,' he said, and he took her good arm under the elbow. Rocky was turning crazy circles around them, totally unaware of drama, knowing only that he was out of the house and free. 'Let's get to this house. Is it far?'

'A hundred yards as the crow flies,' she told him. 'Sadly we don't have wings.'

'You mean it's up?'

'It's up.'

'I'm sorry.' For the first time his voice faltered. 'I don't think I can carry you.'

'Well, there's a relief,' she managed. 'Because I might have been forced to let you help me dress, but that's as far as it goes. You're carrying me nowhere.'

It had been two days since he'd set off from Hobart, and to say he was exhausted was an understatement. The storm had blown up from nowhere and the boat's engine hadn't been big enough to fight it. Sails had been impossible. He'd been forced to simply ride it out, trying to use the storm jib to keep clear of land, letting the elements take him where they willed.

And no one knew where he was.

His first inkling of the storm had been a faint black streak on the horizon. The streak had turned into a mass with frightening speed. He'd been a good couple of hours out. As soon as he'd noticed it he'd headed for port, but the storm had overwhelmed him.

And he'd been stupidly unprepared. He'd had his phone, but the first massive wave breaking over the bow had soaked him and rendered his phone useless. He'd kicked himself for not putting it in a waterproof container and headed below to Tom's radio. And found it useless. Out of order.

Raoul had thought then how great Tom's devil-may-care attitude had seemed when he and Tom had done their Sunday afternoon sail with his bodyguard in the background, and how dumb it seemed now. And where was the EPIRB? The emergency position indicating radio beacon all boats should carry to alert the authorities if they were in distress and send an automatic location beacon? Did Tom even own one?

Apparently not.

Dumb was the word to describe what he'd done. He'd set out to sea because he was fed up with the world and wanted some time to himself to reflect. But he wasn't so fed up that he wanted to die, and with no one knowing where he was, and no reliable method of communication, he'd stood every chance of ending up that way.

He'd been lucky to end up here.

He'd put this woman's life at risk.

He was helping her up the cliff now. He'd kicked his boots off in the water, which meant he was only wearing socks. The shale on the steep cliff was biting in, but that was the least of his worries. He'd been in the water for a couple of hours, trying to fight his way to shore, and he'd spent two days fighting the sea. He was freezing, and he was so tired all he wanted to do was sleep.

But the woman by his side was rigid with pain. She wasn't complaining, but when he'd put his arm around her waist and held her, supporting her as she walked, she hadn't pulled away. She wasn't big—five-four, five-five or so—and was slight with it. She had a smattering of freckles on her face, her chestnut curls clung wetly to her too-pale skin and her mouth was set in determination.

He just knew this woman didn't accept help unless there was a need.

'How far from the top of the cliff?' he asked, and she took a couple of deep breaths and managed to climb a few more feet before replying.

'Close. You want to go ahead? The back door's open.'

'Are you kidding?' His arm tightened around her. He was on her good side, aware that her left arm was useless and radiating pain. 'You're the lifesaver. Without you I'm a dead man.'

'Rocky will show you…where the pantry is…' She was talking in gasps. 'And the dog food. You'll survive.'

'I need *you* to show me where the pantry is. I think we're almost up now.'

'You'd know that how…?'

'I wouldn't,' he agreed humbly. 'I was just saying it to make you feel better.'

'Thank you,' she whispered.

'No, thank *you*,' he said, and held her tighter and put one foot after another and kept going.

And then they reached the top and he saw the house.

The island was a rocky outcrop, seeming almost to burst from the water in the midst of Bass Strait. He'd aimed for it simply because he'd had no choice—the boat had been taking on water and it had been the only land mass on the map—but from the sea it had seemed stark and inhospitable, with high cliffs looming out of the water. The small bay had seemed the only possible place to land, and even that had proved disastrous. What kind of a house could possibly be built *here*?

He reached the top of the cliff and saw a mansion.

Quite simply, it was extraordinary.

It was almost as if it was part of the island itself, long

and low across the plateau, built of the same stone. In one sense it was an uncompromising fortress. In another sense it was pure fantasy.

Celtic columns faced the sea, supporting a vast pergola, with massive stone terraces underneath. Stone was stacked on stone, massive structures creating an impression of awe and wonder. There were sculptures everywhere—artworks built to withstand the elements. And the house itself… Huge French windows looked out over the sea. They were shuttered now, making the house look even more like a fortress. There was a vast swimming pool, carved to look like a natural rock pool. In this bleak weather it was covered by a solid mat.

He wouldn't be swimming for a while yet, he thought, but he looked at the house and thought he'd never seen anything more fantastic.

If he was being honest a one-room wooden hut would have looked good now, he conceded. But this…

'Safe,' he said, and the woman in his arms wilted a little. Her effort to climb the cliff had been huge.

'B… Back door…out of the wind,' she managed, and her voice was thready.

She'd fought to reach him in the water. She'd been injured trying to save him and now she'd managed to get up the cliff. He hadn't thought he had any strength left in him, but it was amazing what a body was capable of. His army instructors had told him that.

'No matter how dire, there's always another level of adrenalin. You'll never know it's there until you need it.'

He'd needed it once in a sticky situation in West Africa. He felt the woman slump beside him and needed it now. He stopped and turned her, and then swept her up into his arms.

She didn't protest. She was past protesting.

The little dog tore on ahead, showing him the way to the rear door, and in the end it was easy. Two minutes later he had her in the house and they were safe.

CHAPTER THREE

THE FIRST THING he had to do was get himself warm.

It seemed selfish, but he was so cold he couldn't function. And he needed to stay switched on for a while yet.

He laid his lifesaver on a vast settee in front of an open fire—miraculously it was lit, and the house was warm. She was back in her dry clothes and after her exertion on the cliff she wasn't shivering.

He was. His feet and hands were almost completely numb. He'd been in cold water for too long.

She knew it. She gripped his hand as he set her down and winced. 'Bathroom. Thataway,' she told him. 'You'll find clothes in the dressing room beside it.'

'I'll be fast.'

'Stay under water until you're warm,' she ordered, and now the urgent need had passed he knew she was right.

He'd been fighting to get his feet to work on the way up the cliff. He'd also been fighting to get his mind to think straight. Fuzzy images were playing at the edges and he had an almost overwhelming urge to lie by the fire and sleep.

He was trained to recognise hypothermia. He'd been starting to suffer in the water and the physical exertion hadn't been enough to raise his core temperature. He had to get himself warm if he was to be any use to this woman or to himself.

'You'll be okay? Don't move that arm.'

'As if I would. Go.'

So he went, and found a bathroom so sumptuous he might almost be in the palace at home. Any doubts as to how close he'd come to disaster were dispelled by the pain he felt when the warm water touched him.

There was a bench along the length of the shower. Two

shower heads pointed hot water at him from different directions. He slumped on the bench and let the water do its work. Gradually the pain eased. He was battered and bruised, but he'd been more bruised than this after military exercises.

With his core heat back to normal he could almost think straight. Except he needed to sleep. He *really* needed to sleep.

There was a woman who needed him.

He towelled himself dry and moved to the next imperative. Clothes. This was a huge place. Who lived here?

The master bedroom was stunning, and whoever used it had a truly impressive wardrobe. There were over-the-top women's clothes—surely not belonging to the woman who'd saved him? He couldn't see her in flowing rainbow chiffon—but the guy's wardrobe was expansive, too. He found jogging pants that stretched to fit and the T-shirts were okay. There were even socks and sheepskin slippers. And a cardigan just like his grandfather wore.

Exhaustion was still sweeping over him in waves, but at least his head was working. It had to keep working. He was dehydrated and starving and he needed to fix it. He found the kitchen, found a stack of long-life milk in the pantry and drank until the hollow, sick feeling in his stomach receded. Feeling absurdly pleased with himself, he headed back to the living room.

She was lying on her back, her eyes closed. He could see pain radiating out from her in waves.

'Hey,' he said, and she turned and managed a weak smile.

'Hey, yourself,' she managed. 'They look a whole lot better on you than Don.'

'Don?'

'Don and Marigold own this place.'

'Not you?'

'I wish.' She grimaced again. 'Actually, I *don't* wish. I've run out of good coffee.'

'You think it's time for introductions?' he asked, and she winced and tried for a smile.

'Claire. Claire Tremaine. I'm the island caretaker.'

'I'm Raoul,' he told her. 'Raoul de Castelaise.' Now surely wasn't the time for titles and formalities. 'Soldier. I'm pleased to meet you, Claire. In fact I can't begin to tell you *how* pleased. Tell me about your arm.'

'I guess…it's broken.'

'Can I see? I'll need to lift your windcheater.'

'I don't have a bra on.'

'So you don't. You want me to find you a bra?'

'I don't care,' she muttered. 'Look at my arm. Don't look at anything else.'

'No, ma'am.' He sat on the edge of the settee and helped her sit up, then carefully tugged off her windcheater. She only had her good arm in it, so it came off easily.

She'd ordered him not to look at anything else. That was a big ask.

Too big.

She was beautiful, he thought. She looked almost like an athlete, taut and lean. Her chestnut curls were wisping onto her naked shoulders.

She looked vulnerable and scared.

He headed back to the bathroom and brought out a towel, wrapping the fluffy whiteness around her so she was almost respectable but her arm was still exposed.

She hugged the towel to her as if she needed its comfort. The bravado she'd shown since the moment he'd met her in the water seemed to have disappeared.

She *was* scared?

Yeah. He was a big guy. Apart from the dog, she seemed to be in this house alone. She was semi-naked and injured.

Why *wouldn't* she be scared?

'Can I tell you that my grandmother thinks I'm trustworthy?' he told her, tucking in the edges of the towel so it made an almost secure sarong. 'She tells the world what a good boy I am, and I'm not about to mess with her beliefs. I *am* trustworthy, Claire. I promise. If only because my grandmother's presence seems to spend a lot of time sitting on my shoulder. You're safe with me.'

And she managed a smile that was almost genuine.

'Scary Granny, huh.'

'You'd better believe it. But I can handle her.'

'And you love her?'

'You can believe that, too.'

And her smile softened, as if she really did believe him. As if somehow his words really had made her feel safe.

'Are you French?' she asked.

'I'm from Marétal. It's a small land-locked country near...'

'I know it,' she said, in an exclamation of surprise. 'Your army's taking part in the international army exercises in Tasmania. I looked it up.'

'You looked it up?'

'I get bored,' she admitted. Her voice was still tight, but she was making a huge effort to sound normal. 'I was listening to the Tasmanian news on the radio. They listed the countries taking part. I didn't know where Marétal was. So you're part of that exercise.' And then her voice grew tighter. 'Are there...are there any other soldiers lost overboard?'

'Only me—and it wasn't an army exercise,' he said ruefully. 'Despite the camouflage, I'm off duty. I took a friend's boat out from Hobart and got caught in the storm. I had two days being flung about Bass Strait, finally made it to the lee of your island and you know the rest. But my friend—the guy who owns *Rosebud*—is in Nepal. He doesn't know I took his boat and I didn't tell anyone I was going. It was a spur-of-the-moment decision. I broke all the rules and the army would agree that I've been an idiot.'

'You've paid the price.

'It could have been a whole lot higher.'

He was watching her arm while they talked. She was supporting it with her good hand, holding it slightly away from her body. Her shoulder looked odd. Squared off.

'Idiot or not, you might need to trust me with your arm,' he suggested. 'Can I touch it?'

'If you don't mind me screaming.'

'I'll be gentle,' he told her, and lightly ran his fingers down the front of her shoulder joint, thinking back to his first-aid courses. Thinking of anatomy.

'It feels dislocated,' he told her.

'It feels broken.'

'It probably feels worse than if it was broken.'

He put his fingers on her wrist and checked her pulse, then did it again at the elbow.

'You look like you know what you're doing,' she managed.

'I've been in the army for years. I'm a first-aider for my unit.

'You put on sticking plasters?'

'Sometimes it's more than that. When we're out of range of medical help this is what I do.'

'Like now?'

'I hope we're not out of range. You said you have a radio. Two-way? We must be within an hour's journey for a chopper coming from the mainland. Tell me where it is and I'll radio now.'

'Or not,' she said.

'Not?'

'No.' She winced. 'I know this sounds appalling… We have a radio—a big one. We also have back-up—a decent hand-held thing that's capable of sending signals to Hobart. But last time he was here Don—the owner—was messing around with it and dropped his beer into its workings. And the main radio seems to have been wiped out in the storm.'

'He dropped his beer…?'

'Yeah,' she said. 'If it had been Marigold it would have

been a martini.' She closed her eyes. 'There's a first-aid kit in the kitchen,' she told him. 'I think I need it.'

'I doubt aspirin will help.'

'Marigold is allergic to pain. *Very* allergic. She's been known to demand morphine and a helicopter transfer to the mainland for a torn toenail. I'm thinking there'll be something decent in there.'

There was. He found enough painkillers to knock out an elephant. Also muscle relaxant, and a dosage list that seemed to be made out for the Flying Doctor—Australia's remote medical service. The list didn't actually say *This much for a dislocated shoulder*, but he had enough experience to figure the dose. He made her hot, sweet tea—plus one for himself—then watched her take the pills he gave her.

'Stay still until that works,' he told her.

He found a blanket and covered her, and watched her curl into an almost foetal position on the settee. Rocky nestled on the floor by her side.

He tried to think of a plan.

Plans were thin on the ground and he was still having trouble thinking straight.

The drugs would ease her pain, he thought, but he also knew that the longer the shoulder stayed dislocated, the higher the chance of long-term damage.

In the Middle East he'd had a mate who had…

Um, no. He wasn't going there.

He did a further tour and found the radio in a truly impressive study. Claire had been right: there was no transmission. He headed outside and saw a wooden building blasted to splinters. A huge radio antenna lay smashed among the timber.

No joy there.

'You're on your own,' he muttered, and pushed away the waves of exhaustion and headed back to the living room.

She was still lying where he'd left her, but her rigidity seemed to have lessened.

He knelt beside her. 'Better?'

'Better,' she whispered. 'Just leave me be.'

'I can't do that. Claire, we're going to have to get that arm back into position.'

'My arm wants to stay really still.'

'And I'm going to have to hurt you,' he told her. 'But if I don't hurt you now you may have long-term damage.'

'How do I know it's not broken?'

'You don't. I don't. So I'm using basic first aid, and the first rule is *Do no harm.* We were taught a method which only sometimes works, but its huge advantage is that it won't hurt a fracture. If there's a fracture the arm will scream at you and you'll scream at me and we'll stop.' He hoped. 'Claire, I need you to lie on your front and let your arm hang down. We'll put a few cushions under you so your arm is high enough to hang freely. Then I'm going to gradually weight your arm, using sticking plaster to attach things like cans of beans…'

'Beans?'

'Anything I can find.' He smiled. 'In an emergency, anything goes. My first-aid trainer said if I ask you to grip the cans then your arm will tense, so I just need to stick them on you as dead weights. Then we'll let the nice drugs do their work. You'll lie back and think of England, and the tins of beans will tug your arm down, and if you relax completely then I'm hoping it'll pop back in.'

'Think of England?'

'Or sunbeams,' he told her. 'Anything to take your mind off your arm.'

She appeared to think about that for a moment, maybe choosing from a list of options. And then she opened her eyes and glanced up at him, taking in his appearance. From head to toe.

'Nice,' she whispered. 'I think I'll think about *you.* If you knew how different you look to Don… Don fills his T-shirt up with beer belly. You fill it up with…you.'

'Me?'

'Muscles.'

Right. It was the drugs talking, he thought. He needed to stop looking into her eyes and quit smiling at her like an idiot and think of her as a patient. As one of the guys in his unit, injured in the field. *Work.*

Nothing personal at all.

But he needed to get her relaxed. He knelt beside her and pushed a damp curl from her eyes. She was little and dark and feisty, and her freckles were very, very cute. Her hair was still damp from her soaking. He would have liked to get her completely dry, but he was working through a list of imperatives. Arm first.

'H… How does this work?' she muttered.

'The socket's like a cup,' he told her. 'I think your arm's slipped out of the cup, but it still has muscles that want it to go back in. If we weight it, and you're relaxed, then your muscles have a chance to pull it back into place.'

That was the theory, anyway. *If* it worked. *If* the arm wasn't broken. But the weighting method was the only safe course of action. To pull on a broken arm could mean disaster. Gradual weighting was the only way, but she had to trust him.

And it seemed she did.

'Do it,' she said, and smiled up at him. 'Only we don't have baked beans. How about tins of caviar?'

'You're kidding?'

'No. But there are tinned tomatoes as well.' Then she appeared to brighten. 'And we have tins of truly appalling instant coffee. It'd be great if they could be useful for something.'

She smiled up at him and he thought of the pain she was suffering, and the sheer courage she was showing, and the fact that she was smiling to make *him* smile…

And he smiled back at her and backed away—because a

man had to back away fast from a smile like that—and went to find some truly useful cans of coffee.

Somehow he stayed businesslike. Professional. Somehow he followed the instructions in his head from first-aid training in the field. He taped on the weights. He watched for her to react from too much pain, but although she winced as he weighted her arm she didn't make a murmur.

He put on as much weight as he thought she could tolerate and then he sat beside her and waited.

'What do we do now?' she asked.

'Relax. Forget the arm. Tell you what,' he said. 'I'll tell you a story.'

'What sort of story?'

He thought about it. He needed a story that would make her almost soporific so the arm would totally relax.

'How about *Goldilocks and the Three Bears*?' he suggested, and she choked.

'Really?'

'Has anyone ever read it to you?'

'I guess…not for a very long time.'

'Same for me,' he told her. 'So correct me if I get the bears muddled. Okay, here goes.'

And he sat by the couch and stroked her hair and told her the story of the three bears. It was a simple story—not long enough—so he had to embellish it. He had Goldilocks as a modern-day Bond girl, escaping from villains. He had his bears trying to figure the villains from the good guys, and he put in a bit of drama for good measure.

In other words he had fun, blocking the fuzziness in his own head with the need to keep her attention. And as Baby Bear found Goldilocks, and good guys and baddies were sorted, and baddies were dispatched with buckets of Mama Bear's too-hot porridge, and they all settled down for toast and marmalade, Claire's arm did what he'd desperately hoped it would do. It clicked back into its socket.

In the silence of the room, between breaks in the very exciting narrative, they actually heard it pop.

The relief did his head in.

It was almost as if he hadn't realised what stress he'd been under until the arm clicked back into place. The sound was like an off switch, clicking in his brain.

For the first time in his life he felt as if he was going to faint. He put his head between his knees—because it was either that or keel over. And Claire's fingers touched his hair, running through the still damp strands. Caressing.

'It's done,' she whispered. 'Thank you.'

'Thank *you*,' he managed. 'I couldn't have borne it if you'd suffered permanent damage saving me. Claire, I need to fix you a sling.'

'Raoul… First… Lie here,' she whispered. 'Please… Just…hold me.'

He'd been in deadly peril for two days. For a few hours earlier today he'd been sure he'd drown.

He was past exhaustion. He was past anything. Maybe Claire knew it. Maybe Claire felt the same.

'Sling first,' he muttered, and managed to tie her arm so it wouldn't slip, but then he was done.

'I need to sleep,' Claire murmured. 'The drugs… My arm… It's all okay, but… Raoul, stay with me.'

She was lying on the huge settee, tousled, part-wrapped in a fleecy towel, part-covered by the huge blanket he'd found. The fire was putting out a gentle warmth.

He fought for sense but he was losing. He managed to toss more logs on the fire and then he stared into the flames thinking…*nothing*. Goldilocks and the three bears seemed very far away. Everything seemed very far away.

But Claire was edging sideways to give him room to lie with her.

There was no choice. He sat down on the settee and she put her hand up and touched his face.

'We're safe,' she whispered. 'Nice. Stay.'

He lay down, but the sofa wasn't big enough to avoid touching. And it seemed the most natural thing in the world that he put his arms around her.

She curled into him with a sleepy murmur.

'Nice,' she said again. 'Sleep.'

He woke and it was still daylight. Was it late afternoon or was it the next day? For now he didn't know and didn't care.

He was still on the settee. The room was warm. *He* was warm. The fire was a mass of glowing embers.

He was holding Claire.

There were aches in his body, just waiting to make themselves known. He could feel them lurking. They'd make themselves known if he moved.

But for now he had no intention of moving. He lay with the warmth of the woman beside him: a gentle, amazing comfort. Her towel had slipped. He was lying on her uninjured side. Her naked body was against his chest and he was cradling her to him. She was using his chest as a pillow.

He had a T-shirt on but it didn't feel like it. Her warmth made it feel as if she was almost a part of him.

He could feel her heartbeat. Her hair had dried and was tumbling across his chest, and her breathing was deep and even.

After the perils, the fear, the exhaustion of the last two days, he was filled with a sense of peace so great it threatened to overwhelm him.

He'd been in dangerous situations before. He'd had moments when he'd ended up sleeping tight with other members of his unit, some of them women. He'd held people when they'd been in mutual danger.

But he'd never felt like this, he thought. As if this woman was *right*.

As if this woman was part of him.

That was a crazy thought, he decided, and he hadn't even taken any drugs. What was going on?

He must have moved a little, because Claire stirred and opened her eyes and shifted a fraction. She didn't move far, though. She was still cradled against him.

Her heartbeat was still his.

'Nice,' she said, as she'd said before she'd slept, and it was like a blessing.

'Nice?'

'The wind's died.'

It had, too. He hadn't noticed.

He had sensory overload.He couldn't get past the feeling of the woman in his arms.

'Pain?' he asked, and she seemed to think about it.

'Nope,' she said at last. 'Not if I lie really still.'

That suited him. They lay really still. Rocky was snuffling under the settee. Maybe that was what had woken them.

Or other, more mundane things.

'I need the bathroom,' she murmured, and he conceded that he did, too. And the fire needed more logs. And, to tell the truth, he was so hungry he could eat a horse—the milk and tea had barely hit the sides—but he was prepared to ignore everything if she'd stay where she was. But now Rocky had his paws up on the settee and was looking at them with bright, expectant eyes.

'That's his "feed me" look,' Claire murmured, and she moved a little so she could scratch behind his ear with her good hand. And then she said, in a different voice, 'I've lost my towel.'

'So you have.' It was hard not to sound complacent.

She tugged back, hauled the blanket up across her breasts and tried a glare. It wasn't a very big glare. Those drugs must have packed a fair punch, he thought. She still looked dazed.

Actually...*beautifully* dazed. She had wide green eyes that seemed to be struggling to focus. She had skin that seemed almost translucent. Her lashes were long and curled a little, and her nose was ever so slightly snubbed.

'You noticed,' she said accusingly, and he shook his head.

'No, ma'am. I've been looking at Rocky all the time.'

'Liar.'

'Yes, ma'am.'

She grinned, and he thought that if she'd had two good hands she might have punched him. But one was still pretty much tied up. He was safe.

'Life,' she said.

'Sorry?'

'We fought to keep it. We might as well get on with it.'

'You mean we need to feed the fire, go to the bathroom, feed the dog, find something to eat ourselves...'

'And think of some way to contact the mainland.' Her smile faded. 'Will people be looking for you?'

He thought of his minders. At midday, when he'd spoken to Franz, he had been supposed to be with his unit. His minders had therefore been off duty. At six that night they'd have rung to check his itinerary for the following day.

He'd have been expected to be back well before six. They'd have rung and someone would have told them he was off duty. Then they'd have contacted Franz. 'He's off duty as of this morning. I believe he's planning on returning home,' he would have told them, and then someone would have been sent to check his kit and discovered it was still where it was supposed to be.

It would have taken his minders about thirty seconds after that to panic.

'What is it?' she said, and pushed herself up, wincing a bit as she moved her arm.

'What?'

'Your face. Someone's looking for you right now. Someone's terrified. Your wife? Partner? Family?'

'I don't have a wife or partner.'

'Family? Parents?'

'My parents died when I was five, but I do have grandparents.'

'Back in Marétal?'

'Yes.' He closed his eyes, thinking of the fuss when his grandparents discovered he was missing. Then he thought of how long he'd been gone. After all this time it wouldn't be fuss. It would be horror. 'I imagine they'll know I'm missing.'

She was sitting up now, blanket tucked to her chin, concentrating on the problem at hand. 'Don't worry too much,' she told him. 'The wind's died. I suspect you'll be mortified, but the Australian Air Sea Rescue services are good. They can probably track the wind and the currents and get a fair idea of your direction. If I was them I'd be checking the islands first. There's only about ten. Any minute now we'll have choppers overhead, searching for one lost soldier.'

He felt sick.

'Don't worry,' Claire said again. 'I imagine it's embarrassing, getting rescued twice, once even by a girl, but you'll just have to cop it.'

'I won't,' he told her.

'Are you going to tell me how you can avoid it?'

'I already *have* avoided it,' he said, goaded. 'I didn't tell anyone I was going sailing. What's more, I took my friend's boat. My friend's currently trying to climb Annapurna Two in Nepal. He won't know I'm missing and he won't know his boat's missing. No one knows I went to sea. I could be anywhere and my…my grandparents will be devastated.'

His grandparents?

This wasn't just about his grandparents, he thought. His bodyguard consisted of two skilled, decent men who'd feel as if they'd failed. The top brass of the army would be mortified. His friends would be appalled. And, back home, the media would be in a feeding frenzy. *Heir to the Throne Disappears!* It didn't bear thinking about.

He would have groaned if it would do any good.

It wouldn't.

'Raoul…'

'Mmm?'

'We all do dumb things,' she told him, and put her good hand on his knee. 'Some dumber than others. But, hey, you've lived to be embarrassed. The supply boat's due next Monday. You'll climb aboard, they'll let everyone know, and by the time you reach Hobart the fuss will have died down. You might need to apologise to a few people and go home and hug your grandparents, but it's no big deal. So one soldier's gone AWOL? If they don't think you've drowned then they'll probably assume you're in a bar somewhere. Or with a woman.'

And then she had the temerity to grin.

'Actually, they're both true. You're very much with a woman, and if you go through that door there's a truly excellent bar.'

'I think I need it,' he said, and she chuckled and tried to stand.

She wobbled a bit and he rose to steady her.

'What did you give me?' she demanded. 'I feel like I've had enough drugs to down an elephant.'

'Or to not scream when your arm went back in. You were very brave.'

'I was, wasn't I?' she said smugly. 'So I'm brave and you're lost. And my arm's back to where it belongs. They're the givens. For the rest…we just have to get on with it.'

'I really can't get off this place until next Monday?'

'We can try and fix the transmitter,' she told him. 'Are you any good with electronics?'

'No.'

'Then I'm vetoing that as a plan straight away,' she told him. 'I have no intention of saving you twice. Now, Raoul…?'

'Yes?'

'Put some logs on the fire while I feed Rocky. We have life to get on with.'

'Yes, ma'am,' he said, because there was nothing else to say. Nothing at all.

CHAPTER FOUR

THIS MORNING SHE'D been bored.

This morning her entire desire in life had been a decent cup of coffee.

She was not bored now, and her desire was taking a new and entirely inappropriate direction.

Maybe she should be nervous. This guy was seriously big. He had the brawn and build of a well-honed military machine. Even washed up on the beach he'd looked awesome.

She stood under the shower and let the hot water run over her battered body as she let her mind drift where it willed.

It willed straight to Raoul.

She was alone on this island with a guy she didn't know. A seriously big guy. A seriously good-looking guy. He was dark-haired and tanned and his grey eyes were creased at the edges. Was the weathering on his face from years of military exercises in tough conditions? She wasn't sure if she was right, but she guessed she was.

He was kind. He was also skilled. He'd managed to get her arm back into place and the relief had been enormous. He was also worried about his grandparents. She could see that. One lone soldier AWOL from the army wouldn't cause a fuss, but she'd seen that he was distressed. Of course the army would contact his family, and of course it distressed Raoul that his grandparents would worry. Because he was…a good guy.

Raoul. Nice name, she thought. Nice guy. And a seriously sexy accent. Almost French, with something else in the mix.

Sexy.

And there lay the rub. There lay the reason why she should stop thinking about Raoul right now.

'Are you okay in there?'

His voice almost made her jump out of her skin and when she landed she had to fight to get her voice in order.

'F… Fine.'

'Dinner's ready when you are. I already ate, but I'm ready to eat again.'

'You already *ate*?'

'Your refrigerator's amazing. Or should I say refrigerators, plural. Wow. I opened one to check and three eggs almost fell into my hand. So I ate them. You do realise eating's been low on my priority list over the last few days? Having had my pre-dinner boiled egg snack, I'm now serious about making dinner proper. But first I'm here to towel my lady's back, if she wants it towelled, because it's occurred to me that one-arm towelling might be hard.'

There were things there for a woman to consider. A lot of things. She was alone on the island with this guy. Every sensible part of her said she shouldn't accept his help.

Raoul had put a plastic outdoor chair in the shower before he'd let her into the bathroom. He'd fussed, but she'd assured him she was okay. She'd been able to kick off her salty clothes herself, and sitting under the hot water had been easy. She'd even managed to shampoo her hair with one hand.

But now… The wussy part of her said she didn't know how she *could* towel herself with one arm, especially as the painkillers were still making her feel a bit fuzzy. And there was a tiny part of her—a really dangerous part—that was saying she wouldn't mind being towelled by this guy.

She was twenty-eight years old. She was hardly a prude. He was…

Yeah, enough.

But she had three voices in her head now. One saying, *Safe*, one saying, *Sensible*, the other saying, *Yes!*

She had an internal vote and *Safe* and *Sensible* were outvoted by about a hundred to two.

'Yes,' she whispered, but he didn't hear.

'Claire? Are you okay?'

'I'm fine,' she said. 'And, yes, please—I think I *do* need help to get dry.'

It wasn't a bad feeling.

Okay, it was an incredible feeling. He had his hands full of lush white towel and he was carefully towelling Claire Tremaine dry.

She was beautiful. Every inch of her was beautiful. She'd emerged naked from the shower. She'd stood with rivulets of warm water streaming down her body and he'd never seen anything more beautiful in his life.

If he hadn't spent the last two days having cold shower after cold shower, he might have seriously thought of taking one now. Instead of which he had to get his thoughts under control and do what he was here for—get the lady dry.

She'd grabbed a towel, too, but with only one good hand she could do little. She dried her face and rubbed her front, which was okay because that meant he didn't have to dry her breasts. Which would have been hard. But he did have to towel her hair. He did have to run the towel down the smooth contours of her back. He did need to stoop to dry her gorgeous legs.

She was a small woman, but her legs seemed to go on forever. How did *that* happen?

She was gorgeous.

When he'd knocked on the bathroom door he'd just put steak in the microwave to defrost and until he'd entered the bathroom that steak had been pretty much uppermost in his thoughts.

Not now. The steak could turn into dust for all he cared. Every sense was tuned to this woman.

Every part of his body…

'I think I'm dry,' she said, in a voice that was shaky, but not shaky in a pained kind of way. It was shaky in a way that told him she was as aware of him as he was of her.

He could gather her up right now…

Yeah, like *that* could happen. This woman had hauled him out of the water and let him into her home. She'd been injured on his behalf. She was still slightly drug-affected. No, make that a *lot* drug-affected. He'd given her more pain-killers before she'd gone to shower.

Hitting on her now would be all sorts of wrong.

But she was looking at him with huge eyes, slightly dazed, and her fingers were touching his hair as he stooped to dry her legs.

'Raoul…' she whispered, and he rose and stepped away fast.

'Yeah. You're done,' he told her. 'Where can I find you some clothes? Something sensible.'

He spoke too loud, too emphatically, and the emphasis on the last word was like a slap to them both. *Sensible*. That was the way to go.

'I… My bedroom… It's right next door. There's a jogging suit in the third drawer of the dresser. Knickers in the top drawer. I'm ditching the idea of a bra. But I can get them.'

'Stay where you are,' he said roughly, and backed away fast.

Because it might be sensible to help her into the bedroom and help her get dressed, but there was a bed in the bedroom, and a man had limits, and his were already stretched close to breaking.

So he headed into the bedroom and found the jogging suit, and then he opened the knicker drawer and had to take a deep breath before he felt sensible again. He picked up the first pair of knickers that came to hand and practically slammed the drawer shut. A pair of sheepskin bootees stood beside the bed. Excellent. They weren't sexy in the least.

He headed back to the bathroom, thought about helping her, then decided it might be hard but she should be able to cope herself and it would be far, far safer if he stayed on his side of the door.

He knocked and slipped the clothes around the door, without opening it wide enough for him to see her. They needed barriers, he thought. Big barriers. Preferably barriers with locks on them.

He stepped away from the door as if it was red-hot.

'Steak in ten minutes,' he said. 'If you're up to it. If the painkillers aren't making you too dizzy?'

'The painkillers aren't making me too dizzy,' she told him, and then she stopped.

And he thought he knew what she was about to say because he was feeling the same.

The *painkillers* weren't making her dizzy, but something else was.

The same something that was doing his head in?

She dressed, and replaced the basic sling Raoul had fashioned for her.

Her arm was still painful, but it was a steady, bruised ache, not the searing pain she'd experienced when it was dislocated.

She was dry, she was warm, and she was dressed. She hauled a comb through her curls and thought she looked almost presentable. Almost respectable. *Yeah.* She looked at herself in the mirror. Her jogging suit was baggy and old. She had on her huge sheepskin boots. Her hair was combed but still damp and she didn't have the energy to dry it. There was no way she had the energy for make-up, either.

'It's take me as I am,' she said out loud, and then winced.

Take me?

What was she thinking?

Rocky was sitting at her feet. He looked up at her quizzically, as if guessing her thoughts, and she gave him a rueful smile.

'You and I have been alone too long,' she told him. 'Four months and one lone guy enters our world…'

One *gorgeous* guy. A guy with an accent to make a girl's

toes curl. A guy who was gentle and kind. A guy who'd lost his parents, who knew what being alone felt like.

A kindred spirit?

'Yeah, those drugs are really doing something to you,' she muttered, and adjusted her sling a bit—not because she needed to, but because adjusting it caused her arm to twinge and she felt she needed a little bit of pain right now.

Pain equalled reality. Reality was good.

Reality was getting this guy off her island and going back to her stint of self-imposed exile.

She could smell steak. And onions. Raoul was cooking for her.

'It needed only that,' she muttered, and took a last moment to try and grasp at a reality that was looking more and more elusive.

And then she went to find Raoul.

'Hey.' Raoul turned as she entered the kitchen.

He smiled at her, his eyes raking her from her toes to the top of her head, and his smile said he approved. Of the saggy jogging suit. Of everything. That smile was enough to do a girl's head in.

'Well done. Feel better?'

'I...yes.' Of course she did. A thousand times better. She was clean and she was warm and she was about to be fed. What else could a woman want?

Who else?

'I feel great,' she said, a bit too heartily, and then blinked as he tugged a chair out for her. All this and manners, too?

'You don't need to do this,' she told him. 'I'm the servant here, remember?'

'The servant?'

'Don and Marigold own the island, but they never come here in winter. They needed a caretaker. Rocky and I applied for the job.'

'Just Rocky and you?' He turned to flip the steaks. 'That's hardly safe.'

'There's also supposed to be a handyman-cum-gardener. What they didn't tell me was that he'd quit. He left on the boat I arrived on, and Don and Marigold headed to Europe without finding a replacement.'

He was organising chips on plates. *Chips!* Yeah, they were the frozen oven variety, but she totally approved. Steak and chips and onions. And baby peas, and slivered carrots sautéed in butter. *Wow,* she thought. *Turn back the rescue boats. I'm keeping him.*

Um…*not.*

Drugs, she reminded herself. She really had had a lot of them.

'Don and Marigold need to wake up,' he told her, organising the plates to his satisfaction.

He flipped the steak and veggies on, then carried them to the table, sitting down before her as if this was something they did every day of the week. Then he looked at her sling and leaned over and chopped up her steak. The sensation of being cared for was almost indescribable.

Yeah, maybe she was bordering on delusional…

'They're breaking every rule in the Occupational Safety Code,' he told her, sitting back down again and turning his attention to his own meal. 'Leaving someone in such isolation. Or don't they have those rules in Australia?'

'They do.'

'So why are you still on the island? Come to think about it, why were you here in the first place?'

She didn't answer for a while. She didn't need to. The steak was excellent, as were the accompaniments. She hadn't eaten since breakfast and she'd had a swim and a shock. She could be excused for making food her priority.

But the question hung. *'Why were you here in the first place?'*

It wasn't his business, she thought. But a tiny voice in the back of her mind said, *Why not tell him? Why not say it like it is?*

She hadn't told anyone. She'd simply fled.

'I've been accused of fraud,' she said.

He said nothing.

So what had she expected? Fireworks? Shock? Horror? At least a token of dismay? Instead he concentrated on his second piece of steak as if it was the most important thing in the world. And, because there was nothing else to do, she focused on her food, too. She ate a few more chips and her world settled a little and she felt better.

Lighter.

It was as if the elephant was in the room, but at least it was no longer inside her.

'It couldn't have been a very big fraud,' he said at last, eying the near empty bowl of chips with due consideration.

'What? Why?'

'You're not in jail and you've taken a job as a caretaker in one of the most inhospitable places on the earth. This might be a great house, but you're not living in luxury. So it was either a very small fraud or you've cleverly stacked what you've defrauded away so you can be a billionaire in your old age.'

'I could have paid it back.'

'I suspect if you'd paid it back you wouldn't be on this island. Do you want to tell me about it?'

No, she thought. And then she thought, *Okay, the elephant's out.* But it was still a very big elephant. Regardless of how trivial this guy made it sound.

'It was big,' she told him. 'Something like seven million Australian dollars.'

He shook his head in disbelief. 'Ma'am, if you're hiding that kind of cash you shouldn't let strange men rifle through your knicker drawer.'

And she chuckled. She couldn't help herself.

She laughed, and then she thought, *That's the first time I've laughed since...since...*

She couldn't remember.

'I didn't do it,' she said, and her desire to laugh died. Her thoughts went back to that last day, standing in her boss's office, white with shock. *I didn't do it.*

He hadn't believed her. Why would he?

'So?' Raoul said encouragingly. 'I believe you. You didn't do it, so…the butler?'

She choked again, and he smiled and took another chip and handed it across the table to her.

She took it and ate it, and he kept smiling at her, and his smile was doing something to her insides…

'That's it,' he told her. 'Nice, greasy carbohydrates. Best thing in the world for trauma. Like telling me all about the butler. Jam doughnuts would be better, but for now we're stuck with chips. If not the butler, who?'

'Felicity,' she whispered, and he nodded.

'Of course. I should have guessed. I was lacking a few clues, though. So tell me about Felicity.'

'She's perfect.'

'You mean she probably has the seven million?'

'I guess.'

'Yep, she's perfect, then. Pretty, too, I'll bet.'

And Claire thought of pretty, perfect Felicity and found it hard not to start shaking. But suddenly Raoul's hand was over hers—big, comforting, warm. Joking was put aside.

'Tell me,' he said, and so she did.

From the beginning. All of it.

Of the tiny town where she was raised, of her single mum, of being treated like trash. Of her mum's death when she was fifteen. Of the scholarship and her determination to get out. Of law school and commerce, a double degree. Of academic brilliance and sheer hard work.

Once she'd graduated she'd taken a job in Legal Assistance. It had been a great organisation—helping the underprivileged with legal advice and representation when they couldn't afford it. She'd enjoyed it. Then she'd won a huge legal case that had received national headlines, and she'd been head-hunted by one of the most prestigious law firms in Australia. She had been stupid enough to accept.

Only she hadn't been *one of them.*

'I was the odd one out,' she told him. 'An experiment. They select their lawyers on the basis of family and connections, but one of the senior partners had the noble idea that they should try something else—hire someone on merit. They broke their rules when they hired me. Three others were hired at the same time, on the old system. They'd gone to the same school and the same universities. They were the best of friends. But there was a fourth, and because of me he missed out on a job. So they hated me from day one. I tried not to care. I put my head down and worked. But the more I got ahead the more they hated me.'

'And then?'

'Then there was a problem,' she said, talking almost to herself. 'Insider trading, they call it. Someone in the firm knew something and passed the information on. There was a deal. Someone outside the company made seven million dollars and the media started asking questions. The company had to point the finger at someone.'

'Was there evidence?'

'Of course there was evidence,' she told him. 'A paper trail leading straight back to me. So I was called into the office of the managing director. I had a choice, he said. I could resign and the company's insurer would repay costs, cover the fiasco and keep the company's name clean and out of the courts. Or I could go to jail.' She shrugged. 'They had the best legal team in Australia covering their backs and I was a nobody. I *had* nobody. It didn't seem like much of a choice.'

'But if it wasn't you…?'

She sighed. 'A week after I left Felicity left. For Paris. I have no proof of anything, but Felicity's partner just happens to be the nephew of the managing director, and Felicity had the desk next to mine. So here I am. I haven't been charged with anything, but the legal fraternity in Australia is tight.

My time as a corporate lawyer is over. I might be able to get back into Legal Assistance, but even there I'm now tainted. I took this job to take some time and think through my options, but I don't have many.'

'You could sue,' he said. 'You could fight.'

'Yeah?' She shrugged, and then gave a rueful smile. 'Maybe I could,' she said. 'But it'd cost a fortune. I'd risk debt, or worse, and I'd also risk…'

'Risk what?'

'Attention,' she whispered. 'The media would be all over it. Ever since I was a kid I knew to keep my head down. To stay unnoticed. It's always been safest.' She took a deep breath. 'When I left to go to university our local publican said, "You'll be back, girl. A girl like you…raised in the gutter…you've got airs if you think you'll ever get rid of the stink." But I gave myself airs and this is where it's left me.'

'I wish you'd punched him.'

And the thought suddenly cheered her. She thought back to the smirking publican and wished, quite fiercely, that she'd had the skills then that she had now.

'I could have,' she said, attempting to lighten her voice. 'I have a black belt in karate. I may like keeping myself to myself, but physically if you mess with me you're in trouble. Even if I'm one-handed.'

He looked at her in astonishment. 'You're kidding?'

'Like the publican said, you can take the girl out of the gutter, but you can never take the gutter out of the girl. I learned karate, and the gym I went to taught me base moves as well. I can fight clean or I can fight dirty.'

'That sounds like a warning.'

She grinned. 'If you like. Rocky knows to treat me with respect.' Her smile faded. 'But respect for me is a bit thin on the ground. Bob Maker was a bully and a drunk, but he did get one thing right. Trying to move away from my roots was a mistake. I'll never try it again.'

'So you won't fight? You'll calmly go back where you came from?'

She smiled again at that, but ruefully. 'I wouldn't fit,' she said. 'Legal Assistance is my first love. It's a fantastic organisation. They helped me when Mum died and I was trying to prove I could live independently, but I'm not sure I can go back there. That's what this is all about. Rocky and I are taking six months to think about it. So what about you?'

'What do you mean?'

'Meaning you don't have a mum and dad. I assume your grandparents raised you? Was joining the army a big step?'

He thought about it for a moment. For a long moment. She'd told him so much about herself. It was only fair to explain his background.

But a part of him…*couldn't*. She was sitting opposite him with total trust. She was relaxed, eating her chips, smiling, and she'd just explained how social class had destroyed her career.

Over the years Raoul had watched the almost grotesque change in people's attitudes when his royal title was revealed. Sometimes people fawned. Sometimes people backed away.

With her background, with her recent hurt and with her desire to stay in the background, he suspected Claire would back away fast, and he didn't want that. An urgent voice in his head was starting to say, *This is important. Give it time. Get to know her on equal terms.*

Had his joining the army been a big step?

'I guess it was,' he said at last. 'I'm an officer. I had to fight to get where I was, and to be accepted.'

And wasn't that the truth? Of course he'd been seen as different. It had taken him years to break down barriers, and every now and then the barriers would rise back up.

Like now. If a normal soldier went AWOL questions would be asked, but unless there was a suggestion of foul play the army usually adopted a policy of wait and see. After weeks of tough field exercise some men got drunk, found women, got themselves into places that took them a while to get out of. No one would put out an international alert on *their* disappearance.

Whereas for him…

He had no doubts about the scale of the hue and cry that would be happening. *Heir to the throne of Marétal disappears.* He closed his eyes, thinking of the distress. The fuss. He'd been so stupid.

'You're still tired,' Claire told him, and he thought about explaining and decided again that he didn't want to. Not yet.

He *was* tired. 'I guess…'

'Let's both sleep,' she told him. 'Leave the dishes. They'll wait until morning. I'm beat.'

'The drugs will still be making you dozy.'

'And being tossed around in a bathtub for two days and almost drowned will be making *you* dozy,' she told him. She rose and took a glass of water. 'Pick a bedroom. Any bedroom but mine. Marigold leaves toiletries for her guests—there'll be razors and toothbrushes…everything you need. Raoul, thank you for the meal. Thank you for everything. I'm going to bed.'

She headed for the door. He watched her go. Then… 'Claire?'

She paused and looked back at him. 'Yes?'

'Thank you,' he said softly. 'Thank you for saving my life and thank you…for just being you. And if I ever meet the appalling Felicity it'll be more than karate that comes into play. It would be my privilege to fight for you.'

She smiled, but absently. 'Thank you, but don't get your hopes up,' she told him. 'It's money and power that keeps the Felicitys of this world out of trouble, and neither of us have even close to what *they* have. But there are compensations. That was an awesome steak.'

And then she raised her glass, as if in a toast.

'Here's to what we *do* have,' she told him. 'And here's to

never aspiring to more.' She gave a rueful smile and turned and disappeared.

He didn't follow. Yes, he'd been battered, but he had already slept and there was no way he could sleep now.

He washed the dishes, because that was what you did. Once upon a time he hadn't known what a dishcloth was, but years of roughing it in army camps had knocked that out of him.

Then he figured he should check the damage to the radio transmitter. He'd look pretty stupid if it was just a case of the antenna falling over. And he also needed something to occupy his mind that wasn't Claire.

That was a hard ask. She'd gone to bed, but in a way she was still with him.

She'd told a stark tale and it had hurt her to tell it. He'd been able to tell by the way her face had set as she'd told it. By the way she'd laughed afterwards. He had just been able to...*tell*.

She was right under his skin.

He wanted to find the unknown Felicity and send her to the gutter in Claire's place. He wanted to ruin the entire firm she'd worked for.

He could. Maybe he would.

He thought of what he had—the resources, the power—and thought he should tell her.

Why? What good would it possibly do for Claire to know now what power he could wield?

She was treating him as a companion. He had no doubt that her dreadful little story wouldn't have been told if he'd first appeared to her in royal regalia. But he'd been in army gear, and she'd have had no way of recognising the discreet crown emblazoned on the sleeve. To her he was just a soldier—someone who'd come up through the ranks. A kid with no parents.

She thought he was the same as she was, and he didn't mind her thinking it. No, he *wanted* her to think it.

Why? Tired as he was, the warning bells that seemed to have been installed in his brain since his parents' death were suddenly jangling. He'd been a loner since then—or maybe even earlier. The royal household was always full of people, but whenever he needed comfort he never knew who it was who'd do the comforting. Whose job it was that week…

He'd learned not to need comfort. People came and went. He didn't get attached.

Why was he suddenly thinking of this in relation to Claire?

He shook his head, trying to rid himself of thoughts that were jumbling. He was overtired, he thought, still battered, still not thinking straight. He needed to be practical.

First things first. He didn't intend to spend the rest of his time here wearing Don's clothes. He found the laundry and put his and Claire's salt-laden clothes in the washing machine.

But that was weirdly intimate, too. He shoved them in without looking at them, but as he closed the machine door and the clothes started to tumble he saw Claire's wispy bra tangling with his army gear.

Maybe he should have hand-washed it, he thought, but then again…maybe not.

He turned his back on the laundry, thinking as he did that it was over the top—a vast wet room with every machine a laundry could ever hold.

How was it all powered? There was no mains power here, and if there had been it would have surely been knocked out by the storm.

He did a quick reconnaissance of the house, avoiding the passage to Claire's self-contained apartment. Claire's apartment was sparsely furnished, but the rest of the house not so much. Every room was enormous. Every room was lavish. He had a choice of bedrooms, all made up and ready. The unknown Don and Marigold might obviously sweep in at a moment's notice with a bevy of guests.

The refrigerators would cope.

But the power…?

He ended up in the basement and found his answer. Here was a vast bank of batteries, presumably linked to solar panels. This explained why the house was still warm, the refrigerators still operating.

It still wasn't safe for Claire to be here, he thought. Not alone.

Which led to figuring out the radio. He'd found the second transmitter in the study. It was huge and it was useless.

Frustrated, he found a torch and ventured outside. The wind was still up, catching him in its icy chill, but he'd been in conditions far worse than this during his service. The antenna had been attached to one of the outbuildings and it had crashed down during the storm. It lay smashed across the rocks, and with it lay the remains of a satellite dish.

This had been some communications system. A much smaller one would have been far less prone to damage.

Someone had wanted the best—so they could tune into a football game in Outer Mongolia if they wished. He stared bitterly at the over-the-top equipment and thought they could even have used this to talk to Mars if there had been anyone on Mars to hear.

But not now. A small radio might have been within his power to fix. This, he hadn't a hope of fixing.

In this day and age surely there must be *some* method of communicating with the mainland.

Smoke signals?

Right.

He'd seen the maps. This island was far away from normal shipping channels. There might be the odd fishing trawler around, but after the storm the sea would be churned for days. Fishing fleets would stay in port until things settled.

He thought of his grandparents and felt ill.

There was nothing he could do about their distress. *Nothing.*

He could go to bed and worry about it there.

He did go to bed—in the smallest of the over-the-top bedrooms. He lay in the dark and decided that worrying achieved nothing. He should turn his mind off tomorrow and simply appreciate that he was in a warm bed, his world had stopped rocking and he was safe.

He did manage to turn his mind off worrying.

He didn't quite succeed in turning his mind off Claire.

CHAPTER FIVE

SHE WOKE AND the sun was streaming into her little bedroom. She was safe in her own bed, Rocky was asleep on her feet—and she was sore.

Very sore. She shifted a little and her arm protested in no uncertain terms.

She opened her eyes and saw a note propped against a glass of water.

Pills, it said. *Pain. When you wake take these. Don't try and move until they take effect.*

That seemed like great advice. She took the pills that were magically laid out beside the glass and forced herself to relax. If she lay very still it didn't hurt.

Some time during the night Raoul had come into her bedroom and left the pills. He'd checked on her.

Maybe it was creepy.

Maybe it was…safe.

She let the thought drift and found it comforting. No, it was more than that, she thought. He *cared.*

For Claire, the concept of care was almost foreign. She'd been an unwanted baby. Her mother had done her best by her, but there'd been little affection—her mother had been too stressed taking care of the basics. Claire had been a latchkey kid from the time she could first remember, getting home to an empty house, getting herself dinner, going to bed telling herself stories to keep the dark at bay.

She'd gone to bed last night aching and sore and battered, but so had Raoul. She'd seen the bruises. She was under no illusion that he was hurting almost as much as she was, and he must be far more traumatised.

And yet he'd taken the time to check on her during the

night. He'd thought about her waking in pain and he'd done something about it.

'I'm a sad woman,' she said out loud. 'One act of kindness and I turn to mush. And he owes me. I saved his life. Or I think I did.'

'You did.'

The voice outside the door made her jump.

'Can I come in?'

'I...yes.'

She tugged the bedcovers up to her chin and Rocky assumed the defensive position—right behind the hump of her thigh, so he could look like a watch dog but had Claire between him and any enemy.

And he could be an enemy, she conceded as he pushed open the door. He was back in his army gear. It was a bit battered and torn but it was still decent. He was wearing khaki camouflage pants and a shirt. His shirt was unbuttoned at the neck, his sleeves were rolled back to make him a soldier at ease, but he still looked every inch a soldier. He was shaved and clean and neat, but he still looked...*dangerous.*

He was carrying juice.

'You have great refrigerators,' he told her, and the image of a lean and dangerous soldier receded to be replaced by... just Raoul. The guy with the smile. 'I poured myself some juice and then thought I might check if you were awake. It seems presumptuous to forage in the fridge without my hostess's consent.'

'Forage away,' she said. 'You gave me drugs.'

'They're *your* drugs.'

'They're Marigold's drugs,' she told him. 'But I'm taking them anyway.' She struggled to sit up, and found with one arm it was tricky. But then she had help. The juice was set on the bedside table as Raoul stooped and put an arm around her, pushing a pillow underneath.

He was so close. He smelled clean. He felt...

Yeah, don't go there.

'How sore? Scale of one to ten?' he asked, withdrawing a little.

And she hated him withdrawing, even though it was really dumb to want him to stay. To want him to keep holding her.

How sore? Less since he'd walked into the room, she thought. How could a woman focus on her arm when *he* was there?

'Maybe five,' she managed. 'Compared to about nine last night. Five's manageable.'

'It'll ease. The pills will take off the edge.'

'How do you know?' she asked curiously, and he shrugged.

'I'm in the army. Accidents happen.'

'And sometimes…not accidents?'

'Mostly accidents,' he told her, and gave that lopsided smile that was half-mocking, half-fun.

She liked that smile, she decided. She liked it a lot.

'I've been in the army for fifteen years and never had to put a single sticking plaster on a bullet hole. But broken legs and dislocated shoulders, cuts and bruises, stubbed toes and hangovers…as first-aid officer for my unit I've coped with them all. Actually, make that especially hangovers.'

'Why did you join the army?' She was propped up now. She'd taken her pills. Maybe she should settle down and sleep again until the pills worked, but Raoul was here, and she hadn't seen anyone for four months—surely that was a good enough reason for wanting him to stay? It surely wasn't anything to do with how good he looked in his uniform. And how that smile twisted something she hadn't known could be twisted.

'Lots of reasons,' he told her. 'The army's been good for me.'

'Good *to* you or good *for* you?'

'Both. Has this island been good for *you*?'

'I guess.' She thought about it for a moment and then shook her head. 'Maybe not. Six months is a long time. You just heard me talking to myself. I do that a lot. I guess I'm starting to go stir-crazy.'

'The least your employers could do is give you a decent bedroom,' he told her, looking round at her bare little room in disgust. 'You have bedrooms here that are so opulent they could house a family of six and not be squashed, and you're in something out of *Jane Eyre*.'

'Hey, I have my own bathroom. I bet Jane never had that.' She smiled, the pain in her arm receding with every second—and it had nothing to do with the drugs, she thought. It had everything to do with the way this man was smiling at her. 'But every now and then I do sneak into one of the guest bedrooms,' she conceded. 'They all have fantastic views. Rocky and I read romance novels and pretend we're who we're not all over again. But I'm here to get my life back to normal, not indulge in fantasy.'

'You can't stay here,' he told her.

She took a couple of sips of juice and thought about it. 'I have a contract.'

'The contract doesn't hold water. It's unsafe to leave you here alone for six months and now the radio's smashed.'

'I can get a new one.'

'Which could get smashed, too. When we figure out a way to evacuate me, you need to come, too.'

'I can't just walk out.'

'I assume you can contact Don and Marigold?'

'I…yes. When I get satellite connection again.'

'Or when you get to the mainland and email or phone them. You've been injured. You have no reliable means of communication. Any lawyer in the land will tell you you're within your rights to terminate your contract. And,' he said, and grinned, 'I happen to know a lawyer right here, right now. Don't be a doormat, Claire Tremaine.'

'I'm not a doormat.'

'I know that,' he told her.

And here came that smile again. *Oh, that smile...*

'I had proof of that yesterday,' he continued. 'But for today you're allowed to be as doormat-like as you want. And speaking of wants…would you like breakfast in bed?'

'No!'

'Just asking,' he said, and grinned and put up his hands as in self-defence. 'Don't throw the porridge at me.'

'Porridge?'

'I found oats,' he told her. 'And maple syrup. It's a marriage made in heaven. It's on the stove now.'

'I thought you said you weren't going to forage without my permission.'

'I didn't need to forage for these guys. Like the eggs last night, they jumped right out at me. Want to share?'

'I…' She stared at that smile, at those crinkly eyes, at that magnetic twinkle, and there was only one answer. 'Yes, please,' she told him. And then she added: 'But not in bed.'

Because breakfast in bed with this guy around… Some things seemed too dangerous to be considered.

The transmitter was indeed useless.

They stood in the ruins of the radio shack and stared at the shambles and Raoul said, 'What on earth was he thinking? He could have had half of this set up in the safety of the house.'

'But it would have been only half of this set-up.'

Claire was dressed and breakfasted. The painkillers were working; indeed they might not be needed as much as she'd feared, for with her arm held safe in the sling the throbbing had eased to almost nothing. She'd walked outside with him to see the damage. The wind had ceased. The shack holding the radio transmitter was a splintered mess, debris covered the terracing, but the storm was over.

'He wanted to take over one of the rooms in the house,' she told Raoul. 'But Marigold wouldn't have it—a nasty, messy radio transmitter in her beautiful house. So he planned to build proper housing, but of course he wanted it straight away, so he was forced to use this.' She looked ruefully at the mess. 'This was an old whaler's cottage, but it's been a long time since any whaler came near the place.'

'Or anyone else?'

'The supply boat comes once a week. They didn't come this Monday because of the storm. I expect they'll come next week, unless the weather's bad. That's why we have decent supplies.'

'Fishing boats?' he said, without much hope, and she shook her head.

'I've never seen any. I see an occasional small plane, out sightseeing.' She hesitated. 'You're thinking of rescue. Are you sure your friends won't realise you were on a boat and be searching?'

'I'm sure,' he said grimly. 'There were reasons I wanted to be alone. I seem to have succeeded better than I imagined.'

'Hey,' she said, and she touched his shoulder lightly, a feather touch. 'Not completely,' she said. 'You're stuck with Rocky and me. Want to come to the beach?'

'Why?'

'To see if anything's been washed in from your boat.'

'You need to rest.'

'I've had four months of resting,' she retorted. 'Come on, soldier—or can't those bootees make it?'

He was wearing Don's sheepskin bootees. He stared down at his feet and then stared at Claire.

She smiled her most encouraging smile and turned towards the cliff path. Maybe she should be resting, she thought, but there was a reason she was pushing him to come with her.

While Raoul had been in charge—while there'd been things to do—Raoul's smile had been constant. He'd buoyed her mood. He'd given her courage. But now, standing in the ruins of the only way to get messages to and from the island, his smile had disappeared. She'd heard bleakness and self-blame in his voice.

He'd helped her, so the least she could do was help him back. Maybe she should dislocate the other shoulder. She grinned, and he caught up with her and glanced across and saw the grin.

'What? What do you have to laugh about?'

'You,' she said. 'I might need to put a training regime in place if you're not to get miserable. You're stuck here for at least five days...'

'I can't stay for five days.'

'Five days until the supply boat's due,' she said inexorably. 'But Marigold has a whole library of romance novels, and Don has fishing magazines, so cheer up. Meanwhile, let's go see if anything's left of your boat.'

Rosebud was an ex-boat.

The last time he'd seen Tom's boat she'd been upturned in the surf. Now she was nothing more than a pile of splintered debris on the storm-washed beach.

The radio shack and *Rosebud* had held his only links to the mainland and both were smashed. He looked out at the still churning sea and knew he had a lot to be thankful for—but at what cost?

'Will your friend be very upset?' Claire asked in a small voice.

He thought of Tom, and thought of the new boat he could buy him, and he thought Tom would give him heaps of flak and enjoy buying a new boat very much.

'I guess,' he said.

'Is it insured?'

He hadn't even thought of insurance. 'Probably. I don't know.'

'Will you have to cover the cost? Oh, Raoul...'

And she slipped her hand into his with such easy sympathy that it was impossible for him to say, *No, it's okay, the cost of this yacht is hardly a drop in the ocean of my fortune.*

Why would he say that when she was holding his hand and looking up at him with concern?

Um...because otherwise it was dishonest?

Maybe it was, he thought, but she held his hand and he liked it, and he thought if he was to be stuck here for days then he wouldn't mind being treated as an equal.

Time enough to be treated as a royal when he got home.

And the thought struck again. His grandparents... They'd have heard by now. They'd be grief-stricken, appalled and terrified.

Something must have shown on his face, because the hold on his hand tightened.

'It's okay, Raoul,' she said softly. 'You can't help any of this.'

'I could have.'

'Yeah, but that's in the past. You can't do a thing about that now. Focus on the future.'

'Like you have? Should I go find me a rock to sit on for six months?'

'You can have this one if you like,' she told him. 'I'm over it. Hey, is that a boot?'

It was. Rocky had found it. He was standing over it, wagging every bit of him in excitement. Raoul let go Claire's hand—reluctantly—and went to see.'

One boot. It was half hidden under a clump of seaweed.

'Let's see if we can find more,' Claire told him, and they hunted at the high tide mark and found the other, washed in after he'd kicked it off in the water. It was dumb, but their find made him feel a whole lot better.

Could a guy with boots walk home? Maybe not, but when they were cleaned and dried he wouldn't be dependent on Don's slippers. And when he was finally taken off this rock...

'You'll look very nice for the journalists,' Claire told him, and he looked at her sharply.

'Journalists?'

'You think if someone finds you that you'll slip back into Hobart unnoticed? Storm...wrecked yacht...marooned in the middle of Bass Strait...' She brightened. 'Hey, maybe you could sell it to the tabloids. All it needs is a sex angle and you could maybe make enough to pay for your friend's yacht.'

A sex angle...

The comment had been flippant. Off the cuff. It had been all about tabloid newspapers and what sold. It wasn't anything to do with what was happening to them.

So why did it seem to stand out? Why did the words seem to echo?'

What *was* it about this woman that was making his senses tune in to nuances that shouldn't be there? She was injured, vulnerable, alone. He had no business thinking of her in any way other than as someone who'd saved his life and was stuck on this barren, rocky outcrop with him until help arrived.

Think of something else—fast.

He bent and picked up a battered piece of timber, the painted registration number of *Rosebud*, and tried to think of a way he could get a message to the mainland. A way he could get a message to his grandparents.

He tried not to think of the woman beside him, of how she made him feel.

'Chuck a message in a bottle?' she asked.

He looked sharply up at her. She'd better not be able to read his mind, he thought. His thoughts were too tangled, and somewhere in there was the vision of Claire as he'd first seen her, struggling in the water towards him, holding him, her lovely chestnut curls tangled wetly around her face.

Claire...

Yeah, empty the mind fast, he told himself. What had she said? A message in a bottle?

'I suspect your supply boat might be faster,' he said, and she grimaced.

'You're right. Your grandparents will be very frightened?'

'They'll know I won't have gone AWOL.' *As will half the world.* He thought of the rumours that would be circulating. His country had had recent threats centred on the throne. The current thinking was that they had come from a crazy fringe organisation with no resources. Marétal was a small player on the world stage, but his disappearance followed by silence would have the media in a frenzy. His grandparents would be beside themselves.

No boat for almost a week…

'If we had the internet we could try and make a crystal radio set,' Claire said thoughtfully. 'I had a friend who made one once.'

'Good idea,' he told her. 'Except we *don't* have the internet and crystal sets receive but don't send. But if we had the internet we could email.'

'Oh.'

'But good thinking.'

'Don't patronise me,' she muttered.

He grinned. She really was extraordinary. 'I guess we could always burn the place down,' he said, deciding to join her in the planning department. 'If the fire was big enough and we did it during the day the smoke would be seen for miles.'

'Yeah, and if it wasn't noticed…?'

'Is there a cave in any of these cliffs?'

'I don't know about you, soldier,' she told him. 'But Rocky and I don't take kindly to caves. We like our comfy beds. And how would I explain a fire to Marigold? I'm caretaker for this place. Burning it down doesn't exactly come into my job description.'

'It was just a suggestion,' he said hastily.

'A bad one.'

'Okay, a bad one.'

'Hmmph.'

They stared at the sea some more. She was so close, Raoul thought. She was obviously thinking.

He should be doing some thinking. He *was* thinking. It was just that the woman beside him was taking up a whole lot of his thinking room.

'What about an SOS in the middle of the island?' she said, and he hauled his thoughts back to sense when his thoughts really didn't want to go.

'SOS…?'

'We could do it in rocks,' she said. 'There's a flat plateau behind the house. It's strewn with small rocks. We could organise them into an SOS. I'm thinking by tomorrow sightseeing flights might start again from Hobart. A plane might fly across.'

'Do they always fly across?'

'There aren't many,' she told him. 'It's winter. Tourists who pay money for flights will be thin on the ground and we don't have a weather forecast so it might be a lot of effort for nothing.'

He thought about it. SOS. The universal cry for help. Was it justified?

They were both well. They had enough supplies to keep them fed for as long as they were stranded and the house was more than comfortable.

'It'd be for your grandparents' sake,' Claire said, watching him. 'And you might get charged for the cost of the rescue.'

He might.

The cost would be negligible compared to the costs his country would be facing trying to locate the heir to the throne.

Claire was watching him thoughtfully. 'Is it just for your grandparents?' she asked, and he thought about telling her.

I'm royal and there'll be a worldwide search…

Not yet. For some unknown reason a voice in the back of his head was pleading, *Not yet.* She thought he was an equal. A soldier, nothing more.

She'd been battered by people who'd treated her as trash. She was feisty and brave but she'd retreated to this island, hurt.

He didn't want her retreating from *him*. He knew he'd have to tell her, but now the voice was almost yelling.

Not yet. Not yet.

'There'll be a fuss and a half when I get off this island,' he told her. 'Part of me thinks I should just stay. But the fuss has to be faced some time, and my grandparents…they'll be pushing for a search, no matter what the cost.'

And that was the truth, he thought. When he thought of the resources they'd be throwing at it… At *him*… And his two bodyguards… They'd be being vilified and it wasn't their fault. Short of burning down the house, he had to try everything.

'Let's do it,' he said shortly, without answering her question, and she looked at him curiously.

'There's stuff you're not telling me.'

'I'm ashamed of myself.'

'Would the army rescue you?'

'Yes.' That would be the best outcome, he thought. If the army could slip in and take him off the island…

'An SOS seen by sightseers is going to hit the media,' she told him. 'Are you prepared to have your picture taken?'

'I guess it'll be both of us.'

'Not me,' she told him. 'Not in a million years. I'm hiding, remember? If you get taken off by a crew of SAS forces abseiling down with parachutes and stun guns I'll be hiding in Don's basement. Tell them you were taken in by a hermit with a beard down to his ankles who fires at the sight of a camera. Better still…' She hesitated. 'Better still, just wait for the supply boat.'

'I don't think I can.'

'Really?'

'Really.'

She looked at him long and hard. Then she sighed and picked up his waterlogged boots.

'Okay, then,' she told him. 'Let's go dry some boots and organise some rocks.'

* * *

He organised rocks. Claire sat on a rocky ledge at the edge of the plateau and watched.

It was kind of peaceful. The wind had died completely. The weak winter sun was warm on her face. Today was one of the few days she'd had here when the weather made her think this was a wonderful place to stay.

Or maybe it was the company. Maybe it was because the ache in her arm was fading. Maybe it was because she and Rocky were safe and yesterday had made her realise how wonderful 'safe' was.

Maybe it was because she was watching Raoul work.

He worked…like a soldier. He'd decided a small SOS wouldn't cut it—he needed to work big. So first off he'd cleared an area the size of a tennis court. That alone had been huge. Now, the rocks he was heaving weren't small. One-handed, Claire couldn't have begun to help, but even if she'd been two-handed it would have been a big ask.

Raoul had simply set to work, heaving rock after rock. After the first half hour he'd stripped to his waist. He sweated a bit as he worked. His body glistened in the sunlight.

A girl could waste a lot of hours watching that body, Claire thought, and as there was little she could do to help she might as well enjoy it.

She did enjoy it.

She'd spent four solitary months here. She'd only seen the guys on the supply boat—two guys in their sixties, salt-encrusted to their toenails, bearded, weathered, cracking up at their own jokes as they tossed her supplies onto the beach and left her to cart them up to the house.

They hardly talked to her—they were men in a hurry, trying to get their run done and get back to Hobart and the pub. They couldn't know how important they'd become to her—two harried boatmen and fifteen minutes' terse conversation, mostly about the weather.

And now she had her very own guy here, to look at all she wanted, and who could blame her if she was enjoying it very much indeed?

'You're making it very big,' she ventured, and he tossed a few more rocks and wiped the sweat from his forehead with the back of his hand. He was magnificently tanned, she thought, or maybe he was permanently bronzed.

He was gorgeous.

'Last S,' he said, and headed to a pile of rocks that loomed over the plateau. He climbed the rocks as if he'd been bred on cliffs, sure and steady on the shale. This was the high point of the island. He gazed down at his efforts and gave her the thumbs-up.

'Want to see?'

'I don't think I can.' She couldn't get the full effects of his artwork from ground level, but climbing the loose rocks with one arm would be asking for trouble.

'That's what I'm here for.' He slid down the slope, reached her and held out his hand. 'Your servant, ma'am.'

'I'm very sure you're not,' she said a bit breathlessly, and he smiled.

'You saved my life. You've taken me in and fed me. Believe me, Claire, I'm your servant for life.'

And he drew her upright and she was too close. But then he turned and started up the shale again.

A part of her didn't want to be tugged up the shale. It wanted to stop exactly where it was and be held.

But that wasn't Sensible Claire thinking. It was Dumb Claire. And hadn't she made a vow to be Sensible Claire forever?

Tomorrow, she told herself. Or the next day. Whenever the SOS worked. Then she'd be alone again and she could be as sensible as she wanted.

But Raoul was tugging her up the rocks, holding her tight, making sure she didn't slip, and the feeling of him holding her was making Sensible Claire disappear entirely.

Sense would have to be left to the soldier.

'What do you think?'

They'd reached the top. He turned and held her at the waist—in case she slipped?—and she forced herself to stop focusing on the feel of his hands and look down at his handiwork.

He'd cleared the plateau. The rocks he'd used were seriously big. No one could fly over and miss the message he'd made.

He could be rescued today, she thought. A plane could fly over right now and within an hour a rescue chopper could arrive from the mainland. He'd be gone.

She shivered.

'You're cold,' he said, and curved his arm around her as if he could keep her warm just by holding her.

As indeed he could, she thought ruefully. Even hot.

'I've been doing manual work. You should have stayed inside.'

'But I love hard work,' she managed. 'I can sit and watch people do it for hours.'

Wrong, she thought. *I can sit and watch you...*

'Inside now, though,' he told her. 'You need to rest.'

'You're the one who was battered for two days.'

'So I was. So we both need to rest. And then… Do you have any movies on that very impressive entertainment system?'

'Indeed we do.' She thought for a bit, which was kind of hard, because he was holding her and he was really close and his chest was bare and his skin felt…

Um…what was she trying to think of? Movies. Movies would be excellent.

'Actually, they're mostly on the net,' she told him. 'And we have no net with the communications down. But we do have a few oldies but goodies on DVD.'

'I'm all for oldies but goodies. Popcorn?'

'Possibly not. Potato chips and nuts?'

'My favourite. You want me to help you down from this rock or would you like me to carry you?'

And what was a girl to say to that?

Luckily Sensible Claire hadn't completely disappeared. Luckily Sensible Claire said that this guy had had a physical battering and carrying a load—*her*—down the loose rocks would run every risk of disaster.

'I'll walk,' she said, and Dumb Claire almost cried.

CHAPTER SIX

THEY BOTH HAD a sleep. Then Raoul foraged in Don's cellar while Claire cooked a simple pasta dish.

He showed her what wine he'd chosen and she pretty near had kittens. 'Do you know how much that's worth?'

'No.' Then he looked at the dusty label and grinned. 'Though I can guess.'

'Raoul, it'll be half a week's salary.'

'But I could be dead. And Don owes you. He's stranded an employee with no back-up on a deserted island. Hey, and you're a lawyer. We're safe.'

'Right,' she said dryly, but she stopped arguing. Who could argue with that smile?

They curled upon the sofa and atc dinner, and Claire found chocolate, and the wine was truly excellent.

There were three settees in front of the vast TV screen, but two were elegant and only one was squishy and right in front, so it seemed foolish not to share.

They watched *African Queen* and then *Casablanca.* The wine was still amazing. The fire crackled in the hearth. Rocky snoozed by the fireside. They hadn't bothered with lights as the day faded to night. The television and the fire gave enough light.

And then the movie ended and they were left with the glowing embers of the fire.

'Another one?' Raoul asked as Humphrey Bogart walked away in the fog.

Claire was too busy sniffing to answer.

'I guess not,' Raoul said thoughtfully, and produced a handkerchief and dried her cheeks.

And she had enough sense left—*just*—to recognise the linen.

'That's one of Don's monogrammed handkerchiefs.'

'There goes another week's salary,' he said, and smiled into her eyes. 'I can't think of a worthier cause.'

'Raoul…' She should pull back, but he didn't. He traced the track of her last tear and suddenly things intensified. Or maybe they'd been intensifying all day and now they were too aware of each other, too warm and safe, too…*aware*?

Wrong word. There must be another, but Claire couldn't think of one. Actually, she couldn't think of anything but Raoul and how close he was.

She put her own hand up and touched his face—the bronzed skin, the creases at the corners of his eyes, the raw strength she saw there. And something inside her wanted. Badly wanted.

'Raoul,' she whispered again, and her body seemed to move of its own accord. Closer.

'Claire…'

'Raoul…'

Raoul's smile had faded but his hands were still tracing her cheeks. When he spoke his voice sounded ragged. 'I'm aware, my amazing Claire, that you're alone on this island apart from Rocky, and that Rocky doesn't seem to be standing guard right now. Don deserves to be tossed in jail for leaving you defenceless, and I will not take advantage. But…' He hesitated. 'I *would* like to kiss you. So, in the cold light of day…'

'It's night.'

'In the warm glow of night,' he continued, and put his finger under her chin and raised her face to his. 'Would you like to be kissed?'

'You ask me that after *Casablanca*?'

'I know I don't rate beside Humphrey.'

'*How* do you know?'

'Just guessing.'

And she managed a smile back. Sort of. 'I'd have to see.'

'Have you ever kissed Humphrey?'

'No, but I've watched him kiss. He's pretty good. It's no small order to try and match him.'

'You're asking me to try?'

'No,' she said, and her voice was pretty much a whisper. She was feeling melty. Warm. Safe. Loved?

It was a dumb feeling—a mockery, a lie. How could she feel so deeply so soon? But it was there just the same, and there was no way she could ignore it.

'No,' she said again. 'I'm not asking. I'm ordering.'

And then there was nothing to be said. Nothing at all. Because he was taking her into his arms—gently, because of her injured arm. Or maybe gently because there was no way this man would force himself where he wasn't wanted. She knew him hardly at all, but she knew that about him at least.

And she knew more. She knew how he'd taste. She knew how he'd feel. She knew how her body would respond as their lips met, as the heat passed from one to another, as her whole body seemed to melt into his.

She didn't know how she knew, but she did. It was as if her whole life had been building to this moment. It was as if he was the other half of her whole, and finally—finally—they'd come together.

It was a dumb thought. Theirs was a fleeting encounter, she thought, with what little of her mind she had left to think. This man was a stranger.

Except right now he wasn't. For this moment, on this island, he was everything she needed and more.

And caution was nowhere.

He kissed…but what a kiss.

He hadn't expected to be blown away.

He'd expected a kiss he'd enjoy. He'd expected—or hoped for—warmth, arousal, passion.

He hadn't expected his world to shift.

It did.

Was it shock?

Was it the fear of the last few days?

Was it that Claire had rescued him?

Who could say? But somehow being with this woman had changed something inside him, and whatever it was it felt huge.

He'd been in the army for years. He'd worked with feisty women—women with intelligence and honour and courage. Back home in Marétal he'd met some of the most beautiful women in the world. Society darlings. Aristocracy and royalty.

Beauty and intelligence weren't mutually exclusive. He'd dated many of those women and most he still called friends.

Not one of them made him feel like Claire was making him feel now.

He'd known her for less than two days. This was just a kiss.

So how did it feel as if breaking apart from her would break something inside him?

And, amazingly, she seemed to feel the same. Her body was moulding to his and her hands cupped his face, deepening the kiss. She was warm and strong and wonderful, and the feel of her mouth under his was making his body desire as he'd never felt desire.

This wasn't just a kiss. It could never be just a kiss. This was the sealing of a promise that was unvoiced but seemed to have been made the moment she'd crashed into him out in the water.

Claire.

If she wanted to pull back now he'd let her. Of course he would. He must, because this was a woman to be honoured.

Honour.

With that thought came another, and it was a jolt of reality that left him reeling.

This woman had saved his life. She'd been injured, battered, drugged, all to save his sorry hide, and now she was sharing her place of refuge with him.

Right now he wanted her more than anything he'd ever wanted in his life, but…

But. The word was like a hammer blow in his brain.

But he was a man of honour…

A prince…

He hadn't even told her who he was. If this went further she'd wake up tomorrow and know she'd been bedded by the heir to the throne of Marétal.

There'd be consequences, and consequences had been drilled into him since birth.

Bedding a woman he'd just met…

But how could he think of consequences? He was kissing Claire and she was kissing him back. How could he think past it?

How could he draw away?

She wasn't sure how long the kiss lasted. How did she measure such a thing? How could she think of trying to measure? All she knew was that she was kissing and being kissed and she never wanted it to end.

His arms were around her, tugging her body to him. Her breasts were crushed against his chest.

It felt so right. It felt as if she'd found her home.

Raoul. Her head was singing it—an ode to joy. *Raoul.*

Was it just that she'd been stuck alone on an island for four months? Was this some sort of Robinson Crusoe syndrome?

Their passion was pretty much overwhelming her. She seemed to have too many clothes on. Raoul definitely had too many clothes on.

Almost involuntarily her hands moved to the front of his shirt, tugging…

a voice hammering inside, pounding out the fact that this was uncharted territory. This woman was special.

This woman had the means to slice through the carefully constructed armour he'd developed ever since his parents died. He didn't need anyone. He'd learned that early. And yet when Claire had surged through the surf to save his life… Yes, he had needed her, and somehow with every moment his body was telling him he needed her more.

But honour demanded that he step away. Honour and the need to rebuild that armour.

And was there a touch of fear in there as well?

No!

She wanted to scream it.

Don't stop. Please don't stop. I want to get close. So close...

But he was putting her back from him. She could see passion in his eyes, a desire that matched hers, but she could also see an almost desperate control.

'Claire… We can't.'

'Why not?'

'It's too soon.' His voice was almost a groan. 'Hell, I want to—I'd be inhuman not to—but you've been injured. You're still shocked and so am I. You're on this island by yourself. I won't take advantage.'

'What are you talking about? You wouldn't be taking advantage. We're both adults.'

'If we'd known each other for such a short time on the mainland…' He had her shoulders, was searching her eyes. 'Claire, would you be sleeping with me tonight or would you … wait a little?'

'I don't … thing in the wor… But I won't. It's not ju… this got to do w… told her. … Claire, more than any- … had right now.

math of battle there's often emotional meltdown. What we've been through is the equivalent. We can't take this further until you're sure.'

And his words made her stop.

I'm sure.

She wanted to scream it from one end of the island to the other, but all of a sudden she wasn't.

He was being sensible. She hated him for it, but he was right.

If the weather blew up again they could be marooned together for weeks. Sense said that she had to keep her emotions under control.

She didn't want to be sensible.

She drew back, feeling foolish, emotional and, yes, if she was honest, humiliated. And he saw it. He reached out and touched her face again, but this time his touch was different. It was a feather touch. It was a caress all on its own.

'Don't feel like that,' he told her. 'Claire, I'm trained to recognise my emotions. I'm trained for sense.'

'And I'm not?'

'I don't know,' he told her. 'All I know is that the way I'm feeling about you is scaring the heck out of me.'

'So you'll run?'

'Only as far as another movie.'

'Raoul…'

'Claire.' He touched her lips. 'You are truly beautiful. You are truly wanted. But we both know that sense should have us building six-foot walls.'

'I guess…' she whispered, and he smiled at her, that smile that undid every single thing he said about sense.

'I *know*,' he said, and it nearly killed her that he was right.

Somehow she slept that night. Somehow she ma[illegible]and breakfast. Somehow she swallow[illegible] got on with getting on.

But she didn't know whether she wanted a plane to come or not.

At dawn she was already tuned in to the sound of engines, but it was midwinter and the storm would still be fresh in people's minds. That storm had swung up from the Antarctic seemingly with no warning. Tourists would therefore be delaying or cancelling their sightseeing flights, so a plane was unlikely.

Somehow she had to figure a way to get through this without going nuts. She needed a way of facing Raoul and not wanting him…

After breakfast—a meal full of things unsaid, of loaded silences—she decided to cook. Cooking had been a comfort to her forever, so why not now?

'Muffins,' she told Raoul.

'Muffins?' He'd been distant over breakfast. He was obviously finding the going as hard as she was. It seemed up to her to find a way through it.

'If you want fresh food on this island you need to cook,' she told him. 'And I even have frozen herbs. So if we want muffins for lunch…'

There was a silence, and then, 'Do you have apples?'

'Tinned.'

'Hmm.' He considered. 'That might be a challenge, but I'm up for it. You make your muffins. I'll make *tarte tatin*.'

'*Tarte tatin?* With tinned apples?'

'I'm a camp cook extraordinaire.'

'Wow!' She stared at him. He was back in Don's pants and the T-shirt that stretched too tight. They'd showered before breakfast. His hair was still damp. He was still a bit…rumpled.

The man could cook.

So they cooked, but if she'd thought it would make things [illegible] between them she had been dead wrong.

[illegible] he made pastry from scratch, his long,

strong fingers rubbing butter into flour as if he'd been doing it all his life.

Wanting him was killing her.

'Who taught you to cook?' she managed. 'Your grandmother? If your mother died when you were so young…'

'Many people taught me to cook,' he told her. 'I was never neglected.'

'It sounds like you came from a wonderful community.'

'I did,' he said, but his answer was curt. Maybe it hurt to go there. 'And you?'

'I taught myself to cook.'

'Not your mother?'

'Mum was on her own. I was an accident when she was eighteen and she had a hard time keeping me. She struggled with depression but she did her best. Early on I learned I could make her smile by having something yummy ready when she got home. She used to clean at the local hair salon and she brought home magazines that had got too tatty. I learned to cook from those magazines. It took me ages to accept that some ingredients were too expensive. I'd write a list, and get fed up when she'd come home with cheddar cheese rather than camembert—but she tried.'

'You both sound…courageous.'

'We weren't courageous. We just survived. Until…'

'Until?'

She shrugged. 'Until Mum couldn't survive any more. When I was fifteen she lost the fight.' She dredged up a smile. 'But by then I could cook—and cook well. I could look out for myself, and I was pretty intent on a career where I could afford good cheese.'

'So you became a lawyer?'

'As you say. I pushed myself hard and libraries were my friend. Study was my friend.'

'Hence the French?' She'd spoken French in the water. He'd hardly remembered, but he remembered now.

'What else was there to do when the nights were lonely?'

she asked. 'Italian. French. Chinese. And cooking—which seemed the most important of the lot.'

'You speak Italian, French and Chinese?'

'Doesn't everyone?' She cocked her head to one side. 'Soldier?'

He couldn't resist. *'Was ist Deutch?'* he demanded. *What about German?*

'Ich spreche Deutsch. Aber ich kann nur verstehen wenn langsam gesprochen wird.'

I speak German but I can only understand if people speak slowly.

'Sie sind eine erstaunliche Frau,' he said.

You are an amazing woman.

She grinned. 'Well, I can understand that. You're not bad yourself. German, French, English… Any more?'

'There might be,' he admitted. 'I have smatterings of a lot. Marétal's official language is French, but it's pretty multilingual, plus years in the army means I've travelled. Want to go head to head with how many languages we can swear in?'

She chuckled. 'No way. Rocky would be shocked. Besides, if we're competing I'd rather cook. Your *tarte tatin* against my muffins?'

'Who gets to judge?'

'Rocky, of course,' she told him. 'And he's a very satisfactory judge. If it's edible he'll give it ten out of ten every time.'

The wind was getting up again. Whitecaps topped the ocean. It was becoming more and more unlikely that there'd be any joy flights over the island today, so therefore why not relax and have a cook-off?

It was an unlikely pastime. If anyone had told him three days ago that he'd be marooned on a rocky outcrop, cooking *tarte tatin* beside a woman he was trying not to go to bed with, he'd have thought they had rocks in their head.

But that was what was happening.

He cooked, but a good half of his attention was on the

woman beside him. She was struggling a little, sparing her bad arm. He'd told her she should rest, that she could watch *him* cook, and she'd reacted as if he'd said she had two heads.

'And let you lord it over me when your *tarte* comes out of the oven? In your dreams, soldier. This is battle!'

It was hardly a grim battlefield. They were watching what each other was doing. Learning. Pausing to watch the tricky bits. And finally they were relaxing.

They were talking about the island and her four months here. The things she'd seen. Her personal quest to rid the island of every bit of fishing line that had ever been washed up there—*'Do you know what damage tangled line can do to wildlife?'* The books she'd read. The story of Rocky—how she'd chosen him from the rescue shelter the day before she'd left for the island and how she'd spent the first month trying to persuade him to come out from under her bed.

She talked of her childhood. She talked of her admiration for the legal assistance organisation she'd worked for and how she never should have left. She talked of its scope and its power. She talked of the disaster of her time in Sydney.

She tried to get him to talk to her.

'Is it the army that's making you silent?' she asked at last. 'They say returned soldiers are often too traumatised to speak. Is that you?'

'That's a blunt question.'

'Hey, I had a mother with depression. I learned early not to sugarcoat things. "Mum, how bad are you feeling? Scale of one to ten." That's what I learned to ask. So there you go, Raoul. How traumatised are you—scale of one to ten?'

'I don't think I'm traumatised.' Though that wasn't exactly true. There had been engagements that he didn't want to think about, and she must have seen it in his face.

'You don't want to go there?' she asked, and he shook his head.

'No.'

'And when your boat turned upside down…?'

'I was too busy surviving to be traumatised. And then along came a mermaid.'

'How very fortuitous,' she said primly. She'd finished her muffins—they were baking nicely—and she'd started on a lasagne for dinner. She was feeding pasta dough into a machine, watching with satisfaction as the sheets stretched thinner. 'So what about your childhood?'

'I don't think I'm traumatised.'

'Not even by your parents' death.'

'I was very young. I can hardly remember them, and my grandparents took over.'

'But you don't want to talk about it?'

'No.'

'Fair enough,' she said, and went back to her lasagne.

He thought she wouldn't press. She didn't sound in the least resentful that she'd just told him all about her and he wasn't returning the compliment.

He *should* tell her about himself.

It would change things, though. Of course it would. The decision not to go to bed with her had been the right one, he thought. Claire could be…his friend?

So if she was just his friend why not throw his background out there and see how it altered things?

He could say… *The reason I wasn't traumatised by my parents' death is that I hardly saw them. They were socialite royals. They had a good time while their child stayed home with the servants. Even after they died my grandparents were distant. The reason I cook is that I spent much of my childhood in the kitchens. The head cook called me* 'mon petit chou' *and hugged me as I licked cake mixture from a spoon. The kitchen was my security.*

But he didn't say it. To admit to being royalty was huge, and what was between them seemed strange, tenuous, uncharted territory. Their friendship had happened so suddenly he didn't know how to take it. He only knew that this woman seemed like a miracle. She'd appeared in the water when he was about to drown. She'd given him life. But then, on land, she'd turned out to be…different. As different a woman as he'd ever met.

A woman who made him feel…vulnerable?

A woman he wanted to protect.

So he said nothing. He fell back into silence as they cooked and Claire was silent, too. She was restful, he thought. She was a woman he could come home to.

Or not leave?

A woman he could stay with for the rest of his life.

Whoa. Where had *that* come from? How crazy a thought was that?

Far too crazy. He needed to get away from here and rebuild his armour—fast. He was a loner—wasn't he?

'Done,' she said, popping her lasagne into the oven and closing the door with a satisfactory click. 'That's timed for dinner.'

'Time for a rest?'

'Why would I want a rest?'

'Your shoulder,' he said tentatively. 'Doesn't it hurt?'

'Only when it jerks, and I'm not jerking. And I don't feel like a rest.'

'Then how about a walk?' More than anything else he wanted to take this woman into his arms and carry her to bed, but there was still a part of him that was rigidly holding back. If a plane arrived now and he was airlifted off the island—what then? What next?

He had to go home.

He could take her home with him.

The thought came again from left field, mind-blowing in its craziness. What was he *thinking*? He'd known this woman for *how* long? *Take it easy,* his sensible self was ordering, and he had to listen, even if it almost killed him.

'A walk would be good.'

She was eyeing him speculatively and he wondered if

she'd guessed what he was thinking. Probably she had, he thought. She seemed…almost fey.

No. In some weird way she seemed almost an extension of himself. She'd know what he was thinking.

And maybe she agreed. If she was indeed some deep-linked connection to himself then she'd be as wary as he was. And as off-balance. And she'd understand his need to rebuild his armour.

'We could go and see the seals,' she suggested, and he tried to haul his thoughts back into order and believe a walk to the seals would be good. It was a poor second to what he'd prefer, but it had advantages.

They were full of muffins. *Tarte tatin* and lasagne were waiting in the wings for dinner. The wind had died a little and Rocky was looking hopeful. A man had to be practical instead of emotional.

But it nearly killed him to nod and agree.

'Excellent idea. Let's go see some seals.'

The seals were on the far side of the island. By the time they reached them Raoul was counting his blessings that he'd found his boots and they were clean and dry enough to be useful.

Claire, on the other hand, was wearing light trainers and was leaping from rock to rock like a mountain goat. Okay, not quite like a mountain goat, he conceded as he watched her. With her arm firmly in its sling, as long as they were off the slippery gravel she was as lithe and agile as a fawn.

'You've been practising,' he told her, and she looked back at him and grinned.

The wind was making her curls fly around her face. She looked young and free and…happy. Something had lifted, he thought, remembering her face two days ago. Yes, she'd been in pain, but there'd been other things going on behind the façade. Things he didn't know yet.

Things he might never know?

How had his presence lifted them?

'I've had four months to practise,' she told him. 'Rock-hopping has become my principal skill.'

'Do you regret coming here?' If he was honest he was struggling to keep up with her. It wasn't strength that was needed here, it was agility—and she had it in spades.

'Yes,' she said honestly. 'I was battered and my pride was in tatters and I wanted to escape. But next time I want to escape, please tell me to choose a tropical island with cabana boys and drinks with little umbrellas.'

'The weather's got you down?'

'The isolation. Rocky's an appalling conversationalist.'

'So will you leave now?'

'How can I leave?' She surveyed a large rock ahead of her, checked it out for footholds and took a jump that had him catching his breath. But she was up on top without even using her hands. Maybe the mountain goat analogy was appropriate after all.

'Because it's not safe,' he told her. 'You're not safe here.'

'I'm safer than walking through King's Cross at three in the morning. That's the red light district of Sydney.'

'So there's another place you oughtn't to be.'

'My chances of getting mugged here are practically zero.'

'And your chances of slipping on a rock and falling and being stuck out here alone, with no one to find you...'

'And being eaten by the seagulls,' she finished for him. 'I thought of that. I'm very careful.'

He watched her tackle another rock. 'Define "careful".'

'I'm safe.'

'You're not safe.'

'You think I should stay in the house and read and cook for the entire time?'

'Don shouldn't have left you out here alone. You shouldn't have come.'

'Okay, I shouldn't have come,' she told him. 'It was a whim when I was feeling black, and, yes, Don told me there was another guy here. I talked to him via radio before I came. He seemed decent. He didn't tell me he intended leaving.'

'And now you're alone with no radio.'

'I can get it fixed. I have the authority.'

'It's smashed. It'll take weeks. Claire, you need to come off the island with me.'

There was silence at that. She paused on the top of the rock she'd reached, looked at him for a long moment and then shook her head.

'Not with you. I'll think about it. But I guess I agree about leaving. Without a radio it's not safe, but the supply boat can take me off. I can stay in Hobart until it's fixed.'

'It's still not safe.'

She turned and started climbing again. 'Define "safe". I thought I was safe in a nice lawyerly job in Sydney and I almost ended up in jail. How safe's *that*? And how safe are *you*? Where's your next assignment? War zones in the Middle East? Do you want to pull out of *them* because they're not "safe"?'

'I'm no longer in the army.'

She stopped then, and turned and stared at him. 'No?'

'No.'

'So the uniform…?'

'Probably needs to be returned—though it does have a few rips. My last pay might be docked.'

'I thought you were AWOL.'

'I'm not. I'm on indefinite leave until I can be discharged. That's why I was out in the boat. I had a last talk to my commanding officer and then went down to the harbour to think things through.'

'So they might not even be worried about you?'

'They'll be worried.'

She nodded, surveying his face. There was a long silence.

'You're not happy about leaving the army?' she said and he shrugged.

'No.'

'But you're safe?'

'Yes.'

'You don't want to be safe?'

'It's time I went home.'

'Because...?'

'My grandfather's in his eighties and he's getting frail. My grandmother worries. They need help.' How simplistic a way was *that* of saying what was facing him?

'Oh, Raoul...'

The wind caught her hair, making her curls toss across her face. She brushed them away with impatience, as if the way it impeded her view of him was important. She was watching his face. She was asking questions she wasn't voicing.

'It's tearing you in two to leave the army,' she said softly, and there was nothing to say to that but the truth.

'Yes.'

'What will you do?' she asked at last, and he shook his head.

'I'm not sure yet. There will be things...that have to be done.'

'Things you don't want to think about?'

'Maybe.'

'Like me when I leave this island.'

'The army's been good to me,' he said. 'This island hasn't been all that good to *you*.'

'Hey, it's taught me rock-climbing skills. It can't be all bad.' She smiled at him—a gentle smile that somehow had all the understanding in the world in it. 'Maybe we're alike,' she said. 'Maybe we just need to figure where our place is in the world and settle. Stop fighting to be something we're not.'

'Like you...'

'A corporate lawyer? Rising above my station? I don't think so. As I said, I'm thinking of getting my job back doing legal assistance, working for the socially disadvantaged. I fit there.'

'That sounds bitter.'

'It's not meant to be.' She took a deep breath and turned to face out to sea. 'I know I'm not socially disadvantaged any more,' she said. 'But I also know where I don't fit. I tried to take a big step from my background and failed. I know where my boundaries are.'

'So if someone asked you to take a huge step…?' Why had he asked that? But he had. It was somehow out there—hanging.

'Like what?' She looked at him curiously. 'Like Don offering me this job? That was pretty crazy.'

'I don't know. Something adventurous. Something fun. All jobs don't have crevices waiting for you to fall into.'

'No,' she said thoughtfully. 'They don't. But it behoves a woman to look for crevices. It behoves a woman to be careful.'

And she turned and leaped lightly to the next rock.

He stood watching her for a moment, thinking of crevices.

Thinking of the royal family of Marétal.

Thinking that Claire Tremaine would think—like him—that royal life might well be one huge crevice.

CHAPTER SEVEN

THE SEALS WERE AMAZING—once you got over the smell. Claire had been there often enough not to be blown away by the aroma, but she watched Raoul's reaction and grinned.

It was a rocky inlet, far too dangerous to swim in or beach a boat, but the seals loved it. The rocks were covered by a mass of seals, mostly pups, basking in the weak afternoon sunlight or bobbing in the sea. A couple of massive bull seals were sitting at either end of the cove, watching over the nursery with brooding power.

'Those guys fight a lot,' she told Raoul. 'They think they're great, but when they're busy fighting I've seen younger males pop in and take advantage. Power doesn't always outweigh brains.'

'You've noticed that?' He shook his head and went back to screwing up his nose at the stink. 'You'd have thought these guys would have sorted a sewerage system.'

'Maybe they don't have a sense of smell. Trust an ex-soldier to go all sensitive on me. Next time we'll pack some air freshener. But come and see.'

This was her favourite place on the island. Her favourite thing to do. The young seals were being joyous, tumbling in and out of the water, practising their diving, sleek and beautiful under the translucent sea and bouncing and boisterous on the rocks. The best vantage place was further round—a rocky outcrop where she could see straight down into the depths. She wanted to take Raoul's hand and tug him to where she intended to stand, but she managed to hold herself back.

She had no right to tug him anywhere, she thought. He was being sensible and she must be, too.

She thought suddenly of the young bull seals, charging

in when their elders were fighting, taking their fill of the females and then leaving. That was what men did, she reminded herself.

But not Raoul. Raoul was different?

Or not different. Just…kind? Not leading her anywhere he didn't intend to follow?

So she didn't take his hand. She headed up to the outcrop herself and willed him to follow. As, of course, he did.

Despite his sense, he was a young bull at heart, she told herself, but she couldn't quite believe it. He was so like her. He was a soldier, a kid with no parents, a man with courage and with strength.

Maybe she could turn and touch his face…

'What's happening?' Raoul asked sharply, and she hauled her attention from thinking about Raoul to the surface of the water.

All the seals were suddenly gone. The water, filled moments ago with tumbling pups, was suddenly clear.

And as they stared a crimson smear bloomed up to the surface. A silver-grey mass swirled underneath and then was gone.

Even the seals out on the rocks stilled. The world seemed to hold its breath.

'Shark,' Raoul said, and his hand slid into hers.

Shark.

She watched the crimson stain spread on the water. She thought of the seal pup, its life over almost before it had begun.

She thought of Raoul in the water two days ago and shuddered.

'You don't swim while you're alone here?' Raoul asked, almost casually, and she shook her head.

'No.'

'I mean…not on this whole island?'

'Only…only when I'm pulling dumb sailors out of trouble.'

'Have you seen this happen before?' His tone was still casual.

'I...yes.' Of course she had. Seal breeding areas were a natural feeding ground for sharks.

'The island's not very big. So there are sharks...*every-where*?'

'Obviously not where *you* fell in,' she retorted, trying to make her tone light.

'But you knew...?'

'No biggie. My lasagne will be cooked. You want to go back and have dinner?'

'Half my kingdom,' he said, and now he'd forgotten to be casual. His voice was thick with passion. 'It's yours. My life... You swam into these waters to give me that.'

'Seeing as you've already spent more than half your kingdom, drinking Don's wine and smashing your friend's boat, that's not much of an offer.'

'Whatever it is, I mean it. Claire...'

'No biggie,' she said again. 'Leave it, Raoul. I might even have done the same for Felicity.

'You're kidding?'

'Well, I might have swum slower,' she admitted. 'I might not have minded if her toes had been a bit nibbled. But, yeah, I'm pretty certain I would have had to do it for Felicity. Not that I'd have enjoyed it.'

'Like you enjoyed rescuing me?'

She gave him a long, assessing look and she grinned. 'I did,' she admitted. 'There are aspects of rescuing you that I enjoyed very much indeed. But I'm putting them on the back burner. You've decreed we be sensible, and sensible we shall be. Home to lasagne, soldier, and then bed. Alone.'

They ate lasagne and Raoul's truly excellent *tarte tatin*. They watched *National Velvet* and *The Sting*. They were excellent movies. They had trouble paying them the attention they deserved, but they had staying power.

At some time during one of the movies they edged together on the settee. There was only one blanket, and the snacks had to be within reach of both of them. It was only sensible to stay close.

The movies came to an end and they followed them with a nature documentary. Birds in Africa. Raoul thought he should abandon the television and head to his separate bed, but he didn't want to break the moment, and it seemed neither did Claire.

So they both pretended the birds were riveting. She was leaning against his shoulder, nestled against him. His chin was on her curls. She fitted into the curve of his arm.

She felt…*right*.

And he had to tell her.

Somehow he'd found himself with someone who must surely be the most wonderful woman in the world. Though that was a crazy thought, he decided. There must be other wonderful women.

But he'd met many women. His grandmother had pushed many at him, many had launched themselves at him, and he'd even pursued some himself.

None came near this woman. None made him feel like this.

But he'd been acting on a lie. Oh, he'd *told* no lies, but this relationship was moving fast, moving hard, moving to places he'd never been before and it was based on trust.

Claire thought he was a soldier. Claire thought he was a kid with no parents.

That much was true.

Claire thought his background wasn't so different from hers, and he'd let her think that.

He sat with Claire nestled against him and let things drift. He was savouring the feel of her, the silence, the peace of this place. He knew what was waiting for him in the outside world. The palace would be frantic. There'd be a worldwide hunt. The media would go nuts when he reappeared.

He'd like to hurl the SOS stones from the plateau and stay here forever, holding this woman in his arms. But his responsibilities were unavoidable. He'd walked from the barracks and climbed on board *Rosebud* because he'd felt overwhelmed by the responsibilities facing him, and those responsibilities hadn't disappeared.

His country needed him.

And Claire?

She had him confused. The armour he'd so carefully constructed didn't seem to be working against her.

He was a loner. He had to walk away from her—a plane might arrive tomorrow—but when he left he didn't want her to think these few days had been a lie.

She needed honesty.

He touched her cheek and she stirred and smiled—a smile that was so intimate it almost tore his heart.

He knew he made her smile. She made *him* smile.

'Claire…?'

'Mmm…'

All he wanted was to take her into his arms, make love to her and block out the outside world. Put it off. Take every moment of this time and let Claire find out when finally she must.

But *must* was now if she was ever to trust him.

'Claire,' he said softly, and traced her cheek with his forefinger. 'Let me tell you who I really am.'

Royal.

The word was drumming a savage beat all through her body.

Royal.

She should have known.

How *could* she have known? She couldn't possibly. It wasn't as if he'd come out of the surf wearing a crown or something.

She choked on a sound that might have been laughter but

wasn't. Raoul's hold on her tightened, but he didn't say anything. After telling her he was simply holding her, waiting for her to take it in.

And Raoul holding her was part of the dream, too.

This whole thing had been a dream.

Hauling a soldier out of the water, the deadly peril, the lifesaving stuff, being carried up to the house, her shoulder being righted, the care, the comfort and then the kiss. The beginnings of love? That was what it had felt like, she acknowledged, but of course it had been an illusion. A two-day fantasy that had culminated in the greatest fantasy of all.

A prince!

She felt very close to hysterics and her thoughts were all over the place. It was frogs who were supposed to turn into princes. Not gorgeous half-drowned soldiers who were perfect just the way they were.

'I never should have kissed you,' she managed, because she had to say something. Somehow she had to move forward from this moment.

'Because…?'

'Because then you'd still be a frog. And I liked my frog.' She took a deep breath and pushed herself up. She sat and looked at him in the firelight. He gazed calmly back—her soldier, the man she'd felt seeping into her heart, the man she'd thought was within her orbit.

'If we're talking fairytales…'

'*Cinderella*'s another one,' she said. 'And I never understood that story. She got to change rags for tiaras, but everyone would always know there were rags underneath.'

'You're not in rags. And tiaras aren't compulsory.'

And suddenly the conversation had changed. It was all about them. It was all about a future neither had even dared to consider until this moment. A nebulous, embryonic future which suddenly seemed terrifying.

'I shouldn't believe you,' she said at last. 'Why *do* I believe you?'

'Because in telling you I risk losing you,' he said.

He wasn't moving. He was leaning back on Marigold's sumptuous cushions, watching her, giving her the space she didn't want but desperately needed.

'And the last thing in the world I want to do is lose you.'

'You never had me.'

'No,' he told her. 'But, Claire… I'm starting to think that what we have might be…possible…'

And she snorted. How did she feel? Humiliated, she thought. And lost. As if she'd lost something she'd never had.

'After two days?' she managed. 'I don't think so.'

'It's true. If I hadn't told you then you'd be still lying in my arms, and that's all I want. But I had to tell you some time. Claire, does it have to make a difference?'

'A difference to what?' Although she knew.

'A difference to me seeing you again, off the island. A difference to taking this friendship further.'

'You're kidding me, right? A kid from Kunamungle? A baby with no known father? A kid brought up on the wrong side of the tracks—and even though Kunamungle's small, believe me, there *is* a wrong side of the tracks? A woman who couldn't even get accepted in a legal firm? A lawyer with no background, no money, no aspirations, and now with the stigma of fraud hanging over her head? You're telling me you're heir to the throne of Marétal and asking if it makes a difference to a possible friendship? *Yes*, Your Highness…'

'Don't call me that.'

'Yes, Your Highness, it *does* make a difference.'

'Why?' he said evenly. 'Claire, nothing has changed. I still feel—'

'It doesn't matter how you feel,' she snapped. 'Haven't I always known that? It doesn't matter how you feel or what you want or what you hope for. It's what you *are* that matters.'

The night was too long. The house was too big. Their bedrooms were too far apart and Raoul knew he had to leave her be. Claire had retired to a place he couldn't reach, and after breakfast the next morning—another silent breakfast—she headed off for a long walk with Rocky.

'If a plane comes I'll come back,' she told him. 'Otherwise I could be some time.'

'Like Oates of the Antarctic, heading out into the snow for the last time?'

'Hardly,' she snapped. 'I'm not about to die in the snow because of one prince.'

And she stomped off towards the cliffs.

He was left thinking that he really wanted to go with her. But he had deceived her. The least he could do was give her space. This would probably be their last day together. Surely a plane would come soon. Followed by a chopper to take him off the island. Followed by the rest of his life.

It was his last day with Claire and she'd left.

He couldn't blame her. Swapping roles, he might have walked himself, he thought. And then he really thought about it. If he'd been a soldier and only a soldier, and she'd been heiress to a throne, how would he have reacted?

He wouldn't have walked. He'd have run.

Even if it had been Claire?

Maybe.

He didn't do ties, and royalty would have terrified him too.

Maybe Claire was right, he conceded. *Cinderella* was a sexist fantasy. Put a woman in a beautiful gown, give her a tiara and a palace and expect her to live happily ever after? It wouldn't work for him—although the gown and tiara analogy had to change—so why would it work for Claire?

It wouldn't.

So that was the end of that.

But at the back of his mind was a harsh, unbendable wish. The end? It couldn't be. It mustn't be because he wanted her.

So soon?

And there was another problem. With the threat of a plane

arriving at any minute emotions seemed to have become condensed. He was so unsure where this was going. He felt as if his armour had been cracked, and it scared him, but the more he saw of Claire, the more he was prepared to risk.

Too much was happening, too fast. The responsibilities he faced back in Marétal were enormous. The adjustment he was facing made him feel ill. He didn't need emotions messing with what was ahead of him.

He didn't need Claire.

So if a plane arrived today he might well never see her again. A prince from Marétal and an Australian lawyer? How many chances would they have to meet?

Never.

He thought suddenly of his grandmother's demand that he bring a woman to the Royal Anniversary Ball.

Claire?

Polite society would have her for breakfast, he thought. His grandmother alone would be appalled.

Impossible. The whole situation was crazy.

The house was empty, echoing. He found himself straining for the sound of a far-off engine, a plane, the signal of the end of something that had barely started.

Surely it didn't have to end yet.

He abandoned the house and headed down to the cove where Claire had swum to save him. The water was calm today, but the beach was littered with debris from the storm and from the battered *Rosebud.* The yacht was now little more than matchsticks. He searched the beach, looking for anything he could salvage for Tom, but he was doing it more to distract himself rather than because Tom would want anything. Tom was free, off climbing his mountains.

Two weeks ago Raoul had said goodbye and had been consumed with regret. He'd wanted that kind of freedom.

He couldn't have it. And now he couldn't have even a friendship with Claire.

Unless he didn't treat her as Cinderella.

His thoughts were flying tangentially, and all the while he was distracted by the thought that a plane could arrive at any minute. Finally he climbed along the side of the cove, where the waves from the open sea crashed against the cliffs and he couldn't see the sky from the south. If he couldn't see the plane it didn't exist, he told himself, and he almost smiled. It was a game he'd played when he was a child, when he'd been forced to sit through interminable royal events. He'd worked out how to look interested and still disappear inside his head, dreaming of where he'd rather be.

He had no choice as to where he'd be.

Did he have a choice in who he'd be with?

Claire...

She was a beautiful woman and she made him feel as he'd never felt before. Yes, it was too soon to think about the future, but his head wasn't giving him any leeway. He wanted her.

She was an intelligent, courageous woman who was street-smart. She was a woman who spoke Italian and French, and he had no doubt she was fluent. The phrase he'd flung at her in the water had been gasped, yet she'd understood it without hesitation.

Marétal's official language was French, but natives spoke a mix of Italian and French with some of their own words.

Claire was smart. She'd pick it up.

She didn't want to be Cinderella. Who would?

And he… What did *he* want?

Besides Claire.

He forced himself to think sideways, to think of the life he wanted as a royal.

He wanted to make a difference.

Claire would never want a job that involved tiara-wearing and nothing else. Well, neither did he. If he had to go home—and he did—then he needed to make something of it.

With Claire?

Don't think down that route, he told himself. *Don't even think about hoping.*

But the ball… He had no doubt his grandmother would still insist it go ahead. He also knew that if he didn't organise a partner his grandmother would attempt to do it for him, and the thought was suddenly so claustrophobic it almost choked him.

Claire was still front and centre. He thought of her as she could be. Someone not royal from birth but truly royal as she deserved to be. Why *shouldn't* the woman who'd saved his life be his partner at the ball? Even if nothing came of it, it would be a night of fantasy. A night he'd never forget.

She'd never agree. Why would she?

She needed a job to do. She needed to be needed.

Something colourful caught his eye, caught on a pile of seaweed. He stooped and picked it up.

It was a tiny plastic building brick figure. It was a miniature construction worker, complete with a hard hat and a spanner in his hand.

He'd noticed it on the shelf above Tom's bunk, taped fast to stop it falling. He'd commented on it on their first day's sailing and Tom had grinned, a bit embarrassed.

'That's Herbert. I've had Herbert since I was six years old. He's my good luck talisman. Where I go, he goes.'

He'd noticed him when he'd gone aboard again five days ago and thought of Tom, gone to climb mountains without Herbert.

He had Tom's good luck talisman.

And imperceptibly, ridiculously, his spirits lifted. 'Sorry, Tom,' he told his absent friend. 'Take care on those mountains, because Herbert's about to work for *me*.'

Maybe…

He dusted the sand from Herbert and tucked him carefully into his pocket.

'Come on, then, Herbert,' he told him. 'I'll send you on

to Tom when you've done your job here. But now *I* have need of you. Let's see what happens if we offer a lady a job.'

'A job.'

Claire had walked her legs off. She'd been tired, her arm had ached, and finally she'd turned back. She'd known she had to face him some time. She might as well get it over with.

She'd found Raoul in the kitchen, flipping corn hotcakes. He had smiled at her as if nothing had changed. He'd asked politely about her walk and then watched in satisfaction as she'd eaten his hotcakes. Okay, she was discombobulated, but a woman could be discombobulated *and* hungry.

And then he'd said he wanted to offer her a job.

She stared at him, all six feet of gorgeous Prince, and felt herself cringe. What was he saying?

'I don't think royal mistress has ever been one of my career choices,' she said carefully.

'Who said anything about you being a royal mistress?'

'I kissed you. I know it's dumb, but now it makes me feel smutty.'

'You could never be smutty.'

He reached over the table to touch her face but she flinched.

'Don't.'

'Touching's out of order?'

'Until I get my head around this, yes.

'Claire, you're my friend. You're the woman who saved my life. You're also the woman who attracts me in a way I don't understand yet.'

'You lied.'

'I didn't lie,' he said evenly. 'But neither did I tell you the truth. Why would I? It would have made a difference. If we'd lain exhausted on the sand after you helped me out of the water and I'd said, *By the way, I'm a prince,* wouldn't it have changed…everything?'

'Yes.' She might as well be honest.

'Well, maybe that was what my dumb attempt to sail in dangerous weather conditions was all about. For the last fifteen years I've been in the army. Working in a tight-knit unit with men and women focused on a common mission. I've been one of many. But the moment I return to Marétal—the moment I step out of army uniform—things will change. As they would have changed if I'd told you.'

'I thought you were like *me*.'

'How could I be like you? You're beautiful.'

She flushed. 'Don't, Raoul.' She closed her eyes and he could see her trying to tear her thoughts away from the personal. 'The SOS…' she said. 'Your grandparents…'

'They're the ruling monarchs. The King and Queen.'

'So the heir to the throne is missing, presumed drowned?'

'Probably presumed kidnapped,' he said grimly. 'There have been threats. We haven't taken them too seriously—my country seems too small to attract terrorist interest—but now I'm missing they'll be being taken very seriously indeed. I can't imagine the resources being thrown into searching for me.'

'But they won't think of here.'

'They won't think I'm dumb enough to take out a boat without letting anyone know, and Tom doesn't know his boat is missing. I'll have a lot of humble pie to eat when I get home.'

'So you're hoping a plane will come today?'

'Yes,' he said gently, and made an involuntary move of his hand towards hers. And then he pulled back again. 'I have to hope that—if just to stop the anguish of my grandparents and the money being spent on searching for me. But when I'm rescued… Claire, I'm asking if you'll come with me.'

'To this job?'

'Yes. Can I tell you about it?'

'Oh, for heaven's sake…' She got up and filled the kettle, then took a long time to organise cups for coffee. 'I must have been banged on the head. This isn't real.'

'It *is* real. Claire, I can't leave you here. This place is unsafe. You have no radio transmission, and as far as I can see it could take weeks to get technicians here to fix thc system.'

'I can order a smaller unit…'

'Which will come by the next supply boat—which might or might not arrive depending on the weather. And you'll still be alone. If you slipped on the rocks… If you swam…'

'I won't swim. Are you crazy? The water's just above freezing.'

'You're quibbling. It's not safe for you to be here and you know it. Don should know it. If you don't tell him then I will.'

'Okay.' She turned to face him, tucking her hands behind her back like an errant child facing a stern teacher. 'I shouldn't have come here,' she conceded. 'Like you, I made a spur-of-the-moment decision and I accept it's not safe. So, yes, I'll lock up and go to Hobart—but that's as far as I'm going. You head back to your royal fantasy. And I'll…'

'You'll what? Look for a job? I'm offering you one.'

'Raoul…'

'I won't let this go,' he said, steadily and surely. 'Claire, this thing between us… I've never felt anything like it and I can't walk away. But I've scared you silly. Plus, it's too soon. We've been thrown together in extraordinary circumstances. If you were Sleeping Beauty I'd see you for the first time, fall in love with you on the spot and carry you away to my castle for happy-ever-after. But that story's always worried me. After the initial rush of passion, what if she turns out to have a fetish for watching infomercial television? Or women's wrestling? What if she insists on a life devoted to macramé?'

'I don't know what macramé is,' she said faintly.

'Exactly. And therein lies the brilliance of my plan.'

'The job?'

'The job,' he agreed. 'Claire, I have a problem. I've upset my grandparents enormously. In three weeks there's a ball to celebrate their fifty years on the throne. I imagine that right now it's been cancelled, but as soon as I turn up alive my grandmother will resurrect it. She's indomitable.'

He paused. Claire handed him a mug of coffee. He took a sip and grimaced, as they both did when they tasted this coffee. There was nothing like caterers' blend to make you rethink your caffeine addiction. But even the truly awful coffee wasn't enough to distract him from what seemed such a nebulous plan.

'And…?' she prodded.

She really shouldn't talk to him of the future, she thought. He was a royal prince. He had nothing to do with her.

Except she'd kissed him and she'd wanted him. Her body still did want him, regardless of what her mind was telling her. Was desire an excuse for keeping on talking?

'I'm expected to have a partner for the ball,' he said in a goaded voice, and she decided she needed to stop wanting straight away.

'So you're going to ask me?' she managed. 'Cinderella.'

'I told you—I don't buy into Cinderella.'

'And I don't buy into balls. Or royalty. Or—on a basic level—being surrounded by people who think they've been born better than me.'

'I would *never* think that.'

'You don't need to. It's bred into your genes. You look down your aristocratic nose…'

'That's insulting,' he said, suddenly exasperated. 'Can you get off your high horse and listen to a perfectly good job offer?'

She thought about it, or tried to think about it, and then decided the only way to think about anything was not to look at Raoul. *Prince* Raoul, she reminded herself savagely, and she plonked her cup hard on the table, spilling about a quarter of the contents, and stared into what remained.

'Shoot.'

'Shoot?'

'Go ahead. Tell me about your job so I can refuse and get on with my life.'

'Claire…'

'Talk,' she ordered. 'I'm listening, but not for very long.'

CHAPTER EIGHT

BUT IN THE end she did listen.

In the end it sounded almost reasonable.

'A couple of years ago one of the Australian soldiers I was on an exercise with told me about his son,' he told her. 'The boy was faced with a lengthy jail term for being immature, gullible and in the wrong place at the wrong time. It seems the legal assistance service you worked for helped him escape conviction and gave him another chance. To my shame I'd forgotten it until you mentioned it, but I know we don't have such a service at home—legal help for those who can't afford lawyers. Claire, if I'm to return as more than a figurehead I'd like to institute a few reforms—reforms long overdue. I've never had the authority to make those changes, but maybe it's time for a line in the sand.'

'A line…?'

'You'd be the beginning of my line,' he told her.

She dared a glance at him and discovered he was smiling. She went back to her coffee fast. 'What do you mean?'

'I mean you would accompany me back to Marétal. You'd be greeted by my grandparents as the woman who saved the life of the heir to the throne. And I'll say I've offered you a job—investigating the need for such a service in our country.'

He held up his hand to prevent her instinctive protest.

'Claire, hear me out. My idea is that you'd spend a month talking to our public services, talking to the people high up in the judicial system, assessing whether our system is similar enough to the Australian system for something like legal assistance to work. Given you'll have access via me to whoever you want to speak to, a month should be sufficient to give you an overview. And then you'd go home.'

She did raise her eyes then. She stared up at him in astonishment. 'I'd go home?' she managed.

'Once you've spoken to my people I'd ask—through diplomatic channels—that you have the same access to yours. Then I'd ask that you put forward a proposal for Marétal. It might be six months' work to put together such a proposal, but that six months…' He hesitated. 'Claire, we could use it. We could just…see.'

'See what?' She was having trouble speaking.

'See where we are at the end of six months,' he told her. 'See if we feel the same as we do now. See whether this relationship has legs.'

'Legs…' she muttered, and managed a sort of smile. 'Slang in how many languages?'

'How many do *you* know?' He shrugged. 'Claire, you're smart, you're strong, you have solid legal training and you know enough about the needs of low-income earners to be empathic. You're what our country needs.'

'Others could do the job.'

'I want you.'

And there it was, out in the open, staring at them like a two-headed monster.

I want you.

She could say the same.

She couldn't.

'The ball…' she muttered, and he gave a slightly shamefaced grin.

'That's the pay-off,' he told her. 'A favour, if you like. Claire, I can't pretend there's nothing between us. There is. We both know it. If you come back to Marétal I won't deny there's an attraction.'

'You think I'd move into your palace? Not in a pink fit.'

He grinned. 'How did I know you'd say that? But my plan's more practical. We could find you a nice little apartment in the legal quarter of the city. You'd start work. There'll be a flare of publicity when we arrive, but it'll settle. It'll be suspected that we have a relationship, so there will be media interest, but it won't be over the top.' His grin turned a bit lop-sided. 'I *have* had girlfriends before.'

She tried not to smile back. She tried really hard.

She failed.

'Really?'

'Really.' And then he did reach out and take her hand, and she knew she should pull back, but she couldn't. Not when it was Raoul.

'And thus we come to the brilliance of my plan,' he told her, and she blinked.

'Brilliance?'

'I could escort you to the ball. My grandmother couldn't object because you're the woman who saved my life. She'll stop throwing society darlings at me for a while. She and my grandfather will have a wonderful ball, which they'll thoroughly enjoy, without my grandmother watching me every minute of the night to see who I'm dancing with. You'll get to wear a very beautiful dress—did I tell you I owe you at least a gown? And then you could go home.'

She stared at him blankly. 'Home. To Australia. I don't get it.'

'You should,' he said gently, and his hold on her hand tightened. 'Claire, I think I'm falling for you,' he said. 'But after this short time of course I can't be sure. To be honest, relationships have always scared me. I've been a loner all my life and I'm not sure I can stop being a loner. If you're feeling the least bit like I am you'll be feeling just as uncertain. Plus, the thought of royalty scares you. I'm not surprised—it still scares *me*. But this scheme gives us time. By the night of the ball you'll have had weeks in the country. Then there'll be the ball, which will be royalty at its most splendid. Afterwards you'll get on a plane and you'll spend a few paid months back in Australia investigating the intricacies of legal assistance on Marétal's behalf. And thinking about me—us.'

'Thinking about you…us?'

'That's my hope,' he said, and threw her one of those gorgeous grins that made her heart twist.

Oh, my... Where were her thoughts? They were all over the place. *Think,* she told herself. *Stop sounding like a parrot and get real.*

'The whole idea's crazy,' she managed.

'Tell me why.'

'If you want to find out about our legal assistance scheme you should send one of your own people out here to see how it's done.'

'I could,' he agreed. 'But if I gave the job to any of my senior people they'd come with prejudices. They'd think they'd be doing the old school lawyers out of jobs, and the younger staff wouldn't have the clout to ask the right questions. Claire, you wouldn't be changing anything. All you'd be doing at the end of six months would be handing over a concept that our people could work with.'

Our people. How had he suddenly transformed into a royal? she thought. Last night he'd been a soldier and her friend. Okay, being honest, he'd also—almost—been her embryo lover. Being honest with *herself,* if he'd taken her to bed she would have gone and gone willingly.

But today…

'If I gave the job to any of my senior people...'

He was speaking as a prince. He *was* a prince. He was as far from her as the sun was from the earth.

He was holding her hand.

'But why? Why me?' she demanded. 'And why now? Surely this legal assistance scheme isn't a priority?'

'It's not a priority,' he agreed. 'But it is a real need, and it's my need, too. And I hope yours. Claire, it's not safe for you to stay on this island. You must see that. Soon we'll be taken off. When we do the eyes of the world will be on us. I'm sorry, but I can't stop that. In Australia I can't protect you from media hype. In my country I can—to an extent.

The palace can call in favours. Yes, there'll be speculation, but we can live with that. The line is that I met you, I was impressed with your legal credentials…'

'You don't know anything about my legal credentials.'

'I do,' he told her. 'How can I doubt that they're impeccable? Not only do I trust you, I can ensure the world will, too. Two minutes after we land in Hobart there'll be a legal suppression order thumped on the appalling Felicity and her friends. If one whisper of improper conduct comes out, your ex-firm will be faced with a libel suit so massive it'll make their eyes water. Claire, what I'm proposing is sensible, but it's not sense I'm talking. It's desire. This way you come back to my country. I won't be able to spend much time with you between now and the ball, but you'll see enough of me—and I'll see enough of you—to decide if we have the courage to take this thing forward.'

'Courage…'

'It *would* take courage,' he told her.

His fingers were kneading hers gently, erotically, making her feel as if she wanted to stop talking this minute and head to the bedroom while there was still time. But of course she couldn't. Raoul was talking sense and she had to listen.

Sense? To fly to the other side of the world with a royal prince? *Her?* Claire Tremaine?

Her head was spinning. The only thing grounding her seemed to be Raoul's hold on her hand, and surely she shouldn't trust that.

'It would take courage,' he said again, as if he'd realised her mind was having trouble hearing, much less taking anything in. 'But what I'm suggesting takes the pressure off as far as I can figure how to do that. You'd stay in my country until the ball. You'd dance with me as my partner.'

He gave another of his lopsided grins and she wished he hadn't. It made her… Well, it made it a lot harder for her to take anything in.

'It would be a favour to me,' he told her. 'It would take the pressure from me. It would make my grandparents happy...'

'That you're dancing with a nobody?'

'They can hardly think you're a nobody when you saved my life.'

'Don't you believe it.'

'Claire, stop quibbling,' he said, firmly now. 'Because straight after the ball you'll have a return ticket to Australia. Ostensibly to research a legal assistance system on our behalf. No—*really* to research a legal assistance system. That will give you time to come to terms with everything you've seen and with how you feel about me. It will give us both time. You can return to Australia with a job to do and we can both take stock of how we feel. No pressure. Your call.'

No pressure.

No pressure?

Her head felt as if it was caving in.

'You don't know what you're asking,' she managed, and he took both her hands then, tugging her so she was looking straight at him. What had happened to their coffee? Obviously that was what happened when you used caterers' blend, she thought tangentially. You got distracted by...*a prince.*

'I *do* know what I'm asking,' he told her. 'And it's a shock. To you, though—not to me. Claire, I knew the moment you pulled me from the water that your life had changed. You don't save royal princes and then get marooned on deserted islands with them for days without media hype. You *will* get media hype, and I'm sorry. But there's also this thing between us—this thing which I'm not prepared to let go. With my plan... I'm trying to rewrite the *Cinderella* story. I'm trying to figure how to get through this with your dignity as top priority. This way you'll come to the palace, you'll meet my grandparents, you'll see things as they are. Then you'll come to the ball as an honoured guest. And, yes, I'll dance with you—a lot—but in real life the Prince has to dance with others, because feelings can't be hurt. And you'll dance with others, too, because men will be lining up. And at midnight…'

'Where's my glass slipper?' she said shakily, and tried to smile.

He smiled back. 'That's where the plot changes to what it should be. At the end of the ball I'll put you back into your carriage, which won't turn back into a pumpkin, your luggage will be waiting and you'll take your return ticket back to Australia. I won't come hunting for you. You're your own person, Claire. If you take this job then you have months of secure employment, doing work my country needs. And then you can work out if you have the courage to return.'

'Why…why would I return?'

'Because, fast as this is, and even though I've known you such a short time, I suspect I'll be waiting for you.'

'But no promises?' she said, fast and breathlessly, and he nodded.

'No promises from either of us,' he told her. 'Both of us know that. But this is a chance…our only chance…to wait and see. If you have the courage, my Claire.'

'I'm not your Claire.'

'No,' he agreed. 'You're *your* Claire and the decision is yours. Will you come home with me and give us a chance?'

And what was a woman to say to that?

How could she look into those eyes and say no?

She might have courage, but her knees felt as if they'd sagged under her—and she wasn't even standing.

'Claire?' he said softly, and put a finger under her chin and raised her face so her gaze met his. 'Will you come with me?'

'Yes,' she whispered, because there was no other response. 'Yes, I will.'

And then the world broke in.

At two that afternoon a small plane swooped low over the island.

After four months of isolation the pilots of such planes, like the captains of the supply boats, seemed to have become Claire's friends. They weren't really. They were people doing their job. She couldn't talk to them, and she didn't even know their names, but she usually walked outside and waved. Sometimes they flew low enough so she could see people waving back.

They'd just finished lunch, a mostly silent meal during which too much seemed to be happening in their heads for talk to be possible. Raoul had talked of practicalities and Claire had listened, but mostly her head was full of one huge question.

What had she agreed to do?

The sound of the plane was almost a relief. She glanced out of the window and hesitated. 'If I go outside and wave they'll think I'm okay,' she told him. 'They might not even see the SOS.'

'No one can miss my SOS,' Raoul told her. 'And if you *don't* go outside we'll have people thinking you might be wounded. I didn't have enough rocks to write a detailed explanation of the problem underneath. Claire, we need to be seen. Together. I assume they know you're usually alone here? They'll see us. The wreckage from *Rosebud* on the beach is self-explanatory. Let's go.'

So he led her outside, and they stood on Marigold's Italian terrace, and Claire waved and Raoul stood silently by her side.

He seemed grim.

And as she waved for the first time it struck her. What he was asking of her was huge, but what he was facing himself was even bigger. He'd been in the army for fifteen years—a rugged life, dangerous, challenging, but obviously something he felt deeply about. He was back in his army uniform now, having decided he wouldn't risk facing the world in Don's gear. But it was more than that, she thought. In his army gear he knew who he was.

She glanced at the set lines on his face and thought again of the reasons he'd walked down to his friend's boat and set out to sea.

This was an ending for him. And end of being who he wanted to be.

The start of his royal life.

'You'll be brilliant,' she said, and he looked down at her, startled.

'What…?'

'As a prince. You'll be amazing. Look at you now—you've had three days lying around here and you could have… I don't know…rested on your laurels, played the royal Prince, ordered me around like anything…'

'As if I would.'

'Exactly,' she said. 'Instead you taught me how to make *tarte tatin*, and if nothing else ever comes of this then I thank you. You've assessed this whole situation. You came over all bossy when you told me I need to leave. But more…you thought of the legal assistance thing—and, Raoul, I know that's partly for us, but it's also for your country. You're thinking of what it needs. If you start that way you'll be brilliant. I know you will.'

'Not unless…' And then he stopped. 'No. I won't blackmail you.'

'Excellent,' she said as the plane swooped low, did a one-eighty-degree turn and swooped again, right over the centre of the island where Raoul's SOS stood out like a beacon. 'Because we both have enough pressure on us already. All we can do is face forward and get on with it.'

CHAPTER NINE

THREE WEEKS LATER, in an apartment in Marétal's secure legal precinct, she woke where she wanted to spend the rest of her life.

She woke in Raoul's arms.

'Let me not move.' She murmured the words to herself, not daring to whisper, hardly daring to breathe. 'Let me hold this fantasy as truth.'

For this *was* a fantasy. This was where Cinderella could have her fairytale, she thought. In the arms of her Prince.

No. She wasn't in the arms of her Prince. She was in the arms of the man she loved.

And almost as she thought it Raoul woke, and the arms that had held her even in sleep tightened. Her body was spooned against his. Her skin was against his. The sensation was almost unbearably erotic. The sensation was pure... fantasy.

'I can't believe it's only weeks since I first kissed you,' he murmured into her hair. 'It feels like months. Or years.'

They'd been businesslike, as planned, even though it had almost killed them. But they'd had to be. They'd travelled back to Marétal together, but as soon as their plane had landed Raoul had been absorbed back into the royal family.

Claire was being treated as an honoured guest. The story was that she'd rescued him and he'd been fortunate enough to persuade this skilled lawyer to take an outsider's look at the country's legal system.

There'd been mutterings from the legal fraternity—'Why do we need such an overview?'—but she was young and non-threatening and the royal sanction was enough to keep the peace.

There'd been more than murmurs from the media—of

course there had: *Prince trapped on remote island with glamorous Australian lawyer.* But Raoul had organised her clothes to be couriered from Sydney. She'd taken pains to appear in the prim clothes she customarily wore for work.

There'd been a lavish dinner held by the royal family to thank her formally for her heroism, and Raoul had sat by her side, but she'd deliberately dressed plainly, with little make-up and her hair arranged in a severe knot. Raoul had been charmingly attentive, but he'd carefully been charmingly attentive to the woman on his other side too, and the rumours had faded.

The media would have killed to listen in on the phone calls Raoul made to her every night, the calls she held out for, but the apartment he'd organised for her was in a secure part of the legal district where privacy was paramount.

'If I so much as smile at you in the way I want to smile at you you'll be overwhelmed,' Raoul had told her, and she'd agreed.

This was the plan. She was here to do a job—wasn't she? Nothing more. And Raoul's calls… They were those of a friend.

Except she knew in her heart they were much more. She should stop them, she thought, but she couldn't bear to.

And the calls were a mere fraction of her day. For the rest of the time she could tell herself they weren't important. She'd buried herself in the work she was here to do, and somewhat to her surprise had found it incredibly interesting. There *was* a need. She could do something useful. Paths had been opened to her through Raoul, and through the interest in her background. She'd learned a lot, fast.

What she'd also learned was how constricted Raoul's life was. He could go nowhere without the eyes of the world following.

But finally, last night, Raoul's promise to keep his distance had cracked. A plain black Jeep had driven up to her apartment and paused for maybe five seconds, no longer. A soldier had stepped out and he'd been inside her apartment before the Jeep had disappeared from sight.

If anyone had been watching—which they probably hadn't, because interest had died down—they'd simply have seen a shadow, and that shadow had disappeared so fast they could never have photographed it.

The shadow had finally risked coming.

And Claire should have greeted him formally, as a friend—no, as an employer—but it had been three long weeks, and the phone calls had become more and more the centre of her day.

And, sensible or not, she'd walked straight into his arms and stayed.

The shadow was now holding her. He was running his lovely hands over the smoothness of her belly. He was kissing the nape of her neck. He was sending the most erotic of messages to every nerve-ending in her body.

Raoul. Her fantasy lover.

Her Prince.

'How long can you stay?' she whispered to him now. She scarcely dared to breathe the question but it had to be asked. This night had been so unwise but it would have to stop. Was this all there was? One night of passion, maybe two, before she returned to Australia?

It had to be—she knew that.

Because she needed to return. She'd known that from day one, when she'd seen the sea of photographers pointing their cameras at her. Raoul was royalty and he lived in the media glare, and even if she was ever deemed suitable for him she had no wish to join him.

Except for the way he held her.

Except for the way she felt about him.

Except for now.

Last night… It had been as if two halves had found their whole. She'd walked into his arms and she'd felt complete in a way she'd never felt before.

Raoul had warned her he was coming and she'd made dinner. Dinner had been forgotten.

Dinner had turned into all night.

Dinner had turned into perfect.

'I'm taking all day,' he murmured into her hair, holding her closer. 'Imperatives be damned. You can't believe how much I've missed you. Holding you feels like it's making something in me complete. My Claire. My heart.'

'I can't be your Claire, Raoul. It's taken you three weeks to find an opportunity to come.'

She didn't say it as a reproach. It was simply fact. She'd learned by now how much his country needed him. But he wanted to explain.

He rolled over, propping himself above her so he could look down into her eyes. 'Claire, you know why. You didn't want to come to this country as my lover. Neither of us wanted that. We had to let the media interest die. But we can't go on this way. Maybe it's time to let the world know what's between us.'

He kissed her then, lightly on the lips. Or he meant to. His kiss deepened, and when it was done he pulled back and the smile was gone from his eyes.

'I want you,' he told her. 'I've never wanted a woman as I've wanted you. I've never needed a woman. Claire, every time we talk I'm falling deeper and deeper in love with you. My days have been a nightmare, a jumble of pressing needs, but every night I've called you, and that's what holds me together. Claire, I know it's early. I know I said you're free to go—and you are. But if you could bear to stay for longer… If you could bear to be seen by my side…'

And the world stilled.

She loved him. She knew she did. Their time on the island had been the embryo of their loving. The flight back to Marétal had made it grow. The long calls every night… The sight of him in the newspapers, discussing the needs of his country, shouldering a responsibility she knew was far too heavy for one man…

But to announcc their love to the world? To let the media in?

'You could face that?' She said it as a breathless whisper and he smiled then—that smile that did her head in, the smile that wanted her to agree to anything he suggested.

Anything? Such as walking out onto the balcony and shouting to the world that they were lovers?

Staying with Raoul seemed right. But the rest… It did her head in.

'Still too soon?' he asked, sounding rueful. 'Claire, I've known you for less than a month and yet I'm sure.'

'But…' she managed, and he sighed and closed his eyes, almost as if he was in pain.

'But,' he agreed. 'I live in a goldfish bowl. It's a privileged goldfish bowl, but that's what it is.'

'You're doing your best to improve your bowl,' she told him, striving for lightness.

Striving to keep the underlying question at bay. Or the underlying answer. The answer she knew she'd have to give.

'The news is full of reports of the discussions you've been having with your grandparents and parliament,' she told him. 'They say you're dragging Marétal into the twenty-first century. You want parliament to have more power. You want the people to have more say. And yet the Queen is arguing.'

'My grandparents have held the rule of this country for fifty years,' he told her, following her lead, maybe realising how much she needed to play for time. 'They've wanted me to share that rule. It's come to the crunch now, though—they *need* me to share rather than *want* me to. I hadn't realised quite how frail my grandfather is and how much my grandmother depends on him. So they need me. But I've told them that if I'm to inherit the throne I'll do it on my terms. Or walk away.'

'*Could* you walk away?'

He'd hugged her around so they were face to face on the pillows—the most intimate of positions. His nose was four inches from her nose. His hands still held her waist. They were talking of something as mundane as…inheriting a throne.

'If they won't agree then I might not have a choice,' he told her. He sighed. 'She's fighting me every inch of the way. Even security for the ball… Our security service is tiny, but it should *be* there. She refuses to have officers in the ballroom. But with so many dignitaries from so many places how can we check? The ball is for my grandparents and she insists on having her way.'

'And if she keeps insisting?' She couldn't help it, a tiny flicker of hope kindled and flared. If he could abandon the throne… If he could just be what he once had been… Raoul. Soldier. Sailor.

Lover.

'I don't know,' he said bleakly. 'I'm trying to think of a path but there's no one else to take it on. I have no cousins, and the constitution states that the country reverts to being a republic if the throne has no heir.'

'Is that a problem?'

'After so many years under a monarchy parliament's weak. Anything could happen.'

'So you're stuck?'

'I think I am.'

The flicker of hope faded. Raoul smoothed her face with his beautiful hands and kissed her on the eyelids.

'Don't look so sad, *ma mie*.' He hesitated. 'Is it possible…?' He drew back a little so he could look directly into her eyes. 'Is it possible that you've already decided you can't be with me?'

How to make him see…? 'Raoul, you know I'd stay—but three weeks…and this is the first time…'

'Because of caution. With no caution I'd have had you in my bed every night.'

'And have the whole world looking down on me?'

'Is that courage speaking?' An edge of anger came into his voice. 'Are you *so* afraid of what people will think?'

'Your grandmother made it quite clear... My dog...'

He managed a smile at that. The Queen had asked Claire to be brought to her straight from the airport. Rocky had just been released from his crate. The royal couple had been on the palace steps to greet their heir's saviour.

'It was me who dropped the leash,' Raoul said ruefully. 'After twenty-four hours in a cage he did what any dog would do. She'll warm to him.'

'He's not remotely pedigree. Like me.'

'What's the reverse of a snob? Someone who's proud of her convict ancestors? That should be you. *I'm* proud of your ancestors,' he told her. 'They produced *you*.'

She managed to smile, but the knot of pain within was killing her. The thought of what he was asking was huge. To stand beside him in the glare of publicity... To pretend to be something she could never be...

'Raoul, I can't do this. I need to go home.'

His smile faded.

'I know you do,' he said softly. 'I did know, even from the start, that asking such a thing of you was grossly unfair. I think I've always known what your answer would be. In your place my answer would be the same.'

He sighed then, and kissed her once more, his lovely hands caressing her body, making every sense cry out that here was her place. But it wasn't. It never could be.

'Don't be sad.' He kissed her eyelids again, and maybe there was the beginning of tears there for him to kiss. 'Let's pretend. Grant ourselves a little more time for fantasy. The ball is on Friday. You need to come to the palace to be fitted for a ball gown. I'm being fitted for my own uniform today. So—a fantasy afternoon with swords and tassels and tiaras and lace. Can you have fun with me? My grandparents are in the country, so we'll have the place to ourselves.' He grimaced. 'Well, that's if you don't count a hundred-odd staff, but we pay them well to be discreet. And afterwards…a picnic in the palace grounds? Out of sight of prying lenses? Rocky's more than welcome. What do you say, my Claire? A day of fantasy and fun before we accept reality?'

How should she respond? She glanced across the room to where her severe black jacket hung on the back of a chair—her legal uniform, her life after this time-out.

Her time with Raoul.

'We should end it now,' she whispered, because she had to. Because how was it fair on Raoul to keep him loving her one minute longer?

'Do you want to?' he asked, and his hands caressed her body, and he touched her lips and smiled. 'Now?'

'Raoul…'

'Another week,' he told her.

'Of one-night stands?'

'I'll take what you give me, my love,' he told her. 'Because the rest of my life is a very long time.'

So there were undertones of impending sadness and inevitability, but at some time during the next few hours Claire gave herself up to the idea of enjoying this short sweet time, taking what she could and walking away with memories.

At least that was what she told herself in the sensible part of her brain. But most of her brain was taken up with simply being with Raoul. The future was some grey, barren nothing. For now there was only Raoul—only the way he held her, the way he smiled at her, the way he loved her.

At midday another Jeep arrived discreetly at her apartment and Claire and her shadow soldier—and Rocky—slipped into the back. Then the Jeep made a circuitous journey to the royal palace, and Claire and her dog and her shadow were in Raoul's world.

They drove past the grand entrance, where the King and

Queen had watched down their noses as she'd stumbled through formal greetings.

The palace was a storybook fantasy—a concoction of white stone, turrets, battlements, and heraldic banners floating from spires. The palace scared her half to death. This time, though, they drove around to the back, winding through formal gardens into a place that seemed almost a secret wilderness. The driveway curved onto gravel, accentuating the sense of country, and the Jeep finally came to a halt at a far less intimidating entrance, built between stables and a massive conservatory.

A servant did come down the back steps to greet them, but he was dressed in smart-casual. He was in his sixties, white-haired and dignified, and his smile was warmly welcoming.

'We're happy to have you back, miss,' he told her, and his tone said he meant it.

'Claire, this is Henri Perceaux—my grandparents' chief advisor,' Raoul told her. 'Anything you need to know about this country, ask Henri. On top of everything else, he's my friend. He taught me how to ride a horse when I was six.'

'That's something I've always longed to do,' Claire told him, and both men stared at her as if she'd grown two heads.

'You're Australian and you don't ride?' Raoul demanded.

'Nor do I pat kangaroos as they hop down the main street of Sydney,' she retorted. She shook her head. 'Stereotypes… Just because I'm Australian…'

'Apologies,' Raoul said, and then fixed her with a look. 'But you *can* surf, right?'

'Um…yes.'

'Then you can still be an Australian. Even if we're about to fit you with a tiara.'

'You're about to fit me with a *tiara*?'

'I've a team of dressmakers organised to discuss what you'd like to wear to the royal ball,' Henri said, sounding apologetic. 'If it's satisfactory with you, miss?'

She took a deep breath. Where was a fairy godmother when she needed one? she thought. One wave of her wand and Cinderella had a dress to die for. Cinders never had to face a team of dressmakers.

'Anything you want, they will construct,' Raoul told her. 'Let your imagination go.'

'My imagination's frozen. I don't know much besides black and jeans.'

'Then let yourself have fun,' Henri interspersed. He cast a covert glance at Raoul. 'That's a lesson that needs to be learned. You can still be royal *and* have fun.'

'Says you,' Raoul retorted.

'If I may be so bold,' Henri told him, 'I've watched your grandparents for many years, and within the constraints of their royal roles they do indeed enjoy themselves.'

'They do,' Raoul said tightly. 'But they have each other. They've been lucky.'

The palace was amazing. Over the top. Splendid. When Raoul would have taken her through the palace grounds first, thinking maybe she'd find the fabulous gardens less intimidating, the little girl in Claire made her pause.

'First things first. I'm in a palace. I need to see a chandelier.'

'They're all in the reception rooms and formal living areas,' he told her, bemused. 'Oh, my grandmother has one in her bedroom—no, make that two—but that's because she likes a bit of bling.'

'Will you show me?'

'My grandmother's bling?' he demanded, startled, and she stopped dead.

'No, Raoul, not your grandmother's bling. Your grandmother scares me. But a chandelier, none the less.'

'Which one?'

'Don't be obtuse. *Any* one.'

'Why?' he asked, curious.

'Because the only chandelier I've seen is a plastic travesty my friend Sophie hangs in her bathroom. And even though Sophie's cut me off because of my dubious legal status, one day I may meet her again and I'd love to be able to raise my brows in scorn because I've met a chandelier bigger than hers.'

'You've truly never met a chandelier?'

'I told you—I come from the other side of the tracks, Your Highness,' she retorted.

He looked down at her for a long moment, as if considering all the things he should say—he wanted to say. But finally he sighed and shrugged and managed a lop-sided smile. 'One chandelier coming up,' he told her. 'But if we're going to do this then we'll do it properly. The ballroom.'

'There won't be people?'

'It'll be empty. Cross my heart. Who goes into a ballroom unless there's a ball?'

'Someone to polish the chandelier?'

'It's the weekend. Chandelier-polishers are nine-to-five guys, Monday to Friday.'

'You know that how…?'

'It's in the "*Boys' Own Almanac of What Princes Need to Know*". Trust me.'

'Why should I trust you?'

'Because I'm a Prince of the Blood and I love you,' he told her, and before she could think of a retort he handed Rocky to Henri to take to the stables for a romp with the palace dogs—*'I'll take good care of him, miss.'* Then he took her hand and towed her through a maze of more and more breathtaking passages until they came to a vast hall with massive double doors beyond.

'Behold, my lady,' he said, and tugged the doors open.

If she only saw one chandelier in her life, this was the one to see. It was breathtaking.

Raoul flicked on the lights as he pulled open the doors

and the chandelier sprang to life. Once upon a time it must have been fitted with candles, but the lighting was now instant, with each individual crystal sparkling and twinkling its heart out.

And there were hundreds of crystals. Maybe thousands. The chandelier was a massive art form, a work of a bygone era when such things had been made by skilled artisans funded by the very richest in the land. This was a work of joy.

She'd never seen such a thing. She stood in the cavernous, deserted ballroom and she gaped.

'It's enormous,' she managed at last.

'There are bigger,' he told her. 'If you're interested, the world's largest is in the Dolmabahçe Palace in Istanbul. It has over seven hundred lamps, it weighs over four tons, and they have a staircase with balusters of Baccarat crystal to match.'

She thought about that for a moment and finally decided to confess. 'I don't know what a baluster is.'

'You know what?' He grinned. 'Neither do I. But that's what our guidebook says. We include the information so we sound modest.'

She looked up again at the glittering creation and shook her head. 'Modest? I don't think so. How can you come from living in the army to living in a place like this?'

'How do you know I didn't have a wee chandelier in my rucksack?' he said.

But he suddenly sounded strained and she thought it had been the wrong question. Chandelier or not, he wasn't where he wanted to be. But then he smiled, and she knew he was hauling himself back to reality. Putting regret aside.

He tugged her around to face her and his smile was a caress all by itself. 'Claire, I refuse to let you be intimidated by a chandelier. They're useful things and that's all.'

'Useful for what?'

'For dancing under. How are your dancing skills? I'm demanding to be your partner for at least one waltz.'

'Only one?' she asked, before she could stop herself.

'It depends,' he told her. 'If I dance with you more than twice the media will have me married to you and be conjecturing on how many children we'll have. I'm not objecting, but...'

'Two dances only, then,' she said hurriedly, because she had to. 'Raoul, we need to be sensible.'

There was a moment's pause. She saw his face close again, but then it was gone. Put away. He was back under control.

'As you say,' he said tightly. 'But the waltz... Claire, the eyes of the world will be on us. Do you need a fast lesson?'

'I can waltz!' She said it with some indignation, but then relented. 'Okay, I don't move in circles where the waltz is common, but my mum could dance and she taught me.'

'I'll feel different to your mum.'

'You think?'

'Try me,' he said, and held out his arms, waltz hold ready.

And she hesitated, because more and more she wanted to melt into those arms and more and more she knew she didn't fit there. But Raoul was asking her to dance under what surely must be the second biggest chandelier in the world and he was holding out his arms...

And this was Raoul.

She smiled up at him—a smile full of uncertainty and fear, a smile that said she was falling—had fallen—so deeply in love there was no going back. A smile that said she knew the pain of separation was inevitable but for now she was so in love she couldn't help herself.

She stepped forward into his arms. He took her in the classic waltz hold, lightly, but as if she was the most precious creature in the world.

They danced.

She melted.

There was no music—of course there was no music—

but the beat was right there in her heart. In his heart. She knew it. She felt it.

He held her and their feet scarcely touched the ground. He moved and she moved with him, in perfect synchronisation. How they did it she would never afterwards be able to tell.

It was as if this man had been her partner for years.

For life.

They danced in the great empty ballroom, under the vast chandelier that had seen centuries of love bloom under its sparkling lights, and that was now seeing a Prince of the Blood fall deeper and deeper in love.

And when the dance drew to an end, as dances inevitably did, the lights continued to glitter and sparkle as Raoul tilted his lady's chin and kissed her.

And as he did so a youth appeared in the doorway. He wasn't a palace employee but an apprentice to the master electrician who checked the chandelier at regular intervals.

The electrician didn't work nine to five—not when there was something as major as a ball coming up. Not when every guest room had to be checked and every facet of palace life had to be seen to work splendidly for this state occasion.

He'd finished checking the chandelier lights that morning, but was missing a spool of wire. 'Check the ballroom,' he'd told his lad. 'Make it fast.'

So the lad had slipped into the room—and stopped short.

He knew the Prince—of course he did. And the girl… This woman had been on the front pages of the newspapers for a couple of days. She'd rescued the Prince. She was here for a royal reception and to do some legal something or other. The media had reported sadly that there appeared to be no romantic attachment.

And yet here they were.

The apprentice might not be the smartest kid on the block, but he knew an opportunity when he saw it. He raised his phone and with one click it was done. Photographed. Safe.

Then he went back to report sadly to his boss that the spool of wire was nowhere to be found.

The kiss ended. They were left gazing at each other in some confusion.

I could let myself stay in these arms, Claire thought. *I could just...try.*

And if it failed? If *she* failed? This wasn't some minor fling. Breaking the Prince's heart would make her seem like a villain the world over. But the alternative…to live in a gilded cage and be judged…

She shuddered, and Raoul saw the shudder and touched her face.

'No,' he said, strongly and surely. 'Today we don't let the future mar what we have. You know what I'd like to do now?'

'What?'

'Take you to the gymnasium and let you show me your karate skills. You did say you were good.'

'I did,' she said, because why use false modesty here? Raoul might admit that his was only the second biggest chandelier, but her karate skills were okay.

'So prove it,' he told her.

She knew what he was doing. The kiss had been intense, passionate—a kiss that claimed—and she'd stepped away in fear. She was falling so hard, so fast. How to keep her sensible self working?

But Raoul must have seen the flash of fear and suddenly emotion was taking a back seat to challenge. Karate. 'I bet you can't throw me,' he told her.

'I bet you I can. Do you really have a gymnasium?'

'Yes.'

'Just for you?'

'The staff use it, too,' he told her. 'This is a large palace and we look after our employees. But I can block out any time I want it to myself. Usually I don't, but today I took the precaution…'

'Because you want me to prove myself?'

'Claire, you don't need to prove a thing,' he told her, his voice gentling. 'You've already proved you're the woman—'

'Not another word,' she interjected, suddenly breathless. 'Not one more word, Your Highness. But, okay, let's head to this gymnasium and see if I can throw you.'

She could throw him.

He lay on his back, stunned, and looked up at the diminutive woman above him with incredulity.

At her first approach he'd allowed her to throw him. He'd learned some martial arts himself—it had formed part of his army training. Then, bemused by Claire's claim to skill, he'd performed a token block—because he suspected that, yes, she really could throw, but he was large and skilled himself, and he didn't want to hurt her pride.

That thought had lasted all of twenty seconds, which was the time Claire had needed to move in, feign an amateurish movement, change swiftly to a move that was anything but amateurish and have him flat on the mat.

She grinned down at him. 'You'll have to do better than that, soldier.'

Soldier. For a moment she'd lost the Prince thing. She was having fun, smiling down at him, laughing at the ego that had had him misjudging her.

So then he got serious. He rose and circled and thought about everything his martial arts sergeant had told him.

As a soldier Raoul was trained to work with any number of different weapons. He could work on tactics, set up a battalion for attack, retreat, advance, camouflage, exist on meagre rations, survive with bush craft…

He could do this.

He moved in to attack, thinking how best to throw her without hurting her.

The next moment he was on his back again, and he didn't have a clue how he'd got there. *Whump!* He lay, winded, on the mat, and she was smiling down at him with the same patronising smile that said this throw had been no harder than the first.

'What the…?'

'I told you I was good,' she said, with not a hint of false modesty about her. 'Believe me?'

'Teach me that throw.'

'Really?'

'Please,' he said humbly, and she put down a hand to help him up.

He gazed at it with incredulity, and then grinned and put his hand in hers. She tugged him up, and he let her pull, and the feeling was amazing. He wanted to kiss her again—very, very badly—but she was in full martial arts mode. She was *sensei* to his pupil and she was serious.

They had an hour during which he learned almost more than in the entire time the military had devoted to teaching hand-to-hand combat. And at the end he still didn't know a fraction of what this woman could do.

Karate was fun.

Dressmakers were scary.

The appointment was for two. Showered in the lavish gymnasium bathrooms, dressed again and with make-up newly applied, she should be ready for anything.

She wasn't.

Henri had come to find them. Raoul had left her for his own fittings and Henri had escorted her to a massive bed-chamber on the second floor.

He swung the door wide and four women were waiting for her, all in black, all with faces carefully impassive.

'You'll take care of Miss Tremaine,' Henri said.

'Of course,' the oldest woman said smoothly, and closed the door on Henri and turned to appraise Claire.

She was a woman whose age was impossible to guess—slim, elegant, timeless. She also seemed deeply intimidating. Her gaze was surely a dressmaker's appraisal—nothing more. Claire shouldn't take it personally. But it was hard not to as every inch of her body was assessed and while the other three women stood back, silent, probably doing the same thing.

'Excellent,' the woman said at last. 'I'm Louise Dupont. These women are Marie, Belle and Fleur. Our job is to provide you with whatever you need for the grand ball and for the preceding official engagements which we're informed you're invited to attend. Belle has a list of the requirements. Would you like to tell us your ideas first, so we have an idea where we're going?'

'Simple.' It was as much as Claire could do to get the word out. 'I'm not royal, and I'm not accustomed to such events. If I could, I'd wear a little black dress…'

'A little black dress to a royal ball…?' Louise's expressionless face almost showed a flinch, and the women behind her gasped.

'I know I can't do that, but I'd like something that won't make me stand out.'

Certainly, *mademoiselle*,' Louise said woodenly, and swathes of cloth produced, and sketches, and a part of Claire was thinking, *What a coward.*

Among the swathes of cloth were brocades, sequins, tulle, lace of every description. But sense was sense. She chose beige for one of the anniversary dinners and a soft green for the other. Matching accessories. Deeply conservative. Then the ball dress…

'I really can't have black?'

'Their Majesties would consider it an insult,' Louise told her, and so Claire fingered the silver tulle for just a moment and then chose a muted sensible navy in a simple sheath design.

It will look elegant, she told herself, and the way the women set about fitting the cloth to her figure she knew it would.

And then Raoul arrived. One of the women answered the door to his tap. Whatever he'd tried on, he'd tried on fast. He was back in his casual trousers and open-necked shirt, but he stood in the doorway looking every inch a prince. He stared at the pinned sheath of navy cloth covering Claire and groaned.

'I *knew* it. Get it off.'

'I beg your pardon?' Louise turned and saw who it was, but her attitude hardly changed when she did. 'I beg your pardon—Your Highness.'

'Do you really think that's suitable for a royal ball?'

'It's what Miss Tremaine wishes.'

'Miss Tremaine wishes for the fairytale—don't you, Miss Tremaine?' He shook his head in exasperation. 'Louise, Miss Tremaine is returning to Australia after the ball, to life as a country lawyer. This ball is a ball to be remembered all her life.'

He strode across to where the remaining bolts of fabric lay and lifted some white lace shot with silver.

'This, I think. Something amazing, Louise. Something that makes the world look at Claire and know her for the beauty she is. She'll be wearing my mother's tiara...'

'Raoul!' She should have used his formal title but she was too gobsmacked. 'I don't want to stand out. Plain is good—and I'm not wearing a tiara.'

'You saved my life. If that's not a reason to lend you my mother's tiara I don't know what is. She'd be proud to have you wear it. You need a dress to match. Something magnificent, Louise. Something fairytale.'

'Would you like us to set up screens so you can supervise?'

'No!' Claire retorted.

Raoul grinned. 'What? No screens?'

'Go away!'

The women stared at her in astonishment—a commoner giving orders to royalty?—but Raoul was still smiling.

'Only if you promise to indulge in the fairytale. The full fantasy, Claire. Remember what Henri said? Have fun. Louise, can you do fairytale?'

'Certainly, Your Highness,' Louise told him, sounding intrigued.

'Then fairytale it is,' Raoul told her. 'Get rid of that navy blue.'

'Raoul…'

'I'm leaving,' he said, still smiling at her, and his smile was enough to have every woman in the room trying to hide a gasp. 'But you *will* have fun.'

'I will have fun,' she said grimly.

'That's my brave Claire. Go for it.'

And in the end she did have fun. Raoul left and she had two choices—she could try and incorporate a bit of bling into her image of plain or she could go for it.

With the women's blatant encouragement she went for it.

'I *do* like a bit of fairytale,' Louise admitted, letting her dour exterior drop.

Raoul had suggested the white lace shot with silver, and after a little thought that was what Louise recommended. The design she suggested was a gown of true princess splendour, with a low-cut sweetheart neckline and tiny slivers of silver just off the shoulders to hold the bodice in place. A vast skirt billowed and shimmered from a cinched waist, and a soft satin underskirt of the palest blue made the whole dress seem to light up.

That was the vision. For now it was only draped fabric, held together with pins, but Claire gazed at herself in the mirror and thought, *What am I doing here?*

She needed to ground herself. She needed to find Rocky and go home, she told herself as more and more of the shimmering silver was applied. To Australia. This fairytale was sucking her further and further in.

But she couldn't leave until after the ball.

At last the interminable measuring was done. 'You'll do our Prince proud,' Louise told her, permitting herself a tiny smile, and Claire tugged on her jeans and blouse as fast as she could and wondered how her presence could possibly do anyone proud. She felt a fraud.

Raoul was in the hallway, calmly reading, clearly waiting for her. He had Rocky on his knee. Rocky bounced across to greet her with canine delight and Raoul smiled—and she was in so much trouble.

'Hungry?' he asked. 'Picnic in the grounds?'

'Raoul, I should…'

'There's a whole lot of *I shoulds* waiting for us in the wings,' he said gently. 'For now, though, let's put them aside and focus on the *I wills*.'

CHAPTER TEN

RAOUL DIDN'T RETURN to her apartment that night, and neither did she stay in the palace. It had been a risk for one night; another night would be pushing things past reasonable limits if they were to keep the media treating their relationship as platonic. As they must.

Claire slept fitfully in her sparse apartment. She woke early, eager to throw herself back into work, which was far less confusing than being with Raoul. She was due to meet the head of Raoul's fledgling social services department. She drank coffee and read her notes from the previous week, trying to block out the fantasy of the weekend. Then, still with time before the car came to collect her, she retrieved the newspapers Raoul had organised to have delivered to her door.

She opened the first one and froze.

The page was entirely taken up with a photograph. Claire and Raoul, underneath the chandelier. The moment their waltz had ended. That kiss. The photograph had been blown up to the extent that the images were grainy, but there was no mistaking the passion.

This was no mere kiss. This was a kiss between two lovers. This was a man and a woman who were deeply in love.

She gasped and backed into the hallway, as if burned, dropping the paper on the floor. She stared down at it in horror.

The headline…

Roturière Australienne Pièges Notre Prince.
Commoner Australian Traps Our Prince.

Scarcely breathing, she picked it up again.

The first article she read had been hurriedly but deeply researched.

When she'd first arrived in Marétal the press had given their readers a brief background of the woman who'd rescued their Prince.

Lawyer taking time out from successful career to caretake an island...

It had sounded vaguely romantic, and the description had been superficial.

There was nothing superficial about *this*. Overnight someone had been in touch with an Australian journalist, who must have travelled fast to the tiny Outback town of Kunamungle. There was an exposé of her childhood poverty and scandal, even a nasty jibe from the publican—*'She always thought she was better than us—she was dragged up in the gutter but ambition was her middle name...'*

More coming! the article promised, and Claire thought of the fraud allegations and what might come out—what *would* come out—and she felt ill.

This was sensationalist journalism and it cheapened everything. She felt smutty and used and infinitely weary.

She flicked to the next paper.

Prince Désire Paysanne...
Prince Desires Peasant.

The phone rang. It was Raoul. He spoke, but she couldn't make herself reply. She leant against the wall, feeling she needed its support. The papers were limp in her hands. She dropped them again and felt as if she wanted to drop herself.

'Claire, talk to me.'

'There's nothing to say,' she whispered. 'I knew this would happen. So did you.'

'I need to see you.' He groaned. 'But I can't. The media have staked out the palace gates. I'll be followed if I come to you and it'll make things worse.' He paused. 'Unless you want to face them down together?'

Together? With all that implied? 'No!'

Somehow she hauled herself together. She was here to do a job and she would do it.

'I have an appointment with the head of your social services department in half an hour,' she told him. 'In this precinct. I imagine the media can't get in here?'

'They can't. You'll still do that?'

'I promised,' she whispered. 'It's what I came here for.'

'You came here for so much more.'

'No,' she said, and anger came to her aid now—fury plain and simple. 'I didn't. I agreed to take on a job. If I go home now then your papers will say that every single thing they've printed is true. That I came here to trap you…'

'We both know that's a lie.'

'I bet that's what they said about Cinderella.'

'We're not basing our relationship on a fairytale.'

'You said it,' she said wearily. 'Raoul, it's impossible. This is real life. We had…we *could* have had…something amazing…but amazing doesn't solve real-life problems. You know I'm not good enough for you.'

And he swore—an expletive so strong she almost dropped the phone.

'Um…' she said at last. 'My translation isn't that good.'

'Claire, I *will* see you.'

'No,' she told him. 'It does neither of us any good.'

'You did promise you'd come to the ball.'

She fell silent then. The ball… She *had* promised. And there was the dress. And there was Raoul. And he'd be in his gorgeous regimental uniform.

Cinderella had *her* midnight, she thought ruefully. Maybe she, too, could have her ball and her midnight. There'd be no glass slipper afterwards, because happy-ever-after only happened in fairytales, but the ball would be something she could remember all her life.

She shouldn't. The sensible part of her brain was screaming at her: *Don't, don't, don't!*

But there was still another part of her—the part that remembered Raoul holding her in the waltz, the part that remembered a dress of shimmering silver, the part that knew for the rest of her life she'd remember one night…

And she had to finish what she'd come here to do. She'd do her work, she'd have her ball and she'd go home.

'Okay,' she whispered.

'Okay, what? Claire…'

'I will come to the ball,' she told him. 'As long as…as long as you don't attempt to see me before then. I won't come to the receptions. Just the ball. And I'll finish the work I'm here to do this week so I can go home straight afterwards.'

'It doesn't make any kind of sense'

'It does,' she said sadly. 'It makes all kinds of sense. It's anything else that's just plain lunacy.'

Raoul read the papers from cover to cover.

They were tearing Claire to pieces. No mercy… This woman wasn't good enough to be the future Queen. The papers said so.

A fury was building inside him—a rage so cold, so hard, that it was all he could do not to smash things. The palace was full of excellent things to smash. Priceless china, artwork that still had the power to take his breath away, precious carpets and furnishings…

Right now he wanted to put a match to the lot of it and watch it burn.

Instead he forced himself to keep reading as he knew that Claire, when her work for the day was done, would read.

Together they could face them all down, he thought. This wasn't insurmountable. In time they'd see…

But she wouldn't let that happen. He knew that with a dull, unrelenting certainty. Claire's self-image had been battered from birth, and the ghastly Felicity and her cronies had smashed it to nothing. He knew how wonderful she was, but she'd never let herself believe it. She'd be miserable here, knowing everyone was looking down at her. Her self-image wouldn't let her go past it.

The whole situation was impossible. He slammed his fist down on his desk, causing his coffee to jump and topple and spill onto the priceless Persian rug.

Excellent. A good start.

There was a faint knock on the door.

'Come in,' he snapped, and Henri was at the door, looking grave.

'I am so sorry, Your Highness,' he told him.

'So am I.' He hesitated, and then thought, *Why not say it like it is?* 'The paper's right. I love her.'

Henri stilled. 'Truly?'

'What do *you* think?'

'This criticism will pass.'

'She doesn't think she's good enough, but she's better than all of us put together. What am I going to do? I can't demand she stay. I can't insist she subject herself to this sort of filth.' He picked up the top newspaper and tossed it down onto the pool of spilled coffee.

'She'd like to learn to ride,' Henri said weakly. 'Maybe you could ask her to come here for a lesson.'

'You think that would be an enticement for her to stay?'

'I...no.'

The two men stared at each other for a long moment. Raoul didn't even try to hide his pain. This man had known him since childhood. It was no use trying to hide.

'She must be really special,' Henri said at last.

'She saved my life,' Raoul said simply. He stared down at the spilled coffee and his mouth twisted. 'She saved *me*.'

'So how can you save her back?'

Raoul shrugged. 'I know the answer to that. I need to let her go.'

'There must be another way.'

'If you can think of one...' He lifted the newspaper he'd tossed and screwed it up. 'If you think the media will quit with this... It's relentless.'

'I'm so sorry,' Henri said gently. 'You know, the palace could put out a rebuttal...'

'Everything they say is true. They're crucifying her for things she had no hand in. They're crucifying her for her birth.'

'Are you thinking of marrying her?' Henri asked. 'Are you really thinking she's worthy of the throne?'

The question made Raoul pause. He thought of the years of isolation, of the armour he'd built around himself. He thought of his relentless quest not to need people. Not to love.

He thought of Claire.

'Are you really thinking she's worthy of the throne?'

She surely was. Of course she was. And then he thought of the throne without Claire and he was suddenly face to face with what he must have known for weeks.

'Of course I am,' he said bleakly. 'She's the woman I need beside me for the rest of my life.'

'Will she agree?'

'No,' he said bleakly. 'She won't, and I don't blame her.'

Claire spent the week working harder than she'd worked in her life. She'd been working to a plan and now she simply continued with the plan—except she worked faster.

She was interviewing as many of the country's movers and shakers in the justice system as she could. She was also talking to the police, prison officers, parole officers, small-time lawyers who worked at the fringe of the system—and to people who'd found themselves in court themselves. People who'd failed to find legal help when they'd needed it most. People whom legal assistance was designed to help.

As an outsider she could never have done this work alone, but Raoul had set it up for her. The people he and his staff had chosen for her to talk to were extraordinary, and to her relief almost none of them had backed out of the interviews because of the photograph and the lurid exposé of her past.

'I thought you wouldn't be here,' a lawyer she'd talked to that first morning had said. 'The papers say your legal work is just a smokescreen for you staying with the Prince.'

'It's not. My legal work is the reason His Highness persuaded me to come.'

'So you and the Prince…?' he'd probed, and she'd managed to smile.

'Legal work is dull. A woman has a right to a little fun on the side,' she'd told him, somehow managing to smile.

He'd stared at her in astonishment and then he'd laughed, and they'd got on with their interview.

So that was how she was managing it—laughing it off as best she could as a bit of fun, pretending it had nothing to do with her work and ignoring Raoul.

He still rang every night, and she answered his calls. She talked determinedly about the work she was doing—there was so much that could be done for his country and her report would be comprehensive—but she refused to talk about anything personal.

'Personal's a mistake,' she told him when he pressed her. 'You know that. And who knows who's listening in on this conversation?'

'No one is.'

'You can't be sure.'

'Claire…'

'I'll come to the ball and then I'm out of here,' she told him. 'My work will be done by then.'

'You know I want you to stay.'

'And it's totally unsuitable that I stay. Raoul, find yourself a princess. I'm just Claire.'

And each night she disconnected from his call with a firmness she didn't feel. She punched the pillows into the small hours and even made them a bit soggy, but there was no way she was relenting.

She had to do what she had to do and then leave.

* * *

Raoul also had to do what *he* had to do. As the week went on he became more and more sure that his decision was the right one. He needed her.

Need…

The knowledge made him feel exposed as he'd never been exposed before. It was terrifying and it was exhilarating and it was inarguable.

He'd lost his parents when he was so young he barely remembered them. His grandparents had been kind, but remote. He'd been raised by servants and then he'd found himself in the army—a place where teamwork was valued but individual emotional strength was everything.

He'd learned to be a loner. He'd thought he could be a loner all his life.

He'd been wrong, and the knowledge left him with no choice. Meeting Claire had made something inside him break and it couldn't be repaired.

A part of him said that was weak, but there was nothing he could do about it. Rejecting her felt like tearing himself apart.

He'd faced the worst of conflicts in the Middle East, but he'd joined the army for a reason. He'd spent a solitary childhood when life had seemed bleak to the point of misery. He thought of that solitude now. He had thought he'd trained himself to accept it.

He hadn't.

Two days before the ball he went to see his grandparents. Their discussion was intense, personal, a far cry from their usual formality, but at the end he knew his decision was the right one.

The King had said little, just looked grave.

The Queen had been appalled. 'You *can't*.'

'I might not be able to but I intend to try. Grandmama, it's the only way I can stay sane.'

'She's not worth it. A commoner…'

'She's worth it.'

'Raoul, think of what you're risking,' she'd wailed, and he'd shaken his head.

'I think of what I'm gaining, Grandmama. We can do this if we work together.'

'You're not giving us a choice.'

'No,' he'd said, and he had glanced at the side table where the morning newspapers were, full of even more vituperative stories about his Claire. 'No, I'm not. The country's condemned Claire and in doing so it's refused the best thing that's ever happened to it. And it's rejected the best thing that's ever happened to *me*.'

Cinderella had her coach at midnight. Claire had her plane tickets. Her flight back to Australia was booked for early in the morning after the ball.

'It's the same thing, except I won't be leaving any glass slippers behind,' she told herself.

She was standing before the full-length mirror in her apartment, staring at herself in awe. She'd been invited to dress at the palace but she'd refused, so Henri had organised a dresser, a hairstylist and a make-up artist to come to her. She therefore had three women fussing about her. A chauffeur was standing by with a limousine in the courtyard.

For this night she was deemed royalty.

One night before the rest of her life…

She stood in front of the mirror and knew exactly how Cinderella had felt.

This wasn't her. This was truly a princess.

Her reflection left her feeling stunned. She looked taller, slimmer, glowing. She looked regal. Her curls were loosely caught up, deceptively casual, so they framed her face, tumbled artfully to her shoulders. They were caught back within a glittering tiara so some curls hid the diamonds and some diamonds sparkled through.

The tiara alone had made her catch her breath in wonder, but there was also a matching necklet and earrings.

'They haven't been worn since the Prince's mother died,' the dresser said now, sniffing faintly in disapproval. 'I'm astonished that he thinks it's suitable to bring them out today.'

And there it was—the whole reason this wouldn't work. This woman had read the tabloids. She knew just how unsuitable Claire was.

'I guess it's a final thank-you gift before I go home,' Claire said, managing to keep her voice light, as she'd fought to keep it light all week. 'And it *is* just a loan…'

'But for him to lend it…'

'Well, *I* think it's lovely,' the hairstylist said stoutly. 'Perfect. And I loved the picture of you and His Highness in the paper, miss. So romantic. Wouldn't it be lovely if it was real?'

'I think I might regret it if it was real,' Claire managed. 'Do I absolutely need to wear this corset?'

'Hourglass figures need hourglass corsets,' the dresser snapped. 'The women I normally dress don't complain. You must make sacrifices for a decent figure'

'You have a lovely figure already,' the hairstylist declared. 'Don't listen to her, miss.'

And Claire wasn't listening. This week had been all about not listening.

She stared once more into the mirror at the sparkling vision in silver and white, at the way her skirts shimmered and swung, at the beautiful white slippers—not glass!—peeping from under her skirts. At her hair, which had surely never been lovelier. At the carefully applied make-up, which made it look as if she was wearing no make-up at all and yet made her complexion glow. At the diamonds and the sparkle and everything in life which didn't represent Claire Tremaine.

'Okay,' she whispered. 'Bring on my pumpkin.'

'Your car's ready, miss,' the stylist breathed. 'Oh, miss, you'll break your Prince's heart tonight.'

'He's not my Prince,' Claire told her, gathering her skirts and her courage. 'He's never been my Prince and he never will be.'

The ball was an hour old when Claire arrived.

Raoul was half afraid that she'd got cold feet and wouldn't show at all, but at this late stage there was little he could do about it. As heir to the throne he opened the ball with a waltz with the Queen of a neighbouring country. Then there were others he needed to dance with. He had obligations to fulfil and there was no way he could disappear quietly to phone her.

All he could do was dance on with the list of notables Henri had told him were compulsory, and hope that she'd find the courage to come.

Finally he was rewarded when a stir from the entrance announced her arrival.

'Miss Claire Tremaine,' the footman announced in stentorian tones.

The ball was well under way. The announcement of new arrivals had become a muted background to the night—no one was listening—but somehow all ears caught this.

The attention of the entire ballroom seemed to swing to Claire.

She was stunning. Breathtaking.

Henri must have orchestrated this late entrance, he thought. Henri was in charge of Claire's travel arrangements. Raoul wouldn't put it past him to have staged Claire's entrance so she had maximum attention.

As she did. She stood in the entrance looking slightly unsure—no, make that *very* unsure. She looked so lovely the entire ballroom seemed to hold its breath.

His grandmother was by his side and her hand clutched his arm. 'You don't need to go straight to her,' she hissed. 'The way she looks…others will dance with her. This is nonsense, Raoul. See sense.'

'I *am* seeing sense,' he told her. 'Grandmama, you know what I must do.'

'Not tonight,' she urged. 'You need to accompany us onto the dais for the speech. You need to be seen as royal. Stay with us.'

'Only if you acknowledge Claire.'

'I'll acknowledge her as the woman who saved your life, nothing more.'

'Then I'll be in the crowd, watching. If you expect me to be an onlooker, so be it. But meanwhile…' He gently disengaged her arm. 'Meanwhile I need to welcome the woman I love.'

It might as well have been a fairytale. For as she stood, uncertain, alone, Raoul made his way through the crowd and quite literally took her breath away.

The ballroom itself was enough to take her breath away. It was transformed by the lights from the great chandelier, by a thousand flowers, by an orchestra playing music that soared, by the throng of nobility in attire that was truly splendid.

But the most splendid of all was Raoul.

He was truly a prince of dreams. He was in full royal regalia, a superbly cut suit with a wide blue sash, medals, epaulettes, glittering adornments of royal blood and military might.

His jet-black hair was immaculate. His height, his build, his dress—he looked every inch a prince at the peak of his power. He was the total antithesis of the man she'd helped from the water.

He was magnificent.

He was smiling as he broke through the throng, and he held his hand out to her well before he reached her.

'Miss Tremaine,' he said as he reached her. 'You are very welcome.'

And her response was something that stunned even herself. She sank into a curtsy—a full gesture that she hadn't known how to make until she'd done it.

He took her hand and raised her fingers to his lips, his eyes dancing with laughter.

'What have I done to deserve this?'

'I've watched too many romantic movies,' she told him. 'In this outfit nothing else seems appropriate.'

'Claire, stay…' The laughter died and his voice was low and urgent.

'For tonight,' she whispered. 'For now.'

If tonight was all he had then he intended to use it. How to hold this woman in his arms, how to dance with her, how to feel her melting against him and know that she willed it to end?

But he knew why. All around them were eyes raised, looks askance, the occasional snigger, the odd snort of outrage. *This* was the woman who would steal their royal Prince. He knew Claire could feel it, and there was nothing he could do but hold her and know there must be a future for them.

A future at a cost…

But he couldn't think of that tonight. He couldn't think of anything but the woman in his arms.

As they danced the titters and the whispers fell away. He held her and her beautiful gown swirled against his legs, and her breasts moulded to his chest and he felt…

He felt as if he was flying.

She loved him. How could she let him hold her like this and know that she had to leave? If she let herself think past midnight then her mind simply shut down.

All she was capable of was dancing with the man she loved. Of holding him to her.

Of loving…

Only, of course, the night wasn't all about dancing. There were formalities scheduled. After the next set the King and Queen were to make their anniversary speech. And as they made their way to the stage they paused by the couple in the midst of the dance floor.

'You should stand by us, Raoul,' the Queen told him, but she said it in the tone of one who knew she was already beaten.

'You know my decision,' Raoul said softly. 'I stand by Claire.'

'Raoul—go,' Claire told him.

'Will we come to the stage as a couple, Grandmama?' Raoul asked, but the Queen shook her head.

'No! This is *not* what I planned.'

'I'm staying here,' Raoul told her.

'Then come onto the stage with us yourself, young woman,' the King told Claire unexpectedly, suddenly urgent. As if he'd somehow emerged from his books and was seeing Raoul's firmness for what it was. 'This country's treating you shabbily and I won't have it.' He put a hand on her arm. 'Come with us. Please.'

'As a couple,' Raoul said.

'No!' The Queen was vehement.

'Then come to assist an old man onto the stage,' the King told Claire. 'Raoul, assist your grandmother.' And he took Claire's arm and held it.

So in the end there was no choice. They made their way to the stage, but not as a couple. The King was escorted up first, leaning heavily on Claire as if he did indeed need her help.

Raoul escorted his grandmother up the stairs as well. But then, as she made to tug at him, to stand beside her on the far side of the stage from Claire, he shook his head.

'Claire, our place isn't here.'

The noise from the ballroom had faded. Attention was riveted on the stage. To reach Raoul, to leave the stage, Claire would have to walk right in front of both King and Queen.

Raoul was on the far side of the stage, waiting for her to return to him. She sent him an almost imperceptible shake of her head and backed into the wings. The curtains hid her.

This was her rightful place, she thought. Out of sight. She was in the wings with the workers, with the people handling the curtains, the workers associated with the orchestra.

Where she belonged.

She leaned heavily against the nearest wall and hoped Raoul wouldn't follow.

Fantasy was over. The King was preparing to speak.

Somewhere below was Raoul. He needed to listen to his grandparents' speech but she didn't need to be beside him.

She couldn't need him at all.

If there was one thing King Marcus had been known for during his long reign it was his long speeches—and he didn't disappoint now. He'd prepared a very meaningful, very erudite, very lengthy speech and the crowd settled down to listen. This was their King. The country was fond enough of their Queen, but King Marcus was seldom seen in public and they were prepared to indulge him when he was.

After a moment's hesitation Raoul backed away from the stage, stepping down into the main hall. He didn't want any attention to play on him. After all, this was his grandparents' night, and he even found it within him to be grateful that Claire had backed into the wings, out of sight. The focus was on his grandparents—as it should be. The time for him to claim Claire would follow.

Around him the guests were listening with polite attention, laughing when the King meant them to laugh, applauding when it was appropriate. The men and woman in the orchestra behind the King were all attentive too. They were giving this pair of beloved monarchs their due.

He had a sudden vision of himself and Claire in fifty years, doing the same thing.

It wasn't going to happen.

He glanced at his grandmother and found she was staring straight at him. He winced and turned his attention elsewhere. To the orchestra on the raised platform behind the royals. Men and women in demure black, riveted to the King's words.

Except one. A young man seated behind the drums. The man seemed to be searching the crowd. Looking for someone?

His attention caught, Raoul followed his gaze and saw the man's eyes meet one of the guests. A man in his mid-forties was standing not far from Raoul. He was formally dressed, as a foreign diplomat, and he was standing alone. There was nothing to make him stand out from so many similar guests.

But the man was watching the drummer, not the King, and as the drummer's gaze met his he gave his head an almost imperceptible nod. Then casually—oh, so casually—he reached down as if to adjust his shoelace.

And then he straightened, his arm outstretched…

A glint of metal…

Years of military training had made Raoul's reactions lightning-fast. Act first—ask questions later. That was the training instilled for when lives were at stake.

Raoul, ten feet from the man in question, dived like lightning and brought him down in a tackle that pinned him to the floor.

The pistol in the man's hand discharged—straight into the polished floor. But that wasn't the only threat. He knew it wasn't. He held the man, pinned him down hard, and looked desperately up at the stage as he yelled. 'Security! Drummer on stage!'

And as the dark-suited security officers streamed in from the foyer, where they'd been banished, he was remembering a letter. It had been pointed out to him by Henri. It had been addressed to the Queen…

If you don't follow our orders we'll kill the King and take you as our prisoner for ransom. You might as well pay the money now. It'll save you grief...

There'd been a similar threat—and a tragedy—in another country a couple of years back. Their security chief had been worried enough to talk to the Queen, asking permission to bolster his team. He'd wanted to increase the royal security presence within the ballroom.

'You can do what you want *after* the ball,' the Queen had said fretfully. 'I won't have my ball marred by a room full of bodyguards.'

He'd then shared his concerns with Henri, who'd come to Raoul. 'Please...talk to your grandmother,' Henri had told him, and Raoul had. But with no success.

'You're not in charge yet,' the Queen had told him. 'This is *our* ball. You won't bring a woman of our choice. We won't have your bodyguards.'

'They're not *my* bodyguards, Grandmama. They're yours—to keep you safe.'

'There is no threat in *my* kingdom.'

But of course there was—and it was here. It was real. A diplomat wouldn't have faced a body-search. He'd have been able to conceal a gun.

We'll kill the King and take you as our prisoner...

There were two threats here, and he'd only disarmed one.

'The drummer on stage!' he yelled again to the men approaching.

'Nobody move!' a voice shouted out—icy, cold, vicious.

And Raoul twisted and stared up at the stage.

The drummer had launched himself in from the wings and grabbed the Queen. She'd been standing beside the dais while her husband spoke. The man dragged her back towards the wings, and at her throat he held a vicious, stiletto-type knife that looked as if it might have been concealed in a drumstick.

And Claire was there as well. At the sound of the gunshot and Raoul's sharp command she'd edged out from the wings.

She was right behind the drummer.

The three of them might well have been alone on stage. The men and women in the orchestra were slightly removed from the main players. The King was standing stunned on his dais.

There was the Queen and her assailant—and Claire.

The drummer was hauling the Queen further back, and as he did so he glanced behind him. He saw Claire.

He flicked her a glance that took in the swirl of her amazing skirts, her low-cut neckline and the gorgeous tiara set in beautifully coiffured curls. His glance was contemptuous—a momentary summing-up that said she was nothing of importance. She was the dirt the media had been speaking of. She was something to be safely ignored.

He had his knife to Queen Alicia's throat and was tugging her backwards.

For the moment Queen Alicia was refusing to move, digging in her toes, dragging passively, surprisingly fierce for someone so elderly. 'Let me go,' she ordered, in a voice as imperious as her regalia.

'Shut up!' the drummer snarled, and then as the appalled hiss from the ballroom faded to stunned silence he raised his voice. 'One move from anyone and I'll kill your Queen. If she's so precious, stay where you are. She's coming with me. And *you…*' He turned to Raoul. 'Let my friend go.'

Raoul was at the far end of the ballroom. He was with the security forces. They had the diplomat in their grip.

Raoul had the gun in his hand. The sound of its explosion was still reverberating through the horrified throng. He raised the gun and then lowered it, watched helplessly as the security officers did the same.

The drummer was holding the Queen hard in front of him. To shoot risked killing her. There was nothing he could do.

'Let him go!' the drummer snarled again, talking directly to Raoul. 'Now!'

There was no choice. Raoul gave a nod and the security officers let the man go. The man started to move up through the crowded ballroom, shoving stunned aristocracy aside.

And Claire's mind was racing. In a minute she'd have two of them on the dais, she thought. In a minute they'd have the Queen outside, in their hold. Raoul was powerless.

A minute…

She needed a second.

And the voice of her *sensei*…

She glanced out at Raoul, one sweeping glance in which their eyes met for just a fraction of a second but the message she gave him was powerful.

And then she had to ignore him. She had to move.

Now.

She kicked off her ridiculously high, ridiculously beautiful shoes and in almost the same movement lifted her voluminous skirts high. She raised her gartered knee as high as she could and with the heel of her bare foot slammed a *yoko geri* side-kick with lethal force into the back of the assailant's knee.

She'd only ever done this in training. She'd only ever known it as practice, and she'd certainly never done it while dressed in a corset and ballgown.

'Do this and you'll rip ligaments, or worse,' her *sensei* had told her. 'The first rule of Karate is not to be present. Where there is trouble, you are not. But if you're ever trapped in a life-or-death situation this will cause extreme pain and do enough serious damage to give you time to escape.'

And there was no doubt that was exactly what she'd done. The guy screamed and started to drop.

There was still the knife. He could kill the Queen if he dragged her with him, but years of training, years of knowledge and practice were flooding to her aid. What followed was almost a reflex action. Even as the guy buckled she had his knife arm by the wrist and was pulling it back, her other hand pressed against his elbow, pushing forward. She pressed hard with both hands and the guy screeched in pain.

'Drop it,' she bit out as his knees hit the floor.

Queen Alicia was crumbling with them, unbalanced by

the change of pressure. The combined mass of royal skirts was making the entire scene surreal—where were crisp karate uniforms when she needed them?—but she was totally focused on her assailant.

The guy's hand jerked, still holding the knife. 'You slut…'

'I'm not a slut,' she said calmly. 'But I *am* a Third Dan Karate Black Belt. Drop the knife or I'll break your arm.' And she applied more pressure. Not so much as required to break it—at least she didn't think so—but enough to have him screaming again.

Enough to have the knife clattering harmlessly to the floor.

She fielded it and kicked it under Alicia's skirts—because who knew who was out there in the ballroom if she kicked it off the dais?

And she kept on holding the guy's arm, pushing him flat to the floor, with his arm still held behind him, because she didn't know if the knife was all he had. And then she didn't have to hold him, because Raoul was leaping up onto the dais with her.

She glanced out over the ballroom and realised he'd got her silent message. The security officers had moved, obviously at Raoul's command. The man he'd had to release had been grasped again.

They had them.

Security was suddenly everywhere. Control was theirs.

The guy was underneath her. The last threat. And Raoul was with her.

It was over.

CHAPTER ELEVEN

AT FIVE THE next morning Claire boarded her plane.

Why not?

There was no reason why not. The ball had ended in disarray. The security team hadn't been prepared to let it continue. Who knew what else had been planned?

The guests had dispersed, vetted as they left, their credentials finally minutely inspected.

The Queen had collapsed in hysterics. Raoul had been taken up with security concerns, with coping with the ruffled feathers and nerves of the invited dignitaries, with the calming of his distraught grandparents.

Apart from one brief, hard embrace when they'd realised the danger was past, Claire hadn't seen him. She'd been whisked outside by the security people and Henri had appeared at her side and asked her if she'd like to use a salon in the palace to wait for Raoul.

'I'd like to go home,' she'd told him, and he'd nodded gravely and organised a car to take her back to her apartment. Because that was what he thought home meant.

An hour later a slim figure in jeans and a windcheater had slipped out of her apartment, carrying her own baggage to the taxi she herself had arranged.

And now she was on the plane, staring fixedly forward while she waited for take-off. White-faced but determined. What a way to end it. Maybe she should have waited, but her ticket was for this morning and there was no point. What had to be said had been said.

Marétal to London. London to Sydney. In twenty-four hours she'd be back in the apartment she hadn't been near for almost six months.

She had work to do—she'd come to Marétal on a contract and she'd fulfil her obligations. The next few months would be busy. But she wouldn't return to Marétal. Her report would be emailed. Raoul and his staff could use it or not.

She felt ill.

'Orange juice?' A steward was moving down the aisle, offering refreshments. 'I'm sorry, but there's a slight delay in take-off. It shouldn't be more than half an hour.'

She closed her eyes. Half an hour. The beginning of the rest of her life.

Raoul. How could she leave him?

How could she not?

She should be exhausted. She should sleep. But of course sleep was nowhere. She was still wired, still filled with adrenalin, still seeing Raoul heading towards the stage to help her. Still seeing the fear on his face.

He loved her. She knew he loved her. And to be loved by such a man…

Such an impossible man.

There was a stir among the passengers and she opened her eyes and glanced out of the window. There were two dark limousines, their windows tinted to anonymity in the dawn light, driving onto the tarmac. They stopped and a security contingent emerged from the second car—suited men, armed, dangerous.

Where had they been last night?

And then the door of the first car opened and out stepped…

Raoul.

Raoul in jeans and T-shirt, carrying a rough canvas duffel. Raoul looking every inch *not* a royal.

There was fierce talk between the men—remonstrance? But Raoul simply shook each man's hand and then turned and looked up at the plane.

She shrank back. If he was here to take her off the plane…

She wouldn't go. She couldn't.

She sat head down, scarcely daring to breathe, but nothing happened. She couldn't see the door from where she sat. There was a murmur of interest from the passengers forward of her and then nothing.

'Prepare for take-off…'

Nothing more was said. She ventured a peek out of the window. The cars were gone.

The plane turned its big nose ponderously out to the runway, the taxiing complete.

She closed her eyes as the plane gathered speed and then they were in the air.

Marétal was left behind.

'Would you like a facecloth?' An attendant was moving down the aisle, doing her normal thing, business as usual.

She offered the facecloth to Claire and Claire buried her face in it.

'Hi,' said a voice behind the attendant—a voice she knew so well. 'Do you think that when you're all washed up you can cope with a visitor?'

The seat next to hers was empty. Of course it was.

That couldn't just be a coincidence, she thought as Raoul sank down beside her, and amazingly she even found space to be indignant. The plane was almost full. How had he managed this?

He was royal. Being royal opened doors.

'Very nice,' Raoul said approvingly as he sank into the business class seat. 'I'm back in cattle class. I had to be ever so charming to the staff to be allowed up here.'

'You're in Economy?' As a first statement it was pretty dumb, but then dumb was how she was feeling right now.

'*Your* travel is funded by the Royal Family of Marétal,' he told her. 'I'm funded by me. And I'm unemployed. We unemployed people need to watch every cent.'

It was too much to take in. 'Why…why are you here?' she managed, and for answer he simply took her hand.

'You saved the life of the Queen of Marétal. Someone

has to thank you. I got busy, and when I had time to look around you were gone.'

'I had a plane ticket.'

'So you did.' His hold on her hand tightened. 'As it happened, so did I.'

'You…?'

'You don't think I'd let you go all the way to Australia without me?'

'Of course I do,' she snapped. She was tired, confused, and starting to be angry. 'Raoul, this was never the plan. Go away.'

'It's a bit hard to go away now,' he said, peering out of the window to the night sky. They were now thousands of feet high. 'I believe I've burned my bridges. Henri's cleaning up the loose ends in Marétal. I'm here with you.'

'Henri…'

'He's good,' Raoul told her. 'He's the new administrator of the country. I'm unemployed.'

Unemployed...

He took her breath away. He was looking endearingly casual, in jeans and a tight T-shirt that showed every muscle his army life had toned. He was starting to look a bit unshaven. The difference between now and when she'd last seen him was extraordinary.

Unemployed?

'I've quit,' he told her, settling in. 'This is very nice indeed. How long do you think they'll let me sit here?'

'As long as you want. You're the Prince,' she snapped.

He shook his head. 'Nope. I need a new title. I've been Prince Raoul. I've been Lieutenant Colonel de Castelaise. Now I need to be just plain mister. Mr de Castelaise? That sounds wrong. *Monsieur?* Yes, but I intend to be an Aussie. Any suggestions?'

She had no suggestions at all. She could only stare. If she went back behind her facecloth again would he disappear? This felt surreal.

She was starting to feel as Cinders must have felt when her coach had turned back into a pumpkin. In the middle of the road surrounded by orange pulp. Stranded.

Hornswoggled.

'You can't…just resign,' she managed at last, and Raoul nodded, thoughtful.

'That's what I thought. I couldn't see how I could. But when it got closer to losing you I didn't see how I *couldn't*.'

'Your country needs you.' Her voice was scarcely a whisper.

'That's what I believed, too,' he told her. 'But over the last few weeks I've been looking hard at how our country's run and seeing things in a different light.'

'I don't understand.'

'I'm not sure I do either,' he told her. 'Not fully. But what I *do* know is that my grandfather wasn't born to rule. Yes, he was the heir to the throne, but his head was always in his books. His parents despaired of him. His country despaired of him. But then he did something amazing. He met and married my grandmother. She wasn't what you might call a commoner—she was Lady Alicia Todd—but she was just the daughter of a country squire and she had no pretensions to royalty. But she married my grandfather, she took up the reins of the country, and she's been a superb monarch. She's fading now. She's ceased to move with the times, but she's still awesome. She's still the Queen.'

'She needs help. You said yourself…'

'I know she does. But when I was thinking this through I wondered… All those years ago, what would my grandfather have done if someone had told him—as I believe many people did—that Alicia wasn't fit to be Queen? And the answer was obvious. He would have abdicated rather than lose her.'

'You're not threatening…?' Still she was having trouble getting her voice to work. 'You're not threatening to abdicate?'

'I haven't threatened anything,' he told her. 'I've left.'

'You've walked out?'

'Hey, I'm honourable,' he told her, sounding wounded. 'How could I just walk out?'

'You tell me. Words of one syllable,' she said, trying hard to glare. 'What have you done?'

'Moved the Crown into administration.' He thought about it for a moment and reconsidered. 'That's a three-syllable word. Thrown the reins to Henri? Henri's still two syllables, but he's the best I can do. This whole situation is the best I can do.'

'Raoul...'

'You see, Henri doesn't want it,' Raoul told her. 'In fact he's still trying to talk me out of it. But we're organising good people around him. It'll take time, and I will have to return to get things into final shape, but we'll make it work. We don't have a choice.'

'But you're *needed*,' she said, flabbergasted. 'Raoul, you know you are.'

'And I intend to stay hands-on,' he told her. 'I'll return every so often, for as long as they need me. If my grandfather's health declines further, then those visits might end up being long, but that's all they will be. Visits.'

'How can you *do* that? They need you all the time.'

'And there's the problem,' he told her. 'I need *you* all the time.'

That took her breath away. She wasn't sure how she could make herself breathe, much less talk, but somehow she must.

'Isn't that...?' She could hardly make herself say it, but it had to be said. 'Isn't that selfish? Your country needs you. Even on so short a visit I could see the difference you'd make.'

There was a moment's silence. His face set, and she knew suddenly that what he was proposing was no whim. What he was saying was the end of some bitter internal battle, and even now the outcome hurt.

'I could make a difference,' he agreed at last. 'I know I

could. But, Claire, the more I see of you the more I know I couldn't.'

'I don't understand…'

'Last week, after that appalling photograph and the ensuing fuss, I went to see my grandparents,' he told her. 'I talked to both of them and I asked them honestly if they could have ruled for so long and for so well if they hadn't had each other. My grandfather, the King, was the first to answer and he was blunt. He said Alicia was his strength, and that he'd never have been able to do it alone. That's what I expected. But then my grandmother decided to be honest as well. She told me that, strong as she appeared, my grandfather was her spine. That without him she believed she'd collapse like a house of cards. That her love for him was what sustained her. And she conceded more. That royalty was a massive privilege but also a massive burden. And she said that, disapprove of you—*and* your dog—as she surely did, if I truly loved you then she understood. She'd fight me all the way to the altar—she would *not* support me marrying someone so patently unsuitable—but she understood.'

'Oh, Raoul…' Where was the facecloth when she needed it?

But Raoul had her fingers under her chin, forcing her gaze to meet his. 'So it's Henri,' he told her. 'It's Henri and our staff, and my grandparents, and me working from the sidelines. In time the country will become a democracy and they'll see they don't really need a monarch. We'll work something out. We must.'

'But *you*?' It was almost a wail. 'Raoul, it'll take years to make Marétal a democracy, and even then the monarchy could stay in place. You'd make a wonderful king.'

'Not without you.'

'That's crazy. I could never be royal. Your whole country thinks I'm a piece of dirt.'

'So my whole country can think we're *both* pieces of dirt,' he told her. 'I dare say they will when they wake up tomorrow. *Prince Absconds With the Love of His Life.* I hope that's the headline.'

'After the events at the ball it could be *Prince's Senses Blown to Pieces.*'

'The Prince's senses are indeed blown,' Raoul said.

He was still tilting her face, and his eyes were now smiling. His appalling decision to leave the succession was put aside. What mattered now was them.

'They've been blown apart by one green girl. Claire, I'm coming to Australia with you, whether you will it or not. Where you go, I go. Your home is my home. I'm not exactly sure what I'll do yet—I'm thinking maybe a job in security? A bouncer at a pub? What do you think? Your career prospects are so much better than mine right now, but regardless...unemployed or not... Claire Tremaine, will you marry me?'

And there was the end of breathing. Who needed to breathe? Who could even *think* of breathing?

'I can't,' she managed at last. She was struggling between tears and laughter. 'Raoul, you know I can't.'

'Why not? Are you too good to marry a bouncer?'

'Raoul, you're a *prince.*'

'I can't be a prince without a princess. I thought I could. I was an idiot.'

'You can't throw it all away.'

'I already have. I booked this flight days ago, and then last night you showed me your *yoko geri* side-kick—that's what our security chief tells me it was—and any last niggles of doubt were gone. My brave girl. My heroine. My heart's yours, Claire Tremaine. I'm your faithful shadow. You can be a lawyer wherever you want and I'll be right there beside you.'

Then suddenly he paused, as if struck by inspiration.

'Wait. I have it. You and I could be a team. We could train Rocky to be our killer attack dog. Attack Dog Security—how does that sound as a family business?'

'Right…'

'It *is* right, though, isn't it?' Laughter faded. Everything faded. 'Claire, I'd give up the world for you. Indeed, I don't have a choice—because you *are* my world. Marry me, my love, and somehow we'll make a future together.'

'Raoul…' But she couldn't say more.

He tugged her into his arms and kissed her and she let herself be kissed. She even melted into the kiss. But when the kiss drew to an end and she managed to tug away her eyes were still troubled.

'I don't know what to do,' she whispered.

'I do,' he told her. 'Marry me.'

'But the future…'

'Will fall into place. It must because it doesn't have a choice. Marry me, my love. My Claire. Please.'

And what was a woman to say to that, when Raoul was looking at her with such a look?

Heart on his sleeve… She'd heard the expression so many times…wearing your heart on your sleeve…and she'd thought nothing of it.

But it was true. Raoul was hanging his heart on his sleeve right now. He was caressing her with his eyes, loving her, wanting her.

What did the future hold for both of them? She didn't know. But sitting beside him in the quiet of the plane, looking steadily into eyes that loved her, she knew she had only one answer to give.

'Yes, my love,' she whispered. 'Come what may, I guess… I'll marry you.'

They stopped to change to another flight in London, sat in the airport lounge and barely spoke. None of the passengers from the Marétal flight seemed to be going on to Australia, so no one knew them.

Claire leant on Raoul's chest and slept.

He sat and held her and felt his world shift and shift again. *What had he done?*

He'd set things up as best he could at home. Henri was in charge. With the army manoeuvres finished, the best of Marétal's army was home again, so Franz himself could investigate the aftermath of the events of the ball.

His grandparents had been devastated at his decision to leave, but at least they understood.

He was free to hold this woman forever.

But he wasn't quite free.

A niggle of doubt still troubled him. He knew sometimes that niggle would become a shout, but still… To take the throne without her… He'd self-destruct—he knew he would. These last weeks had become a tangle of introspection, of self-questioning, and in the end he'd come up with what he knew was the absolute truth. He wasn't a loner, and the throne was essentially one of the loneliest places in the world.

Was it weak to say he knew he'd self-destruct? A lifetime on the throne without Claire? He'd looked long and hard at himself and known he couldn't face it.

He loved her.

He held her in his arms while she slept. His chin rested on her hair. She was trusting in sleep, her mouth curved into a faint, loving smile. He had the woman he loved most in the world right here in his arms and nothing else could matter.

He'd do everything in his power to keep Marétal safe, to see it into a prosperous future, but he couldn't give up Claire. This woman was his and he was hers.

The future stretched ahead in all its uncertainty, but for now… He was with Claire and that was all that could matter.

She shouldn't let him do it. For Raoul to abdicate…for *her*…

He mustn't.

She knew he mustn't but she'd said yes.

How selfish was that?

It was impossible, and yet she couldn't let herself think of impossibility. Soon she'd wake up to reality, she thought as she lay nestled in Raoul's arms, half asleep.

Soon she'd wake up—but not yet. Please, not yet.

Sydney, Australia.

'We can't go to my apartment,' Claire had told him as they landed. 'Firstly it's a shoebox, and won't fit us both, and secondly I've sublet it. I…*we* need to find something else. I meant to go to a hostel…'

'Hostels mean dormitories,' he'd said, and had taken charge.

She woke up after a glorious twelve hours' sleep to find herself cocooned in Raoul's arms, sunlight streaming in through the windows of their hotel room and a view of Sydney Harbour that was truly breathtaking.

'So…so much for being unemployed,' she managed as Raoul stirred with her. 'Five-star luxury… We need to say goodbye to all this.'

'Not this morning, woman,' he growled, holding her to him. 'Not until I'm over jet lag—and I hear jet lag lasts a long time. And there's only one cure. Come here and I'll show you.'

And the spectre of unemployment went right out of the window as she turned within his arms and smiled at her beloved, and then melted as she surely must. *Oh, Raoul...*

They loved and loved, and for the moment the cares of the world were put firmly aside in their joy with each other.

But finally the world had to intrude—of course it did. Hunger had a habit of asserting itself even in the most fabulous of settings.

They made themselves decent—sort of—and ordered breakfast, and Claire gasped when she saw it.

'We can't do this. You've said you're an unemployed bouncer. Champagne for breakfast?'

'If I'm not mistaken you've just agreed to marry me. There are some occasions when even unemployed bouncers require the best.'

And who was arguing this morning? Just for today she could put doubts aside and drink her lovely champagne and eat her gorgeous croissants and look lovingly at this gorgeous prince-cum-bouncer as he finished his own croissant and reached lazily for the newspapers that had been delivered with the breakfast tray.

She watched his face change.

'What?' she said, and rose and went to stand beside him.

They were in the breakfast nook—a curved bay window overlooking the sparkling waters of Sydney Harbour. They were both dressed in the towelling robes provided by the hotel. It was the most beautiful, most intimate of settings—a breakfast to remember—and yet as she watched him she saw the dreamlike quality fall away and reality set in.

'Problems?'

'No,' he told her. 'It's just… I didn't think it'd make the news here. You're going to be hounded again.'

And there it was—a front-page spread—and once again she was in the centre. Claire in her Cinderella dress. Claire in the moments after Raoul had reached the stage, the attackers disarmed. Raoul leading her to safety. Raoul in his beautiful prince's clothes, his arm around her, curved in protection.

And the headlines…

Australian Woman Saves Queen...
Assassination Attempt Foiled...

'I might have known,' Raoul said. 'All media's parochial. Your press will have picked up that there was an Australian in the middle of it and gone with that angle. Claire, I'm sorry.'

'I can live with a few days' media attention,' she said,

and managed a smile. 'Especially if we can stay here. Hunker down. Let the world forget us.'

'We might be able to manage that.' He tugged her down onto his knee. 'That's what you want? For the world to forget us?'

And she thought, *Did she?*

For herself? Definitely. Since when did publicity mean anything good? As a child she'd hated anyone looking at her. The taunts. The active discrimination against the child of a single mum…

Yes, she'd hated it and feared it. And the whole lawsuit thing had terrified her even more.

Raoul had had a lifetime of attention being trained on him. Surely he must hate it, too.

She knew he did, but now he was fetching his laptop from his bag, logging in to the internet.

'I need to see what the papers are saying at home,' he told her.

And she thought, *Home? Home is where?*

He was sitting on the bed and she went to join him. He put the laptop where they could both see.

There'd been two mornings in Marétal since they'd left. Two lots of newspapers.

The first newspapers they read were those published in the immediate aftermath of the drama. There were photographs of the white-faced King and Queen, dignified but clearly shaken. There were fuzzy photographs of the attackers being led away by Security. There were photographs of the King and Queen, and of Raoul and Claire.

Saved by Our Prince! the headline screamed, and Raoul winced.

'That's hardly fair.'

'You stopped him firing.'

'And if it wasn't for you the Queen would have been taken and held for ransom,' Raoul told her, and flicked through to the next day's headlines.

Which were different.

The reporters had had time to figure out the details of what had happened.

There was a photograph of Alicia with the knife at her throat, being hauled back towards the wings.

There was a photograph, slightly blurred, of a make-believe princess, her dress hiked up, her legs bare, her shoes kicked off. The moment her foot had come into contact with the assailant's knee. A second photograph of her grip on his arm.

The third photograph was of Raoul, launching himself onto the stage to help her hold.

And the headlines?

The Woman We Called Commoner...
The Princess We Need.

She didn't say anything. She simply sat as Raoul read out the stark article underneath.

Our Prince and the woman he loves saved our King and Queen. This woman we've condemned has done our country a service we can scarcely comprehend. This newspaper wishes to unreservedly apologise...

And then there was a photograph of a shadowy Raoul being escorted to the plane. And another headline.

Bring Her Home, Raoul.
We need her.

'Is that why you're really here?' Claire asked in a small voice. 'To…to bring me back?'

And Raoul set his laptop aside and turned to hold her. 'No,' he said, firmly and surely. 'The media's fickle. They might now have decided they love you, but *I* fell in love with you approximately two minutes after I met you, and I'm not fickle. Claire, I booked my plane ticket almost a week ago. What I'm doing has nothing to do with how my country's reacting to you now. It's all about loving you.'

'They think you're here persuading me to return.'

'That's because we haven't released a statement yet,' he told her. 'Henri made me wait until I was here, until I'd had time to ask you to marry me, before we made an official statement. He said—and he may be right—that if you told me to go to the devil then I might well decide to head back to Marétal with my tail between my legs.'

'And be a solitary prince forever?'

'Probably.' But he hugged her tighter. 'Luckily that's not an option. You've agreed. Do you think we could sneak out today and buy a ring?'

'Sneak out?'

'We could go out the back way. Get one of those nice tinted limos. Go somewhere innocuous and buy a diamond.'

She thought about it. There was a lot to be said for it.

'We could go out the back way. Get one of those nice tinted limos. Go somewhere innocuous...'

Coward.

The word slammed into her head and stayed.

Coward.

She looked at Raoul—really looked at him. He was her soldier, her lover, her Prince.

He'd offered to give up his world for her.

He'd asked her to marry him and she'd said yes.

But had she said yes to Prince Raoul or had she said yes to the man she'd like him to be? A man disappearing into the shadows because she didn't have the courage to stand beside him?

She thought suddenly of that appalling time almost six months ago, when she'd been hounded by the thought of wrongful fraud charges. Running to Orcas Island.

Becoming a shadow.

She thought of the taunts of her childhood and how she'd hidden in her books. Keeping her head down. Being nothing. Hoping no one would notice.

She thought of her workplace, wearing black or beige. Making no waves. Cringing as she waited for criticism.

Coward.

'Raoul,' she said, in a voice that must belong to her but she barely recognised it. It was another woman's voice. Something inside her had shifted. Or come together.

Raoul met her gaze and she thought it was this man who'd changed her. Raoul had given her this. And she'd take it, she thought with sudden determination. Raoul loved her. What sort of gift was that? What was she about, continuing to run?

'Yes?'

He sensed something had changed. He knew her, this man. He knew her so well.

They could stand side by side forever.

'Would you help me bring Felicity to justice?' she asked, and he blinked.

'Felicity?' He looked confused—as well he might.

'She stole money from my law firm,' she said, clearly now, because suddenly her way was defined and there was no way she could deviate. 'I was blamed, but with decent lawyers I could prove it wasn't me. I chose not to make a fuss. That was partly because I didn't have the funds to fight, but I could have borrowed to do it. I chose not to. I chose to disappear. Felicity and her nasty friends counted on it. But suddenly… Raoul, I don't want to disappear any more, and I don't want an accusation of fraud hanging over my head. Even though they've hushed it up I won't accept it. Will you help me?'

'I…yes. Of course I will. Though maybe you should wait a little. For the next couple of weeks you'll be the target of media.'

'Then media might be able to help me. If an accusation is

made, I'll defend myself.' She took a deep breath. 'If you're by my side.'

'You know I will be.'

'As the proprietor of Attack Dog Security?'

He smiled at that. 'We need to get Rocky out of quarantine first.'

It was harder to get Rocky back into Australia than it had been to get him to Marétal. He was currently one day into a hefty quarantine period.

'That's another thing,' she said diffidently. 'I don't want my dog locked up any more.'

'Australian quarantine is stringent,' he said, cautious now, not sure where she was going.

'But if we decided to get back on a plane tomorrow, to return to Marétal, then he'd spend only two more days in a cage.'

What followed was a moment's silence. No, make that more than a moment. It was long and it was filled with questions and it stretched on forever.

'We?' Raoul asked, and his voice sounded strange. 'If *we* decided?'

'I'm not sending Rocky back without me.' She hesitated, and then she placed the computer carefully out of the way, so there was nothing between them. Nothing at all. She took his hands in hers and held them tight. 'And I won't go back without you. But I will go back.'

'Why?' His voice was laced with strain.

'Because it's right,' she whispered. 'Because I know it's right. Because your place is there and my place is at your side.'

'Claire, there'll be…'

'Media. Intrusion. Lack of privacy. But, hey…' She suddenly cheered up. 'There'll also be an awesome hairstylist. She's lovely, and I bet as a princess I can have her do my hair every time we have a state occasion.'

'She can do it every day,' he said grandly. 'But, love…'

'Mmm?' She'd moved on. She was starting to think about personal hairstylists. And the palace gardens, which surely beat the rocks of Orcas Island. And a library. And chandeliers…

'What are you thinking?' he asked uneasily, and she grinned.

'If the Queen can have a chandelier in her bedroom I don't see why I can't have one.'

'You can have ten.' And then he reconsidered. 'But not as big as the one in the ballroom?'

'No?' She sounded gutted, and he laughed, and then he drew her to him and his face grew serious.

'Claire, what are you saying? You know I love you, but this is huge. You're a private person. You'll be in a goldfish bowl.'

'We can buy curtains.'

'Claire…'

'I just figured it out,' she said, cupping his face in her hands, holding him, loving him. 'It's taken me a while, but I have it. This courage thing… Do you remember in the water? I saved you and you saved me right back? As a team, imagine how much more we could save. Imagine how we could save each other.'

'We could do it here,' he said urgently. 'With our Killer Attack—'

'Don't tempt me.' She put a finger on his mouth, shushing him. 'I've been an idiot. If I have you beside me why do I need privacy? Why do I need anything but you? And you… Raoul, you're needed in Marétal. You know you are. I'll never forget that you've given me this choice, but if you stay here you'll worry about your country. You'll worry about your grandparents. You'll worry about security and whether your people can get legal assistance and proper education and healthcare. And, as much as I know that the Attack Dog Security team could do some vital work, keeping the citizens of Australia safe, I suspect that we could do more in Marétal. If we work together.'

There was another pause—a pause so long she didn't know how to break it.

Raoul's hands gripped hers so tightly they hurt.

'You'd do that?' he asked her in a voice choked with emotion. 'For me?'

'No.' She shook her head. 'I've been stupid. I've been a coward. And I didn't see I'd be doing it for *us*. I'm even thinking Cinders had a point, accepting her Prince's hand on the basis of one glass slipper—though I have to think that she was a wuss, staying in the kitchen waiting for him. I won't wait for you, Raoul. I want you *now*. I want you forever.'

How had things changed so fast? She didn't know. She would never afterwards be able to tell. But all she knew was that they had.

She wasn't a coward. She wasn't the illegitimate kid—the one dressed in secondhand clothes, trying to claw her way up through poverty. She wasn't anyone the Felicitys of this world could stomp over.

She was Claire, and she was loved by Raoul, she thought. She was loved by her man.

And then she forgot to think, because she was being kissed—kissed as she needed to be kissed, as she deserved to be kissed—and she kissed him back. And there was nothing else to be said for a very long time.

And afterwards when the kiss was finally done, when there was room again for words between them—Raoul pushed her back and his dark eyes gleamed.

'Diamonds,' he told her, with all the authority of the Royal House of Marétal behind him. 'This very afternoon. Do you still want the back way and tinted limousines?'

'Not on your life,' she told him. 'I want a chariot or six. Where do you think we can find a pumpkin, a few mice and a fairy godmother?'

CHAPTER TWELVE

THEY WERE MARRIED six months later, with all the pomp and ceremony Queen Alicia could manage. She had decreed that a royal wedding must be a showcase of splendour, and so it was. Every dignitary in the land was there, plus as many of Europe's aristocracy as she'd been able to summon.

But no one had needed much summoning. This was a day of joy, and the world was waiting and willing to share.

The bride arrived at the cathedral in a magnificent, horse-drawn coach, with the Horseguards of Marétal parading before her. By Claire's side was King Marcus.

'A girl has to have someone to give her away,' Marcus had said, emerging from his library to give a decree of his own. 'You've almost single-handedly saved the royal family of Marétal. Unless there's someone else at hand to do it, it would be my very great honour to assist.'

And Claire had joyfully agreed.

Marcus was her future father-in-law.

Marcus was the King of Marétal.

Marcus was her ally and her friend.

She seemed to have lots of friends now, she thought, though she was still dubious about many. There'd even been a fawning letter from one of the associates at her old law firm…

You always seemed such a loner, but I was thinking... we did enjoy shopping together. And I've always been on your side, even though I couldn't say. I needed my job too much. If you need a bridesmaid...

Claire most definitely didn't. That appalling time was best forgotten.

Thanks to Raoul's intervention, Felicity and her partner were now facing a hefty jail sentence, and there'd been an 'undisclosed' amount of compensation paid into Claire's bank account. There'd been media coverage of the entire case.

So now it could be forgotten—and today of all days who would think of it?

There were crowds lining the streets, smiling and cheering.

'Wave,' Marcus told her, and she thought of how anonymous she'd always wanted to be.

But she managed to wave, and Marcus waved, too, and she thought, *We're two of a kind. Two introverts in the royal spotlight.*

And then she stopped thinking, for they'd reached the cathedral. Henri was handing her down from the coach. Henri, too, had become a true friend, as had her gorgeous hairstylist, who was currently fussing over her train.

And then it was time.

The doors to the cathedral were flung wide. The sound of trumpets rose triumphantly to the skies.

'Ready?' Marcus asked.

She took a deep breath and nodded. They trod regally—as she'd practised—up the great steps, in through the nave.

The cathedral opened up before them, magnificent in its age and beauty. It was filled with every dignitary in the land, plus so many people who were Raoul's friends and who were becoming her friends.

Raoul stood at the altar. Beside him was Tom, owner of *Rosebud*—because Raoul had thought, Who else could be his best man? The soldier who'd lent him his unseaworthy boat, which had led to him being saved by Claire, was the obvious choice.

But Raoul had saved her back, Claire thought mistily as the sound of trumpets filled the cathedral, as the congregation rose to its feet, and as Raoul turned and smiled at her.

Raoul's smile…

That was what had got her into this mess, she thought. That was the whole trouble.

That was the whole joy.

He smiled, and the over-the-top setting was forgotten. She'd practised walking in this amazing dress, with its vast train, with its priceless adornments. She'd practised keeping step with Marcus. She'd even practised her vows.

But who could think of any of those things when Raoul was standing at the end of the aisle waiting for her?

Raoul. Her heart. Her destiny.

He was in full royal regalia. He looked magnificent, but she wasn't seeing the uniform. She was only seeing Raoul.

Theirs wouldn't be a marriage like that of Marcus and Alicia, she thought mistily. Raoul wanted—needed—her to share his kingdom and of course she would.

For she wasn't unequal. She was loved. She and Raoul were meant to be forever and ever, she thought, and she managed a tremulous smile back at the man she loved with all her heart.

'You can do this,' Marcus whispered at her side, and she managed to smile at the old man, the King of Marétal.

'Of course I can,' she whispered back, and then there was nothing left to be said.

She made her way down the aisle to be married.

Surely there'd never been a more beautiful royal bride, Raoul thought as he watched Claire and his grandfather walk steadily along the aisle towards him. Even the Queen's eyes were misting with tears.

His beautiful Claire was coming to wed him.

By Raoul's feet sat Rocky. Claire had tried to train him to be the ring-bearer, but in rehearsals he'd proved unreliable to say the least.

'But he needs to be there,' Claire had said.

So they'd organised a velvet cushion to be placed front and centre. Claire had trained and trained him, and this morning a footman had taken him on a run that should exhaust the most exuberant dog. So he now lay by Raoul's side, looking as if butter wouldn't melt in his mouth.

But he was also watching Claire approach, and he wasn't totally to be trusted.

'Stay,' Raoul murmured as he stirred, and he looked up at Raoul and thankfully subsided. He wouldn't jump up on the royal bride.

'She's exquisite,' Tom breathed as Claire grew nearer. 'You lucky man.'

And that reminded Raoul of the final thing he had to do.

In his pocket was the tiny figure made of plastic building blocks. Herbert. Tom's good luck charm.

He hadn't admitted to Tom that he'd found him, but now it was time.

'This is yours,' he told Tom. He handed him over but his gaze didn't leave Claire.

'You found Herbert?' Tom stared down at the tiny figure in astonishment. 'My good luck Herbert?'

'I've had him and I've used him,' he told him. 'But as of today he's all yours. Use him wisely, my friend.'

Tom looked at him in bemusement, and then pocketed Herbert safely beside the royal wedding rings. There were things he wanted to ask, but now wasn't the time.

For Claire had reached her Raoul, and Claire was smiling and smiling, and even a tough Special Forces soldier like Tom was finding it hard not to choke up.

'My Claire,' Raoul whispered, taking her hands and drawing her forward. 'My love. Are you ready to be married?'

And Claire's smile softened to a tenderness that must melt the hardest of hearts.

'How can you doubt it, my love?' she whispered. 'Indeed I am.'

* * *

Marétal's first legal assistance office was opened six months later. A small, nondescript building, set in the part of the capital where it was most needed, it seemed a bizarre setting for the fanfare that went with the opening. For not only were the King and Queen present, but so were His Royal Highness Crown Prince Raoul and his beautiful wife the Princess Claire.

Claire wore a turquoise and white dress from one of Australia's leading designers. For this she was criticised in the media the following day—*Support Our Industries!*

The article beside it also wondered why the royal family was always accompanied by a nondescript fox terrier, when everyone knew the royal dog of Marétal should be the Marétal Spaniel.

Claire read those articles early. For once she'd woken before Raoul and had fetched the papers to read in bed. She smiled when she read them. She then hugged the dog she'd graciously admitted to the royal bedroom—because a woman needed some company before her husband woke.

She thought briefly about the articles and decided that she liked her turquoise and white designer frock very much, regardless of who had designed it. And she loved her dog.

And then she forgot all about them.

For her days were too busy for her to be bothered with criticism. She had better things to be doing than worrying about the day's press.

Things like lying in the arms of her husband. Things like living happily-ever-after.

Finally he was waking.

'What are you doing, woman?'

Raoul's voice was a sleepy murmur as he tugged her down against him. Passion was never far away. Love was for always.

'I'm thinking I might get my toenails painted,' she told him, kissing him with all the tenderness he deserved. 'Louise knows someone who can paint intricate designs on individual toes. Does that seem a good idea?'

There was a moment's pause, and then a fast rearrangement of the bedding while the toes in question were examined.

'They seem good to me now,' he told her at last. 'I like them as they are.'

'They seem like a bare canvas.'

'What would you like on them?'

'Storks,' she said complacently. 'I'm wearing open-toed sandals to my next three functions. I'm wondering if the media will pick it up.'

There was another pause. A longer one.

'Storks?' he said at last, and she chuckled.

'Yep. Mind you, if I do it today I'll need to fit the appointment in well before my meeting with the Chief Justice. It wouldn't do to appear before His Lordship with not-yet-dried toes.'

'I guess it wouldn't.'

But Raoul had ceased his toe inspection. He sat up and gazed at her in bemusement.

Claire smiled at him and thought she'd never seen him look sexier. Mind, it could be the early-morning sun reflected from the crystal chandelier above her head.

No, she thought dreamily. He'd looked just as wonderful back on Orcas Island. Her soldier. Her sailor. Her love.

'Are we by any chance going to have a baby?' Raoul demanded at last, in a voice that was just a tiny bit strangled.

'We might be.'

If she sounded like the cat that had got the cream, who could blame her?

'You're pregnant!'

'Only a bit.'

Ten weeks. It was time she told him—probably more than time—but life was busy, and he'd fuss, and they were so gloriously happy how could anything make them *more* happy?

But she was wrong. What crossed Raoul's face was a flash of joy so profound she felt her eyes welling with emotion. With love.

'Claire…'

'Papa,' she said, and then she could say no more.

She was gathered into his arms and held.

So in the end she had to delay having her toes painted with little storks, and she was sadly late for her meeting with the Chief Justice.

'There's no use being royal if I can't issue a royal decree,' Raoul declared. 'And this morning I decree that my wife will lie in my arms until she's listened to every reason why she's cherished. Are there any objections?'

'No, Your Highness,' she whispered as he folded her into him. 'I can't think of a single one.'

* * * * *

"Why was he kissing you?" Jake wanted to know, regarding them suspiciously, as if he wasn't sure whether or not his father was telling him the truth.

"People kiss without getting married, Jake," Marina told him, her voice deliberately breezy. "It happens all the time." She spared Anderson a look. "It doesn't mean a thing."

Anderson couldn't tell if she was letting him off the hook because of Jake, or if she was really being serious and putting him on notice that the kiss had meant less than nothing to her.

Either way, he knew he should be relieved—except that he wasn't. He felt guilty because he was fairly certain that there were still hurt feelings involved. He was really sorry if there were, but there was nothing he could do about that—at least not without compromising himself in front of his son.

This was getting way too complicated. He had more than he could handle just trying to navigate these new turbulent fatherhood waters. He had no room for the kind of baggage having a girlfriend created. Never mind that she could be something more than that, that somewhere in his misbegotten soul he might even *want* her to be more than that.

Get a grip, man. If you're not careful, you'll be going down for the third time.

* * *

Montana Mavericks:
The Baby Bonanza
Meet Rust Creek Falls' newest bundles of joy!

Why was he kissing her? Jake wanted to know, regarding them suspiciously, as if he wasn't sure whether or not his father was telling him the truth.

[illegible]

[illegible]

[illegible]

[illegible]

[illegible]

[illegible]

A MAVERICK AND A HALF

BY
MARIE FERRARELLA

MILLS & BOON

First Published in Great Britain 2016
By Mills & Boon, an imprint of HarperCollins*Publishers*
1 London Bridge Street, London, SE1 9GF

Special thanks and acknowledgement are given to Marie Ferrarella for her contribution to the Montana Mavericks: The Baby Bonanza continuity.

ISBN: 978-0-263-92015-4

23-0916

Our policy is to use papers that are natural, renewable and recyclable products and made from wood grown in sustainable forests. The logging and manufacturing processes conform to the legal environmental regulations of the country of origin.

Printed and bound in Spain
by CPI, Barcelona

USA TODAY bestselling and RITA® Award–winning author **Marie Ferrarella** has written more than two hundred and fifty books for Mills & Boon, some under the name Marie Nicole. Her romances are beloved by fans worldwide. Visit her website, www.marieferrarella.com.

To
Megan Broderick,
Welcome to the Fun House!

Chapter One

All he had come in for was a glass of water.

Ranching was hard, sweaty work, even in September. Granted, if he was so inclined, he could have easily spent his days just sitting on the porch, delegating work to a myriad of ranch hands and no one would have said anything, but that just wasn't his way.

As far back as he could remember, Anderson Dalton had loved working on the family ranch, loved being one with the land as well as the animals that were kept here. Ranch work wasn't a hardship for him, but he had to admit that there were times, when he got too caught up in what he was doing, that he did wind up working up a powerful thirst.

Walking into the kitchen and wiping the sweat off his brow with the back of his wrist, Anderson made his way to the sink.

But he'd made the mistake of absently glancing toward the wall. Specifically, the wall where the old, faded off-white landline was mounted.

That was when he saw it.

The red light blinking at him like the bloodshot eye of an aging dragon way past its prime but still a force to be reckoned with in its own right.

Anderson kept the landline with its answering machine in service because out on the range cell phone signals had a habit of playing hide-and-seek with him. Not to mention he had a tendency to lose his cell phone while riding and doing the thousand and one chores that a large ranch required. Because he was now a father, he had taken to keeping one close by despite all this.

When he saw the pulsing red light, Anderson's first reaction was just to ignore it and walk out again. But a nagging voice in his head urged him to listen to the message.

You never know. It might be important.

Now that he had an eleven-year-old son to take care of—albeit temporarily—everything was different. He had to be more responsible, more cautious, more aware of things than he'd ever been before.

Fatherhood at best was a hard thing to get used to. Instant fatherhood to an eleven-year-old was a whole different ball game altogether. He'd been discovering that firsthand since this July when Lexie James, the woman he'd had a casual one-night stand with twelve years ago, showed up on his doorstep asking him to take temporary custody of their son while she "worked some things out."

Eager to finally get to know his son, Anderson had agreed without a second's hesitation. He hadn't realized that being a father demanded years of on-the-job training. It wasn't something that happened overnight. But he was trying his best.

Downing the glass of water he'd come in for in three quick gulps, Anderson crossed to the wall phone in a few long strides and hit the Play button.

"You have one new message. First new message," the machine metallically announced. The next moment, the machine's robotic-sounding voice was replaced with a very melodic one.

"Mr. Dalton, this is Ms. Laramie, Jake's teacher. We need to talk. Please call me back so we can make an appointment." She proceeded to leave Rust Creek Falls Elementary's phone number before terminating her call.

Anderson stood there, staring at the answering machine.

"We need to talk."

What the hell was *that* supposed to mean?

Anderson closed his eyes. Glimmers of déjà vu flashed through his mind, propelling him back to his own school days all over again. He'd certainly been a bright enough kid, but his mind was always wandering, going in all different directions at once, most of which were not scholastic in nature. That didn't make him the best student in the classic sense of the word.

His mouth curved a little. Obviously the son whose existence he'd only discovered a year ago was a chip off the old block.

He'd only gotten temporary custody of Jake this July and school had just been in session for a couple of weeks now. How much trouble could the boy be in? Anderson couldn't help wondering.

If it was something major—like accidentally blowing up the boys' bathroom, he thought, remembering an incident out of his own past—wouldn't Paige have alerted him? The fourth-grade class that his younger sister taught was located right across the hall from his son's fifth-grade classroom and he was fairly certain that if anything actually bad had happened, he would have known it by now. Paige would have called to tell him.

Fairly certain, but not *completely* certain.

Muttering a few very choice sentiments about thin-skinned teachers under his breath, Anderson tapped out the numbers that connected him to his sister's cell phone.

On the third ring he heard what he assumed was his sister taking his call. But before he could say a word, he heard, "Hello, you've reached Paige Traub. Between teaching a class of energized fourth graders and chasing after my two-year-old fireball, I'm too busy to answer my phone. Please leave a message. If I'm still breathing, I'll call you back."

Anderson frowned. He hated talking to an inanimate recording—so he didn't.

Terminating the call, he could feel himself getting worked up. What right did this Ms. Laramie have to judge his son? She'd only been his teacher for two weeks. How could she find fault in the kid so fast? Besides, Jake was a good kid. He didn't mouth off, didn't act out. Hell, he hardly made any sound at all. Just his thumbs, hitting the keys on the controller of those damn video games he was so hooked on.

Considering that two and a half months ago, Jake was living in Chicago and now he was here, in Rust Creek Falls, Montana, the middle of nowhere by comparison, the kid had made a great adjustment. Just what did that woman *want* from his son?

Lily!

His brother Caleb's daughter Lily was in Jake's class, he remembered. The thought hit Anderson like a thunderbolt. Maybe *she* knew what was going on.

It took Anderson a minute to remember Caleb's number—but he might as well have spared himself the trouble. He had the same results when he called Caleb as he'd had with Paige's phone, except that this time, he didn't wait for the recorded message to go through its paces. He terminated the call before his brother's message was over.

Two strikes. Now what?

This Ms. Laramie had said to call to set up an appointment but if he found himself on the receiving end of yet another answering machine recording, he knew he'd probably yank his phone right off the wall. He didn't want to risk blowing up or losing his temper.

But he couldn't very well ignore the woman, either. After all, she'd said she wanted to talk to him about Jake. She'd probably get bent out of joint if he didn't get in contact with her.

Besides, he knew he wasn't going to have any peace of mind until this thing with the thin-skinned lady teacher was resolved.

That left him only one option. School was almost over for the day, but the last class was still in session. He'd signed Jake up for after school basketball, so that gave him a little extra time. He was going to go down to that school and have it out with that woman before this thing blew any more out of proportion.

With that, Anderson stormed out of the house, the memory of every teacher who'd ever found fault with him all those years ago spurring him on.

* * *

If someone had told Marina Laramie five years ago that she would simultaneously be juggling a teaching career and single motherhood—which entailed taking care of an infant in creative ways she'd never dreamed possible—she would have said that it just couldn't happen. The very idea of doing both wasn't feasible.

Yet here she was, fifteen minutes after her fifth graders had filed rowdily out, homeward bound, and instead of contemplating a fun evening out the way she would have only a couple of short years ago, she was hovering over her desk, trying to change Sydney's rather pungent diaper as quickly as possible.

Marina sighed, shaking her head. This was not quite the carefree life she'd once pictured for herself—but even so, she wouldn't have traded this life for anything in the world.

"Lucky for you I like kids, muffin-face," Marina said, addressing her very animated daughter, who apparently hadn't yet grasped the concept of lying still. The embodiment of perpetual motion, Sydney was all arms and legs and Marina had to be vigilant to keep the five-month-old from literally propelling herself right off the desk that had been temporarily transformed into a changing station. "Even stinky ones," Marina teased as she succeeded in separating her daughter's bottom from what was now a considerably used diaper.

Moving swiftly, she cleaned Sydney off and then slipped a fresh diaper under her. The old diaper had been tightly packed into itself like an unusual origami creation.

"Are you timing me?" she asked the baby. Reacting to the sound of her voice, her daughter seemed to cock her head and stare at her with her bright blue eyes. "I'm getting better at this. Yes, I am," Marina informed her daughter with conviction. "And I'd be better still if you could find it in that heart of yours not to wiggle all over the place quite so much."

Finished, Marina quickly disposed of the old diaper and deposited it, plus several wipes she'd used, into a plastic bag that she then knotted at the top, sealing away the last of the less than fragrant odor. The janitor hadn't been by yet and she definitely didn't want to gross the man out.

"Now then, let's get you presentable again. A lady doesn't hang around in just her undies—not unless she wants to get in a whole lot of trouble. Remember that, Sydney," Marina emphasized. "Otherwise, someday you just might find yourself changing diapers in strange places, too."

Having finished redressing her daughter, Marina popped Sydney into the car seat she had set up on her desk and tightened every available strap around her daughter—just in case. She knew she was probably being overly cautious, but she didn't want to take a chance.

"When did I turn into this super cautious, neurotic woman?" Marina murmured under her breath. "I used to be so carefree."

A lifetime ago, it seemed.

When he'd turned down the hallway, Anderson had found the door to his son's classroom open. Hearing the same voice he'd heard earlier on his answering machine, he walked in, loaded for bear. He assumed that this Ms. Laramie was talking to someone, but he didn't care. He wanted her to know that he was here and that he was ready to have it out with her about whatever it was that she found so lacking in his son—and he wasn't about to go away until it was resolved.

He hadn't expected to find his son's teacher talking to a baby—or changing its diaper, either. Just how young *were* the kids in this school? he wondered.

The next beat, Anderson realized that the baby she was talking to had to be *her* baby. That in turn had him wondering just how lax things had gotten in school these days. Why would the principal allow a teacher to bring her baby in to school like it was some kind of a class project?

Didn't the woman have any money for a babysitter? Or was she checking her fifth graders out for babysitting possibilities?

In any case, all of this seemed like very unorthodox behavior to him. And this Ms. Laramie had the nerve to tell him that they had to talk about *his* son?

Anderson couldn't wait to give her a piece of his mind.

"There," Marina declared after testing the strength of the car seat straps. "That'll hold you in place, Your Majesty."

That was when she heard someone behind her clearing their throat. Startled, Marina jumped as her heart launched into double time.

She could have sworn that she and Sydney were alone. Apparently she was wrong, Marina thought as she swung around.

The next second, she blinked, not quite sure she was seeing what she thought she was seeing.

There was a six-foot-one dark-haired, blue-eyed

stranger in her classroom. A stranger who looked far from happy.

Neither was she, caught like this, Marina thought, flustered as she quickly tossed the bagged diaper into the wastepaper basket. She didn't like being caught unprepared like this. She was still trying to get her bearings as a working mother and absolutely hated looking as if she was at loose ends.

"Just give me a moment," she requested, struggling to measure out her words.

She was trying to sound as if she was in control of the situation even though she was very aware of the fact that she wasn't.

Not waiting for the stranger to respond, Marina quickly hurried over to the sink where her fifth graders washed their hands whenever they got too into recess and enjoying the great outdoors.

Still flustered, Marina turned the faucet handle too quickly. The next second, she found herself on the receiving end of a water spray that promptly soaked her, if not to the skin, enough to look as if she'd been caught in an unexpected fall shower.

Even the floor beneath her feet was wet.

With a dismayed cry that sounded suspiciously like a yelp, Marina managed to turn off the water, but not before she was completely embarrassed.

She was fairly certain that the tall, dark and handsome cowboy who had just walked in, wrapped in scowling mystery, undoubtedly felt she was the veritable Queen of Klutzes.

"Sorry," she apologized, grabbing two paper towels and drying herself off as best she could. She found she needed two more just to do a passable job. Wadding up the paper towels, she tossed them into the same wastebasket that contained Sydney's diaper. "You caught me off guard."

"Apparently."

Had the word sounded any drier, it would have crackled and broken apart as it left the stranger's rather full lips.

Marina walked back to her daughter, moving the car seat closer to her on the desk before she turned fully and addressed the stranger.

In her best "teacher voice" she said to the man in her classroom, "Now then, you didn't mention your name." She spoke as pleasantly as she could, waiting for him to fill in the blank.

Anderson drew himself up to his full height, aware of just how intimidating that appeared to the casual observer.

"I'm Anderson Dalton," he informed her in a no-nonsense voice. "You left a message on my phone, saying you wanted to see me about Jake."

The name instantly rang a bell. It wasn't that big a classroom, nor that big a town, so Marina didn't have to struggle to pair up the name to a student. But she was a little mystified as to why he felt the need to come in so quickly.

"Well, I didn't mean immediately," she told him, sounding half apologetic if she'd conveyed the wrong impression. "I wanted you to call me back so that we could set up an appointment for a time that was convenient to both of us."

His wide shoulders rose and fell in a careless shrug. Okay, maybe he'd gone off half-cocked and misunderstood. But all that was water under the bridge in Anderson's opinion.

"Well, I'm here now," he pointed out needlessly. "We might as well get to it—unless you want to take some time to dry off some more or maybe change your clothes," he suggested.

She didn't have a change of clothes here. It never occurred to her that she might wind up taking an unexpected bath.

"No, I'm fine."

That was Anderson's cue. He immediately launched into a defense on his son's behalf.

Taking a step closer to the teacher, he all but loomed over her as he began his rapid-fire monologue. "Look, Jake's a good kid, but you've got to remember, he's dealing with a lot right now. It's not easy for a kid his age to go from a big inner city to the sticks. Even so, I think he's doing a pretty bang-up job of it, all things considered. A lot of other kids in his place might have acted out. You just have to cut him some slack, that's all," he told her with feeling.

Marina opened her mouth but again, she didn't get a chance to utter a single word. Jake's father just kept on talking.

"If anything's wrong, then it's my fault. Jake and I hardly had time to exchange two words since I found out about him and bang, suddenly I'm the one in charge of him, making all these big decisions. And hell—heck," he censored himself, casting a side glance toward her infant daughter, "I don't know what I'm doing most of the time. This parenting thing is really tough."

Well, that's putting it mildly, Marina couldn't help thinking. But being a private person, she kept that sentiment to herself. While she was generally friendly and outgoing, there were parts of her life that she considered to be private. Her unexpected entry into motherhood was one of them.

Anderson didn't notice the silence. He kept his monologue going.

"Don't punish the kid because of my mistakes," he implored, growing more emotional. "Whatever Jake did that got you angry, he didn't know any better. Let me talk to him—"

This could go on for hours, Marina realized, dismayed.

"Mr. Dalton, stop!" she cried, raising her voice so that he would finally cease talking and take a breath. "I don't know what gave you the impression that Jake's done something wrong, but he hasn't. You've really got a great kid there, Mr. Dalton."

Anderson stopped dead and stared at her, clearly bewildered. "I don't understand," he finally said. "You said we had to talk."

"And we do," Marina agreed. One hand on the car seat, she glanced at her daughter. Despite the man's verbose monologue, Sydney appeared to be dozing. *Thank heavens for small favors,* Marina thought. "But not because he's done something bad."

The temporary relief Anderson felt quickly gave way to annoyance. "If he hasn't done anything wrong, then why am I here?" he wanted to know. "I've got a ranch to run."

She saw that if she wanted to make any headway with Anderson Dalton, she was going to have to speak up and speak with conviction. Otherwise, the man gave every impression that he would steamroll right over her and keep on going.

"I asked to see you because I am a little concerned about Jake," she told him.

In the corner of her eye, she saw Sydney beginning to stir.

Please go on sleeping, pumpkin.

"Concerned?" Anderson echoed. Was she doing a one-eighty on what she'd said a minute ago? Just what was this Ms. Laramie's game? Didn't the woman know how to speak plainly? "What's there to be concerned about?"

The man was beginning to irritate her. Marina started to wonder if this so-called meeting was ultimately an exercise in futility. But as he'd already said, he was here and since he was, she might as well press on and hope she could get through what appeared to be that thick head of his.

Sounding as friendly as possible, Marina asked, "Have you noticed how quiet Jake is?"

Anderson's eyebrows drew together in what amounted to a perplexed scowl. "Well, yeah, sure. I noticed. Why?"

Obviously the man needed to have a picture drawn for him. She did what she could to make that happen. "I'm worried that your son might be holding back something that's really bothering him."

Anderson shrugged again. *Just like a woman*, he thought. *Seeing problems where there weren't any.* Couldn't she just appreciate the fact that Jake wasn't some loudmouth class comedian?

"Jake's been quiet for as long as I've known him." Which was technically the truth. It was also a roundabout way of avoiding stating outright that the length of time he'd been acquainted with his son could only be deemed long in the eyes of a fruit fly. "Like I said, it's been a major adjustment for him—for any kid," he stressed, "to move from the city to the country. Did you ever think that maybe Jake's so quiet because he hasn't had any time to get to know all that many people here yet?"

Sydney began to fuss in earnest and Marina automatically rocked the car seat to and fro, mentally crossing her fingers as she tried to lull her daughter back to sleep. She would much rather have turned her full attention to Sydney instead of talking to a thickheaded rancher who didn't seem to know the first thing about the son living under his roof, but that wasn't her call. She was Jake's teacher and she owed it to the boy to help him if he did indeed need any help.

She tried again, tiptoeing diplomatically into the heart of the subject. "Mr. Dalton, I apologize if I sound as if I'm getting too personal here." She saw him raise an eyebrow as if he was bracing himself. "But do you and Jake ever really…talk?" she asked, emphasizing the last word.

"Sure we talk," Anderson retorted quickly, even as he thought that this wasn't any of this teacher's business. "We talk all the time."

Marina was highly skeptical about his reply, even though she had a feeling that as far as this man was concerned, he and his son actually *did* communicate.

She paused for a moment, taking a breath. She knew that she needed to tread lightly here. She didn't really know the man, not like she knew the parents of a great many of her other students, and she got the feeling that he wasn't happy about the question she was putting to him. Even so, this needed to be asked and she wasn't one who backed away, not when there was a child's well-being at stake.

"No, Mr. Dalton, I mean talk about things that really matter," she stressed.

Judging by the expression on his face, Marina felt she had her answer before the man opened his mouth to say a single word. But she waited for him to say something in his own defense anyway.

"Maybe not so much," Anderson finally conceded rather grudgingly. He didn't like having his shortcomings placed on display like this. "But I don't want Jake to feel as if I'm pressuring him about anything," he added quickly—and truthfully. He remembered what it was like, being hauled out on the proverbial carpet by one or both of his parents and taken to task for something he'd done—or hadn't done when he should have. He didn't want to make that sort of a mistake with Jake. He wanted Jake to feel like his own person.

He watched as Jake's teacher pressed her lips together and murmured, "I see."

With his back up, he felt his shoulders stiffen. *What a condescending woman*, he thought. How the hell could she possibly "see" when she knew nothing about him, about Jake or about the dynamics of their still freshly minted relationship?

"No," Anderson informed her angrily, struggling to hold on to his temper, "you don't."

The man clearly had a chip on his shoulder now, Marina thought. He hadn't behaved as if he had one when he'd first walked in. Was she somehow responsible for the change in attitude?

"All right," she conceded, giving him the benefit of the doubt. "Then why don't you tell me?"

That was *not* the response he'd expected. Caught off guard and unprepared, Anderson started talking before he had a chance to fully weigh his words.

"For the first ten years of Jake's life, I didn't even have a clue that the kid existed—so I wasn't able to be part of that life," he added, which was, to him, the whole point of his frustration. He should have been there for the boy. To guide him, to support him and to get to know him. "Now that I've gotten temporary custody, I think that Jake's confused and conflicted—not that I blame him," he added quickly. "His whole world has changed and he's discovered that everything that he thought he knew, he really didn't."

He blew out a breath and for a moment, Marina had the impression that he wasn't really talking to her anymore, but to himself—and perhaps to the boy who wasn't there.

"I really regret all those years that I lost because a kid really needs his father."

Marina felt as if she'd taken a direct blow to her abdomen. For just a second, she remembered the disinterested look on Gary's face when he told her that if she wanted to have this baby, she was on her own—as if he'd had no part in it.

The sentiment that Mr. Dalton had just expressed hit far too close to home for her to simply ignore or silently accept.

She did her best not to sound too defensive as she responded to his assessment. "Sometimes, Mr. Dalton, that just isn't possible."

Chapter Two

The moment she said the words, Anderson realized his mistake. He really needed to monitor his thoughts before he allowed them to escape his lips, Anderson upbraided himself. He could see that he'd inadvertently hurt the woman. He glanced down at the baby in the car seat. The baby's father wasn't in the picture for some reason and Ms. Laramie had obviously taken his words to heart as some sort of a rebuke when nothing could have been further from the truth.

Anderson felt a shaft of guilt pierce his ordinarily tough hide. He didn't want Jake's teacher to think that he was criticizing her. That hadn't been his intent when he'd stormed into her classroom. He'd only been trying to defend his son.

"I'm sorry, Ms. Laramie," Anderson said contritely. "I meant no disrespect."

Marina flushed. Of course he hadn't. Why was she being so sensitive and overreacting this way? It was her job to think like a professional, not to turn everything around and focus exclusively on herself. Hormonal teenager girls did that, not state-licensed teachers.

She had to remember that, Marina silently lectured herself.

"None taken, Mr. Dalton," she replied stoically.

"Anderson," he prompted, correcting the petite redhead.

Since they'd just been talking about the ideal parenting situation, the unexpected insertion of his given name threw her. Marina looked at him, puzzled. "Excuse me?"

"Not Mr. Dalton," Anderson told her. Mr. Dalton was his father, Ben Dalton, a respected lawyer. He was just plain Anderson, a rancher. "Call me Anderson."

She'd just met him today and she wasn't accustomed to being so friendly with her students' parents if she didn't really know them outside the classroom.

"I don't think that's appro—"

"If we're going to help Jake," Anderson said, interrupting her, "I think we should be a team, not two polite strangers who sound as if they can't wait to get away from one another."

Marina frowned slightly. Was that the message she was getting across to Jake's father by addressing him formally? she wondered. That had definitely not been her intention.

"All right," she allowed, willing to do it his way. She resumed the point she'd been trying to make earlier. "Regarding what you said previously, Anderson, in a perfect world, every child would be raised by two loving parents."

Without meaning to, she glanced down at her daughter and felt a pang. Sydney was the perfect infant and she deserved to be loved by a mother *and* a father.

I'm so sorry it didn't work out, little one. But it's not all bad. I grew up without a dad, too—mostly—and things worked out for me.

"But the world, as we both know," Marina continued telling Jake's father, "is far from perfect. *Very* far."

He certainly couldn't argue with that, Anderson thought.

"True," he agreed. "I'm very aware that not every relationship can work out." Painfully aware, he thought. "But that isn't an excuse not to be there for your kid. They weren't asked to be born, but they were. The way I see it, the people who caused that birth to happen owe that kid something." He was referring to himself, although he didn't say it out loud.

Marina found herself in complete agreement with Jake's father. She also found herself wondering what had happened in Anderson Dalton's relationship that was so traumatic that his girlfriend wouldn't even notify him for ten whole years that they had had a child together.

It was on the tip of Marina's tongue to ask, but she knew that it wasn't any of her business and it had no bearing on her teacher/student relationship with Jake.

Besides, even if she was brash enough to ask Anderson about it, it might just put the man's back up. She had to remember that the point of talking to Jake's father in the first place was to get him to build a stronger relationship with his son, not satisfy her innate curiosity.

Her whole supposition about the relationship—or lack thereof—between Anderson and Jake's mother was truthfully based on her thinking that the former was a nice guy. At least, he seemed that way to her, but then she wasn't exactly the reigning authority when it came to reading men. When she came right down to it, Marina silently admitted, she didn't just have a poor track record with men, she had an absolutely horrible one.

Gary Milton was a case in point.

She'd been utterly, completely and madly in love with the man who was Sydney's father, convinced beyond a shadow of a doubt that he was The One despite the fact that they hadn't been dating all that long. At twenty-seven, with all of her friends getting married and starting families, she was more than ready to take the plunge to happily-ever-after and she was certain that Gary was, too.

Her own parents had long since been divorced, with her father hardly ever turning up in her life, but she was convinced it would be different for her and Gary.

Vulnerable, eager, she'd felt that all the stars were perfectly aligned for something wonderful to happen that July Fourth night when she and Gary had attended Braden and Jennifer's big bash of a wedding. Indeed, romance was in the air and, unbeknownst to her and most of the guests, a spiked glass of punch—thanks to party prankster Homer Gilmore—was in her hand.

What came afterward seemed completely natural at the time—almost like destiny. She and Gary came together in every sense of the word that night.

She'd expected, thanks to the night they'd spent together, to hear a proposal from Gary. But she didn't. Holding her breath, she watched the weeks go by, but Gary was no closer to popping the question than he had been before their friends' wedding celebration. And then she'd discovered that she was pregnant, and a small part of her had thought that now, finally, Gary would step up. But she was sadly mistaken.

Gary not only didn't step up, he stumbled backward and completely freaked out.

Stunned by his initial reaction, Marina had been struck utterly speechless when Gary had actually accused her of engineering her pregnancy so that she could trap him into marrying her.

Angry, Gary had loudly proclaimed that he was way too young to be "saddled" with a wife and kid. He'd broken off their relationship then and there.

An entire spectrum of feelings had gone careening through her at Gary's declaration of independence, but she'd gone positively numb when he had gone on to tactlessly suggest that she "take care of the problem."

The problem.

As if the tiny being growing inside her was anything other than a miracle, she'd thought.

That was when it had hit her with the force of a two-ton truck. She'd been wasting her time and her heart on a self-centered lowlife, foolishly thinking that this poor excuse for a human being was her Prince Charming. He didn't even qualify to be a frog prince. She'd countered his suggestion by telling him in no uncertain terms to get lost.

And he did.

So completely lost that after Sydney had been born, he'd never come by to see his daughter even a single time.

His loss, Marina had silently declared, and from that point forward, she'd eliminated all thoughts of Gary, all memories of their time together, from her mind. She had better things to do than to spend even a single moment reliving the past, or pining for a future that wasn't in the cards.

And while she was actually eternally grateful that their paths had crossed long enough to gift her with the greatest present of her life—her daughter, Sydney—at the same time, the whole traumatic interlude with Gary had definitely scarred her. In a nutshell, it had shaken her faith in her own ability to know whether or not a person was actually a decent human being or just a deceptively charming rat on two legs.

In his own way, Gary had taught her one hell of a lesson.

"Ms. Laramie, is something wrong?"

At the sound of Anderson's deep voice, Marina roused herself. She realized that she'd allowed her thoughts to take her attention hostage, which was, as far as she was concerned, completely inexcusable behavior.

Clearing her throat, she flushed. "What? No, nothing's wrong. Sorry, something you just said started me thinking." Which was true, but undoubtedly not in the way that Anderson might have thought. So before he could ask her any further questions, she quickly redirected the conversation. "I agree with what you said."

"Great." The enthusiasm went down a notch as he asked, "What part?"

"The part about you not wanting Jake to feel as if you were pressuring him," she told him, glad that Anderson was at least partially intuitive. "Being pressured definitely wouldn't help bring your son out of his shell."

"What would?" he asked, curious to hear her take on the matter.

The blanket covering Sydney's legs slipped and she moved it back into place. Her daughter, mercifully, went on dozing but she knew that wasn't going to last for long. She needed to wrap up this conversation. "I was thinking along the lines of some TLC."

"TLC?" Anderson repeated quizzically.

Marina nodded. "That stands for tender loving care," she explained.

"I know what it stands for," he retorted, insulted. Did she think he was entirely backward and clueless? "What I'm trying to figure out is how would I go about expressing that? Are you telling me you think I should hug him and stuff?"

She hadn't been thinking along those lines, but she gave it some thought now. "An occasional hug wouldn't hurt," she acknowledged, then qualified her answer. "But in general, eleven-year-old boys aren't really into that. They're not big on that sort of parental display of affection. At least not on a regular basis."

"Then what?" Anderson asked impatiently. "I've already got him signed up for some after school sports activities," he said, "so that Jake can be around other kids participating in some bonding sports."

"All that's good," Marina agreed tentatively, not wanting to shoot down the man's fledgling enthusiasm so early in the game. "But I was thinking of something along the lines of a more personal, fulfilling activity."

He looked at her uncertainly. He wasn't sure just what she was suggesting. So far, they just seemed to be going around in circles. "Just what is it you have in mind?"

Since she wasn't sure how open he would be to her suggestion, Marina proceeded with caution. "How would you feel about Jake helping me after school a few days a week?"

Anderson had a feeling that her question wasn't as

straightforward as it sounded, so he tried to get her to clarify it. "You mean like cleaning paintbrushes in the art room and stuff like that?" he asked.

Marina shook her head. "No. Jake's a sensitive, caring boy. Those sort of traits should be nurtured," she told Anderson. "I was thinking that Jake might make a perfect mother's helper."

"A mother's helper?" he repeated uncertainly, somewhat stunned and taken aback. "Isn't that something that, you know, *girls* usually do?" he asked, wondering if he should be insulted on Jake's behalf. Just what was she saying about his son?

Marina was quick to set Anderson straight. The man was stereotyping and she couldn't allow that to get in the way of Jake's development as both a student and a boy-in-progress.

"Not necessarily. All that's required to be a mother's helper is patience—and of course the desire to help. From what I've seen, Jake's equipped with both." She became more impassioned as she spoke. "There's no reason why a boy can't help out as well as a girl and I could really use a hand at home—and even here at school," she added for good measure, thinking that might help tip the scales. She was paying someone to watch Sydney while she was teaching, but she could barely afford that.

"I don't know," Anderson said after giving the whole matter less than thirty seconds of thought. "I really don't think it's a very good idea," he confessed with conviction. "Jake and I are doing okay just the way things are."

Marina banked down her growing impatience. She knew she couldn't push this. Anderson—if he *was* going to come around—was going to have to come around on his own. If she pushed in any manner, she had the distinct impression that he was the type to dig in his heels and resist until his dying breath left his body. The bottom line there was that she'd never get anywhere with him.

This way, by maintaining an open mind and an equally open door, there still might be a small chance that things would go her way. With Jake's well-being in mind, she had to take it.

She wanted to argue about it—to discuss it, actually—but the idea of arguing with the man seemed counterproductive in its own right. So for now, and the sake of peace, she went along with what Dalton suggested.

"All right," she told Anderson gamely. "But if you do happen to change your mind about this, please let me know," she requested with a large smile. "You know where to find me."

He nodded, ready to terminate the conversation. He knew the value of quitting while he was ahead.

"Just like I found you this time," he replied, already edging his way out.

Marina spoke up just as he was about to reach the door. "I just suggested Jake being a mother's helper because I think it might help him if he puts himself out in order to help someone else."

"Someone else," Anderson repeated, then knowingly added, "like you."

She saw no reason to pretend that Jake's father had guessed wrong. Marina certainly wasn't embarrassed by either the fact that she needed help nor that she would have accepted it from one of her students.

"Like me," she replied, then hurriedly tacked on, "And Sydney."

"Sidney?" Anderson questioned, suddenly lost. "Who's Sidney?"

"This lovely young lady here," Marina told him, her voice teeming with affection and pride, albeit quietly, as she indicated the car seat.

"Oh." Chagrined over his misunderstanding—and concerned about the odd sort of attraction he was experiencing—attraction to his son's teacher for heaven's sake—Anderson was practically inaudible as he mumbled, "I thought you were talking about some guy."

"An understandable mistake," she said, the corners of her mouth curving in what Anderson could only describe as an appealing smile that seemed to communicate with some inner core of his. He did what he could to block it, or at the very least, just ignore it.

"Well, it's usually a guy's name," Anderson protested in his own defense, trying to backtrack from his error.

While Marina didn't exactly contradict him, she expanded on his answer. "It's both."

She had a feeling that Jake's father was in somewhat of a combative mood and saying anything to outright oppose him would not be the smart thing to do at the moment. It fell under the heading of discretion being the better part of valor.

"Yeah, I know that," he informed her with a dismissive shrug. All he wanted to do was get out of the classroom, away from Marina Laramie and her sleeping infant. "So, if there's nothing else you want to discuss about Jake, I've got to be getting back to the ranch," he informed her, as he turned to leave. Then just before he exited, Anderson felt a need to add, "Those posts don't nail themselves up."

"I'm sure that they don't," she responded with what he had to admit seemed to him to be a very infectious grin.

He hadn't come here to make trite observations about

Jake's teacher's smile, Anderson reminded himself. He'd come because he had Jake's best interests at heart and he was really trying, in his own less than stellar way, to make up for all the time that had been lost to him. Precious time he wasn't going to ever get back.

"Okay, then, so it's settled," Anderson announced as if they had arrived at a mutual agreement rather than something he was just stubbornly reiterating. "Jake's going to be playing some after school activities." Eyeing Marina Laramie, he waited for the redhead to contradict him.

But she didn't, which surprised him—as well as relieved him.

"You know what's best for your boy," she said.

"That's right," Anderson said as he strode out of the classroom, "I do."

Except that he didn't, and he knew it.

He was feeling his way around and fighting the feeling that he was doing a far from spectacular job at every turn.

Indecision nibbled away at him like a stubborn, persistent mouse. Maybe that Laramie woman had the right idea. Maybe Jake would do better helping her out after school. At least it would get him out of his room and away from those video games of his.

Heaven knew the idea of helping the woman out was not without its appeal or merits, he mused. He wouldn't mind having that job himself.

Whoa, there, Andy. Get a grip, he counseled himself. *We're talking about Jake here, not you. He's the one who could benefit from spending some extra one-on-one time with the lady.*

When he came right down to it, he didn't know why he'd turned Jake's teacher down, or why, as he left the building now, he couldn't shake the feeling of being a chastised grade-schooler. After all, the woman hadn't actually said anything to make him feel like he'd done anything wrong. If questioned, he couldn't even put his finger on one reason why he felt that way. He figured it was probably rooted deep into his past, back to the days when he actually *was* a grade-schooler and everyone was always telling him what to do.

He hadn't taken their advice then, Anderson reminded himself, and he wasn't about to start now by being led around by the nose by that slip of a redhead.

He needed to do more than that, Anderson thought as he climbed back up into his truck. He needed to keep his distance from Jake's bubbly, interfering teacher. Everything in his gut—the center of his very best survival instincts—told him that he needed to steer clear of her if he knew what was good for him and if he intended to get through this time of parental custody intact.

Not just intact, he reminded himself. He needed to do more than to remain intact. He needed to come out a winner when it came to all the matters that concerned Jake.

From the second he had found out about his son's existence, Jake was his number one priority.

As for this Ms. Laramie, the woman might be a real stunner, but she was way off base. Jake, a mother's helper? Anderson silently questioned as he now frowned at the idea. Not *his* boy, he thought. Not if he had anything to say about it.

Chapter Three

In order to terminate the awkward meeting with the fifth-grade teacher, Anderson had told her that he had to be getting back to his ranch. But instead of doing that, he decided to stick around until Jake finished playing basketball. When he thought about it, staying in the vicinity of the school made a lot more sense than driving to the ranch and then back again.

Leaving the building, Anderson got into the cab of his truck and drove around to the back entrance of the school. He told himself it was closer to where Jake would get out once basketball practice was over but to be quite honest, he wanted to be sure that Marina Laramie didn't accidentally look out the window and see him parked out in front. It would just complicate everything.

He had no idea why he put so much thought into this, but he did. For some reason, the woman made him uneasy. Avoiding her seemed the best way to go.

The moment he pulled up the brake and turned off the engine, he began to get fidgety. Accustomed to working hard from the moment he opened his eyes in the morning until he fell into bed at night, just sitting in the truck waiting had him growing progressively more restless with every passing moment.

Anderson was not a man who did "nothing" well.

He was contemplating getting out of his truck and walking around the school grounds until practice was over when the cell phone he'd thrown in the glove compartment of his vehicle—an old flip phone model—rang.

At first, Anderson didn't even hear it.

His cell phone hardly ever rang, so it caught him off guard. It took him a moment to connect the faint sound to its source of origin.

He flipped the phone open and fairly barked, "Hello?"

The annoyed greeting would have been enough to scare a great many people away. Paige Dalton Traub was not one of those people. Younger than Anderson by five years, she was every bit as feisty as her brothers. She had to be. Having grown up with three bossy brothers and two equally bossy sisters, it took a great deal for her feathers to get even slightly ruffled. It took even more for her to become even mildly intimidated, and certainly never by a sibling.

Paige recognized her brother's less than dulcet tones immediately.

Rather than return his less than warm greeting, Paige went straight to the heart of the matter. "So, how did it go, big brother?"

Anderson had no idea what his younger sister was talking about. She might as well have been talking gibberish. Most women, in his limited experience, did.

"How did *what* go?" he countered, irritated.

Paige laughed shortly. "Ah, there's that disposition of a wet hornet that I know and love," she noted sarcastically. "You might recall that initially, you called me, and I assumed that the reason you called had something to do with Marina and your son. Am I right?" she wanted to know.

"Yes," he conceded grudgingly through clenched teeth.

"Well, I'm here now so spill it. Do you know why Marina wanted to see you, and is everything okay?"

Instead of answering her directly, Anderson approached her question from a different angle. "You told me about his teacher having a kid of her own, but you never mentioned that the woman was touchy-feely."

"She *touched* you?" Paige asked, clearly taken aback. She and the fifth-grade teacher had gotten to know one another over the last year or so and while Marina was friendly enough and everyone liked the woman, she wasn't the type to touch a student's parent.

"No," he bit off, annoyed that his sister wasn't following his train of thought. "But she wanted me to get all touchy-feely with Jake." As he spoke, his mouth curved downward into a distasteful frown. "She seems to think that Jake's too quiet."

"I should have that problem," Paige commented with a laugh. "I only wish that at least *some* of my students would be quiet like Jake." After a slight hesitation she asked, "So how did she suggest you do it?" When he didn't say anything, she prodded him a little. "How did she suggest you get closer to Jake?"

He frowned so hard he thought she could literally hear it in his voice as he said, "She asked me for permission to turn Jake into a mother's helper. Isn't that just crazy?" he wanted to know, assuming that his sister would have the same sort of reaction to the other woman's idea that he did.

Paige took him totally by surprise when she replied, "Actually, Anderson, I think that might not be such a bad idea."

It took him a second to collect himself and recover. "What? Is this some kind of a woman thing?" he asked, stunned.

"Only in the sense that women are more intuitive than men," Paige replied brightly, no doubt knowing that her remark would get to him. "But seriously," she continued, the humor fading from her voice, "I think that maybe Jake might be a little too isolated. I've been keeping an eye on him at school and I don't see him interacting with the other kids during recess."

Anderson wondered how long she'd been holding off saying anything to him. Apparently today was the day to tackle the subject.

"He's a sweet kid," she continued, "but he needs to acquire some people skills, Anderson. To that end, I think it might do him some good to take care of another person instead of just being aware of his own small sphere."

"Well, it's not like he's going to go backpacking on some survivalist's journey, fending for himself and that baby," Anderson retorted. He felt disappointed. He'd expected Paige to be on his side, not playing for the opposition. "Jake would be taking care of that baby under this Ms. Laramie's supervision the whole time—at the very least. You can't tell me that she won't be watching Jake like a hawk the entire time."

"Not necessarily. I think that the whole point would

be to give Jake the assignment, exercise a little supervision and then step back to see how he does."

Anderson banked down the urge to laugh at his sister's naivety. "Would you step back if this was you we were talking about and the baby you were leaving with someone was Carter?"

Again Paige didn't answer him the way he thought she would. "If I trusted them to look after my son and felt that I had made myself perfectly clear in my instructions, then sure."

He didn't believe it for a minute. "Well, I'm not as naive as either you or your Ms. Laramie," he informed his sister. "You don't just hand over babies to other babies and expect everything to go off without a hitch."

Paige wanted to move on to the topic that really had her interest, but she knew that she needed to get her ordinarily calm brother back to that state before she could go on. Ever since Jake had moved out here, it was as if she didn't even recognize her oldest brother. Anderson had become a different person. A completely uptight, unsettled, different person who seemed to be perpetually afraid of making the wrong move.

"Jake isn't a baby, Anderson. He's halfway to becoming a man—"

Anderson quickly cut her off. "Not for another ten years."

He didn't believe that, did he? "A lot sooner than that," Paige contradicted. "You might as well get used to the idea. Anyway, I didn't call you to discuss Jake's so-called fragile masculinity—or yours," she added. "I called to find out something else."

"What?" he all but snarled. He didn't feel that he could take on another problem right now.

For the second time since she'd called, his sister caught him off guard when she asked, "What did you think of her?"

"Her?" Confusion all but throbbed in his voice. What was Paige talking about?

"Marina Laramie," Paige said patiently.

Why was his sister asking him something like that? "I guess that she's an all right teacher," Anderson finally conceded, thinking that was what he was being asked.

"No." Paige tried again. "What did *you* think of *her*?"

"Think of her?" Anderson echoed, at this point thoroughly confused by Paige's tone as well as her question.

Paige sighed. Men could be so thick, she thought. "This isn't brain surgery, Anderson. Or a trick question," she added in case that was going to be his next guess. "It's really a very simple question," she stressed.

"It's not a simple question," Anderson contradicted. "It's a prying, complex question. What did I think of her?" he repeated, then before she could make any sort of a remark or reply, he continued by asking her a question of his own. "In terms of what? A first-time teacher? A woman who sounds like she has trouble understanding and relating to boys?"

"As a person," Paige interjected, finally getting a chance to get a word in edgewise. "What do you think of Marina Laramie as a person?"

"Why?" Anderson asked suspiciously. It had taken a while before the red flags had gone up for him, but they were flapping madly in the wind now. "Just what is it that you're trying to cook up in that scheming little head of yours?" he wanted to know.

"I'm not 'cooking up' anything," Paige protested. "I wasn't the one who asked you down to the school for a conference, Marina was. I just thought that...well, now that you've seen her and since you were single and she was single..."

Okay, this had gone far enough, Anderson thought. He needed to stop his sister before she *really* got carried away.

"One and one don't always make two, Paige," he ground out.

In her opinion, one and one *always* made two. "You never know until you try," Paige stressed.

"Oh, I know, all right. Trust me, I know," he told her in no uncertain terms. "Besides, I'm not looking for anything—or any*one*."

She already knew that and she thought it was a terrible waste for her oldest brother to be alone like this. "But if you stumble across it right out there in your path—" Paige began.

"I don't plan to do any stumbling, either," Anderson informed her tersely.

As far as he was concerned, one mistake was more than enough for him. Not that he'd actually had any ideas about a possible relationship blossoming between Lexie and him twelve years ago. It had been just one of those classic things, an enjoyable fling that lasted the span of one night, no longer. And, after dealing with the woman, he realized just how fortunate he was *not* to have wanted any sort of a relationship with Jake's mother. They didn't have very much in common.

Now that he thought about it, he wasn't the kind of guy who did well when it came to relationships. Hardworking and blessed with common sense, Anderson knew his shortcomings and he wasn't looking to get involved with anyone.

Even so, it was obvious to him that his sister had other ideas. He needed to set her straight once and for all.

"Look, kid, I realize that you think that since you have this great thing going with Sutter everyone should be married, but it's just not like that for some of us. I'm glad you found somebody to love you, someone who lights up your world, but that isn't my destiny and I'm okay with that."

But apparently Paige was not about to accept defeat for her brother so easily.

"Just because it didn't work out for you and Lexie—her loss, by the way—" she interjected.

Anderson laughed softly. This was the Paige he was more familiar with. The sister who was fiercely loyal to the members of her family and immediately took offense on their behalf.

"Thank you. You're my sister and you have to say that."

"No, I don't," Paige contradicted. "And stop interrupting. What I'm trying to say is that just because it didn't work out for Lexie and you doesn't mean that it won't work out for you with someone else."

She just wouldn't let this go, would she? Ordinarily, he might just let this go for now, but it was far too important to let her think she'd won, even by default.

"It won't because I'm not looking for it to work out—*with anybody*," he underscored. "Look, Paige, I know you mean well, but really, let it go. I'm happy just the way I am."

Paige dug in. "A year ago, you thought you were happy just the way you were, then you found out about Jake and suddenly you wanted him to be a permanent part of your life. You still do," she pointed out, remembering how dejected Anderson had been when Lexie had denied him custody or even visitation rights.

"Don't try to confuse me with your logic, Paige." He was only half kidding.

"It's not 'my' logic," his sister pointed out. "It's just logic."

Anderson blew out an impatient breath. There was just no arguing with his sister once she got going like this. He didn't want to say something to her that he would wind up regretting, but he didn't want her thinking that she was going to emerge the victor in this argument, either.

And then the cavalry arrived in the form of a lanky eleven-year-old boy. Spotting him, Jake was striding toward his truck.

"Sorry, Paige, I'd love to talk some more, but Jake just turned up. Basketball practice must be over. Time to take him home and put him to work," Anderson announced cheerfully. "We'll talk later," he promised, terminating the call before she could say another word.

Or you'll talk later and I'll have to listen, he silently added, tossing the cell phone back into the glove compartment.

Leaning over, Anderson opened the passenger door for his son.

"Hi, how was it?" he asked Jake cheerfully. Then, just in case that sounded a little too vague to his son, Anderson clarified the focus of his question. "How was basketball practice?"

Jake slid into the passenger seat and dutifully buckled up his seat belt.

"It was okay." The reply was completely devoid of any enthusiasm.

Starting up the truck, Anderson pulled out of his parking spot, his eyes trained on the rearview mirror until he put the transmission into Drive.

"Did you play a game?" he asked in the same cheerful voice.

Settling into his seat, Jake kept his eyes forward. "Yes."

He was not exactly a conversationalist himself, but for the sake of trying to draw his son out, he gave it his best shot.

"And then what?"

"We stopped," Jake said matter-of-factly. Then, as the word just hung alone in the air, he explained, "It was time to go home."

This was not going well. "Do you like playing basketball?" Anderson prodded.

His thin shoulders carelessly rose and fell in response as he continued looking out of the front windshield. "It's okay."

That was not exactly a ringing endorsement of the sport. Maybe he'd pressured the boy into playing something he had no desire to participate in.

"Would you rather have me sign you up for something else? Baseball maybe, or football?" Anderson suggested, glancing at Jake's face for a response.

That was the extent of the after school sports activities that were available and he wasn't really sure about the baseball part. The actual baseball season, he was only vaguely aware, was over and he wasn't sure if anyone was available to coach boys in the off-season. He'd never been one to enroll in any of those sports himself when he was a kid. All he'd ever been interested in were things that had to do with ranching.

“You know, it’s not a bad idea to try to broaden yourself a little bit,” Anderson told his son. He hadn’t been critical yet, but maybe a small bit of pressure wasn’t a bad idea. “Sitting in your room all day playing video games isn’t healthy.”

“I don’t play all day,” Jake answered, finally turning toward him. “I go to school.”

It wasn’t a smart-aleck answer, but it didn’t exactly leave room for a warm exchange. Determined to get through to Jake, he tried another approach.

“You need to socialize, Jake. To get to know people. You need to make some friends.”

“Why?” Jake wanted to know. He wasn’t being belligerent; he was just asking a question.

It was a question Anderson wasn’t prepared for and he had no answer ready, so he fell back to an old tried-and-true response parents had used since time began. “You just do.”

“Oh.” Jake went back to looking out the windshield, watching the desolate scenery go by.

Maybe, Anderson thought as silence descended within the vehicle’s cab, that teacher he’d seen today did have a point.

And then again, he thought rebelliously in the next breath, maybe not.

Chapter Four

"Something bothering you, Jake?"

Ever since his meeting last week with the redheaded teacher, Anderson had been more attuned to Jake's silence. All during dinner tonight his son had been even quieter than usual, but for the duration of their trip into town the boy hadn't said a single word. Anderson was taking Jake with him to the town meeting that was being held tonight and they were almost there.

Granted, his son had looked less than happy about having to make this trip when he'd initially suggested it, but he would have thought that thc boy would have said *something* by now. Kids his age *talked*, if only to complain.

But Jake didn't.

Jake was really a hard kid to figure out, Anderson thought wearily.

A heartfelt, mighty sigh preceded Jake's reply when he finally spoke. "I was just about to get to the next level."

"The next level of what?" Anderson asked, puzzled.

He had no idea what his son was talking about. He and Jake shared a house and they shared bloodlines, but at times it was as if they were from two entirely different worlds. Trips to and from school might hear a word or two exchanged and mealtimes were hardly a hotbed of verbal exchange, either, if it was just the two of them at the table instead of occasionally one of his siblings.

But even so, *something* was usually said, some nominal conversation that lasted a couple of minutes. But not this time. Jake hadn't said a word from the time that he had stepped out of his room for the trip to town.

That was right after Jake had looked at him, clearly confused as to why he was going to this meeting and what he was going to do once he got there.

"I thought it might be a good idea for you to see how people in a small town get things done," Anderson had told his son.

But that was only part of the reason he was taking Jake with him. He was also trying to get the boy to feel more involved in what was going on. He was hoping that if his son felt more a part of Rust Creek Falls, he'd open up a little more.

Jake hadn't protested going to the meeting the way a lot of boys his age might have. For that matter, he hadn't dragged his heels, or thrown a tantrum, or mouthed off. Instead, offering no resistance, Jake had just silently come along—but the boy definitely hadn't looked happy about it.

But then, Jake wasn't exactly the definition of a happy-go-lucky kid to begin with.

Still, the silence had really gotten under Anderson's skin and when his son hadn't uttered a single word the whole half hour trip to the town hall, he'd finally decided to initiate some sort of a conversation. The only trouble was, once Jake had answered him, he didn't understand Jake's response.

"The next level in 'Mighty Warriors,'" Jake explained quietly.

"'Mighty Warriors,'" Anderson repeated slowly, as if tasting the words as he uttered them.

What he was really doing was stalling until he could remember exactly what "Mighty Warriors" was. He really was trying to take an interest in his son's life, but what Jake was into represented a whole new world to Anderson. A new world he was attempting to navigate without a road map or a guide.

"That's the video game I was playing when you said we had to go to this meeting."

Anderson was turning his truck into the first available space located in the large parking lot behind the town hall. Pulling up the hand brake, he turned off the engine and shifted in his seat to face his son.

"Oh. Well, you're a bright guy. You can always pick up where you left off when you play again," Anderson said with complete conviction.

Jake's expression gave away nothing, but even so Anderson got the feeling that maybe it wasn't all that easy to play this game his son was so obsessed with when Jake answered, "It's okay, Dad."

Thinking it safer to change the subject than wade through one that he knew absolutely nothing about, Anderson came around the hood of his truck and joined his son. In a gesture of camaraderie, he put his arm around Jake's thin shoulders before he began to walk toward the building.

Jake looked around as they came around to the front of the building. Since it was evening in September, a bevy of streetlights were on, illuminating the front entrance.

"It looks like there's going to be a lot of people here," Jake observed.

Anderson couldn't help wondering if that was a good thing or a bad thing in Jake's eyes. There was still so much he didn't know about this introverted boy he had fathered.

"Everyone who's interested," Anderson agreed. Which, he silently admitted, probably wouldn't have been him if this meeting had been held six months ago. He would have felt it was sufficient to have one of his siblings attend it and then report back on the highlights.

But now he was a family man—or at least he had a family to concern himself with—and that meant that he had to take an active interest in what was going on in town. Especially when it might affect Jake, just as the subject for this meeting promised to do.

He thought back to the wedding celebration that had been held last July Fourth with its unfortunate incidence of spiked punch. Apparently, possibly because of the wedding and definitely because of the punch, love had been in the air that night. Because of that, a large number of babies had consequently joined the population of Rust Creek Falls. Babies who would eventually grow up into children—children who needed to be educated.

Presently, Rust Creek Falls Elementary was too small

a facility to adequately accommodate all these added children. The focus of the meeting tonight was to determine whether the town council should give the okay to just build onto the existing school—or if it was wiser to build a second school altogether.

Although Jake hadn't been part of that baby boom, he was here now and, with any luck, would remain that way. The boy was definitely going to be affected by what would be decided at the meeting.

"Everyone?" Jake repeated, still looking around. His head was turning from side to side as if he was a searchlight that had come to life.

Anderson thought he detected a hopeful note in his son's voice. What was that all about? Was Jake looking around, hoping to see one of his classmates? A girl, maybe? If so, it was a good sign.

"Pretty much," Anderson answered.

Jake spared him a look that could only be interpreted as hopeful. "Like Ms. Laramie?"

The second his son asked whether or not the woman would be attending, Anderson suddenly spotted the teacher in question approximately fifteen feet away from him, standing near the front entrance of the building—and talking to Paige.

Paige, from what he could tell, seemed to be alone. That meant that his brother-in-law was home with Carter, their two-year-old. Anderson wanted to catch up to Paige to talk about a few things, but not if it meant having to talk to Jake's teacher, too.

Since he and Marina Laramie had that less than productive meeting at the school the other week, he hadn't seen the woman or exchanged any words with her, either. But that didn't mean she'd been completely out of his mind.

As a matter of fact, the exact opposite seemed to be true. For some reason, Marina Laramie kept popping up in his head at completely unbidden times and Anderson didn't even remotely like the fact that she did. It made him feel as if he had no control over his own thoughts.

How else could he view having that woman's face suddenly appear in his head while he was in the middle of thinking of something entirely different from an interfering, feisty redhead who thought she knew how to raise his son better than he did?

Never mind that she probably did and that maybe she was even right in her estimation that Jake needed to get involved in something outside of himself. The bottom line was that Jake was *his* kid, not hers, and he would raise the boy any way that he saw fit.

Suddenly, he felt Jake eagerly tugging on his arm. "Hey, Dad, look. There's Ms. Laramie. Let's go over and talk to her."

But as Jake began to make his way over to his teacher, Anderson caught his son's arm, clearly surprising the boy, who looked at him quizzically.

"Ms. Laramie is already talking to someone else," Anderson pointed out.

Jake took another look just to be sure he was right.

"Yeah, but it's Aunt Paige. Aunt Paige won't mind," the boy insisted, shaking his arm free.

The next minute, Anderson saw his son striding over toward the two women. With his long, lanky legs, Jake had reached Marina and his aunt in a matter of a few quick strides. And, as he watched, just like that he saw his son transform from an abnormally quiet, serious eleven-year-old to an animated, bright, smiling boy who clearly had a lot to say.

"Ms. Laramie," Jake had called out before he'd even reached his teacher. When she turned in his direction, he grinned broadly and asked, "Are you going to the town meeting?"

Marina was clearly surprised to see the boy, but she recovered with grace and offered him a warm smile by way of a greeting.

"Yes, I am," she told him.

"Me, too," Jake declared proudly. "I'm here with my dad. He thinks that it's a good idea for me to come see how people in a small town like Rust Creek Falls get things done."

Marina looked past the boy's head and saw his father coming up behind him. She inclined her head politely in a silent greeting.

Her vibrant blue eyes met Anderson's as she told Jake, "Your father's right. It's always a good idea for you to see how things work firsthand."

No doubt pleased at her seal of approval, Jake beamed. The next moment, he seemed to come to and realized that his aunt was standing right next to his teacher. "Hi, Aunt Paige."

It was obvious by Paige's expression that she was surprised by the boy's animated response to seeing her at what was, essentially, a school board meeting.

"Hi yourself, Jake. So your dad dragged you to this, huh?" she asked sympathetically, reading between the lines. She shook her head.

"He didn't drag me," Jake corrected politely, apparently not wanting to lose any of the points he'd just managed to score with his teacher. Turning to his father for backup, Jake asked, "Did you, Dad?"

Anderson found himself being drawn into this unexpected interaction against his will, but he couldn't very well not be supportive of his son. For some reason, having his teacher think well of him obviously meant a great deal to Jake.

"No," he told Marina, "Jake came right along without a single word of protest."

Which was technically true. It was only the boy's body language that indicated he didn't want to go to the meeting. That and his comment about not being allowed to reach the next level of the video game he'd been playing perpetually.

"Can we sit with you, Ms. Laramie?" Jake asked without warning as he looked at the woman with hopeful, soulful eyes.

The same eyes, Marina caught herself thinking, that his father had.

"Jake," Anderson admonished, surprised by his son's extroverted behavior, "you can't just put someone on the spot like that. I'm sure Ms. Laramie has made plans to sit with her friends." And that, Anderson hoped, was the end of that.

Except that it wasn't.

"Actually, I haven't," Marina contradicted, addressing her response to the boy. "Except for your aunt, of course. Otherwise, I didn't have any plans to sit with anyone in particular." She smiled warmly at the boy who had given her some concern. "You're welcome to join us," she told Jake.

Jake looked positively overjoyed.

Anderson couldn't remember ever seeing his son look so enthusiastic and overjoyed before.

And then it hit him.

His son had a crush on his teacher. There wasn't any other explanation for the way he was acting or why he looked as if he was on the verge of doing cartwheels. This was a completely different boy from the one he'd roused from his room earlier.

"Dad, too?" Jake asked eagerly.

Anderson was completely floored by his son's inclusion. Ordinarily, eleven-year-olds, whether they were male or female, were not nearly this thoughtful when it came to their parents. Or really anyone over the age of fifteen.

He could remember himself at that age. In comparison to Jake, he'd been a thoughtless, self-centered little know-it-all. Granted, he'd outgrown that phase a long time ago, but he'd still gone through it. Jake, however, had somehow managed to bypass all that. It made Anderson realize just what a special, decent adolescent Jake really was.

Even so, if Marina Laramie represented Jake's big crush, he still didn't intend to be put on the spot because of it. He was about to politely turn down the whole invitation before it was even tendered to him, but then he saw a quirky kind of smile curve the woman's lips and heard Marina say, "Sure, why not? Your dad's included, too."

Then the petite redhead turned her very bright blue eyes on him and said, "You're welcome to join your sister and me—and your son—at the meeting if you like, Mr. Dalton."

She'd very deftly—and formally—put him on the spot. If he turned her down, he'd be the villain in his son's eyes. He'd been struggling too hard to be Jake's white knight to risk sabotaging himself just because it would entail spending an uncomfortable hour in the woman's company. Uncomfortable not because he had any real, concrete reason to dislike her—he'd actually begun to think of Jake being a babysitter as a good thing—but because there was something about this woman that made him feel...well, *antsy* was as good a word for it as any, he decided.

She made him strangely restless, like he couldn't find a place for himself whenever she was around.

He knew it was an absurd reaction, but it was *his* reaction and as long as he was experiencing it, he wasn't going to be able to relax, certainly not anywhere around her.

But he supposed that not being able to relax was in reality a small price to pay in exchange for seeing his son looking so happy.

Looking like, he realized, a typical kid his age *should* look.

"Can we, Dad?" Jake asked eagerly, turning his face up to his father's.

Anderson slipped a hand on his son's shoulder in a gesture that spoke of familiarity and hopeful bonding. He reminded himself that this was all about Jake and nothing else, certainly not about him.

"Sure, son," he told Jake, "since Ms. Laramie said it was all right."

"I said it was all right, too," Paige reminded him, pretending to raise her hand like a student who was trying to catch her teacher's attention after being conspicuously ignored.

"I know, but you don't count," Anderson teased.

"You're just my sister. You're supposed to say it's all right."

Paige narrowed her eyes as she gave her brother a dismissive, reproving look. "Yeah, well, maybe I haven't read the little sister, big bullying brother handbook lately."

"Then maybe you should," Anderson suggested, a hint of a teasing smile barely curving the corners of his mouth. And then he deadpanned, "You'll have fewer slipups that way."

Jake looked a little confused and concerned at the exchange he was witnessing between his aunt and his father.

Noticing his expression, Marina placed a comforting hand on his forearm. When he looked at her, his expression making it clear that he was ready to hang on her every word, Marina told him, "They're only teasing each other. It's what brothers and sisters do," she added, thinking of her own younger sister.

"Oh." Jake looked as if he'd just been seriously enlightened. "I don't have a brother or a sister," he explained.

Marina resisted the temptation to tousle his hair. He looked so terribly serious. The boy needed to lighten up just a little.

"Maybe someday, you will," she told him.

He nodded solemnly. "Maybe."

It struck Anderson that his son sounded almost wistful as he uttered the single word.

Chapter Five

"C'mon, Dad, we don't want to be late," Jake urged, all but hopping from foot to foot as he tried to get his father to move faster.

This was a definite change in the boy, Anderson thought. Rather than sitting passively in front of his game console for hours on end, Jake had rushed through dinner and even helped put all the dishes into the dishwasher, all in an effort to get going.

Too bad all this enthusiasm involved something that he personally would have preferred not to have to deal with, Anderson thought.

"It's not like they're going to close the doors the way they do when people are boarding an airplane," Anderson pointed out.

He was doing his best not to sound as reluctant as he felt. After last week's town meeting, where he wound up spending almost two hours sitting not next to Marina—

that was Jake's place of honor—but one seat over, he'd still been close enough to be able to have the woman's perfume fill all the exposed pores of his body. It had certainly filled his head.

Even for days later, he could have sworn that her perfume was lingering on his clothing and on his person, constantly distracting him. It was as if he couldn't shake the scent of her away from his consciousness. That, coupled with his mind conducting unannounced ambushes on him, suddenly conjuring up images of the woman in his head, made him feel as if he had become the victim of a stalker.

Except that in this case, it was his own mind that was responsible for the stalking.

He needed to get a grip, Anderson told himself sternly.

What he *didn't* need was to be thrown back in with Marina Laramie again, this time in a somewhat more intimate setting than he'd been subjected to the last time.

But this was Back to School Night and considering that Marina was Jake's teacher, there was just no reasonable way to avoid spending time in the woman's company—unless he didn't attend the event in the first place.

"You sure you want to go back to school tonight?" Anderson asked, pausing in the kitchen despite his son's best efforts to get him out the front door. "I mean, you were just there this afternoon. To have to come back tonight just doesn't seem fair."

"I can handle it," Jake assured him, puffing up his chest a little.

Yeah, maybe you can handle it, but can I? Anderson couldn't help thinking in response.

By now, Jake was pacing around the room impatiently, moving closer and closer to the front door in an attempt to prod his father in that direction. "You look ready," the boy told him.

He might as well get this over with, Anderson thought.

"I guess I am, then," he replied. The words were no sooner out of his mouth than his son all but dashed out the front door, hurrying out to the truck. "And so are you, I see," Anderson muttered under his breath, following his son out.

It promised to be a long evening, Anderson thought as he got in behind the wheel of his truck.

"What are these things like?" he asked Jake once they were finally on their way to the elementary school. "These Back to School Night things," he elaborated in case he hadn't made himself clear.

"You've never gone to one before?" Jake asked, surprised.

"Never had a reason to go to one before," Anderson replied.

"Not even your own?"

Anderson thought for a moment, then shook his head. "I don't think I ever went to any back then. My teachers used to send notes home, so my parents knew how I was doing without having to go trudging down to the halls of learning in order to find out. So what's it like?" he wanted to know, getting back to his initial question.

Having been through it a total of five times before, Jake dutifully told his father what was involved. "You talk to my teacher and she tells you how I'm doing. Then she shows you some of my work."

Anderson supposed he could see the merit in that—if only it didn't have to involve Marina Laramie. "You mean like your drawings?"

"I'm in fifth grade, Dad," Jake reminded him, suddenly sounding very grown-up. "I don't spend time drawing."

Anderson suppressed a grin. Jake sounded way older than his years when he said that. "Sorry, didn't mean to insult you, old man."

Jake looked at him thoughtfully. "Maybe you'd better not say anything to Ms. Laramie, Dad. Just let her do the talking."

"Deal."

He wanted to go one better and not have to look at Ms. Laramie, either, but that was out of the question. The woman was far too easy on the eyes and he could see himself getting swept away without any effort on his part. As a matter of fact, it was going to take effort *not* to get swept away.

"Hey, Dad," Jake said suddenly, turning in his seat to get a better look at him.

Anderson instinctively braced himself. Now what? "Yes?"

"Do you like Ms. Laramie?"

He'd been braced, but he hadn't been expecting that. Jake's question came completely out of left field and caught him utterly off guard. For a second, he made no response. Was his son somehow being intuitive? Had Jake guessed that despite his best efforts, there was some sort of a strange attraction going on between him and the teacher?

Glancing at his son's eager face, Anderson told himself that he was overthinking this by a mile. Jake wasn't some brilliant, pint-size mind reader. His son was just asking a harmless question to satisfy his own budding curiosity. Maybe he even thought that if his teacher was seeing his dad, then his report card would have straight As.

Anderson did his best to sound honest. "I haven't given it much thought."

He secretly hoped he could be forgiven for taking refuge in a lie in order to avoid any immediate problems and confrontations with Jake. It was very obvious that the boy had a crush on the woman and maybe if he thought that his father liked her, too, he'd be jealous. That was a road Anderson definitely didn't want to go down.

"But if you did give it some thought," Jake pressed, not about to let the subject drop so quickly, "what would you say?" His eyes seemed to be almost dancing as he eagerly waited for an answer.

Anderson turned away and looked out the front windshield. His shoulders rose and fell in a vague, noncommittal response. "I guess she's okay."

"'Okay'?" Jake repeated incredulously. "She's not 'okay,'" he admonished. "She's great!" His voice throbbed with gusto. "She's terrific! She's perfect!"

This was where he just backed away with grace, Anderson thought.

"If you say so." That was supposed to be as far as he was going to go talking about Marina. But something seemed to egg him on. So he paused for a second, fighting his own internal reaction, and then he gave in and finally asked, "What makes her so great?"

Jake had his answer all prepared and didn't even hesitate for a moment. "Ms. Laramie looks out for everybody and makes sure that nobody makes fun of anybody else. That's important," Jake stressed.

He'd said it with such intensity, Anderson had an uneasy feeling that Jake was one of those people who would have been made fun of if his teacher hadn't put a stop to that activity.

He supposed that put him in the woman's debt, Anderson thought grudgingly. He felt stymied at every turn, but if this teacher really was championing his son's cause, he knew that he owed her. And Anderson Dalton was a man who made good on his debts.

"Then I guess she really is pretty great," he conceded.

He was rewarded by Jake flashing a wide, happy grin at him. Anderson thought it was priceless.

The next moment, Jake, looking around, needlessly announced, "We're here."

"I recognize the place," Anderson told him, deadpan.

Sitting ramrod straight, Jake scanned the area, looking somewhat concerned. "Looks like there are a lot of people here already."

"There are a lot of kids who go here," Anderson pointed out, then reminded his son, "But don't worry, they're not all here to see Ms. Laramie."

Jake brightened, flashing an almost sheepish smile. "You're right. Hey, there's a spot there, Dad," he said suddenly, eagerly pointing to the space. "Hurry before somebody beats you to it!"

If that one was snapped up, there'd be another one to take its place, but saying so to his son in Jake's present ramped-up mood seemed like an exercise in futility. Instead, he accommodated Jake and deftly swung his truck into the space—a space made somewhat smaller by a greedy 4x4 that had parked too far over to the left.

Ready to bound out of the cab, Jake was already unbuckling his seat belt before the truck even came to a full stop.

"Hold it, cowboy," Anderson called out, grabbing the

edge of his son's jacket to keep him in place. "There's nothing to be gained by a few extra seconds if you get hurt grabbing them."

Chastised, Jake sat back down in his seat. "Yes, sir."

Pulling up the hand brake, Anderson turned off the engine. "Okay, *now* you can get out of the truck."

Jake didn't need anything more. He was out of the cab like the proverbial shot.

Anderson expected his son to be halfway into the building by the time he got out himself, but he was surprised to see the boy waiting for him on the first step.

"You waited," Anderson marveled as he approached his son.

Jake bobbed his head up and down. "I thought maybe you'd like to go in together."

Anderson smiled, pleased by the boy's thoughtful actions. Maybe this father thing was going to work out after all.

"I'd like that a lot," he told Jake.

The second Anderson reached him, Jake began moving quickly again. Glancing over his shoulder, he saw that he'd outpaced his father again. "Can you walk faster, Dad?" Jake prodded.

Anderson nodded. "I can do that." To prove it, he stepped up his pace. So much so that he swiftly outdistanced his son.

Because Anderson's legs were so much longer, Jake had to fairly skip to keep up with him. Judging by his expression, Anderson estimated that the boy loved it.

Back to School Night, Anderson discovered, was basically an informal event. Parents were milling around the classroom with their fifth graders and their siblings.

There were tables lined up in the middle of the classroom displaying reports written by Ms. Laramie's students and, despite what Jake had said, there were also drawings and paintings done by the class—some of which Anderson thought were rather impressive—hanging on the walls.

"Why don't you show me your work?" Anderson coaxed his son as they wove their way in between the aisles.

"My reports are right here," Jake pointed out, drawing his father over to one of the tables. Within a couple of seconds, the boy had honed in on his folder and offered it to him.

Anderson curbed the urge to just flip through the pages. Instead, because he knew how much it meant to Jake, he went through the folder methodically, giving each page the attention it deserved. He read everything under Jake's eager, watchful eye.

Preoccupied and focused, Anderson still became instantly aware of her the moment she approached him, despite the fact that it was from behind.

"Good, aren't they?" Marina asked. The next moment, she had circled around to face him. And then she smiled at Jake, who seemed to actually *glow* right before his eyes. "Jake has a very gifted way with words." Raising her eyes to his, she said, "You should be very proud of your son, Mr. Dalton."

Anderson's eyes met hers for just a moment. The split second was almost enough to make him lose his train of thought. Exercising extreme effort was the only thing that saved him.

That and looking away.

"I already am," Anderson replied, looking at his son and smiling.

"So," Marina continued, the smile on her lips never wavering as she addressed Jake's father, "now that you're here, is there anything you want to ask me?"

Yes, why are you messing with my head? And why can't you look more like Mrs. Peabody, my fifth-grade teacher who stopped every clock she walked by? And why can't I shake off the scent of your perfume? Why do I want to ask you out when that's the worst possible thing I could do to either of us?

The questions flashed through his head in an instant. Out loud, he said, "No, can't think of a thing." And then something did occur to him. He added the coda. "Unless you can think of something that might need improving."

Jake had momentarily gone off to confer with one of the new friends he'd been making at school. Marina took the opportunity to focus on Anderson and answer his question in a low voice.

"Maybe our relationship."

Stunned, Anderson could only stare at her. "Excuse me?"

"Our relationship," Marina repeated, stressing the words even though they were hardly above a whisper. "Ever since you came storm-trooping into my classroom that day, you've been avoiding me."

"No, I haven't," he protested.

Her eyes narrowed. "I saw you crossing the street the other day to avoid walking by me," she told him.

She'd caught him dead to rights, but he wasn't about to go down without a fight.

"I haven't been avoiding you," he retorted, then lowered his voice when he realized he'd attracted the attention of one of the mothers in the room, who seemed to lean over in their direction, undoubtedly to hear better. "I haven't been avoiding you," he repeated at a much lower decibel. "I just didn't see the need to confer with you over every single little thing that Jake might have said at the dinner table."

Jake returned just then, incurring Anderson's silent prayer of thanks. The woman couldn't continue harping on this point if Jake was around to hear her—right? Okay, so he had been avoiding her and maybe that was cowardly of him, but it was definitely the easier way to go. A confrontation and all that entailed wouldn't be any good for Jake, either.

"You two talking about me?" Jake asked, a guileless grin on his thin lips as he looked from one adult to the other.

No matter what kind of feelings he had about Marina Laramie, his son's fifth-grade teacher was obviously doing the boy a world of good. Though part of him hated to admit it, she had drawn the boy out more in the last few weeks than he had on his own over the entire summer.

If this had been a competition, Marina would have been the obvious winner, hands down. He was man enough to admit that, just not out loud. He hadn't reached the point where he could say anything of the kind to her—yet.

But, if the time came and he had to, then he would. Jake meant everything to him.

"If you have no questions, nothing to share or point out, then this might just qualify as the shortest parent-teacher conference on record," Marina conceded, willing to let it go at that.

Even though she thought it would be beneficial to the boy, she was not about to force Anderson Dalton to talk to her—which he seemed no more inclined to do than he was inclined to have that in-depth conversation with his son she'd urged him to have.

"Unless you count our first one," Anderson reminded her.

A competitive, combative streak shot through her, not allowing her to take his comeback at face value.

"As far as substance goes, this was definitely the shorter one," she informed him, her voice sounding just a little formal and reserved.

"Does that mean that we have to leave now?"

At Jake's question she looked over at the boy, whose eyes were on her, not his father. His brows were knit in sadness.

"Oh no, of course not," Marina assured him quickly. "You definitely don't have to leave. I was just giving your father a way out if he wanted to go."

Her eyes met Anderson's fleetingly. She had no clue as to what he was thinking, whether he welcomed the reprieve or not. The expression on Jake's face, however, had her continuing with what she was saying.

"Your dad's welcome to stay here, talk to the other parents, have some cupcakes," she suggested, gesturing at the plates of the dessert she'd made last night, strictly for this occasion.

"Did you make them?" Jake asked eagerly, already claiming one.

Marina tousled the boy's hair. "Every last one of them."

Jake bobbed his head up and down as he swallowed the bite he had taken. "I thought so."

"Why?" she asked, amused.

"Because they taste so good." To prove it, Jake took another big bite of his cupcake, then grinned as he savored the taste.

"You have a natural charmer here, Mr. Dalton." Marina's eyes were laughing as she regarded her student. "I'd watch him like a hawk if I were you."

Jake, Anderson thought, trying not to stare at the woman, was the only one in his life that he *didn't* have to watch. She, on the other hand, was another story entirely.

Chapter Six

"I see you survived your first Back to School Night." The breezy observation was addressed to Anderson by his sister as Paige stepped out of her Jeep.

Anderson stopped working and frowned.

It was a Saturday morning and he was out on the range, doing one of his least favorite chores: looking for breaks in the fence and mending them. He knew he could just order a couple of his ranch hands to do it, but Anderson didn't believe in asking his men to do anything that he wasn't willing to do himself. So here he was, out under a particularly warm September sun, repairing fences.

He'd paused what he was doing when he'd heard the sound of an approaching vehicle. He'd assumed that it was Jerry, one of the hands, bringing Jake out to help him. His son had gamely volunteered his services at breakfast this morning and Anderson had thought it was a good idea. But he'd wanted to get started really early, so he'd told the ranch hand to bring Jake when the boy was ready.

But instead of his son, he looked up to see his sister Paige, who, he had to admit, was looking every bit as fit as she used to when she'd worked right alongside all of them on the family ranch.

Anderson studied her in silence for a second, then shook his head. "You come all the way out here to tell me that?" he wanted to know.

"Of course I did," she responded, tongue-in-cheek. "I'm your sister, or at least one of them," Paige amended, "and I care."

"If you care so much, sister, why don't you pick up a hammer?" Anderson suggested, holding one out to her. "Make yourself useful. I could use the help."

Instead of taking the hammer from him, Paige demurred. "Sorry, I'm afraid I won't be here long enough for that. I promised Sutter I'd meet him in town in less than an hour."

"Convenient," Anderson murmured, dropping the other hammer before getting back to work. "Say hi to my brother-in-law."

"What's gotten into you lately, Anderson?" Paige asked, being deliberately cheerful in contrast. "You didn't used to be so surly."

"Surly?" he echoed. "And here I thought I was being my usual charming self."

Following him as he moved down the fence, Paige shrugged. "Maybe you're just reacting to the stress of being a new parent," she conjectured. "You might think about getting some help dealing with Jake—just for a while until you get more used to being a dad," she added quickly in case her well-meaning suggestion irritated her brother or set him off.

Lately, she wasn't sure just how to read Anderson. His behavior had been unusual. But she'd been observing him and now she had a theory. A rather rock-solid sort of a theory, in her opinion.

Anderson glanced at her over his shoulder. "You volunteering?"

"Me?" She stared at her brother, stunned. "Sure. In the three minutes I have left over when I'm not chasing after Carter, or helping out taking care of Jamie Stockton's motherless triplets, or, oh yes, teaching a bunch of overenergized fourth graders. I was planning on using those three minutes to nap, but I can just pencil you in instead." She looked a little exasperated that Anderson didn't understand just how very busy almost all of her days were. "Of course I'm not volunteering, Anderson. I would if I could and you know that, but I'm practically sleepwalking through parts of my life as it is."

"And yet, here you are, looking in on me to see how I'm doing," he said with a touch of sarcasm. Paige was up to something, he could feel it. He just didn't know what yet. "They broke the 'sister' mold when they made you." He paused to pick up another handful of nails before continuing. "So who's this helper you're suggesting I contact to assist me over the bumpy parts of being a first-time dad?"

Paige stood behind him as Anderson hammered in the next board. "You could talk to Marina."

Anderson abruptly stopped working and stood up. Now it was starting to make sense. His sister was trying to play matchmaker.

"Marina?"

"Marina Laramie, Jake's teacher," Paige prompted cheerfully.

"I *know* who Marina is. *This* is your suggestion on who should help me navigate through the maze of fatherhood?" he asked incredulously. He really would have thought that Paige would know better than to attempt to play matchmaker or meddle in any way in his life. Obviously, he'd given her too much credit. "In case you hadn't noticed, she's not a father."

"No, but she is a first-time parent," Paige pointed out. "The two of you could pool your information, or maybe even—"

"I don't need to know how to diaper Jake," he bit off, interrupting.

"But you do need to know how to talk to him, how to reach him," Paige said emphatically. "And from what I've seen, Marina's pretty much got that covered. You could stand to learn from her."

"What are you, her publicity agent?" he asked, annoyed.

Paige ignored the sarcastic question. She wasn't about to get sidetracked. From what she—and their sister Lani—had observed, there was a spark between their brother and Jake's teacher and in her opinion, the two made a very good pair. All she had to do was make her thickheaded brother aware of that.

"Whether you realize it or not, you and she do have a lot in common," Paige insisted. "You're both first-time parents and you're both single."

Okay, it was time to make his sister back off, he thought.

"Is that what this is all about?" he demanded, forgetting about the fence repairs for the moment. "Being single?"

"No," Paige immediately cried, afraid that maybe she had overplayed her hand. She knew how Anderson felt about someone trying to set him up. "It's about being alone in this parenting game and admitting that you need to pair up with someone who knows exactly what it's like to be in your shoes."

His frown looked as if it went clear down to the bone. "I don't want her in my shoes," he snapped. "Besides," he continued, his tone lightening just a little, "I'm not alone in this. I've got you and Lani and Lindsay helps when she's not too busy at Dad's firm, and I'm—"

Paige threw up her hands. "No one could ever tell you anything."

Unfazed, Anderson responded mildly, "That's because I'm older and smarter."

"Well, you certainly are older." It was all that Paige was willing to concede. Taking a deep breath, she forced herself to calm down. She'd learned long ago that yelling at Anderson never got her anywhere. "Seriously, big brother, Marina's very good at her job."

"I'm sure she is," he replied dismissively. Turning away from Paige, he got back to work. There was still a lot of fence mending left to do.

Paige could all but see her words bouncing off her brother's head, unheeded. But she wasn't about to give up or go away without saying what she'd come to say.

"And did you see the way Jake lit up around her at the town hall meeting?" she asked. "Every time she said anything to him, Jake positively glowed. You *had* to have seen that."

Anderson paused for a second, but he didn't get up

and he didn't turn around. "I might have noticed," he allowed just before hammering in another nail. Hard.

There were times when he could get her so angry, Paige couldn't see straight. But this was important and she wanted to get her point across before she had to leave. "Look," she began patiently, "it's none of my business, but if you ask me—"

"I don't recall doing that," Anderson told her quietly, knowing damn well that his sister was going to ignore him. She was good like that, ignoring whatever she didn't want interfering with whatever point she was espousing.

"If you ask me," Paige repeated through clenched teeth, "I don't think that boy was getting the right sort of attention he needed from Lexie."

This time, Anderson did get up and turn around. He had deliberately avoided asking Jake anything about his mother. Lexie's behavior was a definite sore point for him, but he didn't want to make either his son or his son's mother think that he was attempting to drive a wedge between them. He knew Lexie would immediately accuse him of trying to gain permanent custody of Jake—something he wanted with all his heart even if he didn't have an aptitude for parenting. He could learn how to be a good parent, but he needed to have his son around in order to learn that. Antagonizing Lexie would definitely cause him to forfeit his custody rights.

"Maybe not." It was all Anderson would concede.

"Well, Jake clearly responds well to the attention that Marina's given him. Given that, wouldn't it make sense to have those two together even when he's not in school?"

Anderson frowned. Just where was Paige going with

all this? "What are you suggesting? That I get Marina to adopt him?"

There were times that her brother was so thick, she could just scream. "Of course not."

"Then what?" he wanted to know impatiently.

"You're the big, smart brother," Paige reminded him, throwing his earlier self-description back at him. "You figure it out."

"Paige—" There was a warning note in Anderson's voice.

She could only lead him so far. After that, he was going to have to figure it out for himself. Otherwise, he'd accuse her of meddling and do the exact opposite of what she wanted to suggest with all her heart: that he go out with Marina and give them both a chance.

Paige pretended to look at her watch. "Oh, look at the time. Gotta go," she announced. With that, she got back behind the wheel of her vehicle. "Tell Jake I said hi—and think about what I said."

"Which part?" he wanted to know, exasperated.

"All of it," she told him just before she pulled away.

"No time," he called after her.

But the truth of it was, he did think about it. He thought about how he felt he was in over his head. Most of all, he thought about the petite redheaded teacher with the startling blue eyes. He was struggling to resist having anything to do with the woman, but he was really beginning to wonder if he wasn't allowing his own fear of any sort of involvement to get in the way of his son's welfare.

If what he'd seen at the town meeting and at Back to School Night were any indication, his son really did have a full-blown crush on his teacher. She could very well be the key to his being able to establish a decent relationship with Jake. At least it was worth a shot, he told himself.

He just hoped that he wasn't also shooting himself in the foot.

It was another half hour before Jerry Holder finally drove up in his beat-up pickup truck, bringing Jake with him.

"I brought my own hammer," Jake announced proudly as he bounced out of the passenger side of the truck. He held it up so that his father could see it for himself. Joining him, Jake looked back and forth along the long length of the fence. "Where do you want me to get started?"

"Why don't you work right alongside me?" Anderson suggested. He thought it best to keep an eye on the boy until he felt that Jake knew enough about the task to be allowed to work at his own pace.

Jake took another hard look at the long length of fencing. His small face puckered up a little.

"Are we fixing all of it?" he asked, sounding somewhat intimidated by the scope of the job.

Anderson looked at the fence, trying to see it through the young boy's eyes. He had to admit that from this angle, it looked as if it went on forever.

"Whatever needs fixing," he told his son.

"Oh." The single word was brimming with emotion. "Are we doing it all today?" he asked,

Anderson laughed. "No, not today. Today we're only going to do a little bit to get started." He pretended to look very solemn as he asked Jake, "That okay with you, cowboy?"

Jake bobbed his head up and down, clearly pleased at

being consulted by his father this way. "It's okay with me," he said, and went to work.

Jake worked quietly alongside his father for close to twenty minutes before he finally and unexpectedly broke the silence.

His out-of-the-blue declaration was not exactly the kind that caused ripples of surprise to go undulating through the air.

"I really like Ms. Laramie," he told his father.

Jake looked so serious, it was hard for him not to laugh, but he managed to pull it off. "Really? I hadn't noticed."

"Well, I do," Jake solemnly confirmed. "I think that she's really nice." He paused then, his hammer dangling from his fingers as he seemed to ponder what he was about to say next. He began carefully, his eyes never leaving Anderson. "Dad?"

"Yes, Jake?" Anderson asked patiently. He'd decided that he was going to be open to anything his son had to say. This was brand-new territory that they were crossing and he didn't want to say anything that would have Jake closing up again.

Jake pressed his lips together as he searched for just the right words. "Do you think that maybe someday, we could invite Ms. Laramie and her daughter to the ranch for lunch or maybe dinner?" he asked.

"Maybe someday," Anderson echoed, knowing full well that it wasn't going to end there.

And it didn't.

"Someday soon?" Jake asked hopefully, rocking forward on his toes.

"Define *soon*," Anderson requested, appearing to continue to hammer down the next nail. In reality, his mind was anywhere *but* on fixing the fence. He was bracing himself for what was coming—and for what he was going to have to say in order to make his son happy.

"I dunno," Jake answered. "Like maybe next week?"

"That soon?" Anderson knew he couldn't surrender immediately. It had to take at least a couple of seconds. "Jake, I don't know if—"

"Did you know that Sydney's never seen a horse?" Jake asked. "Not in her *whole* life," he stressed.

"Sydney?" Anderson questioned.

"Ms. Laramie's baby," Jake explained, his eyes never leaving his father.

Anderson remembered the expression on Marina's face when he surprised her by walking in on her when she was changing her daughter. He recalled the infant's little arms and legs waving in the air.

"Isn't Sydney about five months old?" he asked, taking a stab at the infant's age from her small size.

Again Jake nodded vigorously. "Yes, she is."

"At five months, she could have seen an elephant and I doubt if she would remember once she's a year old. At that age, nothing much registers," he assured his son, waiting to see what Jake came up with next.

He was surprised that his son didn't attempt to spin any yarns. Instead, he was very direct about the matter. "Then you're not going to invite them to the ranch?" Jake asked, looking crestfallen.

When the boy regarded him like that, Anderson knew that he would have moved heaven and earth to get him to smile again.

That was when Anderson resigned himself to losing this battle over Marina's invasion into his life. Jake had somehow, without a single shot being fired, won the war.

His son had somehow managed to get the upper hand here by doing nothing more than being himself.

And, in order to make his son happy, he knew he was willing to do anything, even if it meant having to throw open his doors and invite that woman and her offspring into his home.

"On the contrary," he told Jake, "I am going to invite her to lunch."

Jake's eyes grew huge, brimming with happiness. "When?" he asked eagerly.

"When am I going to invite her, or when is she coming over?" Anderson asked, drawing the moment out.

"Both!" Jake cried.

He'd expected nothing else, Anderson thought. "I was thinking along the lines of inviting her to come to lunch next Saturday. That way it'll be light and Sydney can get to see the horses. Who knows, maybe she'll even get to ride one."

"But she's too little for that," Jake protested protectively.

He would have made a great big brother, Anderson thought. Too bad that wasn't going to happen. At least, not on his side, Anderson thought. Nonetheless, he was pleased to see these qualities in his son.

"Can you tell me when you're going to do it?" Jake asked hopefully. "When you're going to ask Ms. Laramie over?"

Anderson had no problem with that. "Sure, but why?" he asked, curious.

"That way, I can watch and listen. I won't even make a peep," Jake promised.

Then, in case there was any doubt, the boy crossed his heart making an elaborate show of sweeping his fingertips first in one direction and then in the other, forming a huge, albeit invisible, cross over his small heart.

Anderson suppressed a grin. "Okay, now that that's settled, let's get back to work," he suggested.

"Let's!" Jake agreed, beaming as he grabbed up his hammer, looking ready and eager to follow his father anywhere.

Seeing him, Anderson knew he would have been willing to pay any price just to bask in that sort of gleeful approval.

Even if it meant spending the day with Jake's fifth-grade teacher.

Chapter Seven

Out of the corner of his eye, Anderson could see his son in the family room.

Jake was hovering around instead of sitting on the sofa. He had the video controller in his hand, but unlike when he first arrived on the ranch, the boy wasn't playing. Despite the fact that there were lifelike characters flying back and forth across the TV screen, Jake wasn't even pretending to pay attention to them. Not since the boy had seen him pick up the receiver to make thc call.

Anderson could see his son watching him in what he could only assume the boy believed to be a covert manner. Well, it looked like Jake could definitely rule out being a spy from his list of future careers, he thought, the corners of his mouth curving in amusement.

Every time he looked in Jake's direction, the boy would jerk his head down as if something about his controller had suddenly caught his complete, undivided attention.

But Anderson knew better. Jake was watching him. Watching and waiting for him to complete the phone call that would commit him to the fateful path he'd promised his son he would take—the path he didn't want to take. Inviting Marina Laramie and her daughter, Sydney, to come out to the ranch for the day.

C'mon, Dalton, how bad can it be? It's just for one afternoon out of your life. Before you know it, it'll be gone just like that—and you will have made your son one happy cowboy.

Anderson suppressed a sigh. The problem was he didn't want to call Marina. Didn't want to call her for a number of reasons. If he extended the invitation and Marina turned it down, Jake would be devastated and any good that had come from the association of teacher and student would have gone out the window. If, however, Marina *did* accept the invitation, then Jake would undoubtedly want her to come over again.

And again.

And again—until the woman would weave herself into the fabric of both their lives and there would be no escaping her. He knew that he really didn't want to go that route.

And then there were his sisters. Paige and Lani had turned into some sort of an annoying cheering section for the feisty little redheaded teacher, extolling Marina's virtues every time he wound up exchanging more than a couple of words with either of them.

If they caught wind of the fact that he'd actually invited Marina and Sydney to the house, that would be the end of peace as he knew it. He knew his sisters.

They would immediately start planning their wedding no matter *what* he said to them about the invitation being extended to the woman strictly for Jake's sake and not his own.

Then there was that "other" reason. The one that entailed his complete reluctance to occupy the same general area as the vibrant fifth-grade teacher because—well, just because. She made him uneasy, made him remember that when it came to women, he didn't exactly have an outstanding track record. He didn't want to be attracted to a woman because attraction meant that the specter of disappointment and all that entailed would be waiting for him in the wings only a few steps away.

He'd much rather keep to himself than have to go through that. It was demoralizing.

Do it for Jake. This is for Jake, an insistent voice in his head whispered. The only reason he was even in this situation—having to call Marina's cell to tender the invitation—was because he was Jake's dad and it was up to him to extend the invitation since Jake couldn't very well do it on his own and be taken seriously. She was extroverted and properly unpredictable to a degree, but he sincerely doubted that Marina would just pop up on the porch and announce she was staying for lunch because Jake had invited her to do so.

He'd been psyching himself up now for fifteen minutes. Braced as he would ever be, Anderson brought the landline receiver to his ear.

Glancing one last time over his shoulder, he saw Jake watching his every move. At this point, the boy didn't even try to pretend to look away. Instead, with an encouraging grin, Jake gave him the thumbs-up sign.

His son was obviously hoping for the best.

That makes two of us, buddy.

The only problem was, given this particular scenario, Anderson didn't exactly know what "the best" outcome was in this case.

He looked down at the precise numbers that Jake had carefully written down on the piece of paper he'd handed him. The paper contained Marina's cell number, which Jake had gotten thanks to Paige.

He supposed that made sense, Anderson thought now, looking down at the phone number. After all, Paige and Marina were friends so of course his sister would have the other teacher's personal number. He had to shake off this feeling that it was all one giant conspiracy to pair him up with the teacher.

Taking another breath and feeling Jake's eyes all but boring into him, Anderson forced himself to complete the call. As it rang, he silently resigned himself to the inevitable.

But before he could complete his mental pep talk, Anderson heard the phone on the other end being picked up and someone on the other end saying, "Hello?"

The single word sounded like a self-contained symphony.

Anderson came very close to losing his nerve and just hanging up. And maybe he would have if he hadn't felt Jake's eyes all but glued to him the entire time. He couldn't disappoint the boy.

Here goes nothing.

"Hello, Ms. Laramie?"

"Yes?"

He could hear the slight quizzical note in her response. She didn't recognize his voice.

Last chance to bail, he thought, toying with the idea.

But if he bailed, he knew that he'd be disappointing Jake—and besides, bailing was the act of a coward. He knew that he was a lot of things, but a coward was not one of them.

Most especially when his son was watching him.

"Ms. Laramie, this is Anderson Dalton—Jake's father," he added almost awkwardly, as well as, he discovered, needlessly.

"I know who you are, Mr. Dalton," she assured him patiently. "Is there something that I can do for you?"

Transfer to another state before I do something we're both going to regret.

"Actually," he told her, "I'm calling about something that I could do for you."

She paused for a long moment before finally saying—rather stiffly at that, "I'm afraid you have me at a disadvantage."

That makes two of us, Anderson couldn't help thinking.

Belatedly he realized how Marina might have gotten the wrong idea from his response. Anderson cleared his throat, telling himself he needed to start over if this had a prayer of working out—for Jake, he tacked on again. This was all for Jake. He couldn't allow himself to lose sight of that.

"Let me start over," he began.

"Please," Marina urged.

He almost laughed at the unabashed earnestness of the request. He had a feeling she wouldn't have reacted well to his laughing at her and managed to refrain.

"Jake was telling me that Sydney's never ridden on a horse."

"No, she hasn't," Marina confirmed, sounding as if

she wasn't sure if he was being serious. "You do realize that my daughter's only five months old."

"I figured she was around that age," Anderson admitted. He gave no indication that he knew perfectly well that a five-month-old did not belong on the back of a horse—at least not by herself. "But Jake seems really troubled that your daughter's gone all this time without having that experience."

He heard her laugh and he had to admit that there was something almost lyrically engaging about that sound. And he also had to admit that at least part of him was relieved that she didn't think he was either insensitive or crazy to even be talking about the idea of Sydney on horseback.

"You do have a very sensitive, thoughtful son, Mr. Dalton."

Marina smiled to herself as she thought of the boy. She had to bite back the urge to ask if Jake took after his mother. Anderson seemed more like the type to shoulder his way through the world—whether the world wanted to get out of the way or not.

"My 'very sensitive, thoughtful son' would like me to invite you and your daughter to come to the ranch for lunch and a little horseplay."

Marina stepped back into the land of confusion again. "Excuse me?"

"Jake wants Sydney to meet Fury."

That remark was even less clear than the first one. Was he deliberately trying to confuse her? Or was it her? "What?"

Anderson realized that the reference probably meant nothing to the woman, unless she was a trivia expert—

or one of her students happened to be hooked on classic kids' TV shows.

"Jake named the horse I gave him after this old, old TV show he saw on one of those kids' channels." And then, just in case she was worried that the name fit the horse, he reassured her. "Trust me, Fury doesn't live up to her name. The horse makes molasses look like it's moving fast. Jake is a city boy—he likes to make things sound dangerous. But I knew he had to take it slow when it came to riding and Fury is really even gentler than an old gray mare."

"If you say so," she replied, not totally convinced that he was telling her the truth.

But the one thing she was convinced of was that Anderson loved his son. Anyone who was around the two of them for more than a couple of minutes could see that was the case.

She heard what sounded like Anderson clearing his throat. The next moment, he started to speak. "Well, anyway, Jake wanted me to invite the two of you to the ranch whenever it was convenient for you to come out."

Marina noticed how he emphasized the fact that the invitation was coming from his son. If she was reading correctly between the lines, that meant that he was extending the invitation under protest.

"Tell Jake that I think it's very sweet of him to invite us, but I'm afraid Sydney and I will have to take a rain check."

"Oh. Sure. Okay." Anderson would have thought that he'd be relieved. After all, that was what he wanted, wasn't it? To have her turn down his invitation. And he *was* relieved—to some extent.

But he was also experiencing something else. Something, for lack of a better description, that felt akin to disappointment.

It was official. He was going crazy, he thought.

And then, to cinch his impression, he heard himself asking her, "Mind if I ask why?"

Marina had expected Anderson to accept her declination—maybe even cheer a little—and just hang up. He certainly hadn't sounded as if he was eager for her to accept the invitation.

So why was he asking her to give him a reason?

He knew the answer to her declination as well as she did.

"Look, Mr. Dalton, I wouldn't want to put you out," she told him.

"Put me out?" he repeated, completely perplexed. What was she talking about? More than anything, he wished that women would come with some sort of an instruction booklet. It would make life a hell of a lot easier. "What makes you think having you come out to the ranch would be 'putting me out'?"

She sighed. She was beginning to think that the man took a certain perverse pleasure in making things difficult.

"I'm trying to be accommodating here, Mr. Dalton," she began and got no further.

"I don't understand," Anderson said. "If you were trying to be accommodating, wouldn't you have said yes to the invitation?"

"To your *son's* invitation," she emphasized. Didn't he see the difference?

He missed the point for a minute and was about to tell her again that he didn't understand what she was trying to tell him when he managed to successfully play back her words in his mind.

"Wait, what? Why did you just refer to it as Jake's invitation?" he wanted to know.

"Well, isn't it?"

He saw no reason to lie. After all, this had started out specifically because it *was* Jake's idea. "Yes."

The word felt like a burst of cold water, shocking her in its honesty. Well, at least he wasn't trying to snow her, she told herself. Then again, he didn't seem to care about her feelings, either. It would have been nice to have him indulge in even a little white lie.

She discovered that she was having trouble holding on to her temper. That only happened when she had exhausted her own deep well of patience.

"Anyway," she managed to say, "the only thing that should matter to you is that I'm letting you off the hook."

"You keep talking about some 'hook.' I'm not *on* a hook," he insisted, shortly.

"Yes, you are," she countered, digging in. She absolutely hated being lied to. The worst truth was better than the best lie in her opinion. "Jake asked you to invite us and you did, but it's obvious that the invitation to come to the ranch is coming from him and not from you."

The woman was coming close to dancing on his last nerve. "It might be obvious to you, but not to me."

"Don't try to spare my feelings, Mr. Dalton," she cautioned. "It's a little too late for that."

He was about to let it go at that, thinking it was for the best for both of them since he firmly believed that the woman could make a saint crazy. But then he caught sight of Jake watching him, looking so hopeful that it all but stabbed him right through his heart. Because of that, he gave it one more try.

For Jake.

"The invitation is really from both of us," he informed her. Then, before she had a chance to launch into some sort of full-scale rebuttal, he shot down any possible argument she had in her arsenal.

"Do you really think I'd be inviting you to come to the ranch for the day if I didn't want you and your daughter here?"

Okay, so it was a lie, he silently admitted, but it was a well-intentioned one and it had been undertaken for the best of reasons. Namely because something about Marina Laramie not only made his son happy, but made him light up like the proverbial Christmas tree.

He would have extended an invitation to a Tasmanian she-devil if the prospect of having one over to the ranch would have had the same effect on Jake.

He realized that the other end of the line had gone quiet and for a second, Anderson thought he'd lost her because she'd seen through his fabrication—otherwise known as a lie—and hung up. He hoped not because that meant that he would have to call her back.

"Are you still there?" he asked, raising his voice.

"Yes, I'm still here," he heard her say in a voice that was definitely subdued.

He plowed on. "So what's your answer?"

"You're really asking us to the ranch?" she asked, wanting to make sure one final time.

"I could try to get it across with hand puppets," he volunteered. "But you really wouldn't be able to see that over the phone—I'm calling from a landline," he explained, vaguely aware that these days, there were ways for people calling one another on the phone to be able to see the other person.

Personally, he thought that the whole world needed to take a few steps back and have a time-out. There was just too much tech stuff out there for his liking. It interfered with human relationships—when there were any, he quickly inserted, mentally backing away from the subject.

"So, what's it going to be?" he asked her. "What do I tell Jake—and what are you going to tell me?" he added out of the blue.

It was almost as if the words had just come out on their own volition without any prompting or effort on his part.

"What day would you like us over?" she asked him tentatively. What was she doing? She felt as if she was about to make a fifteen-foot dive into a half-filled teacup. Her stomach clenched, even as excitement skittered over her nerve endings.

An inexplicable feeling of triumph volleyed through Anderson. He didn't attempt to analyze it, understand it or even question why it suddenly turned up. Those were all things he told himself he'd deal with later. Right now he needed to nail down the woman's response to the invitation before she changed her mind or had second, paralyzing thoughts. If she did, Jake would be severely disappointed. It was his job to make sure that didn't happen.

That was his story and he was sticking to it.

"So is that a yes?" he asked her.

"It's a yes," she agreed.

"How does tomorrow sound?" he asked. "I know it's

kind of last-minute, but it's a Sunday so I thought you both might be free."

"As it so happens," she told him in carefully measured out words, "we are both free. Tomorrow sounds fine."

"Great. Why don't you and your daughter plan on coming out here around nine and we'll make a day of it." He gave her the straightforward directions, ending with, "You can't miss it."

She laughed softly. "I wouldn't take any bets on that if I were you." Then, before he could interject anything else, she said, "We'll see you there at nine," and with that, she hung up.

Chapter Eight

Marina's sigh seemed to echo all around. Why was she doing this to herself? Sunday was supposed to be a day of rest, not a day of extreme tension.

She shouldn't have said yes.

"This is a mistake." She looked down at her daughter. "Listen very carefully, Sydney, because Mommy's not going to say these words very often during your formative years, at least not about herself where you can hear them. I think I've made a mistake saying yes to Jake's daddy. A really big mistake."

Marina had stopped her futile search within the bedroom of her small apartment. There was no point in looking for the right outfit to wear, she thought, feeling more and more insecure by the minute.

In an effort to calm down, she'd begun talking to her daughter as if she were an equal and a confidant instead of an infant strapped into her car seat on the floor.

For her part, Sydney was following her around the room with her eyes, looking as if she was hanging on every word even as she was trying to shove her tiny fist into her mouth and swallow it whole.

"I know that every woman is supposed to say this sometime in her lifetime," she told Sydney, "but in my case, it's true. I don't have anything to wear."

She'd gone through all her clothes and nothing looked right to her. She was attempting to find something casual, but all she could find were outfits that were either too formal, or looked as if she'd spent the morning scrubbing floors—and gotten the worst of it.

"I know, I know," Marina continued with her conversation, filling in what she felt would have been Sydney's responses if her daughter was capable of making responses. "You want to see the horsies but we can do that some other time—with somebody else's daddy doing the hosting, not Jake's daddy."

Sinking down on the edge of her bed she looked down at her daughter in earnest and for the second time in as many minutes, she sighed.

"You're right, we're not exactly awash in social invitations, are we? But they'll come. Just you wait, they'll come." Sydney made a gurgling sound. Marina blew out a breath, resigned. "But you want to go now, don't you? Okay, Mommy will just have to put her brave smile on and face this like an adult. After all, if I can deal with a roomful of eleven-year-olds, I can certainly deal with one adult. It's not like he's going to bite me or anything, right?"

Sydney gurgled again and this time, bobbed her head a little, which Marina took to be a nod. She got up again. "Good talk, Sydney. Good talk."

Just then, the doorbell rang and Marina could feel everything inside her instantly freezing up. Every insecurity she'd previously experienced was back, bringing along a friend.

"Maybe it's not too late to make a getaway out the back window," she said aloud, glancing toward it longingly. The doorbell rang again and Marina sighed. "Too late." Looking down at the outfit she'd wound up in—worn jeans and a blue-gray pullover—she shook her head. There was absolutely no time to change again. "This is going to have to do."

Sydney jabbered, as if responding to that statement.

"Right, easy for you to say," Marina told her. "You look adorable in everything."

She picked up the car seat and carried her daughter into her living room. Once there, she parked Sydney on the floor beside the sofa.

"Coming," she called out when the doorbell rang a third time.

Opening the door, Marina found herself looking up at Anderson Dalton. For some reason, he looked taller today than he had the other times.

A *lot* taller.

Or maybe that was just her nerves making him *look* taller.

But he smelled nice, she couldn't help noticing. He smelled of sunshine and wind.

Marina felt her stomach tightening and prayed that this outing she'd agreed to wasn't going to be something she was going to regret.

"Sorry it took me so long to get to the door," she apologized. "I was in the bedroom, looking for something to wear."

His eyes skimmed over her slowly—as if appraising what she had on, she couldn't help thinking. "I see you found it," he murmured.

The sound of his voice made the ripples in her stomach increase to storm-warning size. She shifted her eyes to Anderson's shadow, who had moved right to his father's side the moment he heard her voice.

On familiar ground again, Marina grinned at him. "Hi, Jake."

The boy's chest seemed to immediately puff up in response to her greeting. "Hi!"

Only when her eyes shifted back to him, Anderson realized he was staring at her. Marina had divided her hair into two pigtails and looked like a kid herself instead of the mother of one and the teacher of many. He mumbled a greeting, realizing that he hadn't done so when she came to the door. And then he felt compelled to explain.

"When you didn't answer the door after I rang the doorbell two times, I was going to leave," Anderson confessed. "I didn't think you were home, but Jake didn't want to give up so fast. He made me ring again."

"I call that patient stubbornness," Marina told him, smiling fondly at the boy. "It's a very good quality to have." She turned her attention back to Anderson. "That means he doesn't give up right away when things don't go his way."

"Oh, he can be pretty stubborn, all right," Anderson vouched, thinking of how persistent Jake had been until he'd gotten him to invite his teacher over against his own best instincts.

Looking past Marina into the living room, Anderson saw the swinging arms and legs first, then realized that he was looking at Marina's daughter, who, if she hadn't been strapped into the car seat, appeared ready for take-off like a tiny helicopter.

"You need any help with that?" he asked, nodding at the baby. "You know, carrying it?"

What *was* it about this woman that turned him into an awkward, tongue-tripping idiot? He was behaving like the people he held in low esteem or actual contempt most of the time.

"The car seat," Anderson specified as an afterthought.

"I know what you meant," Marina assured him. "And no, I don't. Carrying around this much weight has become second nature to me. I don't even know I'm doing it. And," she added, "truthfully, lugging the car seat around has helped me build up my biceps."

But Anderson had already moved past her and was picking up the car seat with Sydney in it before she had a chance to get to her daughter.

"I've got it," he told her matter-of-factly, as if this was business as usual instead of an outing he would have preferred to have no part of.

"What's a biceps?" Jake wanted to know, practically skipping next to her as they went outside and toward the truck.

The cab of Anderson's truck was large enough to accommodate all of them, including Sydney's car seat. Anderson had checked all that out beforehand. Otherwise, he would have been forced to borrow his sister Lindsay's car for the errand—and that would have required way too much explaining.

Following Anderson to his vehicle, Marina paused for a moment to answer the boy's question. "Make a muscle," she instructed. When he did, she pointed to the tiny ridge that was formed. "There," she told him, "that's your biceps."

Jake turned his head and looked at his upper arm as if seeing it for the first time. "I have one."

Marina never hesitated. "Absolutely. And it'll get to be very big if you do your exercises," she assured him and then added encouragingly, "It looks like you've already gotten started."

Jake beamed in response. "Maybe a little," he confided.

"Well, it's very impressive. Keep it up." Marina turned her attention to Anderson's struggles with her daughter's car seat. "Here, let me." Very gently, she edged him out of the way. "It's very frustrating until you get the hang of it," she said matter-of-factly.

Within a few seconds, she'd untangled the hook Anderson had gotten caught in the back of the seat and successfully attached Sydney's car seat to the truck's seat.

"There," Marina declared with relief. "Done."

He took her word for it. It certainly looked as if it was well secured. "I guess maybe I could use some of the patient stubbornness you were talking about," Anderson observed.

Getting into the backseat next to her daughter, Marina buckled herself in.

"I thought that was where Jake got it from," she said innocently. "You."

Her answer struck him as funny. "Not hardly." Anderson laughed shortly. "He probably developed it trying to impress you."

She was about to deny having anything to do with it when Jake climbed into the backseat next to her. She looked at her student in surprise.

"Don't you want to sit up front next to your dad, Jake?" She didn't want the boy hurting his father's feelings by having so blatantly picked her over him. "Most boys want to be right up front, where the action is."

But Jake, she quickly found out, wasn't like most boys.

"No, that's okay, Ms. Laramie. I'd rather be back here with you."

Marina leaned over and whispered to the boy, "You don't want to hurt your dad's feelings, do you? He'll think you don't like him if you sit back here with me instead of up front with him."

Anderson watched the little exchange in his rearview mirror. Since Marina was whispering to his son, he didn't hear what was being said, but he felt he could make a pretty educated guess.

"That's okay," he assured Marina as well as his son. "I don't mind him sitting back there with you if he wants. Jake is just trying to make you feel more welcome."

Marina wasn't sure if that was actually true or not, but she grasped at the excuse that Anderson had handed her and gave the boy a quick one-armed hug.

"Well, he certainly accomplished that," she told Jake fondly.

Jake's eyes sparkled. "We've got a surprise for you," he confided in what amounted to a stage whisper. "You and Sydney."

"A surprise? I love surprises," she told him with the proper enthusiasm, knowing that was what Jake was hoping for. "I can't wait."

She couldn't have said anything better to Jake if she had tried, Anderson thought, catching sight of his son's face in his rearview mirror.

His son looked proud enough to burst and seemed as if he could hardly contain himself. Jake gave the distinct impression that any second now, he'd go off like a Roman candle.

She had a hell of a great effect on his son, Anderson thought. Maybe having this woman here for the afternoon might turn out to be a good thing after all.

He realized that he could probably stand to learn a few things from her—whether he liked the idea of not.

"Do you want a hint?" Jake was asking, fidgeting in his seat and moving his feet back and forth, like someone who was desperately in need of channeling his energy somewhere.

"Well, I'm pretty good at picking up hints," Marina told her student, urging him on because she sensed that Jake wanted her to. "It won't spoil the surprise, will it?"

Damn, but she was good, Anderson couldn't help thinking. She really looked as if she was having a serious conversation with his son rather than the kind most adults had with children—a few words before they were brushed off.

Moreover, he could tell that Jake was totally eating all this up.

This woman was really worth observing more closely, Anderson told himself. He was rather certain that he could pick up a few pointers from her on how to communicate with his son. With all his heart, he really did want to build a better, closer relationship with Jake. That was, after all, he reminded himself, the reason he'd given in and invited Marina over in the first place.

Glancing up, Marina's eyes met Anderson's in the rearview mirror. For the last few minutes she'd thought she felt his eyes on her and she looked up, thinking perhaps she was just imagining things.

But she wasn't.

Anderson seemed to be watching her like a hawk. Why? Did he expect her to do something to upset his son? The man hadn't struck her as the protective type, but he obviously was. Marina viewed that as a good thing, even though it made her feel as if she was under a microscope. But she would gladly put up with it, for Jake's sake, given this rather delicate situation he found himself in.

"Jake," Anderson cautioned, "why don't you hold off on the hints? I'm sure Ms. Laramie likes to be surprised and she already said that she's very good at unraveling clues. You don't want to spoil her surprise for her, now do you?"

"Uh-uh," Jake piped up, shaking his head from side to side so hard that his straight light brown hair swung back and forth.

"I guess that I'll just have to wait," Marina said stoically, playing along.

"It'll be worth it," Jake assured her, his excitement once again bubbling up to the surface. "You'll like it." He glanced toward her daughter. "So will Sydney." The little girl made a sound in response to her name and Jake declared happily, "Did you hear her, Ms. Laramie? She agrees with me."

"Certainly sounds that way to me," Marina replied, doing, Anderson thought, a more than credible job of keeping a straight face.

She raised her eyes to meet Anderson's again, hoping that there would be something there to give her a clue as to whether she should be braced for something, or if his son was getting excited just because he had gotten caught up in the visit and the promise of the day that was ahead of them.

From the way she saw Anderson's eyes crinkle as he looked at her, she realized that the man had to be smiling.

It was going to be all right, she silently promised herself. Whatever the surprise was, she felt fairly confident that there wasn't going to be something overwhelming going on. She began to relax and lower her guard.

And then it hit her.

The tension she'd felt ever since she'd agreed to this outing and had hung up the phone yesterday was gone. She was actually relaxed and, in a way, even looking forward to spending the day with her daughter on the ranch. She genuinely liked Jake and wanted to be able to help the boy fit into a home-life setting, something that she felt he both needed and deserved.

As for Anderson, he seemed somewhat abrupt at times, but she could tell that he loved his son and, bottom line, that was all that counted.

She rather envied Jake that. He had something that her daughter had been deprived of—a father who cared.

"Dad and I made lunch for you," Jake announced out of the blue. "We did it ahead of time," he added proudly. "Well, Dad made it and I helped."

Now *that* surprised her. "Your dad cooks?"

The tone of her voice had Anderson raising his eyes and looking at her in the mirror again. "Does that surprise you?"

She hadn't meant to say that out loud. Caught, she had to confess. "No disrespect intended but—yes."

"The best chefs in the world are men," Anderson pointed out.

"A handful," Marina allowed. "But that doesn't change the fact that a lot of men aren't sure how to even boil water."

Ordinarily, he would have just disregarded her comment, letting it pass and not caring one way or the other what she believed or thought. But for some reason, he didn't want her having that kind of a negative image of him.

"In my family," Anderson heard himself saying as they neared the ranch, "everyone was taught to pull their own weight and at least knows how to cook well enough to survive."

"Then I'll look forward to lunch," Marina assured him, allowing just a glimmer of her amusement to show through.

"We've got milk for Sydney," Jake piped up, not to be left out, "'cause Dad said that she can't chew her food like I can."

"She can't," Marina confirmed, then explained, "because she only has three teeth."

Jake looked at her, concerned. "The janitor in my old elementary school, Mr. Wilson, he didn't have any of his teeth and he said he lost 'em in a fighting match."

"A boxing match?" Marina supplied, trying to get the details of his story straight.

Jake nodded. "Yeah, that's it, a boxing match. You saw it?" he asked. It was obvious that he thought since she was familiar with the term, that meant that she had to have been there to witness the event.

"No," she told him. "Just a lucky guess."

Jake cocked his head, studying her in fascination. "Are you lucky?"

Was she?

Unbidden, her eyes glanced up and lit on Anderson's in the rearview mirror. Out of nowhere the words slipped out. "At times."

Chapter Nine

"This is all yours?" Marina asked in a voice that was just a little above a hushed whisper.

She had been growing progressively more awestruck as the miles had gone by. The land they'd been traveling on to get here was nothing short of overwhelmingly impressive. Squinting just a little, Marina thought she could make out a corral in the distance. There looked to be several horses milling about within its confines.

"Mine and the family's," Anderson told her as he drove. "I run the place for them but the ranch actually belongs to my father, Ben. Ranching really doesn't interest him all that much and his law firm keeps him pretty busy most of the time." Anderson shrugged good-naturedly. "I have no head for the law, but I like working with my hands, so this arrangement works out to everyone's advantage."

Pulling his truck up in front of the house, Anderson

turned off the engine, got out and then opened the rear passenger door for his guests.

"Well, this is it."

Marina peered out through the window before beginning to remove the straps from around Sydney's car seat. He had pulled up before a one story ranch house with simple, strong lines. It suited Anderson, she thought.

As she began undoing the vehicle's restraining straps, she saw that Jake, after unbuckling himself, was doing the same on his side of the car seat.

"That's all right, Jake," Marina told him. "I can do that."

But the boy continued, pausing only to look up and tell her, "I like helping."

She couldn't very well argue with that. She knew it was a trait to encourage.

"Well, that's lucky, because I like being helped," she responded. "And I very much appreciate yours."

The remark only managed to spur Jake on and he worked quicker.

"Done!" Jake announced, raising his hands up in the air like a rodeo cowboy when he had managed to successfully finish roping a calf.

"Me, too," Marina said, matching his tone. She edged out of the truck, wanting to be on firm ground before easing her daughter out.

But she had no sooner gotten out of the truck than Anderson was moving her over, out of the way.

"Okay," he told her. "I'll take it from here."

Before she could demur or offer any protest, Anderson was taking both car seat and baby out of the back of his truck. Then he ushered her toward the house, still holding on to the car seat.

"Let's go inside," Anderson said. It sounded more like a command than a suggestion. "Jake said he wanted to show you around. I didn't think you'd mind," he said, giving her a way out if she wanted it.

"Well, then, let's get to it," Marina urged cheerfully, placing one arm lightly around the boy's shoulders.

His son, Anderson noted, was now beaming so hard, he had a feeling that if the power in Rust Creek Falls went out, the boy could light the whole town up.

Anderson caught himself smiling as he led the way into the house.

The tour of the ranch house went rather quickly, with Jake doing virtually all of the narrating as they passed from one room to another. Anderson was surprised that his son had actually picked up so much information about the place in the last three months. If anyone had asked him, he would have sworn that Jake was oblivious to everything that was going on around him, focusing exclusively on the small world that existed within the video games he seemed to be so attached to.

Live and learn, Anderson thought, happy that he had turned out to be wrong about Jake.

At the end of the impromptu tour, they ended up in the kitchen.

"And here we are, back in the kitchen," Jake declared just before he quietly slipped away, after giving his father a wink.

Marina shifted her daughter to her other hip and drew closer to her official host.

"Where's he going?" she asked, surprised that the boy had decided to disappear.

"Well, a couple of weeks ago, I would have said that

he's gone to his room to play a video game, but since he seemed so caught up in showing you the lay of the land, I'd say he's gone to fetch the surprise that he got for you."

Marina looked at him quizzically. "I don't think I understand."

"You will," was all that Anderson was willing to tell her.

Did he want her to prod him? "You're being very mysterious."

Anderson didn't debate the matter one way or another. Instead, he just told her, "Jake would be very disappointed if I spoiled his surprise."

That still didn't really address her concerns. So she came right out and asked, "Should I be braced for something?"

Anderson laughed then. It was a genuine laugh, tinged with amusement. The sound seemed to embrace her. Any concerns she might have had began to melt away.

"Lady," he told her, "you strike me as someone who's already braced for anything that might come her way."

She wasn't sure if he was giving her a compliment, but she liked to think that he was.

Jake chose that moment to come back into the room. He had a bag with him from one of the local stores in town and he held it out to her.

"This is for Sydney," Jake told her proudly. "She can't open it, so you have to."

Touched, Marina accepted it, then held up the bag for her daughter to see.

"Jake got you a present, Sydney," Marina told the baby, shifting the tiny girl again so that she could open the bag.

"Dad paid for it," Jake told her, wanting her to have all the details. "But I picked it out."

Marina glanced at the quiet man at her side. "You have an incredibly honest son, Mr. Dalton. Anyone else would have taken all the credit himself," she concluded, looking at Jake. She smiled her approval at the boy.

The latter beamed in response. "Open it, open it," he urged her excitedly.

Marina did as he asked. Reaching into the bag, she took her daughter's gift out.

"It's a cowboy hat," she cried. "A really sweet, tiny cowboy hat." She was delighted with it. "Look, Sydney," she said, holding it up in front of her daughter. "Your very first cowboy hat."

"Here, let me help," Anderson volunteered, taking the hat from Marina and gently slipping it onto the infant's head.

Once it was on, he tightened the drawstrings beneath her small chin just enough to keep the hat from slipping off her head.

"She looks like a real cowgirl!" Jake enthused, visibly happy that he'd been part of the "transformation" process.

Sydney kept turning her head, as if trying to catch sight of what it was atop her head. After several tries, she finally gave up.

Jake suddenly turned toward his father. "Can we take them out to the corral?" he wanted to know, eager to start the next phase of his plan.

"Maybe Ms. Laramie would like something to eat or drink first before we go outside again," Anderson suggested.

But Marina shook her head. "No, we're fine and I'm

sure that Sydney would love to see your horses," she told Jake. "I know I would," she admitted.

"Okay, let's go back out to the truck," Anderson said, beginning to lead the way to the front door.

"Why the truck?" Marina wanted to know, surprised and a little disappointed. "Have you changed your mind about going to the corral and decided to take us home?"

He looked at her quizzically, wondering where she could have gotten that idea. "No, I'm taking the truck so that I can drive you over to the corral," Anderson explained.

"Can't we just walk?"

"Well, sure we can," Anderson agreed. "But I thought that walking all that way over to the corral might be too far for you and the baby."

Just what sort of women was this man used to? Marina couldn't help wondering. Granted, she wasn't exactly pioneer stock, but she didn't fall apart at the mention of a brisk walk, either.

"Sydney and I really aren't that fragile, Mr. Dalton. And walking is a very good form of exercise," she added, glancing at Jake in order to include the boy in this, as well. "I don't get a chance to do it often enough," she confided to Anderson.

Jake looked up at his father. "Can we, Dad? Can we walk there?"

Anderson wasn't about to be the villain of the piece. He'd only made the offer for Marina's benefit. If she wanted to walk, then that was fine with him.

"Lead the way, Jake," Anderson told his son. As Jake took off like a flash, Anderson called after him, "Walk, Jake, don't run."

Jake came to almost a skidding halt, his face flushing slightly as he turned around to look at his teacher. "Sorry. I forgot. You can't run."

"Who says I can't run?" Marina wanted to know. "I just can't run when I'm holding the baby."

"'Cause you don't want to drop her?" Jake earnestly asked.

"That would be a good reason, yes," Marina agreed, doing her best to suppress the laughter that was bubbling up in her throat, threatening to spill out.

"I can take her from you if you feel like stretching your legs," Anderson volunteered. His offer took her completely by surprise.

Marina was about to thank him, but tell Anderson that it was all right, that she would carry her daughter. It wasn't that she didn't trust him, it was just that she didn't know how familiar he was with what it took to walk that distance while carrying an infant—a possibly wiggling infant—in his arms.

But the next moment, she decided to keep the words to herself when she looked at his face. There was something there that allayed her fears about turning her infant daughter over to this man.

So instead, Marina told him, "That would be very nice of you," as she handed her daughter over, placing Sydney into Anderson's arms.

She watched, fascinated, as Anderson's face instantly softened right in front of her eyes. Then and there he seemed to bond with her daughter in a way she would have never expected.

The next second, Jake was declaring, "Race you!" The announcement snapped Marina out of her self-imposed trance.

"You're on," Marina responded and then quickly began to run toward the corral.

Marina was careful to keep up, but to never outpace her student, who gleefully made a beeline for the corral, which was the intended finish line.

They reached it almost at the same time, together, with Jake getting to the corral just a few feet ahead of her.

"I won!" he laughed gleefully.

Marina sagged slightly against the corral, even as she affectionately ruffled his hair. "You sure did," she agreed.

"But you ran good," Jake was quick to add, not wanting to hurt her feelings.

"I ran 'well,'" Marina told him, correcting his grammar.

Caught up in the moment and the win, the correction flew right over Jake's head.

"That, too," Jake said, nodding his head. It caused her to laugh, charmed by his innocent intensity.

"Let's catch our breath while we wait for your dad," she suggested, pointing in the distance to the man and her baby.

Anderson raised his hand in a wave.

As he watched Marina, he couldn't help thinking she didn't run like a stereotypical girl. From his vantage point, she ran like a sleek thoroughbred.

Marina Laramie was a thing of beauty to observe, he couldn't help noting.

Sydney made a noise and he glanced down at the infant he was carrying in his arms.

"You a mind reader, hot stuff?" he asked, amused, pretending that the infant's noise was a commentary on what he'd been thinking. "It was just an observation. I didn't mean anything by it."

In response, Sydney made what sounded suspiciously like a cooing noise.

The sound warmed Anderson and made him sad at the same time. He'd missed experiencing these sorts of small moments with his own son. Missed so much in those ten years that he'd been kept in the dark about Jake's existence. He couldn't find it in his heart to forgive Lexie for that.

He liked to think that he would have made a decent father, if these feelings that he was now experiencing were any sort of indication of what fatherhood would have been like.

"I won!" Jake called out to him gleefully as he approached with Marina's daughter. "Did you see me, Dad? I won!"

"You certainly did," Marina confirmed with a smile. Turning toward Anderson, she held out her arms. "Give her to me. She's got to be getting heavy for you."

But Anderson deliberately ignored her request. "Catch your breath first," he told Marina. "This little charmer isn't heavy at all. I think I can manage holding your daughter for a little while longer."

As a matter of fact, he thought, though he kept it to himself, he rather enjoyed it.

"She does look cute like that," Marina commented, referring to the pint-size cowboy hat atop her daughter's head.

"Can I show Ms. Laramie the big surprise now?" Jake asked excitedly, dancing from foot to foot as he looked at his father.

"Doesn't that boy ever tire out?" Marina asked, marveling at his energy.

"Not to my knowledge. Okay, Jake, bring over the surprise," he told his son. As the boy ducked into the corral and ran off to the stable just beyond, Anderson turned so that he was facing Marina. He didn't want his son to hear. "You let him win."

Marina looked up at him, an innocent expression on her face. "No, I didn't."

"I'm not much of an expert when it comes to a lot of things," he told her. "But you were definitely holding back. No point in denying it, Ms. Laramie. I know what I know."

"Marina," she corrected him.

He looked at her, confused for a moment. And then he realized what she was saying. "Tell you what, you stop calling me Mr. Dalton and I'll stop calling you Ms. Laramie. Deal?"

"Deal," she said, eyeing Sydney. "As long as you give me back my daughter."

"You drive a hard bargain, Marina," he told her, amused. With that, he handed back the infant.

Just in time for Jake to return and bring over his big surprise.

The surprise was trotting right behind him on four very sturdy hooves.

Chapter Ten

Jake's surprise turned out to be a beautiful, chestnut-colored mare.

"This is Fury," he proudly told his teacher. "She's my horse and she's going to give Sydney her very first horseback ride."

Marina knew that the boy meant well, but there was no way she was about to allow Sydney to get on the back of that horse.

She hugged her daughter a little closer as she looked over her shoulder at her host. What was Jake's father thinking? she silently demanded.

As if reading her mind, Anderson told her, "Don't let the name fool you. They don't come any gentler than Lady Fury, here." Leaning over the corral fence, he patted the mare's muzzle.

Maybe the horse was gentle, but the mare was also

very big—and Sydney was very little. "Be that as it may—" Marina began only to have Anderson interrupt her as if she hadn't said anything.

"Since Jake seemed to think it was so important for Sydney to experience her very first horseback ride, I thought that I could hold her in my arms while I rode around the inside of the corral on Fury."

She supposed that was a way to appease the boy and yet keep Sydney safe.

Marina looked at the mare, still a little skeptical about the idea. "And you're sure that she's gentle?"

"No question about it," Anderson assured her. "I give you my word."

"Absolutely!" Jake chimed in enthusiastically. "Dad wouldn't let me ride on any other horse to start with. Fury's so gentle, she's almost poky," the boy told her solemnly.

She didn't want to come across as being overprotective—and they were both doing their best to accommodate Sydney.

"I guess that's good enough for me," Marina told them. She turned toward Anderson. "Hold Sydney while I get on the horse."

That wasn't what he'd just proposed. "You?" Anderson asked.

"Me." She saw the doubtful look in Anderson's eyes as he took the baby. "I can ride a horse. Don't look so surprised. After all, this *is* Montana. What kind of a Montanan would I be if I didn't know how to ride?" Holding on to the saddle horn, Marina swung into the saddle, then held her arms out for her daughter. "The baby, please," she prompted when Anderson made no attempt to hand over Sydney to her.

After what seemed like a long moment, Anderson surrendered the baby. "I wasn't going to drop her," he protested, thinking that might have been the reason Marina didn't want him to take the baby for a ride.

"I know. I wasn't insinuating that you were. I just wanted to be the one to give Sydney her first horseback ride," Marina told him.

"I can lead my horse around the corral for you," Jake volunteered enthusiastically, his eyes shining with excitement.

Marina was about to tell her student that she wanted to just circle the corral herself, but she saw the eagerness in his eyes and couldn't find it in her heart to refuse Jake.

So she didn't.

"I'd be honored if you led Fury around the corral for Sydney and me," she told the boy.

Jake beamed so hard, she thought his face was seriously in danger of cracking. And then he suddenly turned solemn, as if he was about to take on a huge responsibility.

"I won't go too fast," Jake promised.

"I have every faith in you," Marina told the boy as he began to lead Fury around the perimeter of the corral by her bit.

True to his word, Jake led the mare around slowly—almost too slowly.

As they passed by Anderson, who was perched on the top rung of the corral, she noticed the amusement on his face.

"Gentle enough for you, Marina?" he asked.

"The point is that she's gentle enough for Sydney," Marina responded. "And she is."

Anderson inclined his head. "That's all that matters," he agreed.

She glanced down at her daughter, who was cooing with delight. Jake seemed to take credit for her enjoyment, and Marina had a feeling that he would have gone on indefinitely if she'd let him. She let Jake enjoy himself for as long as she thought prudent, and then she whistled.

When he looked at her over his shoulder, she told him, "I think that maybe Sydney's had enough for her first time, Jake. She's getting tired." The little girl had grown quiet and looked as if she'd fall asleep.

Jake reluctantly nodded his head. "Okay."

He led Fury back over to where his father was still sitting on the fence.

"Had enough?" Anderson asked the taller of Fury's two passengers.

"Sydney has. I could go on riding," Marina confided. "It's been a long time since I've had a chance to go out riding."

"Maybe we can do something about that," Anderson said casually as he took the sleepy infant from Marina.

It sounded as if he was extending an invitation for a return visit, Marina thought, then told herself that she was reading things into his comment. He was probably just being kind, nothing more.

It really had been a long time since she'd gotten out, Marina thought. Maybe that was why she was guilty of being a little too eager and of reading things into Anderson's casual conversation.

They went back to the house and this time, they had lunch. Anderson had prepared hamburger patties ahead of time.

"It's our secret recipe," Jake confided to her as his father placed several patties on an indoor grill. Within a few minutes, the air was filled with a mouthwatering, tempting aroma.

"That smells delicious," Marina told her host, realizing how hungry she was. She'd been too nervous to have any breakfast this morning, she recalled.

"That's the general idea," Anderson replied, taking her comment in stride. "Two burgers enough for you?"

"Oh, more than enough," Marina assured him. "I get filled up quickly."

Anderson laughed, glancing at his son. "That's not our problem, is it, Jake?"

The boy grinned from ear to ear, eyeing the burgers' progress. "Nope."

"For a skinny kid," Anderson told her, "Jake's a regular bottomless pit."

Marina glanced at the boy. He was thin and wiry, without an ounce of fat on him.

"A lot of people would kill to be like that," she told both Anderson and Jake.

Her host looked to have everything under control. Still, she wanted to pitch in. "Is there anything I can do?" she wanted to know.

"You can eat," Anderson told her as he flipped the first batch of hamburgers onto a plate. He set the plate down on the table, putting it next to the buns and a platter of sliced tomatoes and lettuce, and a few condiments.

"Besides that," she countered.

Anderson shook his head. "Can't think of a thing," he answered. He arranged a second batch of hamburgers on the grill to replace the first. Glancing at the plates on the table, he gestured at the offering. "Eat!" It was definitely an order.

Marina made no move to obey. "What about you?"

"I'll grab a couple from the next batch," Anderson promised. When he glanced back at her again, he saw that Marina was breaking apart the first hamburger she'd slipped onto her plate. "Looking for something?" he asked. "I've got to warn you, there are no hidden prizes inside the burgers."

"I thought the prize *was* the burger," she deadpanned.

He looked over at the infant a little skeptically. Sydney was back in her car seat, which in turn was on a chair beside her mother. "Isn't she too young for solid food?"

"Not my kid," Marina told him. "Sydney's been eating some solid foods since she was a little old lady of four months."

"And she's all right with it?" he asked, still skeptical. "I mean, there aren't any ill effects of her eating solid food at such a young age? Or am I just showing my ignorance about what babies can and can't do?"

"No ignorance," Marina told him. "You haven't been around babies very much, so how would you know?" she asked. "For the record, baby and doctor are both fine with it, as long as the food's pureed. Do you have a blender around? It's okay if you don't. I did bring a couple of jars of pureed fruit with me, but I'm pretty confident that she'd enjoy something different."

"Got one right there on the counter," he pointed out. "It's a gift from Paige, actually. She likes to mix herself these awful green smoothies when she comes by."

Marina got to work and had a small portion ready for her daughter within a few minutes.

As she carefully fed the baby, Marina took a bite of her own hamburger. She paused, savoring it.

"Hey, this *is* very good," she told Anderson, surprised.

"Told you," Jake piped up.

"Yes, you did," she agreed, "but most guys like to brag about their dads. That doesn't always mean what they're saying is true," she qualified.

"I wouldn't lie to you, Ms. Laramie," Jake told her with solemnity.

"And I appreciate that," Marina assured him, trying to keep a straight face. Her eyes shifted to Anderson again. He had finished making the second batch and was just sitting down at the table opposite her. "These are very, very good."

Her compliment pleased him, although his expression remained impassive. "Glad you like them."

She took another bite. Maybe it was her imagination, but it tasted even better than the first bite. "What did you put into them?" she marveled.

Anderson shrugged. "A little bit of this, a little bit of that."

She'd been a teacher long enough to know evasiveness when she heard it. "You're not going to give me your recipe?"

"Not a chance," he answered with a laugh. And then he looked at his son. "And you, you're sworn to secrecy."

Jake looked really surprised. "I am?"

"Yes, you are," Anderson told him with a straight face. The so-called secret was no big deal, but this was a way to test the boy's loyalties, he thought. "As of right now."

"Oh." Jake looked as if he was digesting this new piece of information. "I guess that means that Ms. Laramie and Sydney are just going to have to come over again if she wants to have your hamburgers, right, Dad?"

He was putting his father on the spot, Marina thought. She didn't want the day to turn awkward, not after they'd all been having such a nice time. She quickly came to Anderson's rescue.

"I don't think you should make your dad feel like he has to invite us back, Jake. It's up to him to extend the invitation—when he feels like it. Right now, I think he should have a chance to recover from our visit at his own pace."

She was trying to get him off the hook, Anderson realized. That made it easier for him to say yes to his son—and himself in the bargain.

"Well, if you ask me, I think that Jake's got a very good idea—unless, of course, you and Sydney have a lot of plans for the next few weeks," he added, not wanting Marina to think he was pressuring her into anything.

Jake turned his soulful eyes on his teacher and said, "You don't have any plans for the next few weeks, do you, Ms. Laramie?"

Marina looked from the son to the father, a smile budding and blooming on her lips. "Well, apparently I do now."

"Then you'll come?" Jake asked excitedly, grinning in total, unabashed glee.

"Yes." Her answer was given not just to Jake but to his father, as well. Maybe even foremost.

"When?" Jake was asking her, his wide blue eyes trained on her.

She gave him a completely innocent look. "That's entirely up your dad," she told him.

She didn't have to wonder long, because Anderson spoke up. "How about next Saturday?" he asked.

"Saturday sounds fine," she answered, delighted. Sydney made a funny little noise. Marina put her own spin on it. "Saturday's fine with Sydney, too," she told the Dalton men.

"Saturday it is," Anderson confirmed, allowing himself a very infectious smile.

"Want any more?" Anderson asked her after she had wound up consuming a second burger with as much enthusiasm as she had spent on the first.

"Only if you want to watch me explode," Marina protested. "I am really, really full." She glanced over at her daughter, who was dozing once again in her car seat. "And so is Sydney, from the looks of it."

Rising to her feet, Marina began gathering the plates.

Watching her for a moment, Anderson asked, "What are you doing?"

It wasn't exactly a mystery, she thought. Still, she answered politely, "I'm clearing the table."

"You don't have to," Anderson protested.

"I know," she answered matter-of-factly. "But I want to. It's the least I can do in appreciation for your hospitality." She looked over at Jake. "Want to help clean the plates?"

Jake jumped to his feet as if he was a jack-in-the-box in training. "Sure," he responded. The single word throbbed with verve.

Anderson continued observing her. He couldn't help admiring the way Marina could get his son to all but trip over himself in an effort to do her bidding.

She made it all look so effortless, he thought. Of

course, the fact that Jake had a crush on her the size of Texas didn't exactly hurt her cause.

Still, it wasn't so much her face—which was damn pretty, he thought—as her personality that motivated his son. He was certain of it. Marina had a way about her that just seemed to pull a guy in, no matter what the age.

He was going to have to watch that himself, Anderson thought.

Although, after what he'd been through with Jake's mother, Lexie, he felt rather confident that when it came to matters that concerned women, he was rather savvy in that department. He wasn't about to be smitten, or led blindly around because of some sort of a surface attraction. The days of his being a gullible sucker who could be taken in by a pretty face were definitely over.

He had become a man who was suspicious of everyone and everything. Including sexy fifth-grade teachers.

"We had a wonderful time," Marina told Anderson later that evening as she stopped at her front door. Anderson was right beside her, his arms full of Sydney's car seat—and Sydney. Turning around, she smiled at him. "Thank you."

The day had turned out to be far more pleasant than he'd anticipated when he'd initially given Jake the go-ahead.

"It was our pleasure, right, Jake?" He looked at the boy, who was right beside him.

"Right!" Jake declared with feeling. He looked up at Marina hopefully. "And you are coming next Saturday, like you said, right?"

Marina solemnly drew a cross over her heart. "I never go back on my word."

Anderson noticed that she hadn't directly answered his son's question. Looking at the sleeping infant in his arms, he made use of an excuse that had suddenly occurred to him,

"Jake, Sydney left her hat in the car. Do me a favor and get it for her."

"Sure thing," Jake said just before he took off.

He waited until he was sure the boy was out of earshot and then he spoke. "I don't want you to feel you have to come next Saturday if you don't want to."

She laughed, amused. "Funny, I was going to tell you that you shouldn't feel pressured into inviting us over next Saturday if you'd rather not."

He looked at her in confusion. "What gave you the idea that I feel pressured?"

She would have thought that *that* was self-evident. "Well, for one thing, Jake didn't exactly leave you any leeway."

He nodded his head, giving her the point. And then raising one of his own. "I could point out the same thing in your case."

That surprised her. "I don't feel any pressure."

"Neither do I," he replied—and then found himself getting lost in her smile.

"Then I guess we'll see each other Saturday," Marina told him.

Anderson nodded his head ever so slightly. "I guess so."

Had Jake not popped up just then, Sydney's hat in his hand, Anderson would have given in to the sudden impulse that came over him to kiss Marina.

Lucky for him, Jake did pop up just then, Anderson thought.

The thing was, he didn't exactly feel all that lucky about it.

Chapter Eleven

It was getting to be a habit, coming to Anderson's ranch, Marina thought as she watched Jake play peekaboo with Sydney. A habit she had to admit that she looked forward to, maybe even a little more each time than the last.

She told herself not to, that she shouldn't—but that didn't change things. The rest of the week couldn't go by fast enough for her.

This was their third weekend here—the invitation had been extended from just one day to two. In order to keep everything light and friendly, she and Sydney went home each Saturday night, only to return the following morning, even though Jake had innocently pointed out that it would be easier on her if she and her daughter just stayed on the ranch and spent the night.

And, she also had to admit, they were becoming closer. All of them. Although she had always tried to keep her professional life separated from her personal one, there was no way she could deny that she and Jake were getting closer.

As far as she and Jake's father went, well, nothing was said but she could *feel* the barriers between them disintegrating. Despite all her promises to herself never to allow another man to get close enough to touch her soul, she knew it was happening with Anderson. Seeing his kindness to her daughter and watching the way he acted toward his son had done that—penetrated her once-impenetrable shield without so much as firing a single shot at it.

"Ms. Laramie." The way Jake said her name made her realize that he'd already said it more than once and was now trying very hard to get her attention.

"Sorry," Marina apologized. "I was thinking about something and I guess I just didn't hear you. My mistake. What did I miss?"

"That's okay, Ms. Laramie." The look on the boy's face told her that he would forgive her anything. "I just wanted to know if it was okay with you to give Sydney a ride in my wagon." He indicated the bright red, shiny wagon that Anderson had brought out to the corral earlier. "I'll prop her up in her car seat and I'll go real slow," Jake promised.

"Let me secure the car seat first," Anderson interjected, taking part in the negotiations. "I've got some rope in the barn—if it's all right with you," he qualified, looking at Marina.

She had to admit that the prospect of what Jake was suggesting made her a little nervous, but she also knew that she couldn't allow her overprotectiveness to get in the way of Sydney experiencing things.

"And you're sure you'll go slowly?" Marina asked the boy.

Jake nodded his head so hard, it looked as if it was bobbing. "Like a poky old turtle," he told her, drawing a cross over his heart.

Marina laughed. She knew he was saying that for her benefit. "That doesn't sound like it'll be all that much fun for you."

The corners of Jake's eyes crinkled. "Oh, it will be," he assured her, then confided, "I like hearing Sydney laugh."

Marina smiled and tousled his hair fondly. "So do I, Jake, so do I." It was little details like this that had allowed Jake to seep into her heart. "There's nothing sweeter than the sound of innocent laughter."

Anderson came out carrying what looked to be a leather harness instead of the rope he'd gone to fetch.

"I think this'll work better in the long run," he told Marina and then proceeded to secure Sydney's car seat to his son's wagon with the leather straps. Testing it to make sure that it wouldn't suddenly come loose or that the wagon wouldn't wind up tipping over if Jake pulled on the leather too hard, Anderson stepped back and looked at his handiwork, a satisfied expression on his face.

"You're good to go, Jake," he informed his son.

In response, Jake looked down at the infant in his wagon. "Here we go, Sydney. Hang on!" And then he looked up in Marina's direction and lowered his voice in order to tell her, "I just said that to get her excited. I'll go slowly, like I promised."

The moment he began to pull the wagon, Sydney squealed with what sounded like sheer delight.

The whole scene completely warmed Marina's heart.

She moved back, standing beside Anderson to watch her daughter being pulled along by her student.

Sydney made another happy noise.

"You know," Marina said to the man beside her, thinking of the way her daughter had lit up this morning when she'd put her in her car seat and began to head out to the Dalton ranch, "if I didn't know any better, I'd have to say that Sydney really looks forward to these outings on your ranch."

Anderson was trying his best to concentrate on watching the children and blocking out his acute awareness of just how close he was standing to Marina.

He was also trying to block out the scent of her disturbingly arousing perfume before it completely undid him. He was also trying to deal with recurring, rather urgent thoughts that kept insisting on popping up in his head. Thoughts that had absolutely nothing to do with either his child or hers.

Just her.

He had to get a tighter rein on himself, Anderson thought impatiently, silently upbraiding himself.

"She's not the only one," Anderson replied, focusing strictly on what she had just said.

The next moment, when Marina looked at him quizzically, he realized what his words must have sounded like to her. He didn't want Marina thinking he was coming on to her, especially when he was busy fighting those very inclinations.

"I mean Jake." He cleared his throat, then continued, "I was talking about Jake's looking forward to you and Sydney coming over."

She'd been wrong, Marina thought, thinking that Anderson might actually have some small, budding feelings for her. She'd misread each and every sign.

Marina felt like an idiot. She searched for a way to save a little face, as well as a shred of her own self-esteem.

"You're a good father," she told him, doing her best to sound natural, yet somewhat removed, "putting up with things just to make Jake happy."

"Things?" Anderson echoed. She'd lost him again. He was getting better at understanding female-speak, but right now, he wasn't following her train of thought. Just what was she talking about?

"Well, yes." When she saw that Anderson still didn't seem to understand her subtle reference, she patiently spelled it out for him. "Sydney and me."

It took Anderson a couple of seconds to put two and two together. She thought he didn't want her here, he thought, astonished.

"What makes you think I'm 'putting up' with you?" He knew that he wasn't exactly the warm, outgoing type, but he was fairly certain that he hadn't said anything to offend her—or at least, he hadn't meant to offend her.

Marina looked at him. Did the man actually need it spelled out for him, or was he just pretending to be clueless? Since men could very easily *be* clueless, she gave him the benefit of the doubt.

"Well, you just went to some great lengths to make it clear that it was Jake who was looking forward to our visits. What that implies is that you *aren't* looking forward to them." She looked at him, daring Anderson to contradict that.

For his part, Anderson could only stare at her incredulously. How the hell had she arrived at that conclusion? Especially since the exact opposite was true—and that in itself was what really worried him. He had caught himself looking forward to Marina's visits—and he knew that ultimately wasn't good.

"You're putting words into my mouth," he told her with a touch of annoyance—then softened his tone just a tad. He didn't want her thinking he was some surly ogre, easily offended by the use of the wrong word. "Trust me, if I didn't want you here, I would have said so—and you *wouldn't* have been here."

Marina looked at him, trying to comprehend what Anderson was actually telling her. She was getting some very mixed signals.

A small frown curved the corners of her mouth as Marina tried to get what was going on straight in her mind.

"So you're not not looking forward to our visits?" she concluded. She watched his expression to see if she'd guessed correctly.

"Isn't that some kind of a double negative? Those are supposed to cancel each other out, right?" he asked, then went on to confess almost a little sheepishly, "Grammar wasn't exactly my best subject in school."

That had to have been hard for him to admit, Marina realized. The man had a great deal of pride. She did what she could to put him at ease.

"It usually isn't anybody's best subject," she told her host. "But yes, to answer your question, a double negative does cancel itself out, making the answer a positive one."

He nodded, appreciating that she hadn't talked down to him when it could have been so easy for her to do that, given her educational background.

"I thought so," Anderson murmured, then went on

to say a little more audibly, "And for the record, I do like having you come by with the baby. I enjoy watching her light up and respond to riding on Fury and the dozen and a half other things she's been encountering."

He looked a little wistful. "I missed all that with Jake," he told Marina, not entirely realizing that he was allowing the sadness he felt over that to come through. "Missed watching him grow, watching him respond to things for the first time." His expression grew even more wistful as he spoke. "All the things that parents wind up taking for granted I never got to experience. I guess I'm trying to recapture that by watching Sydney do all those 'firsts.'"

Anderson paused for a moment, as if weighing whether or not to say what he wanted to say next. "And I guess that I really feel as if I'd been cheated," he admitted bluntly.

His words touched her. She knew how she'd feel if for some reason, her daughter had been withheld from her and she'd been unable to take part in Sydney's formative years.

Her empathy for what Anderson had to be going through grew.

As she watched Jake slowly make his way to the far end of the corral, she lightly touched Anderson's arm to get his attention—and just maybe to form a little more of a bond.

When he turned his head to look at her, Marina said, "I know it won't begin to make up for it, but feel free to experience as much as you can with Sydney."

He had no idea what made him do what he did next. Maybe it was motivated by what Marina had just said, or maybe it was the look in her eyes, a mixture of sympathy and understanding.

Or maybe it was just the woman, standing beside him at the right time, the right place.

Most likely, it was a combination of all of that plus the ache of loneliness that seemed to have taken up permanent residence in his chest. Surrounded by his siblings, his son and the rest of his extended family, not to mention being involved with more physical labor than he could shake a proverbial stick at, by evening's end he still felt very much alone—with the prospect of remaining that way.

It wasn't a prospect that filled him with any sort of even mild joy.

Most of the time, he could put up with it, block it from his mind or ignore it outright. But right now, at this moment, it was different. Right now, that loneliness ate up his oxygen and punched holes in his resolve.

And before he knew what he was doing, that loneliness was making him do it. Making him take Marina into his arms and bring his mouth down to her very tempting one.

It was, he realized, as if he had no choice in the matter. As if somewhere, in some giant book in the sky, this was written down as being inevitable, as needing to happen in order for the rest of the world to go on spinning on its axis.

Because if he didn't do this, if he didn't kiss her, then the world as it existed, as everyone knew it, would cease to be.

Anderson truthfully didn't know who was more caught off guard and surprised by the action—him, or Marina.

What he was even more surprised at was that Marina didn't pull away. On the contrary, she seemed to melt right into him, as if she had been waiting for this, as if she had known, once it happened, that it *had* to happen.

The second their lips touched, he was completely undone. Marina tasted exactly as he knew she would. She tasted of everything wondrous, spellbinding and life-affirming. And something akin to strawberries.

And he wanted more.

So very much more than he could have right at this moment.

Anderson heard her moan against his lips and excitement shot up through the roof, going from high up to completely immeasurable.

All he knew was that it was completely off the charts and far more disturbing and yet more wonderful than anything he had ever experienced or even could possibly anticipate experiencing.

He knew he should stop. A grown man would have called a halt to this even before it had begun—or at the very least, a moment after it had started.

But all he wanted to do was hang in there—hang on for dear life and savor the completely uncharted territory he had fallen, headfirst, into.

The thought gave him no peace. He had to stop. Now, before it got out of hand. Before his son made it back to where he had started his journey and saw him lip-locked with his teacher. He knew how Jake felt about his teacher—the boy had a huge crush on her—and he didn't want to be the source of heartache for his son.

A second longer, Anderson told himself, just one tiny second longer.

He wanted to remain lost in her kiss for just a second longer and then he'd pull away. No harm in letting this continue just a couple of heartbeats longer, right?

Or maybe longer than that?

"Dad, are you and Ms. Laramie getting married?" Jake asked excitedly.

And just like that, the question shattered the exquisite moment he had been sharing with Marina.

Chapter Twelve

He didn't remember doing it, didn't remember separating himself from the woman he'd just been kissing. One moment his lips were firmly pressed against hers, the next, with his son's voice ringing in his head, Anderson found himself suddenly springing away from her as if he'd just been poked—hard—by a cattle prod.

Flushing, struggling to regain his bearings, Anderson looked down at his son.

"What?" And then the boy's question replayed itself in his head. "No," he cried with feeling.

The word vibrated with such intensity that Marina felt as if she'd just been roughly slapped by the man who had just seconds earlier stirred such a wondrous kaleidoscope of feelings in her head. Feelings and sensations that caused her, just for that single instant, to actually forget all the promises that she'd made to herself regarding ever, *ever* letting her guard down.

She'd forgot that she wasn't supposed to.

But the abrupt coldness in Anderson's heartfelt denial that there was anything remotely in the offing as far as their future went swiftly brought reality crashing down all around her.

Marina felt as if she was suddenly standing in a field of ashes.

Somehow, she managed to recover, not for her own sake, but for Jake's. She'd heard the note of hope in the boy's voice. She didn't want him crushed—or led astray.

"Your father's right, dear," she assured the boy, sounding a little formal in order to keep her hurt from breaking through.

"Then why was he kissing you?" Jake wanted to know, regarding them suspiciously, as if he wasn't sure whether or not his father was telling him the truth.

"People kiss without getting married, Jake," she told him, her voice deliberately breezy. "It happens all the time." She spared Anderson a look. "It doesn't mean a thing."

Anderson couldn't tell if she was letting him off the hook because of Jake, or if she was really being serious and putting him on notice that the kiss had meant less than nothing to her.

Either way, he knew he should be relieved—except he wasn't. He felt guilty because he was fairly certain that there were still hurt feelings involved. He was really sorry if there were, but there was nothing he could do about that—at least not without compromising himself in front of his son.

This was getting way too complicated. He had more than he could handle just trying to navigate these new turbulent fatherhood waters. He had no room for the kind of baggage having a girlfriend created. Never mind that she could be something more than that, that somewhere in his misbegotten soul he might even *want* her to be more than that.

Get a grip, man. If you're not careful, you'll be going down for the third time.

Apparently, despite his teacher's disclaimer and the look on his father's face, Jake chose to see things from a different perspective.

"Oh, I don't know, it already feels like you and Dad, Sydney and me are this big happy family," he declared happily.

"Sydney and I, not Sydney and me," Marina corrected him.

But Jake was focused on the bigger picture and not something as mundane as grammar that needed correcting. His eyes lit up. "Then you agree!" Jake exclaimed gleefully.

This was getting away from her. "No, no, I'm just trying to get you to speak correctly, I didn't mean to imply that what you said was right," Marina told him helplessly.

The grin on the boy's face told her that he wasn't buying what she was telling him. It was as if he could see through all the camouflage straight down to the heart of the matter.

"Whatever you say, Ms. Laramie." He all but winked as he pretended to agree with her. Sydney was making gurgling noises and Jake looked at his lone passenger. "I think she's hungry," he announced to the two adults. "Maybe we should go back inside the house and have some lunch before she gets cranky."

Marina slanted a glance at Anderson as Jake began

to head toward the house with Sydney. "Is it my imagination, or did he suddenly become the adult?"

Anderson blew out a frustrated breath as his son walked away. "Jake certainly became something," he reluctantly agreed.

But his mind wasn't on Jake; it was on his own foolish slip. Kissing Marina had turned the ground beneath his feet to quicksand. But he wasn't going to allow himself to get sucked in again, the way he had with Lexie. Pairing up with Lexie had been a total mistake. He'd thought she was a mild-mannered and agreeable woman, only to discover that she was actually a self-centered creature with her own agenda. An agenda that had had little regard for him as a person, much less any regard for his feelings.

Though he wouldn't admit it to anyone, not even his own family, because of Lexie's deception his ego and self-esteem were still very bruised and in serious need of repair. He couldn't risk going through something like that again, not if he wanted to survive. And he *had* to survive, had to do right by his son. Jake's welfare was the only thing that mattered to him. It wasn't just himself he had to think about anymore. He had Jake to consider and put before anything else—and that definitely included putting the boy before his own self-gratification.

All he had to do to get through this afternoon, Anderson told himself, was to avoid making direct eye contact with Marina.

Easier said than done.

For the remainder of the visit, Marina did her best to act as if nothing had changed. But something definitely had.

Two somethings, actually, she thought. The first thing that had changed—and foremost in her mind—was that Anderson had kissed her. Not just a peck on the cheek or a quick, stolen kiss that was over before it had actually even begun, but a long, toe-curling, soul-changing, mind-blowing kiss that had changed the parameters of the world as she knew it.

The second, which she had a sneaking suspicion was a direct result of the first, was that she was acutely aware that for the remainder of the visit, Anderson had withdrawn from her and from the visit in general.

His interactions with her, with her daughter and even with his son were cut down to monosyllabic responses that were given in answer to any questions directed to him.

That was the act of a man who was troubled by something he had either done or was about to do. Marina had her suspicions that it was a combination of both. She tried very hard not to dwell on it and consequently, she was unable to do anything else *but* dwell on it, even though she did her best to put up a good front. She did the latter for Jake's sake because she didn't want him thinking something was wrong until that conclusion was absolutely unavoidable.

She did her best to hold it at bay as long as she could.

Because she didn't want to push her luck—or to have some sort of a confrontation suddenly erupt between Anderson and her—Marina called an early end to their time together.

The event did not go unnoticed.

"But you never leave this early," Jake protested when she announced right after she had cleared away the dishes that she and Sydney had had a lovely time, but now they had to be going home.

Marina had been afraid of this reaction from Jake, but it didn't change her mind.

"I know, honey, but Sydney's tired and I think she might be coming down with a cold. It's best if I get her home and put her to bed." She assumed that was the end of it, but she should have known better.

"We've got beds here," Jake volunteered. "Lots of beds. You could put her to bed here and maybe she'll feel better, right, Dad?" he asked, turning toward Anderson and waiting for his father to back him up.

But he was disappointed. "Jake, if Ms. Laramie wants to take Sydney home and put her to bed, she has a right to do that."

Jake looked crestfallen. "I know, but—"

He hated saying no to Jake, but this was for both their good.

"Never argue with a guest, Jake," Anderson told his son, draping a restraining arm around the boy's shoulders. "Ms. Laramie wants to take Sydney home, so we should let her do that."

The wording about the argument clearly went over Jake's head. "I thought I was arguing with you," Jake told his dad.

"Never do that, either," Marina said softly, adding her voice to the discussion and coming to Anderson's aid. "Being a dad is hard, Jake. It involves doing things that aren't always popular, but that still need to be done anyway."

Jake's face was puckered as he tried to make sense of what he was being told. It was obvious that he was having very little luck with that. Reluctantly, he gave in. "Okay—if you say so, Ms. Laramie."

Gathering her things together, Marina paused for a moment to run her hand along Jake's cheek. "You are a sweet, sweet boy, Jake. Your dad's very lucky to have you as his son," she told him.

The next moment, she snapped out of her mood and went back to gathering everything together. It seemed to her that each time she left, there were more things to take back with her—certainly more than she had brought in the first place. She looked around carefully, making sure she had everything. An uneasiness told her that she wouldn't be coming back.

As usual, Jake was right behind her, carrying as much as his short arms could hold.

And Anderson was behind him, bringing up the rear.

That, too, wasn't unusual, not in itself. He always helped her carry things to her car, but there was never this reserved air about him when he was doing it, the way there was today.

He wasn't saying a word, wasn't joining in the conversation the way he normally did. Instead, he was acting as if he was the odd man out, excluded by choice from the club of two formed by his son and his son's teacher—the woman who had, for one brief shining moment, turned his entire world upside down.

But that world had to be righted and he was determined to be the one to do it.

Jake was shifting from foot to foot, as if he was doing some strange little happy dance that only he was privy to.

"I can't wait for the week to go by and next Saturday

to come," Jake confided. "I'm going to have something special planned for Sydney," he announced happily.

"Oh? What?" Marina asked, trying her hardest to be upbeat, telling herself that she was only imagining Anderson's sudden change in behavior, that she was reading things into it when there was really nothing there to read.

Maybe the thought of being happy worried her. It brought with it its own set of demons that needed to be dealt with. The last time she recalled being too happy for words, it hadn't been long before her world came crashing down around her.

"Can't tell you," Jake answered. "'Cause if I did, then it wouldn't be a surprise for Sydney."

"I promise I won't tell her," Marina said solemnly, crossing her heart for him.

Despite that, Jake was determined to keep the surprise to himself and spring it on Sydney the following weekend.

He shook his head from side to side. "Sorry, I can't tell you. I don't want you to be tempted," he said, sounding for all the world as if he was an adult.

Marina secured Sydney's car seat in the back of her vehicle. Just before she got into her car herself, Marina turned toward Anderson and said, "Thank you for having us over again." Her gaze met his and she added with feeling, "Sydney and I had a wonderful time," even as she wondered if this was the last time she would be standing here like this.

Anderson met her words of thanks with a shrug. If she didn't know any better, she would have said that he looked relieved to see her leaving with her daughter.

"Glad you could come." He said it with as much feeling as he would have exhibited talking about his last month's telephone bill.

There was nothing left to do but leave.

Marina ruffled Jake's hair just before getting in behind the wheel. "See you bright and early in school tomorrow, young man."

Jake's eyes fairly sparkled. "You bet," he cried happily.

He hung on his father's arm as he watched the vehicle drive down the winding road. He watched until he couldn't see it anymore.

And then he had a question. "Why do you think she had to leave so early, Dad?"

Because she knows it's better this way, Anderson thought. Out loud, he addressed Jake's question. "She said it was because she was worried Sydney was coming down with a cold, remember?"

But it was obvious that Jake didn't believe that. He shook his head. "I don't think so. Sydney didn't sneeze or cough."

Anderson found himself wishing that the boy wasn't as insightful as he apparently was. "She's still the baby's mother, Jake. It's best not to interfere in family matters."

Jake sighed and then nodded. "If you say so, Dad." Turning toward the house, he began to take off.

"Where are you going in such a hurry?" Anderson wanted to know. He wasn't accustomed to seeing his son moving so fast once it was just the two of them.

Jake paused just long enough to answer him. "I thought I'd start working on Sydney's surprise for next week."

Anderson thought of the phone call he was going to

make in a little while. "Maybe you should hold off on that for a few days."

Jake stared at him for a long moment, as if trying to come to some sort of a conclusion about what his father was telling him. But after a moment, it was obvious that none had been reached.

"Why, Dad?"

He hated being put on the spot this way, hated being the one to cause his son any disappointment. But some things had to be done in the name of self-preservation. This was one of them.

"You never know when something might just go wrong, Jake. Maybe Ms. Laramie won't be able to make it next week."

But Jake shook his head. "Nothing's going to happen," he said with such total conviction, it gave Anderson pause.

But not for long.

She almost didn't pick up her phone when it rang. She certainly knew she didn't want to.

The caller ID told her that Anderson was on the line and her intuition told her she wasn't going to like what he had to say. So, for reasons of self-preservation, she almost let her machine pick it up.

But that, Marina told herself, was only putting off the inevitable. The longer she did that, the worse it would wind up being for her. So, putting her daughter down in the port-a-crib she kept for Sydney in her living room, Marina picked up the receiver.

"Hello?" she asked almost hesitantly.

"Marina," she heard the deep voice rumble in her ear, "this is Anderson Dalton."

"I know," she replied quietly, "I have caller ID. Besides, I recognize your voice. Is something wrong with Jake? Did something happen to him?" she asked, wanting to get that out of the way first. After all, it wasn't entirely inconceivable that Anderson might be calling about his son.

"No, Jake's fine," he assured her.

So much for a final desperate grasp at an excuse, she thought. "Good." Lord, this felt oddly painful, she couldn't help thinking. More painfully awkward than their first exchange that time he came storming into her classroom after hours.

Marina gathered her courage to her. "Why are you calling, then? Did I forget something back at your place?"

"No." He paused for a moment before continuing. "But I did."

Okay, he'd lost her, she thought. "I don't understand."

"I forgot not to get involved. And I am. Getting involved," he tacked on. "So I think it's best for everyone's sake if we stop getting together over the weekends."

Even though she'd tried to prepare herself for this, she felt as if someone had twisted her heart right out of her chest.

"Does Jake know?" she asked quietly.

"Jake doesn't have to know about it," Anderson said curtly. "I'm the one who make the decisions."

Then act like an adult and tell me what's going on, she wanted to shout. Instead, she said, "I know, but I just thought that since he's so involved with us coming over—"

Desperate, Anderson went to his initial go-to excuse. "People are starting to talk."

"People?" she echoed, momentarily lost. What was he talking about? "What people?"

"People-people," he said in exasperation. "You're Jake's teacher, I'm his father. I don't want anything being said or done that might compromise your job there—or my son's education. Jake needs you too much as his teacher."

"So this is about him."

Her voice was very still. Was Anderson actually trying to get her to believe that he was sacrificing something they might have in order to stop some perceived gossip that hadn't happened yet? Marina doubled her fist at her side.

"Absolutely—and your reputation."

And it has nothing to do with you running scared, she added silently. Out loud she said, "Well, I appreciate you being so concerned about my reputation, Anderson." Her voice was crisp, removed.

"Don't mention it," Anderson said, hanging up before she could say anything else that would make him lose his nerve.

He'd almost lost it twice already.

Chapter Thirteen

"I know what you're thinking."

Marina said the words out loud as she glanced at her daughter. Sydney's huge blue eyes were following her as she moved around the small apartment, trying, through sheer force of will, to somehow fill up the overwhelming emptiness and find a space for herself.

"I said I'd never be in this position again, never leave myself wide open so I could hurt like this again. And yet, here I am, doing it to myself all over again, just like the first time." Marina took in a deep breath, trying to center herself. "But it's not like Jake's dad made any promises to me, not the way I felt that your father did. You wouldn't remember him," she assured the infant. "He was gone before you were born—his loss, honey. All that means is that I'm going to love you twice as much—if that's possible." She never wanted Sydney to feel unlovable the way she had because of her father's absences. Granted, things had changed of late. Hank Laramie had come back into her sister Dawn's life and into hers, apparently wanting to make amends.

All that was well and good, but it was going to take a long time for the emptiness she'd felt while she was growing up to finally fade away. She wasn't emotionally up to taking on something more only to be disappointed. Thinking that it would be different with Anderson was a mistake. She needed to be grateful that she hadn't gone any further, hadn't made an even bigger mistake with the man.

Get over it, Marina, she told herself.

Marina blew out a breath as she sat down on the sofa. She could still feel Sydney's eyes on her. She looked down at her daughter, who, lying in her port-a-crib, was parked on the floor directly in front of the sofa.

She needed to talk this out of her system, she thought.

"But Jake's dad, well," she said wistfully, "I was really beginning to think that you and I had a future with him. He's trying really hard to be a good dad to Jake and I could tell he had a weakness for you—who wouldn't?" she asked with a laugh. "So all that seemed really promising to me. A lot of guys run when fatherhood is sprung on them."

And she would be the first to testify to that, Marina thought, remembering the expression on Gary's face the evening she had told him that she was pregnant with his baby.

"And when Anderson kissed me, Sydney," she said, reliving the very intense moment, "Oh, when he kissed me, I thought that we were both on to something very special. Something with promise." She sighed as she picked up the remote control from the side table. "I guess I just let my imagination get carried away."

Turning on the flat-screen that hung on the wall across from her, Marina began trolling through the channels, searching for something that would be distracting enough to make her forget about the ever growing ache she felt.

"Anyway, it looks like it's going to be just you and me tonight, kidlet. What are you in the mood for?"

Sydney seemed to scrunch up her face and make an emphatic noise.

Marina put her own meaning to the sound. "Yeah, me, too. But Jake and his dad aren't coming over tonight. Or, probably, not tomorrow night or the night after that," she added, sadly. "But we'll get by, you and I." She tried to put as much positive energy into the statement as she could. "We did it before, we'll do it again."

As if in response, Sydney made another noise and Marina forced a resigned smile to her lips. "You're right. I don't believe me, either. But I'm going to give it a really good try. We're *not* going to let this bring us down."

She only hoped she could live up to those words.

It was a small town and, realistically, Marina knew that it was only to be expected that their paths would cross sometime or other. But, despite the fact that she was a full-time teacher and that Anderson was a full-time rancher, for some unknown reason, their paths seemed to be crossing *all* the time.

So much so that it seemed to be happening almost every day.

When Anderson came to pick up Jake or when she made a quick stop at the supermarket, all she had to do was look up and there the man was, almost in her space. And, when she did look in his direction, she saw Anderson ducking his head down, pretending that he hadn't been looking her way.

The hell he wasn't.

It was a ridiculous game they were playing and they both knew it, she thought. And yet, they continued playing it.

The first time she'd accidentally run into Anderson, it was because she'd noticed that one of her students—Hannah McKay—had left her math book on her desk. Since the girl needed the book in order to do the assigned math homework that night, Marina had grabbed it and hurried after the girl, who had left the classroom, along with the other students, less than five minutes earlier.

Hurrying from the classroom, Marina had dashed out into the hallway and out the front door—straight into Anderson Dalton. She'd almost managed to knock both of them down from the force of the impact. Anderson had steadied himself at the last moment and automatic reflexes had him catching her by her shoulders before she fell.

For one prolonged second they looked at one another, each surprised beyond words to see the other. Surprised and almost undone. It took another very long moment before they were able to recover themselves.

Marina did it first, bracing her shoulders and stiffening as she took a very deliberate step back, away from him.

"Sorry," she apologized almost woodenly, "I didn't mean to almost knock you down. I was in a hurry to catch—Hannah!" she called, seeing the girl and trying to get her attention. "I'm sorry," she apologized again, pulling herself entirely out of Anderson's hold. "I need to give this to her."

She held the book aloft as if to offer proof that her story was genuine and not just a mere desperate fabrication.

With that, she pulled herself away and quickly headed in the girl's direction.

Jake had been a stunned, silent witness to the whole thing.

"That was Ms. Laramie," he pointed out needlessly to his father.

Anderson's heart literally felt like lead in his chest as he replied, "Yes, I know."

"Don't you want to talk to her?" Jake asked with a barely veiled desperate note in his voice. His eyes darted from his father to the teacher and then back again.

"Not particularly." It was a lie, but he forced himself to utter it. "I'd rather talk to you," Anderson said, draping an arm around his son's shoulders. "So how was today?"

Jake's momentary lighthearted display of exuberance, Anderson noticed, was conspicuously gone as Jake answered his question, prefacing it with a heavy sigh, "Okay, I guess."

And so began his son's rather pronounced downward spiral.

It grew, Anderson noticed, a little more intense with each day that passed. And, as those days went by, Anderson found himself questioning his own actions and his reasoning behind the path he had decided to take with Marina.

Maybe going this route did prevent him from making any kind of personal mistakes he might find himself regretting in the near future, but this route also seemed to be taking all the liveliness, all the energy out of Jake. Within one short week, they were suddenly back where they started from, with his being the parent of a robot who was far more connected to his video games than he was to him.

The light, Anderson had noticed, had gone out of Jake's eyes.

And then something happened that made his own actions and Jake's reactions to what he'd done seem to be totally moot.

Jake's mother, Lexie, showed up on his doorstep unannounced.

She came breezing up to the ranch just the same way she had when she'd decided—seemingly out of the blue—that Jake needed to spend some "quality time" with his father. That was when she'd just deposited the boy on his doorstep as if he was no more than a package that needed to be posted.

But this time when she showed up, she announced that she was here to take back what she had so carelessly left behind.

"That's right," she said to Anderson in no uncertain terms, "I've come to take Jake home."

Her bluntly stated intentions almost left him speechless. How could she just barrel in like a tornado and take away his son without so much as blinking her eyes? Didn't she realize how destructive that was for Jake's morale? Never mind how it affected him personally.

He tried his best to make her understand, to see beyond her own selfish point of view.

"But this is Jake's home now," Anderson protested.

The annoyed, exasperated expression on her face told Anderson just what the woman thought of his argument. Less than nothing.

"Correction, this was just someplace he was spending some time—until I came back for him. Well, I came back for him," she announced, as if that wasn't already painfully apparent.

Anderson fisted his hands at his sides to keep from wrapping them around her throat and strangling the selfish, thoughtless woman.

"He's not a football you can just punt back and forth," Anderson insisted.

Lexie looked at him as if he was babbling. "Of course he's not. Look, all I did was let him spend some time with you because you were so adamant about spending time with *him*," she concluded as if that answered everything.

"I was adamant a year ago," Anderson reminded her. "And you refused to let me have Jake. Why did you suddenly change your mind twelve months later?" he challenged.

Lexie shrugged her shoulders, a look of disinterested annoyance on her face. "Because I'm big enough to admit that I was wrong. A boy does need to spend some time with his father. But he's spent it and now I'm taking him back."

It all sounded too pat to him. Lexie was up to something; he'd bet his soul on it.

"Is that the only reason?" he asked, pinning her with a look. "And I warn you, there are ways to find out if you're telling me the truth."

Lexie blew out a breath, her hands on her hips. He could see the frustration clearly on her face, no doubt because nothing was going according to her plans. She was a woman who was used to things falling into her lap the way she had hoped. But not this time.

The frustration boiled over and Lexie snapped. "I wanted to spend some quality time with Raul, okay?" she said, telling him the real reason for Jake's sudden transplant earlier in July.

"Raul?" Anderson echoed, confused. "Who the hell is Raul?"

"Raul is history," Lexie answered with finality, "so there's no point in talking about him. What's important here is that I'm putting you on notice," she emphasized. "I want my son back and I'm going to take him with me. Now be a good soldier," she ordered sarcastically, "and tell Jake so that he's ready to go back to Chicago in five days."

And with that, the woman breezed out again, leaving ashes and ruin in her wake.

Anderson stood looking after her, the words *five days* echoing over and over again in his head.

"Jake, if your face was any longer, we'd have to put cones around it to keep people from tripping on it," Marina pointed out kindly the following Monday morning.

The rest of the class had gone out for recess, but Jake, she'd noticed, remained where he was, staring off into space and completely oblivious to what was going on around him.

Marina made her way over to his row and sat down in the seat right in front of the boy. The haunted, sad expression on his face tore at her heart.

Turning around in order to face him, she asked in a kindly voice, "What's wrong, Jake?"

Jake refused to look at her and kept staring off into space. But she could see the sheen of tears forming in his eyes.

"Nothing," he mumbled, saying the word so quietly, had she not been sitting right in front of him, she wouldn't have been able to hear it.

She was not about to give up and let him have his space. This was too important and he was too tortured to leave alone.

"No, I know 'nothing' and this is definitely not 'nothing.' Now out with it," she ordered kindly. "You've been looking as if you lost your best friend or your beloved pet all morning long. Please tell me what's wrong."

Jake raised his eyes to hers and for a moment, she thought he was just going to maintain his silence on the subject.

But then he sighed.

It was a long, heartfelt sigh that seemed to come from the very depths of his toes and raked right over his heart. She could see that saying the words hurt him a great deal. "It's just that I'm not going to be here much longer."

This was the first time she was hearing this and it hit her with the force of a well-delivered punch to the stomach, stealing the very air out of her lungs.

"Oh? Why?" she asked, surprised. "Where are you going?" She wanted to know.

He was clearly miserable as he spoke, staring down at his shoes. It was as if his head felt too heavy to hold up.

"Mom says home, but it doesn't feel like it's home anymore. Is that weird?" he asked her, looking up. "I mean, I've been here just a couple of months and I've been there all my life, but when I think of 'home,' I think of here." The corners of his mouth turned completely down and for a moment, Marina thought that he was going to cry. But then he managed to hold himself together. "Except that I won't be here soon."

To say she was stunned was a vast understatement.

"Are you sure about this?" she asked Jake.

Jake bobbed his head up and down and his expression seemed to just grow sadder by degrees as he replied, "Yes, I'm sure. I heard Dad talking to Mom and she told him that she was taking me back. Ms. Laramie, I don't want to go," he told her plaintively. There was a hitch in his voice, as if he was doing his best not to cry. "Do I hafta?"

It wasn't her place to raise the boy's hopes, or to dash them, either. So, as much as she would have wanted to say something to bolster his morale, Marina forced herself to go for neutral ground.

"What does your dad say?" she asked him, fervently praying that Anderson had told the boy something she could expand on.

Again the small shoulders rose and fell. "He didn't say too much—and he looked kind of sad." Jake's eyes begged her to say something positive he could cling to.

There wasn't much to work with there, but she did her best. "That's because he doesn't want you to go."

The look on his face was just breaking her heart. "You think so?"

In her heart, she all but cursed Anderson for not promising the boy he could stay at his home until all appeals were exhausted—hopefully, by then, Jake's flaky mother would have lost interest in whatever game she was trying to play.

"Oh, I'm sure of it."

But Jake was not a boy to be easily fooled or put off. "Then why doesn't he tell Mom no?"

Although she hated to do it, Marina gave him a one-size-fits-all excuse. "I'm afraid it's not that simple, honey."

Jake refused to let it go. He fought to understand. His immediate future depended on it.

"Why not? I don't want to go and he doesn't want me to go. That's two against one, Ms. Laramie," he pointed out. "Doesn't that win?"

Oh, Jake, if only. "In a democracy," she said out loud, "yes, it does. But I'm afraid that this is different."

Jake clearly didn't understand—and he wanted to. "How?"

She smiled sadly at him as she caressed his cheek and shook her head. "If that were easy to answer, there wouldn't be any need for lawyers in this world, honey."

For the first time in a week, Jake's face lit up. "Dad says that my grandpa's a lawyer. Does that help any?" he asked hopefully.

"That's true," Marina said. "Well, then, maybe that *can* help," she told the boy. "Maybe your dad's going to talk to your grandpa to see if maybe there's a way to convince your mother to allow you to live here—or to at least let you stay until the end of the school year."

A small smile began to curve the corners of his mouth. "That would be good," Jake agreed. "Because I really like school, Ms. Laramie—and I really like coming to your class every day."

She could feel tears stinging her eyes. In such a short time, the boy had managed to burrow his way into her heart.

Like father, like son, she couldn't help thinking.

"Well, thank you, Jake. I really like having you as my student," she replied with feeling.

It was all that she would allow herself to say at the moment. In her heart she knew that yanking Jake out of school just when he was finally getting adjusted to it would be doing a grave disservice to the boy, never mind what it would do to his father or the blow that Anderson would suffer in having to give the boy up again so soon after having finally gained what had seemed like at least partial custody of his son.

It made her wonder about the kind of woman Jake's mother was. Wonder, too, what Anderson could have seen in her in the first place. From what she understood, there had been no long-standing relationship that had turned sour. Instead, there had been a brief interlude and ten years later, Anderson was made aware—by accident—that the interlude had resulted in his son. A son that Jake's mother had no intentions of sharing—until she did.

The woman, Marina couldn't help thinking, had some very serious stability issues. But that wasn't really the point. The point of it—and of everything—was Jake's welfare and making Jake smile again.

She just had to come up with a way, Marina told herself—a way acceptable to everyone—to make that happen.

Chapter Fourteen

Lexie went back on her word.

Anderson didn't know why that even mildly surprised him. After all, it wasn't as if the woman was exactly trustworthy. Initially, she had said that she was going to give Jake five days to get used to the idea of returning to Chicago before she came to get him.

But she didn't give Jake five days, she gave him three. Three days with no warning of what was about to happen.

Just like that, when he was sitting down to dinner with his son, Lexie descended on both of them like some dire, deadly form of the medieval black plague.

She knocked on the front door and when Anderson opened the door, just like that, she made her announcement.

Pushing past him, Lexie looked around the room for their son. When she didn't see him immediately, she turned on Anderson and declared, "He's coming with me *now*."

Anderson stared at her, stunned. He continued holding the door open for a moment longer, hoping she would take the hint and leave.

She didn't.

"You said he had five days," Anderson protested, following her into the foyer.

Lexie's annoyed expression told him that she had no patience with any delaying tactics. "And now I'm saying he doesn't. Why does everything have to be an argument with you?" she demanded.

"I could say the same to you," Anderson shot back.

And then he caught a glimpse of Jake out of the corner of his eye. The boy had followed him out to the living room. Right now, Jake looked as if he was cowering in the wake of their raised voices.

Anderson forced himself to lower his. He wasn't doing Jake any good by fighting with Lexie this way and ultimately, the woman had the law on her side. She was Jake's mother and she was the one who had legal custody of the boy. He was going to do whatever he could to change that, but right at this moment, he knew the end result of tonight's confrontation: she'd take Jake with her.

The thought almost killed him.

"Let him stay the two days, Lexie. What harm could it do?" Anderson asked, trying to appeal to her sense of fair play—even though he was certain that she ultimately didn't have any.

"The 'harm' is that those are two extra days I have to hang around this flyspeck of a town instead of flying back to a civilized world. As it is, I've let you two play house longer than I should have. Now hear this. Playtime is over. I want my son and I want to go home," she bit off angrily. Her eyes narrowed as she demanded, "Make it happen."

Jake grabbed his arm imploringly as he all but hid on his other side, the side away from his mother. "Dad, please don't let her take me. I want to stay here with you and Ms. Laramie and Sydney. Please, Dad. *Please*," Jake begged.

It was as if someone had waved a red flag in front of Lexie. "Who the hell are Ms. Laramie and Sydney?" she demanded hotly. She turned on Anderson. "Just what kind of perverted carryings-on have you been having here, Anderson?"

He dug down deep for patience—and to hold on to his temper.

"Ms. Laramie is his teacher and Sydney is her little girl," he told her evenly, doling out each word one at a time. "Jake wants to feel like he's part of a family unit and they provide that for him."

He couldn't have said anything worse to her if he'd tried. Lexie's complexion reddened as her eyes flashed with anger.

"He *is* part of a family," she retorted, grabbing the boy's arm. "He's part of *my* family." Lexie huffed angrily. "I was crazy to let you have him," she declared. "Let's go, Jake," she ordered.

Jake tried to dig in his heels. "But my things—" he protested.

"Your father will send them," Lexie snapped. Holding on to his arm tightly, she all but dragged the boy to the door.

Anderson wanted to stop her, wanted to grab the boy

and pull him away from this woman he regarded as a she-devil, but he refused to turn his son into the living embodiment of a game of tug-of-war.

So all he could do was appeal to her humanity, which was, he knew even as he did it, a completely lost cause. He did it anyway.

"Lexie, please don't do this."

"What I shouldn't have done," she informed him as she opened the front door, still tightly holding on to Jake, "was go out with you that night twelve years ago. *That's* what I shouldn't have done."

And with that, Lexie stormed out of the house with Jake in tow, slamming the door so hard behind her, it shook.

Rage ate away at him.

Anderson struggled with the almost overpowering urge to go after the woman and take back his son. But that wouldn't solve anything and if he knew Lexie, this would wind up with her getting the sheriff to come back with her and haul Jake away. The whole thing would be very traumatic for Jake and that wasn't something he wanted to do to the boy.

And, though it cost him dearly, he didn't want Jake hating his mother, either. At least not on his account.

But that still didn't keep him from wanting to strangle Lexie.

The palms of his hands itched.

The law offices of Ben Dalton were in a simple, tidy looking one story building near the center of town. The decor was on the masculine side and subtly inspired a feeling of confidence in the average person who walked through the front doors.

As Anderson came through those doors, he found himself hoping that there was something to that.

Nodding at the receptionist who presided over the office's centrally located front desk, Anderson asked, "Is my father in?"

"He has a meeting scheduled with a client in twenty minutes," she told him.

"Then I'll be quick," Anderson promised as he went past her, heading toward his father's office.

Knocking once, he walked in before his father could tell him to enter.

Ben Dalton, tall, distinguished-looking, with a hint of gray just beginning at his temples, wore his age well. He was blessed with a poker face, but he looked surprised to see his firstborn. Anderson rarely made an appearance in his world.

"Something wrong on the ranch?" Ben wanted to know, saying the first thing that came to mind.

"Only in a general sense," Anderson answered. He paused for a second, trying to get his thoughts in order. His brain felt as if it had been haphazardly tossed in the air and he was having trouble thinking. "Technically, this has nothing to do with the ranch. Just with me," he added before finally making his appeal, "Dad, I need your help."

The slight crease in his brow was the only indication that Ben Dalton was concerned. Very concerned. "What is it?"

"I know that this isn't the kind of case you normally handle," Anderson prefaced, "but I need help in getting custody of my son."

Ben squared his shoulders just a tad. This was still a sore point between them, Anderson knew. Not that Anderson had a son, but that he had known he had one for a year and hadn't said anything to his father until the boy had suddenly turned up on the ranch, forcing introductions to be made.

Ben raised his chin. "You mean the grandson I didn't know about until just recently?"

Anderson pressed his lips together. He didn't want to get into that squabble right now. This was far more important. "Yes, that one."

Ben nodded, as if tucking what was being said into its proper corners. "Before we go on, is there anything else you're keeping from me?"

Anderson sighed. Obviously he wasn't going to be able to just set this aside until later. "Dad, I didn't tell you about Jake when I found out because there wasn't anything I could do to even get Lexie to give me visitation rights. I thought telling you about a grandson you weren't even allowed to see was cruel, so I decided not to say anything." He set his mouth hard. "This isn't the time to make me pay for that."

"No," Ben agreed, "You're right, this isn't." He turned his attention to the immediate problem at hand. "It's going to be an uphill battle," he warned his son. "You don't need the extra pressure of my needling you. Let me ask around," Ben proposed, "and see what I can come up with." His face softened with understanding, as if speaking as one father to another. "She just appeared out of the blue and took him, huh?"

Anger creased his features. "Like he was a piece of forgotten luggage she swooped in to pick up," Anderson said in utter disgust.

Ben shook his head. "I certainly hope your taste in women has improved since then." Before Anderson could respond to that, he held up his hand to silence him. "While I'm looking into this, you might try running the details by your sister," Ben suggested.

Anderson's thoughts were still colliding into one another. For a moment, he didn't follow his father. "Which one?"

"The one who's a lawyer," Ben prompted. "Now that she's graduated, Lindsay's joined the firm. She's already got a case," he said with a measure of fatherly pride. "The parents of that baby who was hospitalized after contracting RSV at Just Us Kids day care are looking into the possibility of filing a lawsuit. Your sister's investigating whether the day care center followed proper procedures or if that baby getting sick is a direct result of their negligence."

Realizing that he'd digressed, Ben changed direction. "She's set up her office down the hall and is already hunting for more clients," he told his son. "In the meantime, I'll make some calls about your options and get back to you with what I come up with."

Anderson was already heading out the door to see his sister. "Thanks, Dad."

"Thank me *after* I come up with something," Ben advised as he picked up his phone.

As he headed down the hall, Anderson discovered that Lindsay's door was open. Looking in, he saw that the inside of the small office looked as if it had been hit by a hurricane.

Hurricane Lindsay, he thought with a smile.

Knocking on the door frame, Anderson walked in as his sister looked over her shoulder in his direction. "Dad said I should look in on you."

Lindsay froze. At twenty-five, the five-foot-five

young woman with her long brown hair and penetrating blue eyes was the baby of the family. The position came with perks as well as with a stigma.

"What did I do now?" she questioned wearily.

Anderson shrugged. "Nothing that I know of," he told her honestly. "Dad thought that you might be able to help me."

She was no more enlightened than she'd been a minute ago. "Help you how?"

"Lexie took Jake back home yesterday." No matter how casual he tried to sound about it, saying the words still hurt.

Lindsay stopped putting leather-bound books on her bookshelves and immediately made her way over to her big brother. She threw her arms around him to embrace him in a heartfelt hug.

"Oh, Anderson, I'm so sorry," she said, releasing him and stepping back to look at him as she spoke. "I really liked the little guy."

"Yeah, me, too," Anderson said heavily. "He didn't want to go, Lindsay. Lexie practically dragged him out of the house."

Apparently unable to imagine something so heartless, Lindsay shook her head. "You have lousy taste in women, big brother."

"So I keep being told," Anderson responded with a sigh. And then, desperate, he got down to business. "That's not the point, Linds. I need help in getting custody of Jake."

Far more familiar with the prospect than her father, Lindsay shook her head.

"It's not going to be easy," she told her brother, then got down to the specifics he would be battling. "You're a single dad who works long hours on his ranch and has zero experience with kids," she told him, pointing out all the things that she knew Lexie's lawyer would ultimately cite.

"Lexie's a single mother," Anderson protested. From his point of view, they were both facing the same handicap.

"The key word here is not *single*," Lindsay pointed out, "but *mother*. I don't like it," she admitted, "but unless Lexie has done something really awful that can be held against her, the judge will be inclined to award custody to her if that's what she's asking for.

"But let me look into this," she told Anderson once she saw her brother's dejected expression. "Maybe I can come up with some last-ditch plan. Give me a little bit," she asked.

What choice did he have, Anderson thought. Shrugging, he said, "Sure."

What else could he do?

When Anderson heard the knock on his door later that day, his first thought was to pretend he wasn't home. He wasn't up to seeing anyone, or pretending that he felt like talking.

But then he thought that maybe it was either his father or Lindsay—or both—here to see him about a possible custody strategy. Doing his best to raise his spirits in order to be able to face company—even his family—he went to answer the door.

It occurred to him just a beat before he opened the door that his father or Lindsay were far more likely to call than to just show up on the doorstep even though this was the family ranch, but by then it was too late. He was already opening the door.

And looking at Marina.

He did *not* feel like talking to the woman. Being polite, much less friendly, required far more effort than he had to give.

"If you're here to find out why Jake wasn't in school today, you're too late," he informed her coldly. "He's gone. His mother took him home to Chicago."

She was here for another reason, but Anderson's statement caught her off guard. Her heart ached for the boy. How could the woman have just dragged him away like that?

"I thought she wasn't supposed to be doing that until the weekend."

"Yeah, we all thought that," Anderson responded, making no effort to hide his bitterness. "But apparently she had other ideas. So, if there's nothing else," he began, ready to close the door again.

But Marina deftly slipped across the threshold and into his living room. Turning to look at him, she observed, "You look awful."

He didn't need to be told that, he knew. "Not exactly my finest hour," he told her crisply, then added in a voice that sounded far more forlorn, "I feel like a fool."

"Because she took him from you?" Marina questioned. That didn't make any sense to her. Jake's mother coming to take the boy back to Chicago with her certainly wasn't Anderson's fault.

"Because I actually thought she'd had a change of heart," he corrected. "Turns out she just needed someplace to dump Jake while she went off with her new lover. But apparently that relationship went sour pretty quickly—like so many of her *other* relationships—so she wanted Jake back. And she got him," he concluded with no small bitterness.

"Just like that?" Marina questioned. It took her breath away to think about it. Didn't the woman have any decency? She was traumatizing her own son. "How could she be so insensitive not to see that Jake was actually beginning to adjust to living here? To being *happy* here?" Marina protested.

Bitterness curved the corners of Anderson's mouth downward. "Lexie only sees what she wants to see. The rest she just blocks out at will," he recalled.

"That certainly doesn't sound like she'd be a candidate for the world's greatest mother," Marina told him. There was only one important point here. "You have to get Jake back."

Helpless, Anderson shrugged. *Tell me something I don't know*, he thought darkly.

Out loud he told her, "I don't know what else I can do. Supposedly, I have visitation rights. But if I try to get custody of Jake away from her, Lexie is threatening to revoke those visitation rights and I'll be back to where I was a year ago. Nowhere," he underscored angrily. "Besides," he told her, already resigned to his fate—and hating it, "it wouldn't be fair keeping Jake away from his mother just because I have an ax to grind with the woman."

Was he serious? Jake's mother sounded like she was some kind of a monster. Jake would do well to be rid of her. But Marina knew she couldn't come out and say that, at least not yet.

"Why don't you try to get joint custody?" she wanted

to know. To her, that was the first thing she would have thought of.

"My father and sister are already looking into it for me, but to be honest, I really doubt anything will come of that. Let's face it, with my background, if Lexie fights me on this, the court will side with her and, like I said, if she gets angry enough, she'll pull the rug right out from under me and I won't be able to see Jake at all. This is a case of something being better than nothing," he told her, resigned.

Marina thought for a moment, debating saying what was on her mind out loud. Then she decided to go for it. A boy's happiness was at stake.

Choosing her words carefully, she instantly piqued Anderson's attention when she asked him, "What if, when you applied for joint custody of your son, your situation changed?"

Chapter Fifteen

Anderson looked at his son's teacher, confusion, not to mention frustration over the situation he found himself in, claiming his ability to think straight.

"Exactly what do you mean by 'changed'?" he wanted to know.

Marina spoke slowly, weighing each word as she attempted to decide if what she was about to suggest to Anderson would be welcomed—or rejected—by him. "Well, according to what you just said, it sounds like your chances of getting at least joint custody would be much better if the judge thought that you were a family man."

By some people's definition, just having Jake made him a family man. But he had a feeling that Marina wasn't talking about that.

"And by family man you mean…?"

Anderson still wasn't getting it because he was certain that she couldn't possibly be saying what he thought she was saying.

"I mean the usual thing," Marina replied. She was going to have to spell it out for him, wasn't she? *Okay,* she thought, resigned, *here goes nothing.* She hit the ground running. "A two-parent household with a schoolteacher mom—"

Maybe it shouldn't have, but the description hit him with the force of a two-by-four. He was stunned to say the least.

"Meaning you?"

"Meaning me," she confirmed almost as an aside, and then continued laying out the scenario. "It would certainly hold some sway with a judge and give you the leverage you need to be able to get cust—"

"Wait," he ordered, still looking at her in complete disbelief. "Are you *actually* saying that you would be willing to make this sacrifice for Jake? That you'd be willing to marry me so that I could get joint custody of my son?"

Yes, you idiot, that's what I'm saying. What did you think I was saying?

But she couldn't say the words out loud. She was afraid that Anderson would turn her down after she'd put herself on the line like this for him, or that he would accuse her of having some sort of ulterior motive. Instead, Marina asked him a question of her own.

"How would you feel about that?" She carefully watched his expression to gauge what Anderson was thinking.

"How would I feel?" Anderson echoed incredulously.

"Yes," she replied patiently, "That's what I just asked."

"How would I feel?" Anderson repeated again, stunned as well as overjoyed by the very magnitude of the sacrifice she was offering to make. "I'll show you how I feel," he cried.

Overwhelmed and thrilled by her offer and what it would ultimately mean for Jake, Anderson abruptly dropped his guard as well as his very controlled behavior. He literally grabbed Marina, pulled her to him and kissed her. Kissed her long and hard.

Kissed her with every fiber of the immense gratitude that throbbed within him.

"Lord, I don't know how to thank you," he cried, breathless.

Shaken down to her very core, Marina struggled to sound flippant and blasé rather than like someone who was very close to dissolving like hot candle wax.

"I think you just did," she heard herself murmur.

It was a complete mystery to Marina how she could remain standing upright when it felt as if her kneecaps had been completely melted away in the heat that was generated by Anderson's kiss.

And then, as she watched, she saw Anderson's expression sobering, going from pure joy to solemnity. Instantly, she felt her heart sinking.

"What's wrong?" she asked him.

All sorts of roadblocks were beginning to pop up in his head. "There's still the problem of the no-fraternizing rule at school," he told her.

Was that all? she thought, almost laughing out loud. "Well, that's easy enough to solve," she assured him.

The woman obviously had clearer insight into things than he had, Anderson thought. The tiniest spark of hope began to burn again even as he admitted, "I don't see how."

Anderson was too close to it, she thought. And too consumed with worry to see the actual picture. She did what she could to clear it up for him.

"If Jake's back in Chicago, then I'm not his teacher anymore. And if I'm not his teacher, then I'm not fraternizing with the parent of one of my students, am I?" she asked, spreading her hands as if to bring her point home. "Problem solved," she announced.

For her trouble, Marina found herself being hugged again. Hugged, and whirled around the room and then finally, kissed again.

Maybe it was just her imagination, but each time Anderson kissed her, his lips felt even more lethal to her than the last time. Now it wasn't just her knees but her whole body that felt like it was melting.

She was barely aware of putting her arms around his neck, but she needed to anchor herself to something while the foundation of her very world was rocked down to its bottom layer of concrete.

For the first time in his life, Anderson felt almost giddy. He told himself that the sensation rose out of relief, and not out of the fact that he was going to be marrying a woman who could, just by kissing him, make his mind go completely blank, even while the rest of him craved something far more substantial, far more basic than euphoria.

What she was doing just by kissing him was turning his very world upside down and making him forget every single one of the rules he had laid out for himself. Rules that had brought order to his life and to his very existence.

Those rules did not allow for him to even remotely entertain the idea of falling in love.

He blocked the thought from his mind and focused instead on the pragmatic side of what was happening.

Because of Marina's sacrifice, he was going to be able to have his son back in his life on a regular basis. He knew that he would always be eternally grateful to her for that.

And because he *was* trying to be pragmatic, he forced himself to examine everything, to leave nothing to last-minute upheavals.

"You're sure about this?" he questioned Marina. His eyes all but pinned her down intently. "About marrying me?"

"This would be a terrible time for me to shout, 'April Fools,'" she replied. Then, in case he was actually harboring any doubts, she quickly added, "Yes, I'm sure."

It should have satisfied him, he told himself—but it didn't. Because Lexie had turned on him so abruptly after their one night together, it had left a lasting impression on him. A very sour lasting impression. And that didn't begin to take into account the way she had kept his only son's very existence from him, then denied him any access to the boy once he did know about Jake.

It had made Anderson feel very leery and it caused him to be suspicious of everything. Especially something that seemed to be too good to be true. What if he was being set up for some reason? He couldn't abide something like that. Not again.

He looked at Marina. "What's in it for you?" he wanted to know.

Because her only thoughts were about Anderson and his son, his question completely threw her. "Excuse me?"

Impatience clawed at him. He hated how suspicious he'd become, but there was no getting away from it. His only recourse was to try to pin her down—and to hope she was as selfless as her actions painted her to be.

"Marrying me, giving up for your freedom so I can get custody of Jake, what's in it for you?" Anderson asked.

Obviously he didn't believe she was doing this because she simply cared about the boy. She was going to have to convince him, Marina thought.

"You're not the only one who loves Jake," she said. "I'm doing this—offering to marry you—because Jake has every right to be happy. Because he's a terrific kid and I think he'd make a really good big brother for Sydney." She took a breath, knowing that she was crossing a line. But this had to be said. "And I'm doing it because, no offense, I think his mother is a witch and I'm afraid of how she might wind up warping his soul if she has sole custody of him.

"Jake is a good, decent, sweet kid who deserves to have a parent who puts his needs first, not a parent who sees him as an impediment to her next tryst." She stopped and looked at the expression on Anderson's face. She couldn't quite read it. *Had* she said too much? "What? Did I go too far?" she asked him.

Maybe he was still in love with Lexie despite everything the woman had done to him, Marina thought. Maybe he even resented her criticism of Jake's mother. In that case, she needed to backtrack—but she couldn't.

"I'm sorry," she apologized. "But that's what I think."

"Don't apologize," he told her, his voice stoic and completely unreadable.

"Okay," she said slowly, still feeling as if she was

standing on ground that could, just like that, turn to quicksand. "But you still have this expression on your face that I can't quite make out. What are you thinking?" she forced herself to ask, feeling as if she really didn't have anything to lose at this point.

"What I'm thinking," he told her in very slow, deliberately measured out words, "is that I don't know how I got so lucky."

Marina blinked, certain that she had misheard him. It was just her desperate need to make him understand why she was ready to go through with this for him that had her putting words into Anderson's mouth.

"Excuse me?" she said in a soft voice.

"I said," he repeated, speaking louder, "I don't know how I got this lucky."

Somehow, his words were not penetrating her head. Maybe her own disbelief was preventing her from absorbing what he was telling her. She took a stab at clarifying things for herself. "You mean to get someone to marry you so that you could get custody of Jake."

Maybe she didn't want to put any more emphasis on what was actually happening between them than that, Anderson thought. Maybe admitting that there might be more going on than a simple convenient arrangement was too scary for her.

He could certainly identify with that, Anderson thought, what with the episode with Lexie looming in his past. He'd be willing to bet that Marina had gotten burned herself by the man who'd gotten her pregnant. For that matter, all she really knew about *him* was that he was Jake's father and that he desperately wanted custody of the boy.

Not exactly something to build forever on with a man,

he thought. Especially when that man had suddenly and abruptly severed all ties with her after a month of some pretty good, not to mention intense weekends, he rationalized. Looking back, he realized that he could have handled that so much better than he had.

He needed to make amends for that, Anderson told himself.

He also told himself that right now, it would be for the best if he just went with the scenario that she had handed him. They were both going to do this—to marry one another—for Jake's sake, so that he could come back to Rust Creek Falls.

"Yeah," Anderson agreed. "What you said."

And then, because Marina made him feel so exuberantly happy, Anderson found himself kissing her again.

And again.

Because each time, it was better than the last and it made him want to sample the next time. And the next.

So, just for this very short interlude in time, he did.

Deepening the kiss, Anderson kissed her as if there was no tomorrow, no moments to follow this one. All there was, was now.

But it was enough.

"Last chance to change your mind," Anderson warned her several days later.

They were standing in a room that was right outside a judge's chambers in Kalispell. Instead of being in a church filled with her friends and her sister, Dawn, and Dawn's new husband, Marina would soon be facing a middle-aged man who had only a fringe of hair to call his own and a solemn air about him that made her think of her first elementary school principal, Mr. Oshinsky.

But those were just trappings, Marina reminded herself. Just the mere daydreams of an adolescent girl who was given to romanticizing things. They *weren't* what was really important here.

All that mattered was Jake—and of course Sydney, both of whom, with this one short act on her part, would be getting a kind, loving man as their father. Jake would be getting him because of course Anderson was his father, and Sydney would be getting him because both Jake and Anderson were crazy about her. They would make certain that her little girl would be getting a loving home out of this arrangement.

So, if she was sacrificing bells and whistles, as well as a misty dose of romance and all the things that went with it, well, she was a big girl, Marina told herself. The benefits to be gotten out of this union far outweighed what she was giving up.

"Marina?" Anderson softly prodded, obviously waiting for her response to his question.

Embarrassed to be caught mentally adrift this way, Marina flushed and apologized to him quickly. "I'm sorry, what?"

Anderson repeated his question, concerned that maybe she didn't answer because she *didn't* want to go through with this arrangement after all.

"I asked if you're sure about going through with this."

Marina raised her chin defensively. "Of course I'm sure. I wouldn't be here if I wasn't," she told him with conviction. "My only regret is that you couldn't get Jake to be here."

He didn't want to think about the conversation he'd had with Lexie just yesterday. The memory of the sound of her voice would be enough to put him in a bad mood and Marina deserved better than that for the sacrifice she was making for him.

All he would let himself say was, "Lexie's not convinced it's going to happen and she didn't want to allow Jake to fly out here until after she was sure we'd gone through with it."

That was one highly suspicious woman, Marina thought. Everything she'd heard about Lexie so far had her thoroughly disliking her.

"Didn't you tell her that you'd pay for the plane ticket?"

"I did." It was the first thing he'd said when he called her. The first thing Lexie had said to him was *No*. "But that didn't seem to make any difference to her."

"I was right," Marina concluded. "Jake's mother really *is* a witch. I'm glad we're saving him."

"We're not," Anderson corrected. When she started to question him, he told her, "You are."

She was pleased that he thought that, but she'd never been one to take credit as her due. "Not without you, I'm not."

Just then, the judge's legal intern peeked into the room where they were waiting. The hint of a smile was on her thin lips.

"Judge Wyatt is ready to marry you now," the young woman told them.

Anderson rose to his feet, then turned toward Marina and put his hand out to her. When she wrapped her fingers around it, he drew her up so that she was standing right beside him.

Marina could feel her heart pounding. Adrenaline was doing double-time in her veins. It was really happening, she thought.

"I guess this is it," Marina murmured.

Anderson nodded. "Showtime," he told her.

The judge's intern, Josephine Vickers, said, "This way, please," as she turned on her neatly stacked heel and led the way back into the judge's chambers.

Tucking Marina's arm through his, Anderson lowered his head to hers and apologized in a hushed whisper. "I'm sorry this isn't in a church." He sensed that she would have preferred the latter.

But if she was disappointed, Marina gave no indication. "We would have had to wait too long and every minute that goes by is another minute that Jake believes that he was abandoned by the people he thought loved him."

Anderson turned toward her before they crossed the threshold into the chambers. He wanted one more moment in private with Marina.

"You really are a very rare woman," he told her with admiration.

Marina smiled, her heart warmed by his praise more than she could possibly begin to tell him. Instead, she turned to humor.

"I'm a fifth-grade teacher," she told him. "It comes with the territory."

The judge looked somewhat impatient as they entered his chambers. It was obvious that he had somewhere else to be.

"Mr. Dalton, Ms. Laramie," he said, greeting them each in turn with a nod. "I'm Judge Wyatt and I'm pressed for time, so shall we get on with it?" he asked, looking from one to the other.

He really wasn't asking a question; he was putting them on notice.

Some very short notice, it turned out, because as he began to officiate the service, his rather monotone cadence seemed to speed up and he said all the words of the ceremony so quickly, they barely had time to register before he uttered the final ones.

"And I now pronounce you husband and wife. Thank you and good luck!"

And just like that, they were married.

Chapter Sixteen

He was grateful to Marina, he really was. Because of her, he felt that he at least had a shot at getting his son back in his life, if only on a part-time basis.

She deserved something better than a quickie wedding ceremony in a brusque judge's chambers, even if this wasn't a real love match.

Feeling slightly sheepish, Anderson looked at her as they walked down the steps of the courthouse less than half an hour after they had entered the building. "Not exactly the wedding of your dreams, was it?" he asked Marina.

She wasn't going to dwell on what it wasn't, only on what it was. "It got the job done," she told him brightly.

"That's not what I asked you," Anderson pointed out tactfully.

He appreciated the fact that she didn't carry on about

how lacking the ceremony was. In her place, he knew Lexie would have gone on about it for hours, possibly days. But that still didn't make the actual occurrence any better.

Standing at the bottom step, Marina was forced to admit, "I doubt that any woman dreams of standing in front of a frowning, balding man in a suit with a soup stain just above his breast pocket, listening to him say the words that are meant to bind her forever to someone in the eyes of the law."

He laughed shortly as he shook his head. "Very pragmatically stated. Soup stain, huh?" On top of everything else, the woman was incredibly observant, he thought.

She nodded. "Just above his breast pocket," she repeated. "A faint one." And then she shrugged philosophically. "Like I said, it got the job done. In the eyes of the law, I am your wife and we are a unit." She began to walk over to his truck. "A family. I've got a very good record as a teacher, you're a good, hardworking man." Marina got into the vehicle on her side, then closed the door. She waited until he got in on his side before continuing. "There is no reason in the world why you wouldn't be granted at least partial custody of Jake," she told him, buckling up.

Anderson paused, listening to the woman he had just made his wife. They had just gotten married for very practical reasons. This was supposed to be more of a covenant, an agreement, than anything else, and yet, he could swear that because of what she said and her gracious behavior in a less than ideal situation, he could feel himself falling in love with her. Falling in love with her selflessness, with the way he'd observed her acting around Jake.

She wasn't just a good teacher, she was a born mother. And there was no denying the fact that he was attracted to her. When he kissed her—well, all he knew was that he'd never known two friends to kiss this way. As the old expression went, she certainly lit his fire. And yet, all the while, all she seemed to think about or focus on were Jake's and Sydney's needs, not her own.

For that matter, she was putting him before herself, as well. It was as if she didn't count in this grand scheme of things.

He had never met anyone quite like Marina.

"Tell me, how would you feel about going on a honeymoon?" he asked her out of the blue.

Her hand froze midway in securing her seat belt. It took her a couple of seconds to absorb what he was asking her. Her mind had been going in an entirely different direction.

Marina blinked as she looked at him incredulously. "A what?"

"A honeymoon," he repeated, amused at the bewildered expression on her face. She looked almost adorable. "You know, what a couple goes on after they get married."

She couldn't tell if he was just pulling her leg, or if he was actually serious. How was she going to train herself not to have any feelings for this man if he kept derailing her like this? If he kept throwing out thoughts that teased her and caused havoc with the mind-set she was trying so hard to assume? She would have loved to go on a honeymoon, but that wasn't what all this was supposed to be about.

"Conventional people," Marina pointed out. "The kind who are focused on each other and just having fun, not gearing up to do battle over custody issues with the Wicked Witch of the West. Besides," she gently reminded him, "Sydney is still an infant. I can't leave her for a week, much less two," she protested, then, after a moment, she added in a much quieter voice, "No matter how nice the idea of a honeymoon might seem."

The selfless practicality of the woman astounded him. "All right, then how about an overnight stay at Maverick Manor?" he suggested, not ready to just give up on the idea of doing *something* to show Marina how grateful he was. "I know someone there who can get us a very nice suite." He put his key into the ignition, but still held off starting his truck. Instead, he looked at Marina. "It doesn't seem right for a couple to get married and then just plunge back into their daily lives without at least *some* sort of an acknowledgment that something different has happened.

"Unless, of course, you don't want to," he suddenly qualified, realizing that maybe Marina didn't want any more attention brought to the fact that they were married.

If you only knew how much I want to go on that honeymoon, Marina thought. *You'd be knocked right out of your boots.*

"Why wouldn't I want to?" she questioned out loud, curious as to his thought process.

He didn't have a gift with words, he never had. That was why he preferred being a rancher and hadn't followed his father into a career as a lawyer. The fact of the matter was he didn't really know how to express himself, but he knew he had to give it a try.

"I thought that maybe you'd want as little attention called to our, um, 'arrangement' as possible," he finally said.

Her eyebrows drew together as she tried to find a reason why he would think this way. Try as she might, she came up empty. “Isn’t that the whole point of this? To call attention to the fact that we’re married and can create a good home for Jake?”

She had him there. “I guess you’re right.” He thought for a moment, then went back to his last proposal. “So, since you can’t be away from Sydney for any great length of time, why don’t we do what I suggested and just go for an overnight stay at the hotel?” he asked, watching her face to see how she really felt about the matter. “Would that be all right?”

Marina really wished she could gauge how *he* felt about the idea of a honeymoon. But, since she couldn’t, she felt she could at least tell him what she thought of his suggestion.

“That would be perfect.” She did her best to try to curb her enthusiasm. She didn’t want to scare him away. “I can get Dawn to babysit Sydney overnight. She’s already told me that she would be more than willing to take the baby for a night when I dropped her off earlier today.”

Or two, Marina silently added, recalling her younger sister’s words. She had a feeling that Dawn was trying to see what kind of a parent she’d make before taking the plunge and becoming pregnant herself.

“Then it’s settled,” Anderson said, pleased. “I’ll give my friend at Maverick Manor a call and as long as your sister’s available for the job, we can leave right after school’s over tomorrow—sooner if you want to take the day off,” he added.

She did, but she didn’t feel that it was right. “I already took today off. I don't want the kids to think I've abandoned them."

Absolutely incredible, he couldn't help thinking. *The woman's a saint.*

"Fair enough," he told her out loud, finally starting the truck. "I'll come by tomorrow and pick you up from school, Mrs. Dalton," Anderson added after a beat, then realized that, again, he'd wound up taking something for granted. "Unless, of course, you want to continue being called Ms. Laramie."

But Marina shook her head. She loved the idea of taking his name, but again, she didn't want to scare him off so instead she said, "That might confuse everyone."

Anderson was more than happy to accommodate her. "Mrs. Dalton it is."

He had to admit, he liked the sound of that.

She might not have had a dream wedding. But in all the fantasies that she did have about the man she might someday marry, the husband she envisioned definitely paled in comparison to the man who walked into her classroom the following afternoon.

Anderson Dalton, at six foot one, with his slightly shaggy light brown hair and his electric blue eyes was just the kind of stuff that fantasies were made of. She felt her pulse skip a beat when she looked up and saw him standing there in her doorway.

"Ready?" he asked, his deep voice rumbling and filling up all the space around her.

"Ready," she echoed, closing the middle drawer of her desk and locking it. "I just have to grab my suitcase. I packed a few things," she explained. "If that's all right."

"Sure it's all right." Why would she even doubt that?

he wondered. "I'm not kidnapping you, we're going on a honeymoon. An abbreviated one," he qualified, "but still a honeymoon. I didn't assume you wanted to rough it—any more than you already are," he added with what sounded like an apologetic note.

She was nervous, but his apologetic tone put her a little more at ease.

"Let's go, then," she said, picking up her suitcase from behind her desk.

"Let's," Anderson echoed as he took the suitcase from her and walked behind her out of the classroom.

Her nerves were back, growing progressively more pronounced the closer they came to the hotel. By the time she found herself standing before the honeymoon suite, her nerves had grown to towering proportions.

Opening the doors for them, the hotel attendant smiled politely and then silently withdrew, leaving them alone in the suite.

Anderson couldn't remember the last time he had felt nervous, but for some reason, he realized that he was nervous as he waited for her reaction. Pleasing Marina had suddenly become important to him.

"Do you like it?" he asked, intently watching her face.

"It's big," Marina acknowledged. It seemed like a safe thing to say. Looking around, it all began to sink in for her. This was real. She was married to Anderson Dalton and standing in the honeymoon suite—and she hadn't a clue how to act. Did she let him realize that she loved him? Or did she do her very best to act as if she was just going through the motions?

She continued talking about the suite because it felt safe. "I think it's bigger than my apartment." She moved around the room, gauging the size. "You could have a party in here," she told him. Her nerves were practically strangling her.

"A party for two," Anderson replied. Realizing that sounded as if he was putting pressure on her, he immediately attempted to do damage control. "I mean, if that's what someone wanted to do. It is, after all, a honeymoon suite."

This wasn't coming out right. He cleared his throat and tried again, wanting to make sure that Marina didn't feel that he was thinking of taking advantage of her because they were legally married now. "The suite has two rooms."

She looked at him, thinking that sounded rather odd. "A honeymoon suite with two rooms? Isn't that strange?" She'd only been in a hotel room once, and it had been a tiny thing. Even so, there had been two beds shoved into it. Hardly room for a person to walk, she recalled. Here, they could have installed a bowling alley if they'd been so inclined.

"One's a bedroom," he told her, feeling more awkward by the moment, "the other is where they can share a private meal if they want to. It's got a couch so I can sleep on that if—" The knock on the door interrupted him, bringing with it a wave of relief. "That's got to be room service," he told her.

"Room service?" she repeated. "Did we order room service?" She didn't recall either one of them doing so. They'd just walked in. There had to be some sort of a mistake.

"Yes, we did," Anderson assured her as he went to the door. "I thought that a little privacy might be nice.

But we can eat down in the restaurant if you'd rather do that," he told her, wanting to stay entirely flexible for her.

"Room service is fine," she told him, doing her best not to let her nerves get the better of her. It wasn't easy.

Room service was more than fine, it was exquisite. She couldn't remember ever having a meal as sumptuous as the one Anderson had ordered for them.

The man might look like a cowboy, she thought, but somewhere in that broad chest beat the heart of a man with sophisticated tastes.

Along with the filet mignon and the lobster tail came a bottle of champagne that seemed to heighten all her senses and make her acutely aware of just how much the man sitting across from her at their small table for two actually aroused her.

By the time they had gotten to dessert—a chocolate parfait—she felt as if the temperature in the room had gone up more than ten degrees—and was getting steadily warmer.

"I had no idea you could eat so much," Anderson said as the last bite of parfait disappeared behind her lips. He was extremely pleased that she'd enjoyed the meal he had ordered for them.

"Neither did I," she laughed.

"I can order more," he offered. "Maybe another dessert?"

"Oh please, I couldn't take another bite, not without possibly exploding," she confessed. And then she smiled at him. "This was all just perfect."

No, she was perfect. The meal was just good, Anderson thought.

Putting down his napkin, he glanced at his watch. He

hadn't realized it was so late. Talking with Marina, time had just managed to escape him.

He pushed the table aside and rose to his feet. "It's getting late and you're probably tired. I should let you get to bed."

Marina was immediately up. "Where are you going to sleep?" she asked.

She was testing him, wasn't she? Anderson thought. "Well, like I said, there's a couch here."

She looked at it. It was a lovely piece of furniture, but it was curved. Definitely not the sort of thing a person over the age of nine could sleep on.

"That can't be comfortable," she told him. "There's hardly enough room to stretch out."

His mind hadn't really been focused on the sofa. Now that he looked at it, she was right. "There's always the floor," he pointed out.

But she shook her head. "Even more uncomfortable," she told him. "There's a king-size bed in the other room," Marina reminded him. "It's certainly big enough for two people."

The idea of sharing a bed with her was far too tempting—resisting her now was already hard enough for him.

"I'm not so sure about that."

She looked at him for a long moment. She supposed what she said next she could have blamed on the champagne, but that would have been a lie. Because she'd thought about one thing ever since she had agreed to marry him.

"I am," she told Anderson quietly.

He could feel his heart quickening, but for her sake, if not his own, he had to talk some sense into her. "You don't know what you're saying, Marina."

She was already threading her arms around his neck, already bringing her body up against him, standing so close that a whisper wouldn't have been able to get through.

"I think I am," she told him, her voice low.

Did she realize how hard she was making this for him? "Marina, I'm only human. You keep standing so close to me like this and I'm not going to be able to do the right thing."

"I think you're doing the right thing right now," she told him, her warm breath gliding seductively along his neck and his skin. Cocking her head ever so slightly, she looked up into his eyes. "I'm your wife, Anderson," she whispered.

"I know that." If this was some sort of a test, he was failing it, he thought, feeling himself slipping. "That's what the wedding certificate says."

Her eyes never left his and he could feel himself getting lost in them. "I want to be your wife in every sense of the word, not just on paper."

This was a great deal more difficult than he had ever imagined. No, scratch that. It was beyond difficult. It was next to impossible and getting more so by the second.

"Oh damn it, Marina, I can't keep holding you at arm's length—"

"Then don't," she urged, rising up on her toes and kissing him.

She felt it instantly, felt him giving in to her, surrendering. Felt the kiss deepening and with it, the charade that they were both pretending to take part in ceased to exist.

Felt him wanting her.

Wanting her just as much as she wanted him.

She could feel a small whoop of joy echoing within her as her anticipation increased tenfold.

Their marriage was about to officially begin.

Chapter Seventeen

Marina admittedly had never been very experienced when it came to having sex. To her, the idea of doing it if love wasn't involved was completely off-putting, so her partners over the years had been less than a handful. Moreover, it had been over a year since she had even felt a man's touch. Since her affair with Gary had ended so badly she hadn't even been tempted to make love with anyone. It was a complication she wanted no part of.

She thought—assumed—that she was just fine on her own. She actually felt content in the fact that it was just her and Sydney against the world. There was no need for her to yearn for a man in her life.

And yet, right at this moment, she couldn't think of anything she wanted more than to make love with Anderson, than to have him touch her, kiss her, possess her and make her his in every exquisite sense of the word.

Marina gave herself up to the sensation and sealed herself to her destiny—and Anderson.

She didn't remember just how or when their clothes had come off, didn't remember how they had gotten from the one room to the bedroom, much less into the king-size bed that dominated the room.

All she was aware of was this burning need to love and be wanted, to be taken up beyond the boundaries of the mortal world and into a realm where there were only two individuals who made up the population.

Anderson and her.

"Am I going too fast?" he'd asked her at one point, just before they'd landed on the bed.

"Your timing is perfect," she'd managed to get out. She found that she had to concentrate in order to get her breathing under control.

It was all he needed to hear to inflame him and urge him on to higher plateaus.

That was when it actually hit him, that it all became crystal clear to him: he didn't ever want to let Marina go. Not because she was helping him get Jake back—that was part of it, but it wasn't the main part. He didn't want to let her go because he was in love with her. In love with a beautiful, pure woman who wanted nothing from him, nothing but to help him.

How could he have possibly gotten so lucky?

He wanted to tell Marina how he felt, to shout about the glorious feelings going on inside him from the highest rooftops. But he was afraid that if he let her suspect how he felt, it might just ultimately frighten her away. So all he could do was *show* her. And he intended to, for as long as she would let him.

He made love to her with a vengeance.

* * *

Something had changed.

Marina could feel it. Or maybe it was just the champagne that was finally kicking into high gear.

Whatever was at the root of it, she could have sworn that Anderson's lovemaking had escalated another notch—maybe even several. His lips were everywhere, making her crazy, branding her, causing her very skin to feel as if it was on fire. And the hotter it felt, the more she burned for him.

Her head was spinning and a stray little voice within her was whispering, *This is special, this is something unique. This is definitely a man who could easily rock my world.*

What "could"? she mocked herself. There was no doubt that he already was doing just that.

It suddenly occurred to her that she didn't want him coming away thinking she was only there to take from him. She needed to let him see that she was just as capable of giving back.

So she did.

Somewhere deep inside her, something very basic rose to the surface. It was bent on pleasing Anderson, on making him not regret this marriage of convenience they had struck up.

She wanted to make Anderson want her every bit as much as she wanted him.

Marina found herself acting on instincts she never even knew she possessed. Instincts Anderson had, just by making love with her, by arousing her with his skillful foreplay, brought out of her.

And just like that, she was giving him just as much

pleasure as he had been giving her. Hearing Anderson moan acted like a catalyst and ignited her.

Marina had no idea where any of this came from, she only knew that suddenly, she had skills that had never been there before, fueled by urges that had never existed before.

Empowered, exhilarated, she reacted to it all as if it was perfectly natural for her to do so.

Anderson had had no idea, when he had walked in on his son's teacher that first afternoon in her classroom, that beneath this woman's cool, classic exterior resided the soul of a tigress.

His own personal tigress.

Foreplay lasted longer than he ever thought himself capable of maintaining. He pleasured Marina for as long as he could hold out, until his self-control was about to break apart. He needed to join with her *now*!

Rolling over so that Marina was beneath him, Anderson primed her with openmouthed kisses all along her smooth, writhing body until neither of them could hold back even a fraction of a second longer.

His heart pounding wildly in his chest, Anderson entered her, making them one unit—for now and for always.

Tapping into what he knew was his last drop of self-control, Anderson began to move slowly.

And then faster.

And faster still, until he thought the tempo they reached was as close to the speed of light as humanly possible. And they were doing it together. That was all that seemed to matter, that they were arriving at the very peak of the mountain they were scaling together.

Standing at the top of the world together.

And then the very final thrust came, bringing all the stars raining down around them.

He clung to her, amazed at how hard his heart was beating without breaking through his ribs and shattering his chest wall.

He was even more amazed at how much he wanted her—again. Wanted her with every fiber of his being even though there wasn't a single ounce of energy left within him.

Marina reveled in the incredible magnitude of the feeling she'd just experienced, reveled in the fact that he was still holding her as if she was the most precious part of his world rather than just rolling away from her because he was done.

She could feel his heart mimicking her own and she had a surprising reaction to that.

A feeling of safety.

She'd never felt so safe, so secure in her entire life, not even when she'd been a child. Marina thought that she was probably reading things into this moment, but for now, she was content just to enjoy the sensation. To enjoy the feeling of his arms around her. To enjoy the calming pretense that she was Anderson's wife and that Anderson was her husband.

To enjoy the pretense that she was one half of a couple.

Reality would be on her doorstep all too soon, but not now. Not yet.

Marina resisted waking up.

The dream she was having, had been having, was too strong, too good to release. She wanted to hang on a little longer, cling to it and pretend that it was real for just a few more moments.

But something nudged at her consciousness, reminding Marina that the rest of her life was waiting for her. With a reluctant sigh, she opened her eyes—and saw that Anderson was lying next to her, propped up on his elbow and watching her.

"What are you doing?" she asked self-consciously. Was he regretting marrying her already? Had another plan occurred to him, one in which he didn't need her to play the role of his wife? Had he realized how disappointing she was in bed?

These and so many other thoughts assailed her as she struggled to get her bearings.

"I'm watching you sleep. And now," he continued with a smile she found infinitely sexy even with her nerves vibrating at top speed, "I'm watching you wake up."

Maybe it was going to be all right? It struck her as a question rather than a statement. "Are you that bored?" she asked hesitantly.

"I'm not bored at all," Anderson told her, allowing his fingers to slowly trail along the hollow of her throat. Arousing himself, arousing her. "Not by a long shot." His lips slowly made their way to the other side of her neck. "Last night was eye-opening," he whispered softly, his breath arousing her further.

She was having a very difficult time just lying there, having him doing what he was doing without responding. She didn't want him thinking that she demanded anything from him in any way.

"How so?" she breathed.

His voice was low and incredibly seductive. "I had no idea you were so talented, so skilled in so many different ways."

"You're laughing at me," Marina said, struggling to keep her eyes from shutting, to keep herself from drifting away.

"I might want to do many things with you, Marina, but laughing at you is definitely not one of them," he told her.

She was trembling again. Maybe she hadn't disappointed him last night and what had happened between them wasn't an isolated occurrence.

Her heart was hammering hard as she whispered, "What kind of things?"

"I'm a man of few words, Marina. I'm a lot better at showing what I mean rather than saying what I mean," he said.

Her pulse was practically beating right out of her body as she whispered, "Well, then I guess you'd better show me."

His smile went straight to her inner core as he said, "I thought you'd never ask."

Marina felt as if she had somehow unwittingly stumbled into a dreamworld. For one week, one wondrous week, absolutely everything was perfect. She didn't think it was humanly possible to be happier.

She moved in with Anderson, went to work every day to teach her students and came home each night to her little family. A family that she had every hope would be increased by one very soon.

Even Sydney, who had always been such an easy baby, seemed somehow happier than usual. And Lindsay had found them a lawyer who was certain that with everything that was going on, winning partial custody of Jake was all but a done deal.

And then on the afternoon of the eighth day, everything changed.

Marina drove up in her car to see another, unfamiliar vehicle parked right in front of the ranch house. Seeing it brought along a sense of vague uneasiness. She was familiar with all the cars and trucks that the members of Anderson's family drove and this vehicle didn't belong to any of them.

It could just belong to one of Anderson's friends, someone she wasn't acquainted with, but for some reason, she didn't believe that. Instead, all sorts of bells and alarms insisted on going off in her head.

Something was wrong.

She could feel it in her bones.

Part of Marina wanted to turn around and drive right back to school, to find some paperwork she'd forgotten about and needed to finish—except that she knew that there wasn't any. She was, among other things, conscientiousness personified. Her reports were always in ahead of time and never just under the wire, much less forgotten about.

Besides, if there *was* something going on, she needed to face it. Running away didn't make it disappear; it just prolonged the inevitable moment when she had to face whatever it was that was happening.

It was probably nothing.

It didn't *feel* like nothing.

The argument in her head went on for a prolonged moment, and then Marina forced herself to walk into the house.

Rather than enter and brightly announce, "I'm home," the way she had been doing for the past week, Marina quietly let herself into the house, all but tiptoeing in. Not because she wanted to catch Anderson doing something he shouldn't, but because if there was something going on she needed to be prepared for, having a moment to observe what that something was might be helpful.

The next moment, as she soundlessly approached the living room, she could hear two people talking. And just like that, she could feel her soul shrinking back not in fear, but in total distress.

One of the voices belonged to Anderson, the other to some woman.

A woman whose identity quickly made itself known by what she was saying.

The other woman was Lexie, Jake's mother. And Anderson's former lover.

The thought throbbed over and over in her head: Lexie was standing in the living room.

In *her* living room.

If her heart had sunk down any farther, it would have gone straight through the floor.

Rather than step forward, Marina remained frozen in the shadows, listening to what they were saying. It quickly became apparent that the woman had gotten here only a couple of minutes ago.

And Lexie did not sound as if she was leaving.

The next second, Marina realized that the woman had brought Jake back with her. Maybe this wasn't as bad as she'd thought. Maybe things were finally falling into place.

But the knot in her stomach didn't think so.

"Jake," Lexie said, "why don't you go to your room? I want to talk to your dad."

Anderson knew his son, having just gotten here, was

reluctant to go anywhere. He wanted to stay near his father. "Can't I stay with you, Dad?" he pleaded.

"You *are* staying with him, Jake," Lexie told her son impatiently. "Now listen to me and go to your room," she said. Her voice softened the next moment as she added, "Just for now."

"Do as she says, Jake," Anderson told his son, releasing the boy after he'd hugged him. "We'll talk in a few minutes," he promised.

"Okay." Jake reluctantly obeyed and shuffled out of the room and then up the stairs.

"All right, Lexie, you've gotten the boy out of the room. Now what's this big thing you want to say to me that you can't say in front of Jake?" Anderson wanted to know.

There was a long pause, as if Lexie was searching for the right words—or her courage. "I wanted to apologize," she finally told him stiffly.

"For?" Anderson asked, somehow managing to hide his surprise.

This was obviously hard for her, but Anderson wasn't about to make it any easier. He stood there in silence, waiting for her to go on.

"For using you," Lexie finally said.

"You're going to have to be more specific than that," he told her gruffly. "What you just apologized for wasn't a onetime deal."

"When we…had that one night together," Lexie began, struggling with each word, "I was seeing someone else at the time."

Over time, Anderson had assumed as much. "Go on," he instructed.

She closed her eyes for a moment, searching for

words. “When I realized I was pregnant, I panicked. I figured I could pass the baby off to my boyfriend as his. For a while, he wasn’t the wiser and I really didn’t think you’d care one way or the other—after all, it was just a fling between us,” she reminded Anderson. “Anyway, my boyfriend and I got married and for a while, everything was good.” Her expression became more somber. “But it didn’t last. To be honest, I don’t think that Jake remembers him at all.”

She took a breath, then continued. “I guess what I’m actually apologizing for is keeping Jake and you apart all this time. A boy needs his father. I can see that now. Ever since I brought Jake back home with me, he’s been completely withdrawn and sullen. I realized that it’s because he misses you so much.”

“So you’ve decided to give me partial custody?” Anderson asked hopefully. He couldn’t see this heading in any other direction, but he took nothing for granted when it came to Lexie.

“Better than that,” Lexie told him, smiling broadly for the first time and obviously very pleased with herself.

“Go on,” he urged when she paused to bask in what she was about to tell him.

“I wanted you to know that I’m making a fresh start, Anderson. I’ve decided to move here to Montana so that you and Jake can see each other on a regular basis.”

The cry of dismay escaped Marina’s voice before she could stop it.

Chapter Eighteen

Hearing the stifled cry, Anderson immediately left Lexie and went around the corner that separated the living room from the foyer. He was surprised to find Marina standing there.

"Marina, when did you get home?" he asked, puzzled why she hadn't just come in when she heard him talking to Lexie.

Marina was trying her very best not to look flustered. She would have loved to have just disappeared into the woodwork, and silently upbraided herself for calling attention to herself this way.

"Just now," she answered, hoping she didn't look as upset as she felt, especially when Lexie stepped into the foyer.

What she had just overheard had knocked the very air out of her lungs. She felt numb. If Lexie was moving here to Montana, to live somewhere close to Anderson so that Jake could interact with his father, then there was no need for Anderson to remain married to her. Just like that, she had outlived her usefulness.

"Ms. Laramie?"

All three adults turned at the sound of the high-pitched, elated cry. Jake came flying down the stairs and went straight to Marina.

"I thought I heard your voice!" he cried happily, throwing his arms around her waist and hugging her as hard as he could.

Lexie looked completely put out by her son's obvious display of affection.

"Jake, I thought we told you to stay in your room," she said, clearly annoyed that Jake had disobeyed her. "See what I mean?" she asked, turning toward Anderson. "He doesn't listen to me anymore. He *always* listened to me before he came out here," Lexie lamented.

"Maybe you're mistaking listening for just not hearing you," Anderson tactfully pointed out, much to the other woman's obvious displeasure. "When he first came here, he was completely consumed with video games. Someone could have told him he was on fire and he wouldn't have paid any attention. It was Marina who turned him around, who got him to pay attention and to study. She saw the lonely kid that neither one of us realized was there and found a way to reach him."

Marina, still hugging Jake, looked at Anderson, utterly stunned and totally pleased. She had no idea that any of this had actually registered with Jake's father. She had just assumed that Anderson thought his son had come around on his own. She certainly wouldn't have pointed it out to him. She had never been out for any credit; she only wanted the boy to be happy. The sadness in his eyes had made her determined to turn him around.

For her part, Lexie looked completely surprised at the revelation.

"Is this true?" she asked. Her question was open-ended. As it stood, it could have been intended for either her son or for Marina.

It was Jake who replied. He looked up at his mother, answering her question almost shyly.

"Ms. Laramie talks to me. She makes me feel good about myself, like just because I didn't know what all the other kids knew didn't mean that I couldn't learn."

Lexie looked taken aback and somewhat humbled. "Is this true?" she asked, looking at Marina.

Marina was at a loss as to how to answer. She really didn't want to sound as if she was bragging, or trying to come between either Jake and his mother, or Anderson and Jake's mother. But she didn't want to lie, either.

She settled for something simple and vague. "Every child just needs a little guidance to help access his or her full potential. That's my job as a teacher," Marina said.

Lexie's expression softened somewhat. She even smiled a little.

"So I guess I did a good thing by bringing Jake here," Lexie said. "Thanks," she told Marina and then turned toward Anderson. "I was thinking of leaving Jake here with you so he can enroll back in school while I go back to Chicago and make all the necessary arrangements to move our things out here."

Suddenly Marina felt as if she was intruding on family business. "Why don't I just go see about getting dinner ready while you two talk logistics."

•

Jake popped up in front of her. “Can I help?” he asked her eagerly.

Marina thought that Jake was probably better off staying with his parents, but he looked so enthusiastic, she didn’t have the heart to turn him down.

“Of course you can,” she told Jake fondly, putting her arm around the boy’s shoulders. “Have you seen Sydney yet? I know that she’ll be so happy to see you,” Marina told him as they walked into the kitchen.

Jake looked surprised by the news. “Sydney’s here in the house?” he asked happily. “Where?”

The playpen had been empty when she’d entered the living room. “Well, since I didn’t see her when I walked in, I guess your dad probably put her down for another nap in her room.”

“Sydney has her own room here?” Jake asked her, surprised and clearly excited by the news.

That was when she realized that Anderson probably hadn’t told his son that they were married. She was tempted to tell him herself, but that would have been selfish of her, done for ulterior motives. This wasn’t her story to tell.

Besides, maybe Anderson didn’t want to tell Jake that they had gotten married. There was no longer a need for that charade to continue and maybe it was just easier for him not to say anything at all about it. That way, the boy wouldn’t get confused, she reasoned, doing her very best to be objective about the situation rather than emotional. But it was hard to deny the way she really felt.

Jake, she realized, was still waiting for her to explain why Sydney had her own room here. “It’s easier when she goes down for a nap to put her somewhere that she won’t be disturbed,” Marina explained.

"Oh." The excuse seemed to satisfy him. "Want me to set the table?" he volunteered brightly.

She was throwing together pulled chicken, which she had already prepared the night before, along with several vegetables that just needed to be steamed. All that was really left to be done was to mix everything together in a big pot on the stove and warm it up. That wouldn't take very long.

She gave Jake an encouraging smile. "That would be very helpful."

The moment Jake left the room, his arms loaded down with dinner plates, Marina felt her eyes beginning to sting.

She wasn't going to cry, she told herself. She was going to hold it together for Jake's sake and then, after dinner, she would collect her daughter and go back to her apartment. She'd given her notice to the landlord at the beginning of the week, but if she appealed to the man's better nature, he might allow her to rescind it. That meant that she could just go back to living in the apartment.

And, with any luck, she could get her life back on track in about a dozen years or so, she thought as a tear spilled out.

Damn it, she wasn't going to go to pieces. She wasn't, she told herself sternly. The last thing she wanted was for Anderson to feel sorry for her—or to have him be shamed into letting her remain on the ranch.

For all she knew, now that Lexie was back, maybe he would even pick up their relationship where it had dropped off twelve years ago. Stranger things had been known to happen. After all, they did have a child together.

Marina heard a noise behind her. Jake was back for the rest of the dinnerware, she thought. The boy moved fast.

"Don't forget, knives on the right, forks on the left," she told him automatically. She kept her back to him, not wanting Jake to see her cry. There would be endless questions if he did.

An amused voice asked, "And where do the spoons go?"

Caught off guard, Marina dropped the spatula she was using to stir the pulled chicken. She whirled around to face Anderson.

"Sorry," she apologized, immediately lowering her eyes. "I thought you were Jake. He's setting the table."

"Actually," he corrected her, "I sent him upstairs to look in on Sydney. She should be waking up from her nap around now."

She saw that Anderson had come into the kitchen by himself. She looked around, but no one else came in behind him.

"Where's Lexie?" she asked.

"On her way back to the airport," Anderson answered. "Why?"

She shrugged vaguely, feeling progressively more uncomfortable. "I just thought she'd be staying for dinner—that is, unless you thought it might be a little awkward to explain to her what I was doing here."

"Why would it be awkward?" he asked her, confused. "Where else would my wife be but in our house?"

Marina looked at him in surprise. "You told her that we got married?"

It was clear why he didn't understand why she looked so surprised. "Among other things, yes. Why?" Even as he asked, he couldn't come up with a reason why Marina wouldn't want that.

Marina shrugged again, feeling at a loss. "I just thought you wouldn't want her to know."

That obviously cleared up nothing for him. "Correct me if I'm wrong, but wasn't that the initial point of our getting married? I mean, that was why you first made the suggestion, right?"

Why was he making her say this? Making her spell it all out? "Yes, but now that Lexie's moving here, I figured that you wouldn't need to keep up pretenses and telling her might just get her angry."

"Pretenses," he repeated as if he wasn't sure what she was trying to say.

Did he realize that he was torturing her? Marina wondered. "Well, yes."

"But we *are* married, so that's not a pretense."

"No, but—"

Anderson was getting a bad feeling about this. "Are you saying that you don't want to be married?" he asked her point-blank.

"No, I want to be married," she told him. She felt as if her thoughts were getting all jumbled up. "But you don't."

"I don't?" he questioned. What was she talking about?

"No," she cried. Why was he making her say this? Didn't he realize how much it hurt? "I know that the only reason you agreed to marry me was because you needed to prove to the court that you had a stable home environment, with a wife and even a baby, to offer Jake. But now that Lexie's going to be moving to Montana, everything's changed."

"Everything?" he questioned, repeating the word slowly.

"Well, yes. You can be together with Lexie if you want to—"

Anderson stopped her right there. "Oh, Lord, no, why would I want that?"

Marina was completely dumbfounded. "You don't want that?" she asked, bewildered.

He was a man of few words—but more than a few were needed here to fix this. He gave it a try.

"Marina, all I want is to stay married to you and to be a dad to Jake and Sydney. It doesn't matter to me where Lexie is, Chicago or here. You're the one I want, the one I love. I'm not going to force you if you don't want to be married to me, but—"

"Not want to be married to you?" Marina repeated as if he had said something she couldn't begin to comprehend. "Of course I want to be married to you. There's nothing I want *more* than to be married to you. I just didn't want you to feel obligated to continue with this if your heart wasn't in it—"

"My heart," he told her, taking her into his arms, "is exactly where it's supposed to be."

She smiled up into his eyes. "Mine, too."

"Good to know, Mrs. Dalton," he murmured just before he kissed her. "Very good to know."

* * * * *

Look for the next installment of

the new Cherish continuity

MONTANA MAVERICKS: THE BABY BONANZA

When tycoon Walker Jones faces off in court against Lindsay Dalton, he finds her a formidable opponent—and an irresistible one! Can she make him see the error of his ways?

Don't miss

MAVERICK VS. MAVERICK

by

New York Times *bestselling author Shirley Jump*

MILLS & BOON®

EXCLUSIVE EXCERPT

Emma Carmichael's world is turned upside-down
when she encounters Jack Westwood—her
secret husband of six years!

Read on for a sneak preview of
A COUNTESS FOR CHRISTMAS
the first book in the enchanting new Cherish quartet
MAIDS UNDER THE MISTLETOE

'You still have your ring,' Jack said.

'Of course.' Emma was frowning now and wouldn't meet his eye.

'Why—?' He walked to where she was standing with her hand gripping her handbag so hard her knuckles were white.

'I'm not very good at letting go of the past,' she said, shrugging and tilting up her chin to look him straight in the eye, as if to dare him to challenge her about it. 'I don't have a lot left from my old life and I couldn't bear to get rid of this ring. It reminds me of a happier time in my life. A simpler time, which I don't want to forget about.'

She blinked hard and clenched her jaw together and it suddenly occurred to him that she was struggling with being around him as much as he was with her.

The atmosphere hung heavy and tense between them,

with only the sound of their breathing breaking the silence.

His throat felt tight with tension and his pulse had picked up so he felt the heavy beat of it in his chest.

Why was it so important to him that she hadn't completely eschewed their past?

He didn't know, but it was.

Taking a step towards her, he slid his fingers under the thin silver chain around her neck, feeling the heat of her soft skin as he brushed the backs of his fingers over it, and drew the ring out of her dress again to look at it.

He remembered picking this out with her. They'd been so happy then, so full of excitement and love for each other.

He heard her ragged intake of breath as the chain slid against the back of her neck and looked up to see confusion in her eyes, and something else. Regret, perhaps, or sorrow for what they'd lost.

Something seemed to be tugging hard inside him, drawing him closer to her.

Her lips parted and he found he couldn't drag his gaze away from her mouth. That beautiful, sensual mouth that used to haunt his dreams all those years ago.

A lifetime ago.